Love Is The New Religion

Silas J. Lees

Copyright © 2018 Silas J. Lees
All rights reserved.

Book layout by www.ebooklaunch.com

This book, its logo and strapline, or any part(s) thereof may not be reproduced, replicated, or copied in any form, stored in any retrieval system (electronic or otherwise), or transmitted in any form by any means — electronic, mechanical, photocopy, photograph, recording, video, or otherwise — without the express prior written consent and permission of the author, except as provided by United Kingdom copyright law.

For permission requests, write to the author at love@loveisthenewreligion.com

The Winged Heart logo and strapline, 'Love is the New Religion', are copyright protected and trademarks of Silas J. Lees. As such, they are not to be reproduced in any way without the express written consent and permission of the author.

Visit the book's website at
www.LoveIsTheNewReligion.com

Praise for
Love is the New Religion

Rarely do we encounter spiritual insights, hidden historical facts, and a kindling hope for humanity's awakening that is cleverly masquerading as a gripping novel. This is one of those times.

The reader is kept in that pleasant tension between wanting to turn the page and see what happens, and wanting to stay on the page they have already read.

As we become engrossed in the fast-paced turn of events, we become the fans who cheer on the main characters, but we are also their apprentices in the arousing of the hero within. One can rightfully suspect that this has been the author's secret plan since the conception of this novel: keeping us entertained, so that the seed of knowing and courage is planted and remains nearly imperceptible. Once it flowers, it may be too late for the forces of stagnation to stop its proliferation.

Aleks Mikic
Author - USA

An addictive read. The perfect book to get lost in.
A real page-turner, full of wisdom, insight, love and adventure.

Suzy El-Shazly
Soulful Entrepreneur - UK

Some books have the power to make you reconsider life, to reflect on your view of the world and transform previous assumptions about religion, war, love and purpose. Love is the New Religion is such a book.

This well-written novel offers a tense and moving journey following a group of special unit soldiers on a mission that takes a most unexpected turn, the results of which cause them to question everything about their lives to date.

In a way that only this author could deliver, you are persuaded to look at the reality of your existence and the world around us through different eyes. Although quite controversial at times, this does provide an inspiring and heart-lifting look at life, love, and what it means to be human.

A thoroughly enjoyable read with a thought-provoking message that has the ability to change your world-view perspective, as well as your internal purpose.

Craig Gravil
Property Investor and Speaker - UK

This book is jammed packed with wisdom, cleverly constructed in a style that beautifully weaves powerful messages within its storyline.

This book highlights controversial issues facing the world today and the atrocities the human spirit is capable of when not being true to its core. When we go against our true being of love, we cause suffering to ourselves and others.

This book also provides a beacon of light, that the human journey, through its fear-driven choices, is a process leading to enlightenment where more and more individuals are connecting to their true self: that of unconditional love.

It closes with a reminder that God is Love, we are one with God, We are Love, We are One.

Dawattie Basdeo
Author - UK

Disclaimer

This body of work should be considered as entirely fictional and is for entertainment purposes only.

Any references to people, names, events, characters, businesses, places, locales, conferences, incidents, and circumstances within the book are entirely products of the author's imagination and/or have been used in an entirely fictitious manner. Any resemblances, likeness, similarities or correlations to actual persons, living, dead, or spiritual or actual events or circumstances is purely and entirely coincidental and shall have no bearing on the reputation, character, or personalities of any person(s), living or dead, event(s) or any circumstance(s) in the known universe.

This body of work is entirely for amusement and entertainment purposes only. No part of this book should be considered as any form of medical, legal, or professional advice in any capacity whatsoever. This book is not intended to be, nor is it to be considered, a replacement or substitute for the professional medical advice of a doctor, physician, or medical practitioner, or any other suitably qualified professional.

The author and publisher do not assume and hereby fully and completely disclaim and disavow any and all liability to any party whatsoever for any loss, and/or damage, and/or disruption howsoever arising and howsoever caused whether by any errors and/or omissions and/or admissions resulting or extending from negligence, accident, harm of reputation, or any other cause

Dedications

Writing this book has been both a highly enjoyable experience and the most testing activity I have ever undertaken. I can honestly say it would not have been possible without some absolutely incredible people in my life who have supported and encouraged me along the way. My thanks and appreciation goes to the following people:

Suzy El-Shazly, who has dedicated scores of hours to reading, re-reading, and editing this work. Thank you for helping to make this book what it is and for showing me what it is to practice many of the principles in this book in the face of personal adversity.

The amazing people who devoted their precious time to read the earlier drafts of this book and provide some much-needed feedback: Helen Watson, Dan and Peggy Hoover, Aleks Mikic, Avril Oenone, Craig Gravil, Dominique St. Leger, Ed Strachar, Lisa Bowen, Robin Shaw, Dawattie Basdeo and Dr Emer Garry - my love, gratitude and appreciation goes out to you all and I thank you so much for all your help and assistance.

Fifi and Mirana, for introducing me to the Madré and for guiding me through my Ayahuasca journey.

GOD for creatively channelling his words through me to create this body of work.

My dear friend, Alex Hickman, for all the knowledge he has shared from his own life journey and for the many deep and esoteric conversations we have enjoyed together that have both expanded my mind and challenged many of my personal viewpoints and beliefs.

My Facebook friend, Jason Christoff, who continues to educate me every single day through his dedication to awakening those who dare to look beyond The Matrix.

My parents for all the love and devotion they shared with me during our life journey together. May you both now rest in peace.

My brothers, Gareth and Johnathan, for their love and support.

My celebrity crush, Katrina Kaif, who inspired me so much with her effortless femininity in the movie 'Ek Tha Tiger', that I have modelled many of the qualities and characteristics of 'Sana' in her honour.

And, finally, Neo; my furry four-legged canine companion and best friend who has shown me what it is to be unconditionally loving and happy every single day. I promise to take you on more walks now this book is finally complete!

Table of Contents

Disclaimer i
Dedications iii
Table of Contents v
Introduction vii
Chapter 1: The Black Widows 1
Chapter 2: Terrorist Camp Attack 8
Chapter 3: Escape 21
Chapter 4: Suspicious Orders 27
Chapter 5: Truths Deep Within 38
Chapter 6: Desert Heat 51
Chapter 7: Ambush 63
Chapter 8: Penance in Paradise 72
Chapter 9: Healing Begins 83
Chapter 10: The Heart Knows 99
Chapter 11: A Journey of Truth 119
Chapter 12: A Mission for Souls 138
Chapter 13: A Plan for Love 149
Chapter 14: Chrysalis 160
Chapter 15: Beginning the End of Hate 178
Chapter 16: The Truth 200
Chapter 17: The Plan 225

Chapter 18: A Crack in the Matrix 233
Chapter 19: The Pendulum 255
Chapter 20: Capture 277
Chapter 21: Rescue and Reveal 294
Chapter 22: The Devil's Breath 310
Chapter 23: A Revolution for Peace 324
Afterword 352
Resources 363

Introduction

Firstly, welcome to the Love is the New Religion family and thank you for purchasing a copy of this book.

The book is a result of a real turning point in my life. Like many of you reading this, I have been through a number of challenging circumstances in my life that resulted in a less healthy mindset and belief system. For one reason or another, I suffered from a deep sense of personal shame: a debilitating condition where I have lived my life feeling continually in danger of being exposed as some sort of fraud.

In an attempt to address these deeply negative emotions, I started numerous businesses, became a property investor, public speaker, mentor, coach, and author. I worked as many hours as I could and lived on a diet of caffeine, alcohol, and sugar to try to keep myself going. However, the more I seemed to accomplish, the more exposed I felt, so I became locked in a continuous spiral of exposure and achievement, ultimately hoping that the dark emotions I was feeling would shift one day and I would finally feel whole, complete, and loved.

Then disaster struck…

In a catalogue of events that began in late 2014, my life began to unravel when I experienced a series of 'failures', as I couldn't maintain the exhausting efforts required to juggle all my projects. As events unfolded, I ended up closing down three separate businesses and stopped public speaking, mentoring, and coaching. This only served as more evidence that I was feeling like a huge failure!

I retired to bed one morning in late January 2015. I was exhausted, and I literally stayed there for a period of three months living on Guinness, Netflix, and Dominoes Pizza! What was even more disheartening was the fact that I didn't hear from the scores of friends I felt I had at that point in my life, save for a few dear souls. More evidence of failure! I was sad, scared, depressed, and very isolated.

One day I got up and decided to take the empties to the recycling bin outside. It was only when I counted the number of empty beer cans I had consumed the night before that I realised I might have a problem. I reached out to a close friend of mine and told her what I was experiencing. She helped me to understand what was going on and prompted me to enlist the support of an excellent cognitive behavioural therapist who showed me the spiralling patterns in my mind. Once I understood this, the dominant critical voice in my head that had run the show for years (*"You're a fake/fraud/failure"*) began to quieten down.

A short time later, and in a very convoluted way (which I have since discovered is how the universe/God works in unveiling their plans), I found myself doing a three-day Ayahuasca retreat. Now I must point out that I have never been one to expose myself to any recreational drugs (save for alcohol), so this was very out of character for me. However, the Shaman told me I had been guided to them to work with the Madré (the mother spirit of Ayahuasca).

Over the next three days and nights, I had the most incredible visions and experiences including basking in the feeling of Unconditional Love. The feeling was truly out of this world! During this time, I had the experience of meeting God, who planted in my mind the seed of Divinity for the title and the messages contained within this book.

Finally, out of a deep pit of personal anguish, I felt like I had a mission to achieve and, through a practice of meditation and listening to uplifting music late at night, the words began to flow through me and on to the page. I started channelling the book in August 2015 after my Ayahuasca experience, and the messages kept coming.

Please don't get me wrong, I am not trying to play the hero, or recommend or promote Ayahuasca as a panacea for anyone who might be struggling with personal problems. The point of sharing this with you is to say that it allowed me to listen to the messages from the universe and follow my intuition for my personal life journey. In short, I stopped looking for external validation of who I was or what I had achieved (my previous life and businesses), and instead learnt to be ok with who I was in myself. In essence, my path had strayed from my true life journey as it was not congruent with who I am at the core and placed me on a different track that now feels much more in alignment.

It would be entirely disingenuous of me to suggest that this work hasn't also been coloured by the many personal development resources I have been exposed to in my life journey so far. I have read scores of books, attended many seminars, researched information on the internet or social media, worked at many places, and all my encounters with others. Many people have shaped who I am today and all of these interactions have been distilled into this book.

My own personal experiences and spiritual growth have also filtered into the book somewhere, although I have tried very hard not to make it about me or let my ego get too involved. I am restricted by my own human limitations; I'm mildly dyslexic (thank goodness for spell-check and some very generous souls who took the time to review previous drafts!), and I still suffer with the fear of how others might judge this book or me for putting my name to this work.

It has taken nearly three long years, thousands of hours of work, and wrangling with my innermost demons to complete and publish this book. I have chosen to deliver the authentic message in its entirety, even if it contains the occasional spelling mistake or grammatical faux pas! It is my sincere hope that this book will inspire and motivate others who may be struggling with the same fears or limiting beliefs to take action on their hopes and dreams despite that nagging inner critic suggesting we're not good enough. If it inspires just one person, I shall feel incredibly blessed.

Looking back over the last few years and beyond, I can now see the beauty and wisdom in God's plan. I had to experience all my previous hardships to find the path I am on now - one of continual learning and growth. I've certainly realised that pain and hardship can have a beautiful side if we choose to learn from them and we remain humble.

I've also learnt that nothing we ever want in life comes to us in a straight-line, A to B, process. Despite what others may say, I believe each of us has an individual path that will take us to what we truly want in life if we only have the courage to persist in walking it. I don't believe anyone else can tell us what that path is; it can only come from quietening the mind and listening to that inner knowing as your journey through life unfolds. All I can council you on is to not take too much notice of others, especially the plethora of people on social media promoting themselves as living the dream. If they are, fair play to them, but I would guard against using anyone else's life as a yardstick for your own (especially some 'guru' on stage), as no one, and I do mean no one, is uniquely you. Only you can walk the path that's meant for you. When you do this with courage, who knows what the future could hold?

Whilst this book is a work of fiction, perhaps there may be some messages within that will resonate with you and your own journey through life. Those of you looking to enjoy the content as a recreational read will no doubt enjoy the story; the truth-seekers amongst you may well see an element to the teachings that escapes the uninitiated. Either way, I believe there is something of value here for everyone.

Once again, thank you for purchasing this book and investing your time to read it. I hope the different insights and ways of looking at the world will prove fruitful for you. I do encourage you not to take everything in this book at face value. Instead, tune into your own heart and you'll know if a message resonates with you or not.

If you have any feedback for me after reading the book, please do feel free to email me via love@loveisthenewreligion.com

Love and light always,

Silas J. Lees

Chapter 1

The Black Widows

LOCATION: Baku, Azerbaijan
DATE: 24th April
WEATHER: Warm and humid

The blacked-out Lynx helicopter thundered across the night sky, swooping in a large arc as it approached its drop-off target.

"Let's get these terrorist fucks," Commander James Wedmore shouted over the intercom system.

The cheer of his elite Special Forces soldiers indicated they were ready to go into battle. It was clear from their adrenaline-charged state that they were going in heavy and taking no prisoners. They all had the determined look of one that would give their lives for each other. They did not intend to do so, as they had certainty that they would emerge victorious. The team weren't known as the Black Windows for nothing, given they were named after the lethal black widow spider.

"Thirty seconds to drop-off," came the voice of the pilot over the radio. Each soldier gripped their machine gun and gritted their teeth. The humidity of the night air caused beads of sweat to roll off their brows and necks, trickling uncomfortably down their backs and soaking their camouflaged uniforms. They had no time to feel uncomfortable; from the moment of the drop-off,

they could be engaged in a fire fight to the death with some of the most ruthless terrorists the world had ever seen. A touch of discomfort was nothing compared to the searing pain of a white-hot bullet ripping through their flesh; a feeling that more than half of the squad had experienced several times in their lives. You didn't get to this level of elite combat without your body taking at least one round of ammo and living to tell the tale.

The chopper descended quickly in the cover of darkness to its drop-off position. The downdraft of the rotor blades caused the long grass to flatten against the ground, resembling a manmade crop circle. The pilot held the helicopter steady a few feet above ground as the exit door flew open and the crew of six leapt out in night vision goggles. They squatted whilst peering into the darkness, rifles at the ready should any hostile hosts be there to welcome their arrival.

Arriving under the cover of darkness gave some protection to the troops, but the thundering noise of the helicopter could easily give away their location, especially in this remote part of countryside in Baku. As soon as the last troop had exited the helicopter, Commander Wedmore bellowed *"All clear"* over the radio, competing with the noise of the blades. The pilot rose quickly into the night sky and made a quick exit from the scene. It was all about efficiency and being as invisible as possible so the mission could be completed with the element of surprise in their favour and as few casualties as possible for Commander Wedmore's team.

The Black Widows had completed many missions deep within enemy territory and were part of an elite, highly confidential crack squad that did not exist as far as the governments of the western world were concerned. How they actually received their instructions and targets was never straightforward or clear; they existed to 'assist in negotiations' with the Middle East and to ensure that the status quo of the world continued in flawless harmony, at least as far as the average citizen on the street knew. The Black Widow team was legendary amongst the military forces of the western world. The particularly rigorous selection process generated members from the SAS, Navy Seals, RAF, Black Ops, CIA, FBI, and secret services. The tales of their adventures were the stuff of campfire talk amongst regular squaddies who inspired by the achievements of this elite group of men.

You would not be able to tell who belonged to this band of mercenaries if you met them in the street because they looked ordinary, unless you looked deep into their eyes. This is what made them so lethal; that they could go undetected in broad daylight to complete their mission as well as they could under the cover of darkness with full combat gear at the ready. Their missions usually involved straightforward elimination, taking no prisoners, and leaving no evidence. Their work was rarely reported by the world media and was usually staged to make most tragedies look like an accident, or a disappearance. The military reformist that drowned after falling overboard from his private yacht, or the terrorist leader that disappeared off the face of the earth without a trace. Only to those in the know, and there were precious few people, would you be able to tell that the Black Widows had been involved.

As the chopper roared off into the night sky and the silence returned, the team remained silent. They were focussed on their respective patch of darkness as though expecting someone to jump out at any moment. Tension filled the air. Missions like this had only one outcome: kill or be killed. A bullet fired from a long-range silenced rifle could strike them down and they wouldn't even hear it coming. Blending into the darkness was their only course and not moving ensured they wouldn't give away their location.

They remained steady in their position for at least ten minutes as they scanned the surrounding areas for any signs of imminent danger. They kept silent and their radios were off. Then, without a word and in perfect harmony, as though subconsciously connected to one another, they collectively crept gently backwards into a closed group with their backs to one another, their intense gaze never moving from their segment of observation.

As the group came together in a close huddle, they switched their radios on and ran over their action plan one more time. It would take them approximately three hours of trekking across the countryside and forest to reach their target on the edge of town where they would take out the Hezmat terrorist group that had recently claimed their involvement in the disappearance of the UN and UK foreign policy ministers and their clerical entourage. The disappearance wasn't the only issue; graphic video footage of their torture and execution had been posted on YouTube, which quickly circled the globe causing a media frenzy and public outcry. People were living in fear over the threats made to repeat a 9/11 style attack on the US and UK. Normally the western world would brush these threats off, yet this group's the recent actions were threatening the stability of the relationships between the West and Middle East. It was decided that their elimination would be the best thing for all involved.

Their leader, Mohammed Guisu, was notably extreme and was linked to the possible contamination of a local water supply through viral infection, which could result in the death of up to twenty million local people after ingesting the tap water. He also had low tolerance for threats from the west and ordinarily acted in spite of the possible consequences by killing all prisoners rather than negotiating at any level. Guisu had created a following of local people who intensely hated America and the UK and were no doubt planning something big as a statement of their dislike for the west.

Commander Wedmore, on the contrary, was an extra-ordinary, no-bullshit leader of the Black Widows who had an intense dislike for anything that threatened the western dream. An Englishman by birth, Wedmore married an American diplomat who he was very much in love with. Despite being in the UK Special Services and having a keen sense of awareness about the dangers of his wife's job, she was victim to a taxi bombing in Pakistan on an international peacekeeping mission between the American and Pakistani governments. The bomb had been planted by a terrorist group that sought freedom from the control of America on the country's economic system and trade deficit. Wedmore was devastated by the loss of his loving wife and was committed to doing all that he could to rid the world of 'terrorist scum' for as long as he was alive. He transferred out of MI6 as soon as he could and took up his position within the Black Widows, quickly rising in rank due to his unquestioning dedication and thirst for the eradication of all terrorist organizations on the planet. He quickly gained the respect of his colleagues and superiors and stood for a better version of the world without the influence of such dark forces on the planet.

Wedmore was a legend in the armed forces. His story was tragic, yet the fire raging inside him spurred him on every time he went into a combat situation. He was fearless, some even claimed he was invincible, as he continually put himself into situations that seemed lethal, yet he walked away without a scratch. Some believed his invincibility came about from the spirit of his wife whom he prayed to shortly before every mission. Whilst not the 'spiritual type', Wedmore was intrinsically linked to his love for her and he wore her locket around his neck at all times. The archetypal man's man, he was almost never afraid, carrying with him a keen sense of duty towards God and the Queen. There was no doubt that Wedmore had a huge influence on his own team and anyone who had heard his name - they would all lay down their life for him and they all trusted his combat decisions implicitly.

The Black Widows huddled tightly together to finalise the plan before setting off on their three-hour hike. Hans Weaker, the blonde haired 6'4" German affectionately called 'Hitler' amongst the Black Widows, was in charge of communications and their extraction once the job was complete. At times of intense night combat, it was especially important that the group communicated well with one another to ensure none were caught by enemy fire. Attacking at night brought many logistical problems on the ground due to limited visibility and the noise of gunfire and explosions interfering with communicating one another's movements. Hitler informed the group that he had communicated the exit procedure to base to ensure everyone was aware of it just in case he went missing in action (MIA). The possibility of going MIA was always high and no one wanted to make it out alive if their teammates were struck down.

Randy 'Kamali' Burns, the American contingent of the team, was poised to lead the team through the forest towards the Hezmat headquarters. Kamali was of Red Indian heritage and had an uncanny knack of tracking people over long distances as well as having incredible intuition of predicting a dangerous event before it happened. The team always looked to Kamali to keep them safe and prevent them from facing a fire fight if it was avoidable. One of the great things about being part of the Black Widows was that there was no subscription to traditional armed forces' dress codes or haircuts. This suited Kamali well as his hair was jet-black, thick, and always kept in a long ponytail down his back. His heritage endowed power in having long hair and he believed this gave him intuition that had saved his life, and the lives of many others, on more occasions than he could count.

Kamali was a master marksman and could hit a pinhead at over a thousand feet. He was equally at home with a crossbow or bow and arrow as he was with a sniper rifle or machine gun. He had been recruited to join the Black Widows after he lost family members in the 9/11 atrocities. Although he was never in the military before, Kamali's reputation as a marksman and a tracker had spread far and wide. He also had many skills that allowed him and his team to live off the land when times were particularly desperate and they needed to lie low for several weeks until they could evacuate. He also had a sense of smell that was keener than most dogs and could sniff out food or an enemy at great distance. All in all, Kamali made an essential part of the team and everyone was glad he was with them.

The squad checked their map and compass before heading off with Kamali leading the team. Ever alert and ready, their ears and eyes were peeled for any sign of danger or impending attack. As back up to Kamali's skill set, Pedro Gonzales, the Mexican-born, Cuban-blooded Thai boxing champion turned military assassin had his heat-seeking night vision goggles on and continually scanned the distance for any sign of human movement. His nickname was 'Gringo Gonzales' amongst the squad who seemed to take great pleasure in racial, religious, or cultural slurs wherever possible. It was considered as bonding and an affectionate sign that they were like a family. Gringo would be the first to signal any sign of movement up ahead if Kamali hadn't already sensed it. It all seemed to be quiet and it looked as though their arrival had gone unnoticed. They were free to proceed with caution towards their target and complete their mission.

Chapter 2

Terrorist Camp Attack

LOCATION: Baku, Azerbaijan
DATE: 25th April
WEATHER: Warm and humid

The cool night air chilled the brows of the soldiers as they moved towards their target. The entrance to the forest was eerie, particularly in the darkness and the strange noises in the distance. Even to the most hardened of elite warriors, there was always something uneasy about treading this terrain and their minds played tricks on them. The presence of venomous snakes, scorpions, and poisonous spiders added an extra element of danger to the mission.

Progress was slow as each step was purposeful to cross the uneven terrain so as not to disturb the surrounding wildlife, which would easily give away their position. After an hour of trekking, all appeared very quiet and the group paused for a water break. In this humidity, it was imperative for the troops to stay fully hydrated, as failure to do so would ultimately compromise their performance. Jimbo 'Springbok' Pattison handed out ration packs to the team whilst they checked their bearings with the map and compass, cross-referencing with GPS tracking to make sure they were right on track. Sometimes the old ways were still the best.

Springbok, the South African weapons specialist, ensured the team was well equipped for the mission. Every team member had their own personal weapons choice, but Springbok made sure that everyone had additional advantages for tactical attacks in the form of long-range sniper rifles, landmines, and explosive-linked tripwires. Sometimes it was necessary to ensure the enemy could be eliminated from long range before engaging in close combat. Hollywood movies always showed adrenaline-fuelled action scenes with millions of rounds per second being dispersed, with the hero emerging unscathed, but the reality was very different. Every time the Black Widows engaged with the enemy, they knew there was the very real possibility that some wouldn't make it home alive or completely intact. Their personal safety was always paramount. Bulletproof body armour was never fully effective against modern weaponry where machine guns firing several rounds per second could cause serious impact damage alone without any of the bullets actually penetrating flesh.

Canadian-born Joe 'The Doc' Murdoch administered any field dressings and patched the crew up after a gunfight, but it was never easy keeping wounds clean and ensuring the troops made it back to safety before blood loss from a serious impact from a bullet or explosion took their lives. The team knew Doc's skills could only swing the balance of survival so far; after that, it was down to the laws of nature as to who survived and who didn't. Being the medic of the group carried huge responsibility to save his fellow troops whenever the chance arose and sometimes this weighed heavily on him. His method of coping always involved a heavy drinking session after every mission, regardless of whether he needed to save anyone's life or not. Fortunately, being part of the Black Widows meant the team were highly successful at taking out the enemy and rarely required medical treatment in the field.

Confirmation of the team's position showed that they would reach their location by 2am. This was prime time for attacking the enemy. It was usually dark enough to get into position to co-ordinate a quick and deadly strike on the enemy without being seen. They could also lay a deadly trail of explosives and then retreat to safety before luring the enemy out with some gunshots, letting their panic and fear do the damage for them. They knew all terrorist groups were usually poorly organized and had little military training, making them easy to rattle under fire before taking them out. That said, they were almost always inhumane in their capture and treatment of western soldiers or civilians; frequently torturing, maiming, or killing them as a show of strength to strike fear into the hearts of the west. It was this display of frequent brutality that drove every member of the Black Widows to do what they did best: take these people out and make the world a better place.

The Black Widows set off across the dark and treacherous terrain once more towards their enemy. Luckily, the clouds had started to clear and the full moon helped to light the way. The crew kept their senses at the ready realizing that one momentary lapse in concentration could result in their death. They were not expecting to run into any trouble throughout the forest, but they could never be too careful. The Black Widows knew that mistakes in battle cost them their lives. No further incentive was required to remain vigilant.

"These fucks are going to pay for dragging me through this fucking forest," Doc said over the airwaves to his comrades.

"I know what you mean," Gringo said. *"I'm looking forward to my black beauty getting some action,"* he said kissing his matt black AK-47 rifle.

"Quiet, you guys," Wedmore said. *"We've come this far, let's not give away our location now. We never know who might be listening."*

"True that," Hitler replied. *"These rag-heads aren't as dumb as we might think. Let's keep it on the down low until we complete the mission."*

The troops continued in silence as they approached their target towards the edge of the town. The three-hour hike had left them all soaked with sweat from the extreme humidity. They all took a cautious and final drink of water before advancing. The compound where the terrorists were believed to be hiding showed little sign of activity. A few lights were on in a couple of the temporary buildings around the site although there were no obvious signs of life. Even the makeshift watchtower constructed of timber poles was unoccupied. Over to the right of the site, a lone bearded man dressed in corduroy trousers with brown boots and a checked shirt stood smoking a cigarette; the pale red end of his cigarette partly illuminated his face in the darkness as he inhaled. He seemed oblivious to the six pairs of eyes staring intently at him.

"What's going on here then?" Wedmore whispered over the radio to his colleagues.

"Beats me!" Gringo said. *"Looks like we're too late!"*

"I can't believe that. Our Intel said this is exactly where they are based," Doc said.

"We're definitely in the right place," Kamali said. *"Can't you smell them?"* he asked rhetorically, his sense of smell picking up the unseen.

"It's all just a little too quiet for my liking," Gringo added. *"Do you think someone might have tipped them off that we were due to pay them a visit?"*

Right at that moment, as the squad lay close to the high ground overlooking the compound, a light came on in one of the temporary buildings. A middle-aged man in a white t-shirt with blue jeans and white sneakers stepped out of the building and crossed the courtyard towards the man finishing his cigarette. He pulled out his own supply of smokes and offered his colleague one. They engaged in small talk as they both lit up their cancer sticks and puffed away, completely unaware that they could be struck down by gunfire at any moment.

The Black Widows did nothing for a whole ten minutes while they observed everything around them. It was too quiet. Something just didn't make sense. What could possibly be going on was the question racing through everyone's mind. It would be too easy to hit the camp, take everyone out, and retreat to safety but it felt like something was missing. The team knew to always trust their gut instincts at times like this. It was far easier to lay low for an hour or two and retreat without engaging the enemy rather than going unprepared into an unexpected situation. That's when mistakes and causalities happened. Besides, time was on their side and they could gather further intelligence before returning to base, so the mission would not be a complete waste.

The smoker in the checked shirt reached into his pocket and pulled out his mobile phone to answer a call. He was too far away for the call to be heard, but it seemed to rouse them into action as they both walked towards the large gate to the compound and opened it. In the silence of the night, the rumble of a fleet of heavy military vehicles could be heard approaching the compound in convoy, their headlights dancing over the bumpy, earthy track as they sped towards their destination. There were three large canvas-backed Rheinmetall MAN military vehicles preceded and followed by two long wheelbase Land Rovers being driven at speed towards the compound in almost perfect military formation. It was only as they approached the gate to the compound did they ease up and slow down to enter. As they entered the yard, they circled around a stockpile of oil drums before screeching to a halt with their engines still running and headlights illuminating much of the courtyard for the Black Widows to observe what was going on around them. The two smokers flicked ash from their cigarettes before closing and bolting the entry gate.

Two armed men bolted from the front vehicle and quickly climbed up the wooden ladder into the watchtower to turn on the spotlight and aim it at the rear of the third MAN vehicle whilst three armed men in casual dress pulled back the canvas tailgate and two more aimed their guns inside the vehicle.

"What the fuck is going on?" Gringo asked.

"Patience," Kamali reassured. *"All will be revealed shortly."*

It was clear that there were people in the third vehicle. The occupants in the back of the wagon were dragged out onto the courtyard, hands bound behind their back and gagged. They were visibly terrified from the ordeal. Men and women between 30 and 45 years of age in casual dress were ordered to stand in line as they exited the vehicle. Assault rifles were waved in their faces to ensure their full co-operation. A fully decorated general stepped out of the first Land Rover and marched towards the first two MAN vehicles. He ordered more armed men out of the rear of the vehicles who disappeared into the temporary buildings, switching on more lights to illuminate the darkened rooms in preparation for the new arrivals.

The Black Widows looked on at the entourage of troops and hostages. Clearly, the situation had changed considerably from what they had been told to expect. Intel suggested that there were around a dozen armed terrorists occupying the camp and no hostages were reported. There was always the chance that things would change, but hostages were a seriously different matter. Attacking the camp in their usual way could result in the deaths of innocent civilians, which they did not want on their conscience. It had now clearly turned into a rescue mission and the stakes were now considerably higher.

The team continued watching the hostages. It was unlikely that they would have been brought back to the camp to be killed, but the team couldn't risk that assumption. If they were to rescue them, they had to act fast before casualties occurred. The hostages were led to a green-painted temporary building with three windows overlooking the courtyard. The incandescent light bulbs swinging in the air shone light on the faces of the hostages to reveal looks of horror. Each hostage was led to a single metal military style bed, each bearing a stained, thin mattress, which they were thrown onto. Most of the hostages had tear marks streaming down their dust-covered faces. They struggled against the force of their oppressors as their feet were bound with rope around the bed frame to prevent them from escaping. Despite the struggling, not one of the hostages sought to break free, as the threat of being shot dead was imminent. It wasn't too long before all the hostages were bound to the beds and the gunmen left the building, turning off the lights and locking the door to reconvene in the courtyard, leaving their sobbing captives behind.

Now they knew where the hostages were being held, Commander Wedmore signalled to his team to pull back into the cover of darkness to discuss the attack strategy.

"We need to do something about this situation," Wedmore said. *"It's clear the game has changed somewhat."*

"I vote we go in hard and heavy," Gringo growled. *"We need to teach these scum a lesson!"*

"I would advise against that," Doc said. *"The hostage situation could turn ugly quite quickly."*

'I agree," Kamali replied, ever the source of calm and tranquillity. *"We don't need any more bloodshed than necessary on a mission like this. We should approach it tactically to take out the armed guards first so we can release the prisoners and evacuate them.*

We need a co-coordinated attack if we are going to be successful with this one."

"How do we get into the compound without being seen?" Hitler asked.

Wedmore stepped in. *"We need someone to take out the tower guards after we have breached the camp walls. Kamali, I'm allocating that job to you with the sniper rifle. You can also watch from up there and help to pick off anyone that we might have missed. Springbok, you and the Doc will be responsible for breaking into the hostage building so we can release them as soon as possible. Me, Gringo, and Hitler will attack the other buildings to take out the troops after we have planted some explosives around the entrance to each unit. It's going to be intense in there as we need to ensure we don't tip them off by accident and get a nasty surprise."*

Without another word, the crack commandos headed back to the high ground to finally observe proceedings before taking positions to launch the attack. The good news was there were plenty of vehicles to make an escape with, as they now had to extract a number of civilians. The bad news was those same civilians were a liability as they could be struck by crossfire from any direction or an explosion. Within the compound, the armed guards were all receiving instructions from the general. It seemed as though this regime had some unexpected military organisation as terrorist groups were notorious for recruiting amateurs to join their ranks. Perhaps this one was different.

Kamali was the first to take position with his sniper rifle. He watched the two watchtower guards through the scope of the silenced sniper rifle before the rest of the team moved out. The team felt reassured by Kamali, as he never missed his target. He could reposition and switch targets quicker than anyone else they had ever met, so with him on the high ground keeping a watchful eye over proceedings, it took a certain amount of pressure off the rest of the team. The remaining team of five crept gently downhill taking care to keep close to the ground and in the shadows.

The movements of the team were unheard over the noise of the engines still running and the general barking orders to his guards as they ran about the courtyard and took up patrol situations around the camp. Twenty-four armed guards could be seen, plus the general and the two smokers who had now retired back to one of the temporary buildings. It wasn't clear if they were also military men or just hired hands, but it was always safer in these situations to never take any risks.

The Widows arrived at the perimeter fence in the darkest corner of the camp that was sheltered by a large oak tree helping to shield their location. The boundary fence was a simple enough to get through as it was constructed of nothing more than metal fence posts and chain-link fencing. What wasn't clear was whether or not there were any tripwires and hidden landmines that might take them out of the game. The team meant were experienced enough to look for any such possibility.

Springbok drew his laser wire-cutting device from his tool belt and used it to form a small opening in the fence. The team crawled through on their stomachs to enter the campsite then split into two teams and went their separate ways. Doc and Springbok remained in the cover of the shadows around the edges of the camp, as they moved closer to the hostage building. They were the first to arrive into position, with machine guns at the ready and watching every step the enemy took.

Wedmore, Hitler, and Gringo moved silently towards the huts containing some of the enemy; the smell of stale cigarettes filled their lungs. They hid under the elevated huts and lay low. Kamali could hear the deep breathing and raised heartbeats of his colleagues over the radio as they went about their tasks, all the time keeping his rifle trained on the soldiers in the watchtower in case they should spot his colleagues in the campsite.

The watchtower spotlight was now scanning the courtyard as four of the guards marched in unison to check the camp's perimeter. They did not suspect that they had visitors. Four more soldiers took up positions around the building containing the hostages whilst the remainder and the general looked as though they were heading to their bunks for the night. One by one, they filed up the short timber staircases with Wedmore, Gringo and Hitler listening to the sound of boot steps and chatter just above their heads. The doors closed, followed by the sound of metal-framed beds creaking under the weight of each occupant as they rested for the night.

Once they saw the lights go out in each of the soldiers' buildings, Wedmore's team decided to make the game a little more interesting by planting claymores facing the entrance doors to each hut, which would take out any enemy rushing out to support their colleagues under attack from gunfire. It took a few short minutes until everything was in position then Wedmore's team retreated to better vantage points ready to take on the opposition. Once they were at a safe distance, Wedmore scanned the camp to assess the position of his colleagues before issuing the command to commence the attack.

Just as Wedmore was about to issue the go-ahead, the camp spotlight shone on Springbok, revealing his location to the tower-guards, who instantly sounded the alarm. Kamali took the first shot, hitting a guard square in the back of the head and dropping him from the platform in free fall. His colleague turned the spotlight around to shine it in the direction of the attack, only to be greeted with a bullet straight between the eyes, leaving him slumped over the spotlight, which was now pointing at the floor of the watch tower. As soon as the alarm went off, the lights instantly came on in the guardhouses. The guards surrounding the hostage building had taken up battle positions around the building, peering out into the darkness and confused at the commotion in the watch tower. One of the patrolling guards set off a flare into the night sky to illuminate the area so they could see what they were up against now the camp spotlight was out of commission. Just as his flare gun went off, a silenced round from Kamali's rifle hit him in the chest, knocking him to the ground.

Springbok, who had been temporarily dazzled by the searchlight, had lost part of his night vision so the Doc leapt into action picking off the guards surrounding the hostage building before anyone could be harmed. The doors to the troops' buildings flew open and they ran down the steps to see what was happening, only to be greeted by the exploding claymores, which took out the terrorists and sent flames ripping through the digs causing screams of pain. The four patrolling guards in the courtyard had run for cover and were now firing aimlessly into the night, clearly panicked by what they had witnessed. The flash of fire from the ends of their rifles revealed their position to Kamali who swiftly silenced them.

The burning remains of the soldiers' hut drew any surviving soldiers from the building. Unarmed and ineffective, they were covered by Gringo's and Hitler's rifles who knew well enough not to open fire on unarmed people, no matter how evil they were. They moved in close and made them surrender quickly, handcuffing them with ratchet straps to prevent them from causing trouble.

Springbok and the Doc moved towards the hostage building. Muffled murmurs and sobs of shock were coming from inside as the Doc forced entry and turned on the lights with

Springbok quickly in tow. The looks on the faces of the hostages said it all; they were deeply traumatized by everything they had experienced so far and the only saving grace was that they hadn't suffered for very long. Springbok took the knife from his boot to cut the bonds of all the hostages whilst the Doc checked them for any wounds requiring emergency medical aid.

Wedmore and his team scanned the remainder of the campsite, which was now illuminated orange by the burning remains of the terrorists' huts, to ensure there were no more threats and that they had rounded up all the unarmed men who had surrendered. One thing bothered them; as the flare had been fired together with the noise of explosives and gunfire echoing through the night sky, the team had a strong feeling further hostile company was to be expected very shortly.

"Get two of those vehicles ready to go," Wedmore ordered over the radio to Springbok and Gringo. *"We need to make a sharp exit. Hitler, get that gate opened whilst Doc and me get these people on board the trucks. Kamali, I need you to meet us at the entrance to the compound pronto!"*

"What are we going to do with the prisoners, boss?" Gringo asked.

"I'm tempted to say fuck 'em, but we'd better take them with us," Wedmore replied. *"They can probably answer a few questions about this organization back at base."*

"Roger that," Gringo said. *"I'll get the trucks up and running and then get them on board."*

Wedmore and the Doc reassured the hostages once again that everything was fine and they were here to help, before leading them out of the building towards the vehicles. They all piled into the front vehicle whilst Gringo rounded up the prisoners and helped them into the back of the second truck. Kamali was silhouetted against the ground, moving down the slope towards the entrance of the camp as Hitler flung the gate open to make a swift exit. Headlights beaming and with everyone on board, the team stepped on the gas. There was only one road out. The Black Widows knew they needed to get to the crossroads towards the local town and harbour or be caught in a fight. The window of opportunity could be counted in seconds and the adrenaline was pumping through the veins of the Black Widows as they sped along the single-track road to make their escape.

Chapter 3

Escape

LOCATION: Baku, Azerbaijan
DATE: 25th April
WEATHER: Warm and humid

The vehicles tailgated at high speed along the bumpy country track with headlights illuminating a few short meters in front of each vehicle as rain started to fall heavily. As the wheels bounced out of the deep ruts and puddles, muddy water covered the windscreen of the trailing vehicle.

"Slow it down a little," Hitler yelled over the noise of the engine revving and the rain pounding the tin roof.

"We need to make a sharp exit out of here, my friend," Gringo shouted. *"I've got this, just relax!"*

The forest road took several twists and turns towards the local town. The Black Widows needed to find the road to the harbour as the possibility of encountering oncoming deadly force was imminent. If any vehicle approached them on the current road, the only option was to engage it. The team was too experienced to take their chances in a fire-fight; besides, with the newly rescued hostages on board, there would invariably be heavy losses if stray bullets ripped through the canvas sides of the trucks and would totally defeat the purpose of the rescue mission.

Time was passing too quickly and it seemed to take forever for the harbour road to appear. The hostages, already shaken from their ordeal, were holding on for dear life in the back of the vehicle as it bounced along the road. Their bloody and dirty faces showed anxiety and fear as they contemplated their fate. A few of the hostages bowed their heads in silent prayer of some desperation, hoping that their God would save them from further trauma, unrest, and upset. Others had tears streaming down their faces that streaked through the grime.

Suddenly, the road forked and the lead vehicle slammed on the brakes, skidding and sliding to a halt on the muddy track as the trailing vehicle did its best to slide to a standstill alongside it.

"Which way, Kamali?" Wedmore shouted so that the occupants of both vehicles could hear his authority.

"We need to head left and pronto!" Kamali had already detected that there was danger fast approaching and they needed to get out of there quickly.

"You take the lead this time with the cargo! Hitler, get in here!" Wedmore commanded. *"We'll follow you and give you cover."*

Hitler jumped into the back of the first vehicle as Gringo and Kamali drove off into the darkness towards the harbour. The Doc and Wedmore joined Hitler whilst Springbok drove in hot pursuit. Intuition told them what was coming. It was best to attack any vehicle that was following them at the first opportunity. They prepped their machine guns to open fire on any vehicle that might try to block their progress.

They didn't have to wait long. As they looked intensely into the dark night, they saw lights flashing in the distance from military vehicles driving at speed down the same road. Their plan was pretty simple; shoot out the headlights to cause them to crash, or pump as much lead as possible into the engines of the pursuit vehicles to cause them to grind to a halt. They knew that if the vehicles caught up with them, there was virtually no chance of survival as they would be severely outnumbered and outgunned. The vehicles gained ground quickly despite Springbok's fast driving. It seemed they had kamikaze drivers in this part of the world.

"Fire!" Wedmore shouted.

The team aimed for the headlights with some degree of success. The first headlight went out immediately, followed by the second after a few more rounds. The moment darkness was forced upon the enemy vehicle, the driver lost control after hitting a big puddle and swerved across the track, slamming into a nearby tree, which turned the truck on its side and partially blocked the road for the remaining vehicles. The screeching brakes could be heard above the continued shots from the Black Widows who were keen to maintain their small advantage. It was imperative to keep the enemy at bay whilst gaining ground towards their destination.

Suddenly, the sound of bullets penetrating metal could be heard close to the Black Widows as they realized response fire was coming from the fast approaching enemy vehicles that had successfully negotiated the obstacle of their fallen comrades. There was only one thing for it. They had to lace the track with several grenades that would hopefully take out the tyres of the pursuing vehicles, whilst they maintained a steady stream of fire to keep them guessing. The Doc and Hitler pulled the pins from a handful of grenades whilst Wedmore increased the number of rounds coming from his machine gun. Travelling at such speed, there was no need to throw the grenades; they just dropped them from the back of the speeding truck into the mud of the track and watched with anticipation as flames and fireworks from the explosions would tell them how accurate they had been.

The second enemy vehicle lit up like a gasoline-fuelled bonfire moments later, causing the third vehicle behind it to crash into it, completely blocking the track. The Black Widows sped off into the night feeling a sense of relief for at least the time being. There was no way any surviving enemy soldiers could catch them on foot at this speed. They only hoped that they would encounter no other traffic so they could evacuate the prisoners via the harbour quickly and effectively.

Within ten minutes of driving, the team arrived at the harbour and brought the vehicles to a halt. As they pulled up towards the water's edge, they jumped out of the trucks to help unload the prisoners.

"Reminds me of a time I went skinny dipping with that hot blonde from San Diego," Gringo said with a wry smile and a look that left little to the imagination.

"Is that the one who told you 'It's like a penis, but smaller'?" Springbok replied with a sense of razor-sharp wit that brought a little chuckle from the rest of the team.

"Come on now, guys, we have important work to do!" Kamali said.

"Hey Gringo, he said important, not impotent!" Springbok said, ever the comedian in high-stress situations.

"Alright, boys, knock it off," Wedmore said. *"Let's get these guys and girls to safety then you two can spend all night playing kiss-chase with one another."*

The team helped the prisoners out of the vehicles onto the small cobbled harbour where the Doc checked them all for any immediate injuries sustained in the road trip with his head torch. There was an assortment of minor bumps, bruises, and scrapes, but nothing that would stop them from making the escape effectively or that needed immediate medical attention. The adrenalin running through their veins would keep them from feeling the pain for a good hour or so, which was long enough to be well away from danger.

Kamali and Hitler were already getting a large fishing boat up and running ready to take the hostages and the team out of harm's way. There was zero security around and no boat alarm system was going to stop these guys from doing what they did best. Hitler and Springbok also made sure they had rounded up plenty of extra fuel from the adjoining boats to take with them on the journey just in case. Kamali turned the engine over and it started first time. The boat seemed seaworthy enough from what could be seen, and it had capacity and space to get everyone out of the danger zone quickly and effectively without arousing too much suspicion.

As the hostages boarded the ship, the Doc, Gringo, and Wedmore ran around the harbour gathering as much drinking water as possible to ensure they could hydrate the prisoners and themselves after such an epic ordeal. They loaded six five-gallon drums of water onto the boat just as Kamali and Hitler raised the anchor and revved the engine to leave via the gap in the harbour wall.

"We need to be careful as it's low tide right now," Kamali said. *"Let's head out to sea as quickly as possible and get to safety."* He glanced briefly at the water-borne compass on the captain's desk and then looked at the stars to navigate more effectively. *"Intuition is always the best guide,"* Kamali said as he noticed Gringo watching him.

"C'mon man! You can't tell me you believe in all that stuff?" Gringo asked.

"Have I ever let you down before? Trust in something bigger than you. There is intelligence at work that knows far more than each of us. Have faith, brother!"

Gringo turned and walked away shaking his head playfully with a smile on his face.

The boat danced gently over the waves of the peaceful ocean. The bright stars provided a welcome distraction for the team who had just successfully completed their mission with zero casualties. The Doc went below deck to check up on everyone. If he could keep them calm, they would be in a much better position to cope with the aftershock of their ordeal rather than be fearful or hysterical.

Wedmore congratulated the team on a job well done before taking a few moments for quiet reflection. When he stopped for a moment and took his mind off the fighting and adrenaline, he realized what a beautiful place the world was and how lucky he had been to see so much of it on his various missions. It always weighed on his conscious that each visit to a new place was tarnished with the blood of another human being. He calmed himself with the thought, *"Well, they're the bad guys, so it's ok!"* Deep inside his heart, however, something was beginning to shift.

Chapter 4

Suspicious Orders

LOCATION: London, England
DATE: 27th April
WEATHER: Grey and overcast

Commander Wedmore was stirred from a deep slumber by the noise of his phone vibrating loudly on his bedside table. His room was sparsely decorated save for a few photos of his late wife. He reached to grasp the phone. His eyes barely opened from lack of sleep and a groggy feeling consumed him. *"Hello?"* Wedmore mumbled as he answered the phone.

"Hello, James," came the stern voice from the other end. *"How are you feeling?"* It was Agent Rosehill; the exceptionally dry and disciplined voice of ruthless efficiency and reason that can only come from years of service to the FBI and various other underground secret agencies within the United States. Rosehill had been transferred to a specialist anti-terrorist division within the US military based in London that was unknown, unheard of, and definitely not in the domain of public knowledge. The organization was known as CGI (Control of Government Intelligence), which controlled the missions of various off the record military subgroups, including the Black Widows. Rosehill issued all mission instructions to the Black Widows via Commander Wedmore, but as neither organization officially existed, there was never any paper trail or link between the two,

nor any links to the military or governments of any kind. It had to be this way for missions to be sanctioned.

No one asked too many questions and everyone followed orders, otherwise they would be cast aside, which was never a good thing for anyone reliant upon the money they earned in these positions. They were paid well and no one bothered to ask where the money came from. Some rumoured it came from taking out drug lords who were sitting on large quantities of cocaine, who watched from the afterlife as they witnessed their spoils being seized by the US government, only to be sold by the people in charge who pocketed the money to enrich their own lifestyle. Others questioned the sanity of this suggestion, yet the question of what happened to all the drugs that were seized remained. There certainly wasn't any evidence of drugs being incinerated, which was the official story sold to the public!

Either way, the money was very good. Where else could you earn £2,000 a day in cash, pay no taxes, and have all your living expenses taken care of? The main outlet for the money was their bad habits of drinking hard liquor, smoking cigars, or riding fast motorbikes, which most of the Black Widows indulged in after each mission. It was a way to let off some steam and adrenaline and to bury some very deep emotions that accompanied ending somebody else's life or witnessing the atrocities in the war-torn countries they were frequently sent to for their missions. What the public never understood, particularly in the west, was that the harsh realities of war are very, very different from the media's pictures of shaky images and explosions with some presenter wearing a bulletproof vest, or the images most teenagers experience in video games. They were just too removed from actual reality.

They have no idea what it is like to take the life of someone, whether a sworn enemy or an innocent bystander who gets caught in the crossfire, and then have to live with the haunting consequences. All of the Black Widows had watched people they care about be killed in combat and some had even held longstanding friends in their arms in the heat of battle as their hearts stopped beating and their souls slipped away. There were never any words to describe that experience and no matter how tough or battle-hardened you were. Watching it all unfold in front of your very eyes was always traumatic and tugged at a part of your heart that twisted your gut, much like wringing water out of a towel.

Despite common perceptions, being a military person did not mean you were devoid of a conscience or you didn't feel pain; quite the opposite, in fact. Many of the soldiers who returned from Iraq were suffering from what was dubbed 'Gulf War Syndrome', which was passed off as chronic fatigue and stress from taking part in battle. However, no-one seemed to take into account the effect it has on a person when they take the life of another human being, no matter how evil they may appear to be or how justified it is. The toll it takes on the human body, mind, and spirit is enormous and some soldiers say that a part of their own soul died too with each person they killed.

Wedmore had experienced this on too many occasions to count. Despite being driven into battle to take out the people who were responsible for the death of his loving wife, he had learnt that mental detachment was the only way to cope without suffering the consequences of the many nightmares that followed in the weeks and months after every field operation. There had been many times when he had woken up startled from another nightmare in a bed that was drenched with sweat where he lay questioning if it was all worth it. There had been other sleepless nights, wrangling with his conscience that prompted the same line of questioning, but when morning came, duty called, and it was business as usual.

The hole gnawing inside Wedmore was getting bigger and bigger, and required more and more energy and alcohol to suppress it. Each time he suppressed the emotions to go into battle during a mission, they always found a way to creep back up and make their presence felt afterwards. He often questioned his own sanity and his ability to cope, wondering if he actually was in the right profession, but what was the use? He was a trained military machine who took care of the world's problems behind closed doors so innocent people didn't have to live with oppressive leaders, or be brutally slain just because of their religious differences. Still, he couldn't escape the truth that his heart and soul were trying to communicate to him, that it's inhuman to be inhumane.

"I feel fine," came Wedmore's gruff reply, knowing that to admit what was really going on for him would fall on deaf ears and ultimately lead to his abilities being questioned and him being dismissed from duty.

"I hope our friends in Azerbaijan took care of you. I wouldn't want you getting soft on us now!" Rosehill replied in a dry, sarcastic tone. *"Listen, I need you to come in to talk about your next operation. Meet me at my office at 1400 hours."*

"Sure thing," Wedmore replied. *"I'll see you then."*

The anticipation of meeting with Rosehill always filled Wedmore with apprehension. No matter how many times he had been called into meetings about operations, he always felt like a school boy being sent to the headmaster's office. Rosehill had a way of interrogating you just by looking at you and was always looking for chinks in the armour of people to exploit to ensure they remained 'in his pocket'. It was clear he trusted no one, which made him a difficult person to work under, as there was always a strong element of suspicion. Rosehill wanted to know the people working with him were trustworthy, but was caught in the paradox of not trusting anyone, which made everything a little difficult to manage.

Rosehill had been betrayed by someone who posed as his best friend for eight years. The two were very close and had supported one, even spending Christmas with one another's family and children. Little did Rosehill know that his best friend, Thomas Hillcrest, was working for a counter-intelligence agency for the Iraqi government and he had been compromised on a number of occasions. Rosehill finally realised Hillcrest was working for the Taliban only after Hillcrest had kidnapped Rosehill's wife and held her to ransom. Rosehill had to share several codes to FBI computer systems in exchange for his wife's release. This compromised many international American military missions and revealed the identity of several FBI agents who had successfully infiltrated foreign terrorist organizations, leading to their public execution.

Rosehill had been scarred for life and had become so mistrusting of people that it had eventually cost him his marriage a few years later. Even though he dearly loved his wife, he could not get over the fear of losing her or learn how to trust someone again. Heartbroken and angry, he worked at the CGI working for 18 hours a day, seven days a week, pledging to stamp out those that dared to challenge the political dominance of the west. In a way, this unspoken bond united Wedmore and Rosehill in the success of their missions, but Rosehill always relied upon Wedmore and his team to deliver the message personally whilst he sat safe in his ivory tower far away from the imminent dangers of life.

Wedmore arrived at the CGI HQ in the London 20 minutes before the rendezvous time. *"Old habits die hard,"* he said to himself as he entered the lobby and approached the security desk. He smirked at the sight of the security that ran the place; the main guard, Dave, was at least 11 stone and looked like he had never seen the inside of a gym. Wedmore pressed his thumbprint into the security scanner and walked through the gate catching the elevator to the 11th floor.

As he exited the elevator and walked towards Rosehill's private office, he saw a smart looking gentleman leaving. His instinct told him something was amiss with the visitor; his frame stooped slightly and his energy was off. Wedmore had spent enough time with Kamali to understand how the personal energy of people was linked to their intent. Whilst Wedmore linked it to warrior instinct, Kamali explained it was intuition linked to the infinite intelligence of the universe, which each individual's subconscious mind was inextricably linked to.

"Once a person starts tuning into their intuition," Kamali explained, *"they become as powerful as God himself as they can access the universal truth and power that lives in the ephemeral unseen."*

Wedmore had initially been sceptical, but he had seen him use it to great effect many times, sifting friend from foe on several occasions and leading the team to safety without maps, compasses, or knowing where they were in enemy territory. Intuition, or gut feeling as Wedmore believed, was more powerful than most people knew. The feeling deep in the pit of his stomach led him to believe that the visitor was a sinister man.

Wedmore paused out of sight farther down the corridor, pulled his phone out, and pretended to take a call whilst he observed what was happening. Rosehill and the visitor shook hands as Rosehill assured him, *"You have my word. I will take care of this matter personally."*

A wry smile spread across the pale face of the hunched visitor as he turned and shuffled off down the corridor, unaware that his every move fell under the watchful hawk-like eye of Wedmore.

Rosehill too, was unaware of his presence. The visitor then pulled his own phone from his pocket, hit a few buttons, and said hauntingly, *"It is done."*

Wedmore's gut wrenched. Something didn't sit right and that was not usually a good sign. He paused for a few moments pondering the situation before he knocked on Rosehill's door ten minutes early for their meeting.

Rosehill greeted him with a stern look over the top of his half-rim glasses as he glanced up from the paperwork on his desk.

"You're unusually early, Wedmore," Rosehill said.

"It sounded important that I get here promptly," Wedmore replied. *"Who's the visitor?"* he asked taking a seat in the leather chair opposite Rosehill.

"Need to know basis, Wedmore, and you don't need to know," came the stern reply.

"Are you still trying to peddle me that bullshit?" Wedmore spouted who was clearly upset at the remark.

"I'm sorry, it's just the way it is. You know what working for these bastards is like. All rules, regulations, and secrecy crap! If I had my way, they'd all be out of a job!"

"That's not a bad idea at all. Bloody pen pushers! Do they have any idea what's going on in the real world?" Wedmore asked.

"They seem to be making all the rules about who the bad guys are and who we need to take care of, strictly off the record of course! Speaking of which, we have new Intel on the location of your friend from Hezmat. Your orders are to take him and his tribe out and make it all look like a rebel assault within their underground HQ. Do you think you can do that without causing a stir?" Rosehill said.

"You know it's what we do best," Wedmore replied with a distracted half-smile. He rose from the chair and walked towards the large plate glass window that overlooked the city. His mind was clearly on occupied as he gazed at the people walking the streets below, minding their own business as they went about their day.

"What's on your mind, Wedmore?" Rosehill asked.

"Have you ever stopped to question what's really going on? I mean, what we are really fighting for? Something you've just said is in my mind and I just can't shake it off. What if we're wrong? What if the guys at the top giving the orders are wrong in their assumptions? I mean, they've never been to war, they've never watched another person die by their own hands, they've never gone through the many sleepless nights in the aftermath of returning from a mission. They just sit in their ivory towers and get guys like us to carry out their orders. How do we know they're right? How do we know we're not fighting to please their whims?" Wedmore asked, his mind clearly anxious about the forthcoming mission.

"We're not paid to question authority, Wedmore. We're paid to follow orders!"

"That's precisely my point! We never question anything! We just follow the official line that we're told and get on with it all. No questions asked!" Wedmore exclaimed as he faced Rosehill. There was a faint hint of tension in his voice as he looked across the room deeply into Rosehill's eyes.

"What's the matter? Don't you like your job all of a sudden? It's what you're paid to do. You clean up the government's problems without anyone asking any questions. Is it all getting a little too much for you?" Rosehill asked with some empathy.

"It's just… Do you think those people down there actually have any idea what's going on?" Wedmore asked.

"They haven't got a fucking clue! They are all too busy going about their daily grind with their minds occupied by trivia fed to them by TV. They don't think for themselves. They are too busy being programmed by the media telling them what to think, what to eat, what to drink, what to wear, what to tell their friends about, and which mind-numbing program to watch next. They're all getting fat and lazy in their soul-destroying jobs, getting paid just enough to keep them from leaving but not enough to actually do anything with their lives. You know what J.O.B. stands for, right? Just Over Broke! You know why they're called 'sheeple'? They're sheep to the system being herded wherever the system wants them to go! It's a system that you and I are paid to protect and keep in place. Lord only knows what would happen if they knew how to think for themselves and they knew what really was going on! You know how the system works as well as I do and we're faced with being part of it or not. Take my advice, don't bite the hand that feeds you!" Rosehill lectured.

"I know all too well about the system! I've given the best years of my life to protecting it and taking out the enemy along the way. There's a part of me that just can't help but wonder if we're really doing the right thing. I can't explain it…it's just a feeling I have inside me. I can only describe it as intuition or 'gut feeling' that's making me start to ask questions," Wedmore said.

"Listen, Wedmore. I am a very busy man and as much as I would love to discuss this further, I have a meeting in 10 minutes, so do you want this job or not?" Rosehill barked.

"Hmmmm…ok, I'll do it. When I come back though, I'm going on leave for a few months to straighten myself out. I need some time to rebalance."

"Rebalance?" Rosehill mocked. "You're starting to sound like a fucking hippy, Wedmore! Get your shit together, do this *mission, and we'll talk more when you come back. Here are your orders and don't fuck this up! The world media will be watching this one. Get it wrong and you're totally on your own. You know you guys aren't even supposed to exist."* Rosehill handed Wedmore a sealed brown envelope. *"The drop point, destination, and formal ID of the Hezmat leader are all in there. Share it with your team, and only your team, then destroy it,"* Rosehill commanded.

"Aye, aye Cap'n!" Wedmore replied sarcastically as he took the envelope and headed for the door.

"Just one more thing, Wedmore. It doesn't pay to question authority, you know. If you have concerns, just resign and disappear. You can't expect to change the world. It's too big. There are forces at work that you don't know about or understand. I don't profess to understand them all either. One thing I do know is what happens to those who do question authority and get out of line, and it tends to be the same thing that happens to people you and your team are sent to deal with. Just keep your head down, get on with it all, and you'll be fine," Rosehill explained.

"Thanks for the heads-up. I appreciate it. We'll talk when I am back. I have a feeling about this mission and you're going to want to know all about it later on. See you in a few weeks."

Wedmore stepped out into the corridor whilst stuffing the envelope inside his leather jacket. The door closed behind him as he walked towards the elevator, his mind still evidently on the last remarks of the conversation with Rosehill. What on earth did he mean about 'forces being at work that I don't know about?'

He punched the call button and waited patiently for the lift. He couldn't shake off the feelings the conversation had left him with and the prospects of the forthcoming mission. He and the rest of the Black Widows were now being ordered to take out the leader of the most wanted terrorist group and the whole world would be watching. It was a big ask. He knew the team was more than capable, but he couldn't shake the feeling that something wasn't quite right. Something deep within him was telling him to be on his guard. He knew from bitter experience not to ignore a feeling like that, as every time he had done so previously, it had backfired on him and his team.

Wedmore walked across the marbled reception area, out of the building, and onto the street. He looked at the crowds of people and recalled Rosehill calling them 'sheeple'. He paused for a couple of minutes and let his mind wander with thoughts of where they were all going and what their lives were really like. Was it really possible that they were all doing just what the system told them to do? Was it really possible that they had been told what to think, eat, drink, and wear? It certainly gave him an introspective view of his own life and raised a few questions over the choices he had made. What if he had made the wrong decisions? What if what he was doing was plain wrong but he had been led to believe he was fighting for good causes?

It was clear to Wedmore that things were getting on top of him and he needed to let off some steam. He pulled out his cell phone and called Kamali, letting him know that the team would be assembling tomorrow to plan the mission and get their kit together. Now it was time to sink a few drinks to take his mind off what was happening and maybe find some female company for the night before meeting with the team at 1000 hours.

Chapter 5

Truths Deep Within

LOCATION: London, England
DATE: 28th April
WEATHER: Sunny spells with some drizzle

The alarm sounded at 0700 hours as Wedmore opened his eyes to the morning sunrise that shimmered through the chink in his bedroom curtains. He had to admit that waking up in a comfortable bed was far more appealing than the floor during missions, and the five hours of alcohol-fuelled sleep he had embraced was far better than the two or three hours of adrenalin-fuelled passivity he was used to.

He pulled back the duvet and walked to the en-suite to take a cold shower to sharpen his mind and help take away some of the muscular aches and pains of military duty. Although he was advancing in years, he physically felt better than ever before.

He reflected on how his night had escalated into a full-blown nicotine and alcohol state in an attempt to stave off some haunting images that had flashed through his mind from a previous mission in Belgrade. What was supposed to be the routine procedure of a textbook assassination of an activist went horribly wrong and two innocent children and their mother were killed in the crossfire between Wedmore's team and the activists' security forces. The images of seeing the mother crying over the death of her babies as she bled to death on the street haunted Wedmore on more than one occasion and added to his lack of sleep and waking up in a pool of his own sweat. These were the times when he most hated what he did for a living and he would not wish the after effects on his worst enemy.

He managed to get into a semi-meditative state to take away the images through a combination of deep breathing and focusing on his heartbeat whilst quieting the mind. It was a technique he had recently learnt from Kamali, which helped him to remain calm and centred even in the most heated of battles with bullets flying everywhere. He wished he had found it years earlier. It would have saved him a lot of heartache and wrestling with his conscience over what he did.

Why were some people allowed to live and some were resigned to die early? Would he himself have been on the receiving end of a bullet from a gun had he been unfortunate enough to be born in another country? Or if his chosen path had been to do what was right rather than what he was paid to do and was told was right? As time went on, there was an inescapable feeling of uneasiness that gripped his heart and conscience.

He looked at himself in the mirror for the first time in a long time. He came face-to-face with Commander James Wedmore and all that he stood for. He looked at the lines on his face, the grey hairs in his sideburns, the chapping of his lips, the three-day stubble growth, and bloodshot eyes. He looked down at his arms and hands as they rested on the sink in front of the mirror, observing the hairs, the scars, the wrinkles and the subtle tan that faded from his forearms into his biceps. He saw the faint imprint on his finger where his wedding ring had been for so many years. He looked deep into his own eyes for several minutes, captivated by what he saw.

As he looked deeper into his eyes, his mind suddenly went still and all thoughts stopped. Time stood still as the silence fell all around him and he became present with his own soul. His gaze led him past all the distractions in his conscious mind and, as the silence descended, his blackened soul stared right back at him. He knew, for the first time in his entire life, that his heart was speaking to him and he didn't like what it was saying. He knew what he was doing wasn't right and things needed to change. He knew he was born for something much deeper than killing people and being paid for it. What had happened to the dreams of his childhood? What had happened to the young man who joined the military to fight for Queen and Country? What had happened to the man who fought for justice and took the lives of those who would take the liberties of others? He was living a false life and he knew it. Something felt very, very wrong indeed. Tears began to form in his eyes as the realization began to set in. Was this what a wasted life looked like?

He told himself to snap out of it as he picked up his razor and turned the tap on. He punished his momentary lapse of composure by dry shaving himself. As he did so, he became more and more angry for allowing the thoughts to creep in in the first place. How could he be so weak? This was inexcusable conduct for a highly decorated military officer and a member of an underground tactical government agency. He patted his face dry before returning to the bedroom and dressing.

Breakfast consisted of a large glass of orange juice, two double espressos, and a cigarette. It wasn't his usual form but he needed it this morning. He gazed out of the kitchen window at the world, which had now started to go about its business. Again, he pondered if they had any idea what was actually going on. Here he was, about to go and take out the most wanted man in history under a covert military operation in order to protect the freedoms of someone that didn't know who he was or probably what he was fighting for. Did they understand that they were inadvertently asking him to put his life at risk for their liberties? Not a chance did they have any conception of what was really going on because even he had absolutely no clue of what was really going on. His instincts were struggling to get through to him against the background of his military conditioning and his deep thought processes. He was certainly feeling a little uncomfortable and couldn't shake off the bad feelings. Perhaps, he reasoned, things would become clearer once he was with his team and they were on their way to carry out the mission. Otherwise, he could always wait until he returned to get some time alone and figure out what was really troubling him so much.

What he felt was his conscience trying to speak to him. An inner knowing that something wasn't as it seemed. Was it the fact that this next mission was probably going to be the toughest of his entire life? Or maybe his last? Or was it that he was just getting too old for fighting and killing people? Perhaps he was exhausted from too many missions and not enough time out. What did he need time out for though, he thought? He didn't have any family and the only friends he had were doing the same thing he was.

He reflected on his life for a moment; the last 10 years had been all about expressing the intense rage that had built up inside him after losing his wife to terrorists and he felt that this had now largely run its course. His energy levels were depleted and he no longer had that burning sensation in his gut to terminate as many oppressors as possible. Had he wasted the last 10 years? Had he spent a huge amount of energy fighting something externally rather than coming to terms with what had happened and being at peace with himself over the loss of his wife? Surely no one deserved to go through that level of pain for something they hadn't done wrong? What could possibly justify the actions of those who took his wife away from him and caused his entire world to collapse? So many questions were left unanswered and Wedmore began to realize he could not continue to suppress the emotions any longer. Something needed to change and change drastically.

He recalled previous conversations he had with Kamali regarding achieving a state of inner peace through meditations, which Kamali claimed would be very useful for Wedmore following his tragic loss. Wedmore had dismissed it as he was just too angry to even engage with the practice and wanted to completely justify the hurt and suffering he had endured by taking the lives of those who had taken the most precious thing from him. Kamali had tried to reassure Wedmore of the tranquillity and calm that could come as a result of just stilling the mind.

"The mind is a poor master but an excellent servant," Kamali had said. *"You must recognize that there are just too many distractions in this world and your mind will be pulled all over the place. If you engage in letting the mind run the show, you will almost certainly lead a life of quiet desperation."*

When Wedmore questioned what Kamali had meant by 'quiet desperation,' he went on to say, *"The majority of people on this planet live lives of deep unfulfilment. They get distracted by the media, their cell phones, Facebook, social media and all the other things that are going on in their lives. Their mind gives them a picture of how things are supposed to be, but life isn't regimented and therefore doesn't fit into the mental pictures of man. So they become continually frustrated by the inconsistency between their mental imagery and what the reality of their life really looks like."*

"To add to this, the majority of people are not following their childhood dreams. There is a complete mismatch between what they dreamt of doing when they were younger and what they are now doing in their adult lives. Their dreams were given up on and died as they went through the schooling process that encouraged social obedience over individuality. So, the level of

frustration within themselves is huge. Their spirit knows what they were born to do in this world, what they were born to do with this precious gift they were given called life. Instead, they chose to do some job to put food on the table or to please their parents or satisfy their ego. Their dreams died inside them and their spirit reminds them every once in a while, which intensifies their frustration. They have not made peace with themselves for giving up on a part of them that was once very important. They are too distracted with life and won't take the time to own every part of themselves through deep personal reflection and meditation. So instead, they sedate themselves through caffeine, alcohol, nicotine, or drugs."

"That's pretty deep, Kamali," Wedmore had replied to what seemed like an assault on his very being.

"You think that's deep?" Kamali scoffed. *"If you want to go really deep, I could talk to you about the full system of control and suppression that exists in modern society, but you're not ready for that yet. No offence, friend!"*

"What are you talking about, Kamali? There's no system of control in place. We live in a free country! We're paid to go abroad to bring freedom to other countries, and remove dictators who would oppose the rights and freedoms of native people," Wedmore replied, obviously shocked at what Kamali had said.

"Brother, look at me," Kamali said. He had never ever used the word 'brother' before when addressing his superior officer. *"Do you honestly think that I would lie to you about something like this? I know that we bring freedom to others in certain cases, but the bigger picture of what is happening in the west is much darker. There is no doubt in my mind that we are allowed a certain amount of freedom, but I cannot call us free people. Not by a long way. I'm not going to suggest to you what is really going on, but take a look around you. Take a look at the*

number of government security organizations that have been created over the last few years. Take a look at the number of CCTV cameras that have been cropping up in every town and city in the west. Heck, even our phones and computers have spy cameras on them and our phones have tracking devices. They call them 'smart phones' because we're dumb people. We pay huge amounts of money for a device that constantly occupies us and spies on everything we do! Why do you think I never got involved with this modern tech? It's not my scene! I'm gravely concerned about what is happening, my brother, and I cannot shake the feeling that something bad is coming."

As Kamali spoke, he looked deep into Wedmore's eyes with a sense of determined kindness that let Wedmore know that what he was communicating was deeply personal and important to him and that his concerns were not just the flights of fantasy of someone who was not firmly grounded in reality. Wedmore knew how seriously Kamali took his spirituality and 'groundedness' with Mother Earth, as he called it. He also knew how Kamali could always sense what the enemy's next move was going to be before it actually happened. He definitely possessed a sixth sense or an intuition that guided him and this was clearly an important issue for him. Time and again, he had to remind himself how many times Kamali had saved the team from a fate worse than death by being intuitively one step ahead at all times. It was funny that Wedmore recalled this conversation now whilst there were so many emotions going on for him. Could it be that his own sense of intuition was awakening and he had begun to tell right from wrong? Only time would tell as the next few weeks unfolded and the end of the mission was in sight.

Commander Wedmore pulled up to the RV point at 0945 and was pleased to see the rest of the team were awaiting his arrival. He loved the fact that he could count on their punctuality, which was vital in a combat situation.

"Hi team!" he said with an undercurrent of joy in his voice. *"Great to see you guys again."*

It was the presence of his team members as they stood there organizing kit on the workbenches that gave him some mental and emotional relief from the earlier part of his day. He wondered if it was possible they could sense something wasn't 100% right with him as he looked at each of his team in turn, holding their gaze for a split-second longer than was ordinarily comfortable. There was no doubt that the pressure and expectation of their forthcoming mission was getting to him and he took a few deeper breaths to steady his mind.

"Everything ok, boss?" Kamali asked as if he had read Wedmore's mind.

"All present and correct, I see," Wedmore replied in an attempt to shake off any further prying questions from Kamali or the rest of the team. *"Are you all ready for this next mission?"* Wedmore asked.

"I was born ready!" came the cocky reply from The Doc with a smile. He quickly followed up with; *"If you stay ready, you don't have to get ready!"*

"I wonder if you will experience maturity some day, Doc," Gringo quipped.

"Easy gentlemen," Wedmore said. *"We have a big mission ahead of us and we need to make sure we don't fuck this one up! The whole world will be watching us!"* Wedmore placed his large well-worn duffle bag on the floor next to the workbenches and threw the leather jacket he was carrying on top of it. *"Hitler, put the kettle on and let's have a brew whilst I brief you on this one. I need your full attention."*

As Hitler turned to walk towards the tea station, Wedmore shouted after him; *"And make it a proper strong English brew, not your usual cup of weak piss!"*

"*Aye, aye, Captain,*" came the reply.

Wedmore enjoyed the bond between him and his team, which was somewhere between a schoolboy lavatorial sense of humour and the greatest of friendships that can only exist from going through the most testing of times together. He felt the connection when they were together and missed it when they were apart.

Hitler returned with six battered tin mugs full of steaming hot tea for his comrades as they formed a circle to listen to their commander outline the proposed operation. A sense of calm fell over the group as they listened with their full attention on Wedmore.

"Listen, team, this next mission is not going to be an easy one. I'm not going to beat around the bush here, but we have been given orders to take out the leader of Hezmat. We have been given the location of his HQ, where we are to infiltrate it and assassinate him without anyone knowing. The powers that be believe this will disrupt their operation and cause the balance of power to shift in favour of the west, whilst ridding the world of a barbaric terrorist."

"Are you fucking kidding me?" Gringo said. *"This guy will be armed to the teeth with a whole bunch of his terrorists scum mates protecting him! We won't have a chance! We can't carry that much firepower to defeat them all."*

"Gringo's right," Doc said. *"It will take a huge amount of firepower to infiltrate their camp, defeat the enemy, and take out their leader."*

"This is not up for discussion guys!" Wedmore retorted. He knew all too well about going into battle with his team when they weren't in the right headspace. In fact, he had often thought that most battles were won in the mind before they were ever won on the battlefield. If their minds were thinking

negative thoughts before they went into battle, they would almost certainly lose. He knew that he had to quash their thoughts and feelings of defeat before it infected the group and fear took over. Fear was the biggest killer in any battle situation, so this had to be eliminated immediately.

"Listen, guys, I would not risk my life on a mission like this if I didn't trust you all implicitly. I know you have my back as much as I have yours. There is no doubt this is our biggest mission ever but I also know we can handle it. It's not going to be easy, but it is going to be worth it. Imagine what the world would be like without this scum of the earth creating a reign of terror. Imagine being the ones that bring peace to the world and allow others to live lives of freedom. This is what we're here to do and I know in my heart we can achieve this. Yes, we need to carefully co-ordinate our attack, but it's nothing we're not used to doing in all our years of experience. I know working as a team we can achieve this, so let's make it happen! Agent Rosehill has given us explicit instructions to take the enemy out and make it look like it was an accident or an inside job. The media will then do the rest to celebrate the downfall of this villain."

"I'm with you and I believe we can make this happen," Hitler said.

"Me too," Kamali said. *"What's the plan?"*

"I've got a map of the area. We will need to cover the majority of the way on land as an air drop is way too risky and we'll be picked up well before we get anywhere near close enough. We're going to have to cross part of the Saudi Arabian Desert, which we can do in the Land Rover. From then on, we will have to approach on foot, take out the enemy strategically, and retreat under cover of darkness."

"Sounds like a good plan, boss," Gringo said with a light-hearted smile, "but you know no plan survives first contact with the enemy! What happens if they pick us up before we get anywhere close?"

"Frankly, this is a one-way mission if we get picked up too soon. We're off the record, so we can't request an emergency evacuation. We need to go in, do a good job, and then head home. If we fail, we're done for. So let's not fail!" Wedmore replied.

"I'm in, if it means we can rid the world of these extremists," Gringo said with an air of machismo. "We're pretty much invincible judging by the missions we've done previously. We'll be fine on this one."

"We need to be clear and level-headed about this mission," Kamali counselled. "We know they are heavily armed and aren't afraid to use captives for public execution for their cause. I can sense something about this mission. We need to keep our wits about us. It's us, versus them, with no halfway house. We can't trust anyone. There are no friends in this harsh desert, especially for six heavily-armed foreign soldiers."

"I'll start pulling the kit together then, boss," Springbok said. "I'll mix in the heavy firepower with long-range rifles and some ground explosives. We're going to have to carry plenty of fuel and water in the Land Rover if we're to make it across the desert. I'll make sure it all happens."

"Great work, team! We'll pull the kit together today, load the Land Rover, and drive to the RAF base and fly to the international airbase in Riyadh tomorrow. From there, we'll head northwest into the desert and on towards Medina. Their base is hidden on the outskirts of 'The Empty Quarter' where we must arrive unannounced to complete our mission. We're going to be away for the next three weeks potentially, so call your wives, girlfriends, and lovers to let them know you're going to be away for a while!" Wedmore said.

The team jumped up and started pulling together their kit and uniform for the next few weeks, carefully checking and oiling their weapons prior to leaving. Operating in the desert always presented added dangers as the hot, sandy environment often led to weapons jamming if they weren't carefully cleaned on a regular basis. The desert presented additional challenges such as lack of water and resulting dehydration and heat exhaustion, huge distances to cover, and sandstorms that caused disorientation, none of which helped in combat situations.

The Land Rover Defender 110 was fully equipped for desert operation with oversized tyres and a roof rack for carrying large quantities of supplies. Tents and sleeping bags, water, fuel, and ammunition all needed to be taken with them. To the side and rear of the vehicle were plenty of holding points for jerry cans that would carry the diesel they needed. They would also have to hide the vehicle in the desert and so they carried desert camouflage, which could be quickly hauled over it to shield it from the eyes of enemies who might hijack the vehicle for their own uses, or even worse, destroy it and leave them stranded in the middle of nowhere.

The Black Widows worked in silence and in perfect harmony carrying out their individual tasks for the greater good of the group. The additional firepower was loaded into the back of the vehicle, with each team member taking charge of their own weapon to ensure it was to their standards. Their guns were an extension of themselves and needed to be set up perfectly to be part of their anatomy, so they could point and shoot without even thinking about it.

Wedmore took particular pride in carrying his 'last line of defence', which was a Bowie survival knife so sharp that it would cut you just by looking at it. The knife was strapped to his right calf when he went into combat situations, so it was always close to hand. He also carried the Desert Eagle .50 sidearm to use in close combat situations, although he rarely did as it immediately gave away his position due to the noise it made with each shot fired. He always chose to carry it with him, as he felt naked and unprotected without it.

Gringo packed a large rucksack full of ration packs. Initially everyone who tasted the rat packs said they tasted like cardboard, but they were nutritious and were easy to hydrate without having to be cooked. He then filled ten five-gallon containers full of water and strapped them to the roof of the vehicle. He drew a reflective sheet over the water to protect it from the sunlight. Unfortunately, any bottled water exposed to the heat of the desert would quickly turn stagnant, and consumption would cause sickness and diarrhoea, not ideal in a combat situation.

Each team member also lightly packed their burgeons, which they would carry with them as they continued their journey on foot. They would need to carry their sleeping bags and personal survival blankets too; the desert was scorching hot in the day and temperatures plunged to sub-zero after dark, making it particularly taxing on the human body. Coping with both extremes whilst packing light was never easy, but experience proved a useful guide. The other concern was encountering scorpions and poisonous snakes in this hostile land, which could pose a serious medical emergency. The Doc carried some anti-venom injections with them, but these were never guaranteed to work.

The kit was loaded onto the vehicle and a final check conducted by all team members to ensure they had everything they needed. Once it was all secure, they took up their positions within the vehicle and headed off in the direction of the RAF base at Feltwell. Gringo was driving fast and blasting out some AC/DC as they sped along the motorway. Everyone seemed to be in high spirits and enjoying their last few hours of England's green land before being sent out to the harsh desert.

Chapter 6

Desert Heat

LOCATION: Riyadh, Saudi Arabia
DATE: 29th April
WEATHER: Unrelenting desert sunshine

As the military plane touched down in Riyadh, the team continued in silence as they mentally prepared themselves for what lay ahead. They knew the intensities of travelling through the desert and it was important to keep themselves in a peak mental state before undertaking their mission. The Black Widows carried out a final vehicle check before reversing the Land Rover out of the back of the plane into the scorching heat of the morning sunshine. Every team member donned their shades in an attempt to deal with the intensity of the sunlight, a far cry from the grey English skies.

The team took their positions before they were ushered out of the airport via a secure gated area and out onto the highway. They joined the traffic, sticking out like the proverbial sore thumb against the civilian traffic, even though the vehicle looked like an Arabian military SUV, complete with desert paintwork and localized number plate. Gringo was driving as the team settled into the faux leather seats, which were quickly becoming slippery with their sweat. It was like being placed inside an oven and opening the windows wasn't doing a great job of cooling them down.

They drove for around ten miles along the highway before exiting onto a minor side road, which led them away from civilization and towards the desert. Their expected itinerary was to spend a day travelling 60% of their way towards their target location, camp the night in the desert, and then continue on foot for the next 48 hours towards the terrorist HQ where they would carry out their mission. Their main issue was ensuring they had enough water to carry them there and back. Keeping hydrated was important, as research reported that even 2% dehydration very quickly led to co-ordination issues and mental exhaustion. They had a method of effectively recycling urine, which would cut down on some of their necessary water needs, but they knew they could only really use this in extreme cases and it was highly unlikely that they could rely on this for more than about 24 hours. The other possible salvation was finding an oasis in the desert, which they knew would allow them some respite if they needed it. Physically getting to it if the enemy was pursuing them was another thing entirely.

After an hour of driving, they turned onto the desert dirt road following their map and their military grade GPS device that would confirm their exact location. Travelling through vast expanses of sandy nothingness without landmarks for reference points was not going to be easy. There was little conversation between the team as they cruised along the bumpy desert road, sand clouds billowing out from the back of the Land Rover as they sped along. They estimated that a four-hour drive along the winding desert road at their current speed would see them set up camp for the night. The hostility of the environment meant that they were unlikely to encounter many people so they felt safe as they drove towards their destination.

"Just another day in paradise, boys!" Gringo joked as he manipulated the vehicle along the dirt track. *"How y'all feeling?"*

"I know one thing. It's fucking hot here!" Doc said as he took a swig of water from his bottle, the beaded sweat on his brow forming marks across his dusty face.

"We sure do get the best jobs," Gringo replied.

"How much farther do we have to go?" Hitler, who was visibly uncomfortable in the hot vehicle, asked.

"About another four hours driving before we get to rest up for the night. Enjoy the heat, boys, it's gonna get a whole lot colder tonight," Gringo replied with a smile.

The road continued to wind through the mountainous sand dunes that remained untouched from the gentle breeze blowing in the desert. The remainder of the trip continued in silence as they headed towards their camp area. As they approached their destination, they estimated they had at least two hours before the sun dipped below the horizon and plunged them into darkness. This gave plenty of time to set up camp, eat, and drink before sleeping soundly for the night.

Gringo pulled up adjacent to a large sand dune that provided shelter from any harsh winds or storms that might blow up during the night. As the vehicle ground to a halt, the team jumped out and stretched their bodies, releasing the clothes that stuck to their bodies from the sweat during transit. They began to unload the tent and cooking implements to hydrate a few rat packs, which would be their feast for the evening.

Wedmore co-coordinated the erection of the tent whilst ensuring the area was free from bugs, snakes, spiders, and scorpions. They arranged the ground sheet in place and secured this whilst the tent was erected next to the sand dune. The Doc set about boiling some water for the food and serving the team with a strong brew of English breakfast tea. As they sat around in a circle enjoying their food and drink, they were treated to a majestic and brilliant red sunset. Head torches at the ready, the team prepared for their last proper night of sleep before they made their approach to enemy HQ.

"Kamali, you're on guard duty for the first part of the night," Wedmore said as he headed into the tent to make himself comfortable for the night. *"You're on for the first two hours, and then it'll be the Doc and then Gringo. Are you all clear?"*

The team agreed as they watched the last remnants of brilliant red sunshine disappear over the horizon and the night sky became illuminated by stars.

"Fine by me," Kamali replied. *"I'm going to enjoy this wonderful starry sky."*

It was now 2200 hours and time for the team to get some sleep. They carried their assault rifles into the tent as Kamali made himself a seat at a higher vantage point on top of the sand dune and looked all around him. It was so peaceful and quiet. The moonlight beaming down from the cloudless sky illuminated the sand dunes and vast expanse of the desert with a warm silver glow whilst the stars twinkled in the sky. The lack of light pollution made it very easy to see the vastness of the universe, the stars, the constellations, and all the boundless emptiness of space in between. Kamali let his mind drift onto some of the unanswered questions, such as where we come from, why we are here, the meaning of life. And what about the possibility of our celestial brothers and sisters being close by? Did they exist and, if so, why could we not see them?

The sounds of his teammates settling in for the night soon ceased and for the first time he was confronted with the deafening silence of endless nothingness all around him. He could hear no breeze or sound of wildlife or other people. They were in a remote and secluded position and he enjoyed being alone with his thoughts and wondering at the beauty of Mother

Earth. He leaned back into the sand dune, interlocking his fingers behind his head, and gazed up into the night sky.

"Thank you, God! Thank you for the abundance you provide. Thank you for my health and fortitude in life. Thank you for the opportunities you have given me. Thank you for taking care of the people I care about. I am blessed!" Kamali whispered, speaking simultaneously with the Almighty and himself.

Kamali always believed that his soul was visiting earth for a specific reason and that he would one day return home. He continued gazing into the night sky looking for a sign from the star that shone most brightly in the sky. Doing what he did for a living was never a pleasant activity, but he reasoned that this was his life purpose: to rid the planet of evil when he could and leave it a much better place.

He spotted a star shining more brightly in the sky and it drew his attention. He felt warmth in his heart and a smile spread across his face as he closed his eyes. He intuitively knew this was home and he basked in the energetic connection to it by imagining a bright rainbow-coloured light radiating from the star, bathing his whole body and connecting him deeply with Mother Earth. The legendary belief of his people was that those who mastered this method of connecting with the Heavens and Earth could actually revitalise and heal their body of almost anything. It was known that no one in his tribe had ever died from a western degenerative disease.

They knew the Universal Law that everything in the universe is energy, and all energy can be transformed. So darkness could be transformed into light and illness transformed into health. No matter what the situation, they knew there was a way to heal themselves through this practice of letting Divine consciousness take over. As a result, his ancestors frequently lived to well over 120 years of age. He lay there basking in the glory of the rainbow light covering his body and embracing the knowledge handed down through the generations. He wasn't suffering with illness, but it wouldn't do him any harm to enjoy the benefits of connecting with home for a few minutes and receive any intuitive downloads for the next steps of his journey whilst restoring his body to maximum vitality.

Without realizing it, Kamali slipped into a deep sleep in his enjoyment of the moment. His beliefs were such that at every stage of his journey through human life, he would receive further instructions on how to live his life and certain situations and life events would change as a result, eventually leading him to his destiny. This energetic state led to many intuitive nudges and solutions for problems that Kamali had been wrestling with. It was almost as though this state gave him access to a sixth sense, which helped him to avoid certain unpleasant situations or solve everyday issues. His mind slipped into a dream state as his body relaxed into the sandy mound that fully supported him as he slept.

As Kamali dreamed, he saw visions of a man and a child playing peacefully with one another, a scene of destruction and devastation, and the intuitive nudge of a possible attack coming at an unexpected time. He stirred from his slumber as he heard a rustling noise in the distance. As he woke, he stared into the night looking for signs of anyone or anything that might be approaching the camp. He knew that his night vision was very good but he couldn't see anything. He sat up, reaching for his flask to take a sip of water as he felt the uncomfortable cold of his damp clothes pressing against his skin as the chill from the desert night set in. He looked around again, but couldn't see anything. It could easily have been some wildlife or a freak gust of wind. It was unlikely they would meet anyone else in this location.

As Kamali peered deeper and deeper into the night, he vaguely made out the shadowy silhouettes of sand dunes in the distance and what could possibly be the presence of a large owl circling in the air no doubt looking for prey. He scanned the horizons from left to right very carefully taking everything in. More important than just looking, he was 'feeling' his way around his environment and searching for any signs of unusual activity or movement. Guard duty was never the best, especially as all his other teammates were sleeping and he was alone with only the cold and solitude of the desert night for company.

He heard a grunt come from the tent where one of his comrades was audibly dreaming and a faint snore coming from another. He chuckled to himself and thought how easily these noises would give their location away if they were behind enemy lines! A wry smile passed his lips as he reminisced on the adventures they had been on over the last few years and how lucky he was to have five warrior brothers who he knew would give their lives to protect him.

Civilians rarely understood the bond that men who fight battles together and who come into close contact with death form; it was certainly something that he had never found with other relationships in his life. Even though he was close with his own family, they had never been as close as he was to his brothers in the Black Widows. How curious that six random people could be brought together to form this team and would willingly die to save the life of another. Blessed he was that God had brought these awesome people into his life and allowed him to feel loved, valued, trusted, and respected.

As the memories of past missions and bonding moments passed through his mind, he heard the sound of a faint whistle in the desert night. He knew this was man-made and not the sound of wildlife or the wind. He reached down to place his night vision goggles on to see if there was any credible threat of danger, or if it was a desert shepherd making noises in his sleep. As he looked around, he spotted movement on top of one of the sand dunes around a mile away; it was the head of a man wrapped in desert attire. His intuition gave him an uneasy feeling that all was not well. The sinking feeling in his gut told him to wake the others.

"Hey guys!" Kamali shouted as he banged on the side of the tent, keeping his eyes clearly fixed on the position of the movement he had observed. *"Wake up!"*

Wedmore was the first to respond. *"What's up, Kamali?"* he asked in a post-sleep slurred tone.

"Get out here now, Commander! Something's not right."

The Black Widows scrambled out of their sleeping bags, grabbed their rifles, and made their way out of the tent, ensuring they didn't switch on any torches to highlight their position. Wedmore slid up next to Kamali with his back pressed up against the sand dune looking out into the night sky in the same direction as Kamali.

"What's happening, Kamali?" Wedmore asked.

"I have a really uneasy feeling that we are about to be attacked. I just heard a faint whistling noise and saw some movement on the top of that sand dune over there. Here, take a look," Kamali said as he handed Wedmore the night vision goggles and pointed in the direction of the sand dune. Wedmore slipped the goggles over his head and peered through the green-tinted optics. He reached up to adjust the goggles and zoomed in closer to the top of the dune, scanning up and down and side-to-side. He saw nothing.

"I'm not seeing anything right now, Kamali. When did you see the movement? What's spooked you?" Wedmore asked.

"About ten seconds before I woke you guys up. I had a feeling earlier that things weren't quite right. I wanted to be sure that we didn't hit a nasty surprise."

"I don't see anything. Team, how about the rest of you? Keep your eyes peeled," Wedmore commanded.

"Nothing here, boss," Hitler replied.

Just then, they heard a dull thud, followed by a hissing noise. They noticed the silhouette of the Land Rover behind them move slightly. Moments later, another dull thud and hiss could be heard. They realised the tyres were being shot out by a long-range sniper with a silenced rifle. The team were caught off-guard by the surprise attack in the middle of the night in the vast expanse of desert land. Worse still, they could not see their enemy leaving and felt very exposed.

Seconds later, the tyres on the other side of the vehicle were shot out. It was clear that they were surrounded and the shots were coming from higher ground. The team could not see any moonlight glinting off a rifle telescope or the signature flash of a round exiting the muzzle of a rifle against the darkness of the night.

"What are we going to do, Commander?" Gringo asked, unusually shaken.

Wedmore scanned the horizon once again looking for any sign of the attackers. *"Keep your heads down team and look for where the shots are coming from,"* Wedmore said, frantically calling upon his years of military battle experience to work out a plan of counter-attack or retreat. They were always the ones that used darkness for the element of surprise; to have it used against them felt very uncomfortable. Who are these mystery attackers and why would they attack them in the dead of the night in this remote spot? It didn't make any sense.

As Wedmore rapidly contemplated their next steps, he saw flames against the night sky. It was the tail end of a rocket launcher heading towards them at rapid speed.

"Incoming!" Wedmore yelled. *"Take cover!"* he shouted as they all scrambled to run for safety. The rocket impacted the side of the Land Rover with a mighty explosion, which lit up the area all around them. The vehicle was thrown up in the air amidst a ball of flames and secondary explosions were heard as the reserve fuel within the jerry cans caught fire from the impact. The Black Widows ran as fast as they could across the sand as they heard the remains of the vehicle crashing on its side against the ground. The Black Widows were spread in all directions, their night vision was ruined from the brilliant explosion, and the burning carcass of their transport lying on the ground behind them.

They were very exposed now their vehicle was gone along with the majority of their ammunition, their means of communication with the outside world, and their water rations. All they had was the ammunition in their machine guns, which gave them about 100 rounds each. Firing aimlessly and randomly into the darkness of the night would be massively ineffective in this situation.

The burning vehicle gave off more explosions as their ammunition went up in smoke. The dispersed team ran towards a smaller sand dune, approximately 500 metres away from camp, where they reconvened, all panting breathlessly from their sprint across the sandy terrain.

"Holy fuck!" Springbok bellowed as he slumped up against the sand dune. *"What the fuck was that?"*

"I have no idea," Wedmore said, *"but I don't like what just happened one bit. There's no reason for us to be attacked like that out here. We're miles from anywhere! It's almost like they were expecting us."*

"Expecting us?" Doc asked. *"Surely no-one knows about us being in this location other than Rosehill?"*

"We must have been tracked here," Kamali said. *"We are clearly not welcome and I suggest we need to get moving right now."*

"Do you remember where the oasis is located?" Wedmore asked. *"We're fucked if we stay here, so let's head in that direction and hope that God is with us and we can make it safely."*

Kamali looked up at the night sky to find the North Star. *"From memory, it's about 10 kilometres east of here."* As the words fell from Kamali's mouth, the familiar sound of a bullet impacting the sand just one metre away from them was clearly audible.

"Let's head that way then! Kamali, you lead and let's double time it!" Wedmore shouted.

The Black Widows jumped to their feet and ran towards the next sand dune to get out of the line of fire, as the impact sound of rounds hit the ground behind them. Whoever was firing on them had the upper hand and everyone knew it. They now knew what it must have felt like for their enemies when they appeared out of nowhere to launch a surprise attack.

They hurried across the desert sand with the faint moonlight guiding their way. The impact sounds of the bullets burying themselves deep into the sandy desert floor chased them as they went. The only way to make it safely to their destination was to run in a zigzag pattern across the sand to avoid being hit by the sniper who was totally in control of the situation. They ran as fast as possible, tacking their way carefully towards their rendezvous. *Thud, thud, and thud,* the impact noises of rounds hitting the ground kept them from tiring or slowing down. As they convened behind the next sand dune out of the line of fire, the team paused momentarily to get their breath back.

"Keep going, guys!" Wedmore said between gasps of breath. *"We'll make it."*

"There's something odd about this situation," Kamali said. *"This guy is clearly good enough to hit us in the dark, but none of us have been taken out. It's like we are being pushed in one direction somewhere."*

"Whatever he's doing, it's working!" Doc said in between taking huge gulps of air.

The impact sound of another round hitting the ground near them got the whole team on their feet again, running east in a zigzag pattern, spreading out in order to give one another space to cover the ground they needed to escape the attack. They fled and kept running no matter how breathless or tired they became. At some point soon, they would be out of the sniper's range and could gather their thoughts. As they were running, Gringo slipped on the sand and crashed to the ground. Hitler was closest to him and he ran across to help him back on his feet as they heard the impact of yet more rounds penetrating the sand adjacent to them. He grabbed Gringo's upper arm, heaving him to his feet, and they ran together towards their teammates. They could not afford to make mistakes. Into the darkness they ran, hopeful that they would soon escape the onslaught.

Chapter 7

Ambush

LOCATION: The Empty Quarter, Medina
DATE: 30th April
WEATHER: Cloudless sky and sub-zero temperatures

After half an hour of running across the sandy desert, the shooting stopped and the team took a moment to gather themselves. They huddled closely together, sharing what little water they had. Wedmore checked with his troops to see how they were all doing. Apart from being breathless and shook up, everyone was ok.

"The oasis must be close now," Wedmore said. *"We'll hydrate and work out our plan from there. We can't carry out our mission now, so getting the fuck out of this desert has to be our primary objective. Let's hope we don't encounter any more mystery snipers. I still can't work out who the fuck would do that."*

"We have plenty of enemies," Hitler said. *"No doubt Hezmat has plenty of guardians keeping this area clear of foreign intruders."*

"It doesn't make sense to let us live," Springbok said. *"We were clearly in this guy's sights and he didn't hit any of us. Why do you think that is, Commander?"*

"I have no idea, but I'm glad we are all ok," Wedmore said. *"Let's head over to the oasis and see if we can get some help."*

The team set off together, walking in line with their rifles across their chests, ready to draw them at a moment's notice should they come under attack again. The moon shone brighter than before and illuminated the ground in front of them. A desert snake slithered by in front of them. Everything was still again in the desert, but Kamali couldn't shake the feeling that their every move was being watched.

As they crested the top of a hill, they saw shimmering silver moonlight reflect off the ground letting them know the oasis was close by. Adjacent to the oasis were a number of white desert tents, some illuminated from within, casting silhouettes of the occupants against the sides. A sense of relief came across the team as they had at least found water and civilization in the dead of the night.

Before they had even formulated their plan of approach to the oasis, they heard rustling all around them. Four figures emerged from the desert sand with laser pointers aimed at the Black Widows.

"Do not move!" came the broken English command spoken with a thick Arabic accent. *"And put hands up."*

The Black Widows did as they were commanded. One of the gunmen approached the team from the rear, drawing his razor sharp scabbard, which he used to cut through the webbing straps of each team member so their rifles fell to the ground. The gunmen's laser pointers danced across their chests as the Black Widows kept their arms high in the air. They were in no position to argue so surrender was the most appropriate course of action to follow.

As the last rifle fell to the ground, another gunman approached from the rear and took away the handguns and knives strapped to their sides leaving them completely exposed.

"Very good. Now move!" the Arabic-English voice said again. The two gunmen at the front moved to one side allowing the Black Widows to walk downhill as the Doc and Gringo were poked hard in the back with rifle barrels encouraging them to walk. They kept their hands up and walked towards the oasis, the gunmen following close behind with their laser pointers trained carefully upon them as a reminder not to do anything foolish. The sandy surface slipped beneath their boots as they walked, making it difficult to maintain their balance.

"Keep it calm, fellas," Wedmore whispered. *"Let's see where this goes."*

"We're right with you, boss," Gringo said, trying his best to fake some confidence.

The team were marched down to the edge of the oasis where they could see a large campfire burning with some wooden seats close by. As they approached the fire, the light from the flames illuminated their captors dressed in traditional Arab smocks. Only their eyes were visible as the fabric scarves wrapped closely around their faces and concealed their faces.

"Wait here!" the Arabic-English voice commanded as he motioned towards the timber seats. The team sat down, whilst the leader headed towards the tents, leaving the three remaining gunmen surrounding them in a triangular formation to minimise their chances of escaping. The Black Widows welcomed the heat from the fire as they leaned towards it in an attempt to dry out their clothes, now soaked with perspiration from the desert run and chilled by the freezing night temperature. As they had scrambled to exit their sleeping bags, the remainder of their clothing had been left behind. The team

looked at one another with an element of camaraderie and disbelief that they found themselves in this situation.

The leader of the desert gunmen walked into one of the illuminated tents, leaving the canvas door flapping gently behind him as he entered. The team knew that there must have been a reason for their capture rather than being shot dead. They were grateful for this fact. Without their weapons, they would have to see how each step unfolded from now on and exploit any opportunity they could to find out why they were there. The problem of being stuck in the middle of a hot, dry desert without water, ammunition, or food remained. As bad days went, this was about the worst the team had encountered together. They weren't used to being vulnerable and without the upper hand.

Their pulse rates slowed as the adrenaline subsided and each team member was caught up in their own thoughts. The usual first step in this situation was to observe their surroundings and see what was going on to learn as much as possible about their environment. All information they gained at this stage would certainly help them plan their escape and with six of them observing, they were sure to capture every detail.

"What now?" the Doc asked.

"Quiet!" came a commanding voice from the darkness, a laser pointer illuminating his chest in case he had forgotten the situation he was in. Silence filled the air again as the team carried on looking around them. Arabic voices could be heard coming from the illuminated tent and little else was happening around the oasis. The flickering light from the fire cast dancing shadows against the sides of the tents and the sand dunes that surrounded the camp. Kamali looked across the water to see the starry sky reflected upon its tranquil surface. The sounds of camels groaning in the background could also be heard. The population of the oasis people could not be more than a few

hundred at most, although it was still a mystery why there would be gunmen awaiting their arrival.

The team waited in silence; the sound of Springbok clearing his throat occasionally breaking the calmness lingering in the air. At that moment, an elegant hand pulled back the canvas as a slender figure exited the tent carrying a clay urn. It was clear the person walking towards them was a woman; her hips swayed delicately as she walked across the sandy path towards the Black Widows. A second female figure followed behind carrying a tray of small clay pots. As both women approached the troops in silence, the woman offered a clay pot to each team member as the first woman poured fresh water for them to drink. Each lady did so in complete silence. The tray bearer bowed in front of each man in turn to indicate she was at their service. The urn bearer did the same.

There was nothing visibly distinctive about each desert lady, as they were both wrapped in white desert dresses with only their hands, feet, and eyes visible. Wedmore took a deep look into the eyes of the urn bearer and connected with the most beautiful eyes he had ever seen. As he held the kind gaze of the desert woman, he felt a quickening of his heart and his stomach churn slightly. He noticed dark eyes, almost as black as her pupils, and the longest eyelashes in the world. Adorning her eyes were perfectly sculpted eyebrows. The flickering flames of the fire helped illuminate the moment between them, as she looked deeper into Wedmore's eyes, stirring his very soul to a point of intense internal agitation.

After pouring his water, she stood up and moved towards Gringo, her hips sashaying like the body of a snake under the speechless gaze of Wedmore. This was all just too much for him. How could he be in this situation? He was expecting some difficulties as they got closer to their target, but certainly not this. Who were this mysterious group? More importantly, who was this desert woman who had just instantly stirred up deep emotions he had kept hidden for so long?

As the women completed their duties, they walked back to the tent in silence. The team all drank their water, except Wedmore who stared longingly after the desert lady. As she was now out of sight, he shook his head to regain his composure and drank most of his water, splashing the remainder onto his face in an attempt to bring himself back to reality.

"You ok, boss?" Hitler whispered noticing his odd behaviour.

"Silence!" boomed a voice from behind him. It was clear their captors didn't want any conversation. Wedmore just nodded his head in response to Hitler as they all sat there in silence.

Time passed without any sign of the lead gunman returning. Occasionally someone would appear out of the illuminated tent to throw some more timber onto the fire and then return to the tent. The flames danced in the night sky with the sound of crackling timber interrupting the silence. With nothing to do or say, the Black Widows became weary after their run across the desert. Their eyelids started to get heavy and their heads bowed as the adrenaline subsided and they started to succumb to the onset of sleep enhanced by the warmth of the fire. The Doc was the first one to fall under the influence as his head slumped forward; his eyes closed and a grunt emanated from his throat as his shoulders hunched forward. One of the gunmen stepped forward and prodded him in the neck with the cold barrel of his rifle to wake him up. Sleeping was also against protocol. They did their best to keep themselves awake, the odd dig in the ribs with a desert boot letting them know when they had failed.

After a few hours, the lead gunman reappeared from the tent and walked towards his comrades. He uttered something in Arabic before gruffly telling the Black Widows to get up. The team did as they were instructed and followed the lead gunman along a desert path. They walked past a row of tents before arriving at the entrance to another illuminated square tent at the end of the row, which they were ushered into.

"Now you will sleep and we will talk in the morning," the lead gunman commanded. *"My friends here will keep you safe,"* he continued, gesturing towards his comrades who took positions around the tent. Reading between the lines, the intimation of 'safe' meant 'do not try and escape or you will be shot'. The Black Widows entered the tent to see it had been set up for their comfort with plenty of space, and soft pillows for them to rest their heads on as they slept.

The ground was covered with intricately designed rugs woven with deep red colours intermingled with gold and silver threads. Sheets of the finest Egyptian cotton were positioned in small piles next to the pillows. In the centre of the tent was a table with a large glass fruit bowl containing grapes, bananas, kiwi fruits, dragon fruits, and papaya. Next to the fruit bowl were six ornate crystal glasses, and two large water jugs filled with fresh chilled water. Hanging from the centre of the ceiling was a solar powered light shining brightly in their eyes, which were still adjusting after hours of darkness.

"Looks like we just found paradise!" Gringo joked.

"I've been in a lot worse situations," Hitler said as he shook his head in disbelief.

"What are you thinking now?" Kamali asked Wedmore.

Their eyes connected and Wedmore realized he had been in a dazed state for the last five minutes. All he could think about was the desert woman who had held his gaze for just a moment too long. He was clearly not concentrating on the situation the team had found themselves in. He snapped back into the position of leader and took a moment to compose himself.

"*Are you ok?*" Kamali asked, looking at his superior for confirmation.

"*I'm fine, thank you,*" Wedmore replied in an unusually calm and soft tone. He glanced rather sheepishly at his teammates under his eyebrows. "*Let's make ourselves comfortable for the night.*"

"*Shouldn't we be making a plan to get out of here?*" the Doc asked. "*This wasn't part of the plan to end up here and now we are defenceless without our weapons or supplies to keep us going. What are we going to do?*"

Wedmore took a deep breath and straightened his back. He looked around once more to his comrades. "*It's precisely for those reasons that I feel we should see how things unfold. I don't feel that these people mean us any harm, otherwise we would be dead by now.*"

"*What are you talking about?*" the Doc asked. "*They blew up our truck and chased us through the desert shooting at us!*"

"*First of all, we don't know if it was the same group who were firing on us in the desert. Secondly, anyone who can make those shots over long range in the dark and hit the ground around us is an expert marksman who could have killed us at any moment. They didn't. That tells us something. I think they want us alive and I don't think they want to do us any harm. Trust me on this one,*" Wedmore replied.

"*You're the boss, and we'll do what you say,*" Hitler said as he threw himself into a pile of pillows like a child in a ball pit. Compared to previous situations they had found themselves in, this was definitely the lap of luxury.

"*Guys, get some sleep and make sure you hydrate. I have no idea what tomorrow brings, but we will all handle it better with rest and keeping ourselves sharp. Let's all bed down for the night and sleep. We can see what unfolds in the morning and* trust that God will take us along the journey as it's meant to be," Wedmore said.

"*Trust in God?!*" Kamali said. "*Sounds to me like all those conversations about Higher Intelligence have started to register with you, my brother,*" Kamali continued with a twinkle in his eye and a kind smile on his face.

"*Maybe,*" Wedmore replied. "*Maybe.*"

Wedmore stepped forward to the table to take a glass of water and greedily sank it in one, before guzzling a refill just as quickly. The rest of the team did the same. With that, Gringo reached up and turned a dial on the solar lamp to dim it down so the team could sleep. They all stretched out and made themselves at home. They were willing captives in this moment and enjoying the kind privilege granted to them by their captors. Moments later, Gringo, Hitler, Springbok, the Doc, and Kamali were asleep.

Wedmore clasped his hands behind his head and gazed up at the ceiling of the tent whilst taking a deep breath. Something was going on within him that had stirred the very deepest emotions of his soul. Something had caught his interest about the desert lady that he couldn't shake from his mind. He was enjoying the feeling of calm and serenity that had spread over him. He smiled again, whispered "*Thank you,*" to the heavens and closed his eyes. A feeling of goose bumps followed by contentment spread throughout his body as he slipped into a deep slumber. For the first time in a very long time, it felt like his sleep was going to be deep, peaceful and tranquil.

Chapter 8

Penance in Paradise

LOCATION: Somewhere in Medina
DATE: 30th April
WEATHER: Hot and sunny

The Black Widows were woken from their sleep by the sound of a cockerel's dawn chorus. As they opened their eyes, they could already see their tent was being illuminated by the early morning rising sun. They looked around at one another in a scene that resembled a sleep over at a friend's house when they were teenagers.

Gringo was the first to speak. *"Morning, guys!"* he said. The team replied in unison *"Morning!"* as they stretched out their bodies across the floor and rubbed their eyes to shake off the last remaining affects of sleep. The Doc got to his feet first and poured water for the rest of the team and threw everyone a banana for sustenance.

"I'll take some grapes too, mum!" Springbok said with a smile.

"They're not suppositories!" the Doc replied as quick as a flash. This brought a mild murmur of laughter from the rest of the team as they set about drinking and eating. The Doc looked towards the entrance of the tent and saw the shadow of one of their captors being cast against the canvas. *"Looks like our

welcome party doesn't want us to leave," he said to his teammates as he motioned towards the shadow.

"I feel we may be here for a little while," Kamali said.

"Tell us what you know," Wedmore asked Kamali.

"I can honestly say I know no more than you, Commander. I just feel that we will be here awhile," Kamali replied.

The team started to stretch and move their bodies. Although they were in an unknown situation, they knew that keeping themselves at the peak of their physical and mental health would be of paramount importance here. They had the space in the tent to conduct their physical workout and took advantage of the cooler morning temperature to do so before the heat of the sun took full effect.

As they were working out, the canvas entrance to the tent was pulled back and the tray bearer entered carrying a selection of flatbread, hummus, and olives as well as a large glass pot of black tea, which was clearly freshly brewed. She set the tray down and without saying a word, poured six cups of tea. There was a small jug of goat's milk left on the side. As quickly as the tray bearer had entered the tent, she turned to leave. They watched this elegantly dressed woman leave the tent before picking up their steaming hot cups of tea. There was certainly no expense being spared in the hospitality presented to them. They sat cross-legged in a small circle together enjoying their feast.

"Sure seems like we are welcome here," Hitler said. *"The missus doesn't treat me this good at home!"*

"Perhaps it's because you're not 'emotionally intelligent'," Springbok jibed.

"What does that even mean?" Hitler asked.

"It's what women want nowadays," Springbok said with an air of sarcastic superiority. *"They want men who are more emotionally intelligent and available to meet their emotional needs. You know, for conversation and shit."*

"I have no clue what she's talking about sometimes," Hitler said. *"It seems like a real mash-mash of conversations that jump from one thing to another without rhyme or reason!"*

"Hello, bro! Why do you think I'm a player?" Gringo said. *"No need to worry about that conversation stuff or meeting their emotional needs. Just wham, bam, thank you ma'am."*

"They don't call you the one-minute wonder for nothing," the Doc teased.

"Now, boys, let's not belittle the fairer sex," Wedmore said. *"Let's behave like adults. I think we should get the focus back to the present moment and make a plan. We need to establish exactly what is going on here, so we must all keep our eyes, ears, and minds open to gaining as much information as possible about our present situation. Assuming we will get out of this tent some point soon, observe everything around you and make a mental note of any weaknesses in their present structure so we can see what we can do to get out of here."*

No sooner had the words left his mouth than the entrance canvas was quickly pulled back as the lead captor entered. He looked down at the collective gathering in the middle of the tent and then looked around to observe how they had enjoyed their night of sleep.

"I trust you slept well?" he asked his captive audience. The Black Widows were taken aback at the apparent friendliness of the man who stood before them. Last night, he had appeared hostile, yet this morning he seemed visibly pleased to see them. Was this a trap? Was this the good cop, bad cop routine being played out by one person?

Wedmore replied, *"We did, thank you."*

"Good! You are required outside now. We have duties for you to undertake."

The Black Widows looked at one another as they got up and followed their captor outside where they were greeted by the intense brightness of the morning and the significant temperature difference between the outside world and the inner climate of their cooler tent. The team squinted as their eyes adjusted to the sunlight so they could observe their new surroundings. There were scores of beautiful white square tents neatly positioned on three sides of the oasis, the surface of which rippled as people nearby filled clay urns with water. There was a hive of activity around a much larger central tent, although it was too far away to see exactly what was going on. What had seemed like a small settlement adjacent to the oasis when they had arrived under cover of darkness was evidently a much larger settlement of possibly several hundred people happily going about their morning routine, unaware of the new arrivals who had appeared during the night.

The lead captor led the Black Widows over to a large pile of wood complete with two axes. *"Here you will undertake your duties this morning. Our village needs the wood for fires at night to keep the cold at bay and to embrace a sense of community. Chop it here and then it needs to be stacked over there. You strong men will manage this no problem,"* he said with a dry smile.

The Black Widows looked at him. He was around 5'6" tall, his skin was visibly dark and leathery due to the intense sun exposure over many years. His face exhibited a dark wispy beard and moustache; Wedmore made a mental note to call him 'Blackbeard'. The lines around his eyes suggested that he had endured a life of some hardship. He pointed with his veiny left hand to a location several hundred metres from the place they would be chopping the wood, his traditional Arab desert dress sleeve riding up as he raised his arm. There was a big gold ring on his middle finger and a gold chain around his neck with a small locket. *"Any questions?"*

"What do you want with us?" Wedmore asked. The rest of the group knew to keep their mouths shut and leave the talking to their leader.

"We want you to chop wood!" came the cheerful reply. *"My friends here will see that you get the job done,"* he continued as he gestured towards the three gunmen who were still standing strong despite being on guard duty all night. With that, Blackbeard turned and walked away back towards the tents with one of the gunmen following him.

"Looks like we had better do what we are told, chaps," Wedmore said as he looked at the enormous pile of wood in front of them. There must have been around ten tonnes of wood, which would take them at least a week to cut and stack by hand. The two remaining gunmen took up positions in the shade, on slightly higher ground in order to observe and make sure they did as they were told. Although there was no verbal communication from them, it was clear what would happen if they didn't carry out the wishes of the village.

Wedmore and Gringo picked up the axes whilst the Doc, Kamali, Springbok, and Hitler positioned the wood on the ground ready for chopping. As the axes started to swing and strike the timber and logs were being split, Kamali and Gringo started to walk back and forth to the woodpile, stacking the wood neatly in position. They worked like a well-oiled machine, without conversation and all doing their role in synchronicity with one another. As the sun rose in the sky, the work they were undertaking became intensely physically exhausting in the dry heat. They took it in turns to rotate their roles between chopping, organizing, and carrying the wood.

They were happily caught up in their own thoughts as they went about this manual task. They also took the opportunity to observe their surroundings and see what was going on. The cries of babies could be heard above the grunts and groans of camels in the background together with the hustle of people busily going about their business. The smells of fresh meat being roasted over an open fire wafted towards the men as they worked, instantly reminding them of the energy they were expending on this task.

The men laboured tirelessly in the heat under the careful watch of their silent supervisors. After two hours, three more gunmen appeared from the centre of the village and silently replaced the original gunmen who must have been desperate for some sleep after being awake for many hours. As the midday sun approached and their labour had continued for what seemed like hours, the heat and physical exertion really began taking its toll. Their progress became protracted and sluggish as their exposed skin turned bright red in the blazing sunshine.

At the point when the sun seemed highest in the sky and they were all but drained of their energy, Blackbeard appeared again followed by the tray bearer bringing water and bread to the team and announced break time. The team drank their water hastily and stuffed their mouths full of freshly baked bread, which had a faint buttery taste. Never in their lives had bread and water tasted so good.

"Good work, friends," Blackbeard said with a smile. *"You like wood duty?"*

"Not really," Gringo said in a moment's lapse of concentration, forgetting to allow his superior to respond on their behalf.

"Very well, friends. We have something that will be more to your liking. You will like this, yes?" Blackbeard said with a smile. He turned his back on the team and pointed to a large sand dune behind the cluster of tents. *"The sand dune needs to*

be made taller to shelter the tents from the wind. You can do this before nightfall."

The rest of the Black Widows looked angrily at Gringo, as they knew the fate that awaited them. Armies around the world had frequently used this method for breaking their soldiers and enemies alike against insolence. The task involved filling a bucket with sand at the bottom of the sand dune, running up the dune and emptying the bucket at the top before returning to the bottom to start the whole process again. It was a mind-numbingly boring never-ending task due to the very granular nature of sand and it was physically exhausting. Many troops had been known to die from being subjected to this soul-destroying treatment and a few hours of it was enough to break even the toughest of spirits.

The Black Widows finished their water and food before being led over to the large sand dune with the gunmen following. At the base of the dune, which must have been around ten metres in height, were six heavy galvanized steel buckets together with six large wooden-handled spades. It was clear that no matter what they had said, their captors already had this next step in mind to break their spirits.

One gunman ran to the top of the dune, the sand sliding and moving beneath the weight of his feet as he did so. Doing this exercise in their desert boots was going to mean sandpaper-like-socks that would chafe and blister the softened, sweat-soaked skin of their feet. It was highly likely that they would not be able to walk very far in the morning.

"Enjoy, friends," Blackbeard said with a smile as he motioned to the Black Widows to pick up their spades and buckets. He watched as each team member reluctantly began the relentless and thankless task of filling their buckets with sand and walking to the top of the sand dune to empty them. The temperature was unbearable and their clothes were already saturated with sweat.

"Feels like being a kid at the beach again!" Gringo joked in an attempt to raise spirits and win favour for seemingly putting them in this situation.

"Hush your mouth before I bury you in this dune, Gringo!" The Doc said with a mixed sense of anger and joviality at the situation they found themselves in. The temperature was getting to them and this dune was particularly exposed to the sun, which absorbed the light before emitting heat like a blast furnace. They went about their task under the observation of the gunmen.

Hours seemed to pass as they carried on walking up and down the dune without breaks or water. Each attempt at climbing back down the dune resulted in at least one of the team slipping and sliding in the sand. The depth of the sand frequently covered the top of their boots and they felt the uncomfortable grit getting between their toes and around their heels, rubbing against the hot leathery inside of their boots. Their shirts were saturated with sweat and their hands and forearms were grazed from trying to prevent themselves falling against the sand dune. The skin covering their knuckles was broken, and the blood was prevented from flowing because the sand had entered the open wounds. It was a miserable existence under the relenting heat with no respite or water to quench their insatiable thirst.

As they climbed the dune to empty their buckets, the Black Widows were treated to a better view across the tops of the tent village and surrounding area. Oceans of orange-gold coloured sand unfolded in every single direction they looked. They realized this was all part of their captors' plans to break their spirits and make them realize how alone they were in this desert prison. Even if they attempted to make a run for it, they wouldn't last long in this harsh environment without water and the only available source of it was right next to the closely guarded village. The gunmen watching them knew that the Black Widows would now be unlikely to make a run for it or overthrow them in any way. There were no signs of vehicles at the village and the only transportation appeared to be the camels. They watched people milling in and out of the main central tent and listened to the children laughing and playing close by. Everyone in the village seemed oblivious to the fact that there were six very sweaty military men climbing up and down a sand dune emptying buckets of sand in the intense heat.

Wedmore looked around at his team who were visibly exhausted. Their lips had already started to swell and crack from the affects of excessive heat and dehydration as their squinting eyes struggled to cope with the brightness of the desert sun reflecting off the sand all around them. Battered and bruised from the exercises of the day, he felt helpless that he had led his fellow men into this situation. He himself was exhausted from all his physical effort in the most demanding environment he had ever been in and he was struggling to think. He knew that they couldn't keep this process up for more than a couple of days before they perished in the heat.

Why had they been led into this position and why were they being held here? They had been given no instructions as to why they were being treated like this. War and military combat were never 'fair places' to operate, but they were used to going through at least a few rounds of questioning with the enemy before being subjected to this kind of treatment. The sunburn on his hands and face started to throb as the intense sun exposure continued.

Willpower was never long lasting in these situations; they would either have to find a way to escape, or perish in the heat. No other options seemed available. They had clearly been lulled into a false sense of security with their kind hospitality. Now they were subject to the most detestable treatment.

The Doc was the first to fall and slide part way down the dune without fighting to get back up. It was clear that he had passed out from the heat. Gringo was closest to him and he rushed over as fast as could. As the gunmen observed this, they stood up from their positions and raised their guns towards the Doc and Gringo. A shot hit the ground a few inches away from the Doc as a warning to leave him where he was. Gringo turned around and looked up at the gunmen standing at the top of the hill with visible outrage. He changed direction in anger and started to make his way uphill towards the gunmen. Wedmore looked at Gringo and then at the gunmen who both aimed squarely at Gringo's chest.

"Gringo! STOP!" Wedmore shouted. *"Don't do it!"* he started to run across the hill towards Gringo and continued shouting *"Gringo, STOP! And that's an order!"* A shot hit the ground just a few inches in front of Gringo as he heard his commander's voice. He continued to stand there breathlessly seething at his captors. Kamali, Springbok and Hitler looked up from the bottom of the dune and were left feeling somewhat helpless. Gringo clenched his fists as he continued looking up at the gunmen, his chest puffed up and a wide stance showing he was ready for battle. *"I'll get you, you fucking bastards!"* he shouted.

Kamali, Springbok and Hitler turned around as they heard people moving behind them. They saw two men in traditional Arabic desert dress carrying a stretcher running towards the Doc. They quickly flipped him onto the stretcher and climbed down the dune with the agility and expertise of mountain goats, the Doc looking limp and lifeless on the stretcher as they did so. They ran across the flat sandy plane before disappearing into a nearby tent. The five remaining teammates looked at one another in disbelief. They had never allowed themselves to be separated by anything before and now one of their own had been taken away from them in a situation that was totally beyond their control. They looked up to see the gunmen still holding their rifles up, pointed directly at the Black Widows. They gestured for them to continue with their task of carrying the sand up the dune. Gringo refused and instead turned his bucket upside down on the dune and sat on it sullenly. As he bowed his head, the gunman on the ground fired a shot, which hit the side of his bucket around an inch below his testicles, and exited the other side of the bucket before burying itself in the soft sand. The impact vibrations on the bucket shook through his backside and legs causing him to jump to his feet. As he did so, his now holey bucket turned on its side and began to roll down the hill. He looked down at the gunman who had fired on him and then towards his bucket that was moving away from him. He looked back at the gunman with hate in his eyes and frustration from being out of options. He was completely exposed and no matter where he turned, guns were watching him ready to strike him down at any moment. As angry as he was, he reluctantly walked down the hill, kicking the bucket farther down the slope to the bottom.

The bucket landed near Wedmore's feet, as he was finishing topping up his own bucket ready for another ascent. As Gringo walked closer to him, Wedmore whispered, *"Cool it!"* to his comrade and friend, with a very stern look in his eyes.

It was clear that tension was brewing here and Gringo would be quick to let his judgmental loathing overtake him if things didn't calm down very quickly. It was intensely difficult to keep calm in the situation and Wedmore himself was sitting on a hot bed of anger and resentment.

"I think I have a plan, so don't ruin it!" Wedmore continued. He knew the importance of keeping morale high in this situation and even though Wedmore himself knew they were powerless and did not in fact have a plan, he needed his men to fall in line and not make the problem any worse.

"Take some deep breaths and get it together," he said as Gringo picked up his bucket and continued the pointless, heartbreaking task.

Chapter 9

Healing Begins

LOCATION: Somewhere in Medina
DATE: 30th April
WEATHER: Scorching sunshine followed by a cool evening

The team continued to work for another three hours in the heat of the afternoon sun, getting slower and more lethargic as their vital energy drained from their bodies. They were walking zombies, delirious with exhaustion as their bodies struggled to operate. As the sun dropped, Blackbeard appeared again and silently ushered the remaining Black Widows into the same tent the Doc was carried into.

As they entered the tent, they were greeted with a sight of sheer opulence. Tables were set with an abundance of food, water, and wine. Through bleary sunblind eyes, they saw the Doc sat on a very luxurious cushioned seat sipping water. They observed the tray bearer, accompanied by three other friends who handed the men water. The men greedily guzzled it to quench their arid thirst, water spilling over the sides of the glasses and dripping from their chins, washing in with the dust and filth that had accumulated from their desert toil.

"It is thirsty work, no?" Blackbeard said with a smile. Before anyone could say anything to the contrary, he continued, *"Please, my friends, eat!"* He spread his arms and hands out as he gestured to the plentiful supply of food that lay before them.

They picked up plates of solid gold and started to pile food high upon them. They were so ravenously hungry, they crammed food into their mouths as they simultaneously piled their plates. They walked over to the Doc who was visibly pleased to see them and were clearly feeling better to be in the shade enjoying the bountiful supply of food and drink available.

This situation was no doubt confusing; why would they be treated so well and then treated with such hostility? There was no sense to it. The team ate like starving men; the four ladies of the desert brought them more food and water. They ate enough between them to feed a small army, as there was no way they were going to give this opportunity up. The pain emanating from their sunburnt lips and skin was not enough to stop them filling their rumbling stomachs with nourishment.

As they came towards the end of their eating spree, they handed their plates to the serving ladies and took refills of water to sip as their eyes grew heavy. It had started to go dark within the tent as the sun dipped towards the horizon, so candles were lit to provide additional light. Blackbeard, who had been observing the feeding frenzy, approached them with a smile on his face. *"My friends, you must be tired now. Please rest for an hour before we continue."*

"Continue what?" Wedmore asked in staggered disbelief.

"So many questions, my friend. Do not worry. You will see soon enough," Blackbeard replied, clearly getting some kind of thrill from playing both good cop, bad cop roles. *"Sleep off your food for an hour and then we will be back."* With that, they silently exited the tent leaving the stunned Black Widows alone. The draft from the flaps of the tent caused the candlelight to flicker as silence once again fell on the room.

"Gentlemen, I suggest we get some sleep. We need to get our energy back after today's gruelling tasks," Wedmore said.

His teammates did not need any encouragement as they all closed their eyes in unison within seconds and passed out, completely exhausted from their efforts. Within moments, the sound of snoring filled the air as they slept under the soft candlelight.

An hour later, they were rudely awakened by the banging of a stick against a metal pot as Blackbeard entered the tent alone. The Black Widows stirred and looked through bleary eyes at the silhouetted figure standing in front of them. They began to sit up with grunts and groans as the pain from the sunburn, their overworked muscles, and heavily chapped lips began to kick in.

"My friends, you are feeling sore, yes?" Blackbeard said with a twinkle in his eye. Although angered by the question, the team nodded their heads whilst simultaneously wondering if this guy was enjoying torturing his captives. He crouched over them and looked at each one in turn.

"Shall we get you, how you say, 'fixed up', my friends?" Again, the team did their best to nod to the current master of their fate. Blackbeard stood up and said, *"Follow me, friends."* With that, he turned and walked out of the tent as the Black Widows groggily and painfully stood up to follow him.

As they left the tent, they realized there was no sign of the gunmen and Blackbeard appeared to be on his own. He led them through a complex of tents, taking great care not to trip over the guide ropes and pegs hammered into the soft sandy ground. They came to a standstill by some timber stalls where four men were waiting for them.

"Ok my friends, now you will undress and my friends here will wash away your sorrows," Blackbeard said.

The Black Widows looked at one another before starting to peel off their layers of clothing in readiness for a much-needed shower. As they stripped off their boots and trousers, grains of sand fell from every part of their body. Their arms and legs were covered in grazes and bruises from their ordeal and their tan lines were highlighted by brutal sunburn from the desert sun. They stood naked apart from their boxer shorts and military dog tags.

Blackbeard ushered them into the small timber stalls, which offered little privacy, where they were ordered to remove the remaining items of clothing before the four men began to gently spray their bodies with warm water. They felt totally exposed as the warm spray hit their skin, and they could feel the warmth of the evening air. The experience was somewhat grounding as the water began to wash away their recent experiences. As the water ran down their bodies, carrying the dust and filth away, it seemed to bathe their souls and instantly relieve the feelings of exhaustion, fatigue, and sunburn. Their troubles almost melted away in that moment as they enjoyed the feeling of the warm water hitting their bodies, cleansing them before it returned to Mother Earth.

As two of the men continued to spray water, the other two men foamed up large soft horsehair brooms and gently rubbed them up and down against the naked bodies of the Black Widows. The brushes felt incredibly soft as the lather built up over their bodies, helping to remove the last traces of dried sweat, dust, and filth, and leaving them feeling like new men. The soap carried a soft lavender fragrance that helped turn their feelings of anxiety and hatred towards their captors to peace and calm. The sense of relief felt by all was incredible and the pain from their sunburn had already begun to lift.

The four Arab men handed the Black Widows shampoo for their hair as well as soap for the more sensitive body parts, allowing them to wash themselves. Once they were clean, they stepped out of the stalls into soft towels made of luxury Egyptian cotton before slipping on sandals and white cotton desert shawls to preserve their modesty. The feeling of 'going commando' was certainly freeing and they walked away from the timber stalls to Blackbeard who was smiling as usual.

"My friends, it has been a long day for you! Come now, and we will take shelter by the fire."

Blackbeard led them back to the original campfire they had spent the morning chopping wood for and bade them to sit down in a semi-circle facing towards the fire. They sat on some beautiful woven rugs with silk embroidered cushions to separate them from the desert floor.

"As you can see, we are making good use of your labour for the firewood!" Blackbeard joked as he took his place in the middle of the semi-circle. He smiled again at each team member, taking a deliberate amount of time to look everyone in the eye and connect momentarily with them. The Black Widows were mesmerized by their captor's presence and were admittedly on the back foot by his treatment, which switched between royalty and slave labour.

"My friends," Blackbeard continued, *"I am sensing you are in some physical pain. Can we help relieve that for you?"*

"How exactly do you propose to do that?" Wedmore asked. *"I don't see a hospital or medical professional for miles! No offence, Doc!"* he said, careful not to alienate his comrade.

"We have our ways. We are people of the desert and we are well connected with the God Allah, and the ways of the Infinite Intelligence," Blackbeard replied. *"If you will allow me, we can heal you all very quickly and take away your pain. Would you like that?"*

Wedmore looked at his team for reassurance as the thought of the practice of Black Magic filled his mind. He had heard rumours of the abilities of desert people before, but his main concern was putting the lives of his men in the hands of Muslim terrorists.

Blackbeard interjected, *"We are not terrorists, my friend, nor do we preach Black Magic!"* As the words fell from Blackbeard's mouth, they completely stunned Wedmore, throwing his train of thought. *'How the fuck did this guy just read my mind?'*

"It is easy when you know how, Commander Wedmore," Blackbeard said.

Wedmore couldn't remain silent anymore. *"How…How do you know my name?"*

"I know more about you than you think," Blackbeard replied. *"But, my friends, we are getting distracted. Shall we heal your pain first and then we can talk more?"*

In a state of stunned disbelief, Wedmore nodded and looked around to reassure his teammates in a way that suggested he needed the reassurance more. The Doc, Gringo, Springbok, and Hitler were all looking perplexed, whilst Kamali just smiled.

"Very well, my friends," Blackbeard said. *"Let the healing commence."* At the clap of his hands, two tray bearers and three other women appeared from a nearby tent, walking in a gentle arc behind them. They took handfuls of a faintly scented lemon cream and began liberally applying it to their sunburnt bodies.

"Relax, my friends, and allow them to do their work. This is the first stage and then I will guide you through the next few steps. You have to keep an open mind to what we are about to do, but if you go with it, you will completely heal your sunburn, pain, and bruising in the next two hours. Are you with me?"

The team nodded as they felt the cold cream spread over their skin leaving a slight tingling sensation in its wake. Instantly, they began to relax as the fragrant lemon scent filled their lungs. The Doc started to get visibly anxious about what they were about to do. As if to read his mind, Blackbeard spoke directly.

"I can see that you are worried, my friend, however do not be alarmed. Western medicine still has a lot to learn." He touched his nose with a knowing wink in the Doc's direction as he spoke. *"Trust me, brother,"* he continued, speaking in a way as though they had known one another for many years. *"What we are about to do, you will not have perhaps done before, but it is very effective at healing the human spirit. Once the spirit is healed, physical healing will take place also very quickly. So my friends, this is not like traditional western medicine where you lie on a table and I fix you. You are all capable of performing miracles, you just need to be shown how. The key is to silence and still the mind, so the heart and soul can take over and do what they need to do to bring healing. When the mind is too busy, it blocks the channels for ultimate healing and it will not work. So, my friends, are you ready to try this?"*

The squad all looked to Kamali for guidance in this moment. He gave a knowing nod of agreement to the words that Blackbeard had just spoken. The squad then turned to face Blackbeard. Wedmore said, *"Please continue."*

"Ok, my friends. Please follow these instructions very carefully as you are about to watch miracles happen right before your eyes. Whatever you want to be cured, we can deal with it now in this session, even if it has been bothering you for many years."

Blackbeard looked to see that his audience were captivated and willing listeners before he started.

"Please close your eyes and take a few moments to be still. Take some deep breaths now. Innnnnnn annnnnnddddd ooouuuuuttttttt. Take a deep breath in now and hold it for five beats of your heart, then breathe out through your mouth, very softly. As softly as you would blow into the ear of a new born baby. And repeat."

Blackbeard looked at his audience of finely honed physical men sat cross-legged with their hands on their knees in the meditative lotus position. With their eyes closed and heads gently bowed, their chests rose and fell with each breath that coincided with the flaring and dilation of their nostrils and the pursing of their lips as they exhaled. They were good students for their first attempt at spiritual healing.

"Breathe in again and hold it now for ten beats of your hearts before breathing out. Still your mind of any thoughts and place yourself in stillness. Focus only on your breathing and nothing else. Give up the need to want to speak at this moment; be in the moment and be still, calm, peaceful. You are doing well. Keep going."

As the minutes passed, a strange phenomenon occurred as the whole squad and Blackbeard began to breathe in and out in unison with one another. A bond of connection between them all had been formed as calmness filled the air. The only noise that could be heard in the desert was the gentle cracking of the flames of the fire against the tinder-dry wood. In and out they continued. In and out. For the first time in their lives, the Black Widows felt a sense of calmness and tranquillity enter their minds and their thoughts slowed right down. No longer were they in the adrenaline-fuelled heat of the battle. They were sitting as one with someone who could be friend or foe, being guided through a meditative healing ritual. Their breathing continued in unison, no one wishing to break the blanket of silence that had descended upon them, all of them aware of one another, yet blissfully unaware at the same time. It was a beautiful place to be.

Blackbeard broke the silence with a calm and gentle voice; *"Ok, gentlemen, you are doing well. I want you to now continue breathing in and holding it for twenty beats of your heart before you breathe out."*

As they held their breath for longer periods between breaths, the calmness continued to deepen and the tranquillity could be felt all around them. Whilst the temperature had dropped noticeably since the sun had disappeared, this bothered none of them as they sat in their thin cotton desert dress completely exposed to the elements. The fire helped to warm the surrounding air, but the real warmth could be felt by an increase in the personal vibration of every individual in their own energy body. As the peace and tranquillity set into their minds, they became detached from their feelings associated with external reality. They had never experienced this feeling before and it felt like they were walking upon the clouds of heaven.

"Good work, my friends. I can feel your presence and the state of calm you are in. Keep breathing now and I want you to breathe right into the centre of your heart as you breathe in. Hold the breath before breathing out gently as before. Keep the mind still. You are all doing great," Blackbeard said.

As the following minutes passed, he began to tap into their level of consciousness and could feel that each man was starting to find the elixir of inner peace.

"My friends," he whispered softly so as not to disturb their mental clarity, *"in order to take things to the next level, I will need to open the door of higher level consciousness so that you may walk through it. I can only show you the door, you will have to walk through it yourself to achieve your healing. Do*

not question what we are about to do, just go with it and you will be fine."

He carefully observed the squad to ensure they were comfortable with the next step before continuing. *"Keep breathing gently now. Using your heart only to project, and without thinking about it, I want you to project an energy pyramid that surrounds where you sit. Very good. Now, project a pyramid surrounding the top half of the earth where we are right now. Great! Now another pyramid around your pineal gland in the centre of your head and finally tiny pyramids within each and every cell of your body. Keep the mind still and do this with the heart engaged rather than the mind."*

Scanning his audience and intuitively sensing them all, he prompted them to keep their minds still and free. *"To a mind that is still, the whole universe surrenders, so this is where we must get to. Focus your mind on each breath and do not get wrapped up with any thought. Ok, I want you to imagine your star in the sky right now. This is your heaven and we are going to connect to the rainbow-coloured light coming down from the star, through your body, and connecting deep into the centre of the earth. The star is your Father Heaven and the earth is your Mother Earth. You are all beautiful beings of light created from both Heaven and Earth."*

"Next we need to put five energy balls in place; the first between your head and Father Heaven, the second in your mind around your pineal gland, the third in your heart, the fourth just below your navel and the fifth deep into the centre of Mother Earth. Then pull the rainbow coloured light down from Father Heaven, through the five balls and your heart and project it out through both feet and the base of your spine deep into Mother Earth."

"You're doing well, my friends. Now, I want you to smile broadly…that's it…and now I want you to project that smile

throughout your body, starting at the top of your head and all the way down to your toes and back up to the top of your head. This should feel very good as you do it."

"Very good, my friends! You are all naturals at this! Keep the mind still. As you project the light deep into Mother Earth, she will welcome this and, like all good mothers, will return it seven-fold back up to you. As she does so, allow the light to pass back up through your heart and pass it onto Father Heaven. As Father Heaven receives it, like all good fathers, he will embrace it and return it to you seven-fold. Allow it to come back down to you and centre in your heart. Keep channelling the light from Heaven deep into Earth and back again for a few minutes. You will be able to feel it within you."

As Blackbeard talked his audience through the instructions carefully, he observed their bodies and noticed that they were all very gently shaking as the powerful energy of Heaven and Earth combined within them and began to rapidly raise the energy vibration of their bodies. The more they did so, the more their bodies began to vibrate and it was a clear sign that the healing had begun and was working. He noted that the redness of the sunburn had begun to dissipate a little and their personal auras became so much brighter.

"Keep going, my friends," he said with friendly encouragement in his voice.

Every team member was shaking as they went about their meditation and it was noticeable enough that they all felt it. The semi-circle of war veterans were opening themselves up to something that they could not explain or had ever experienced before. Even though Kamali was used to meditating, he was being introduced to a much deeper and more interesting world than he had previously ever experienced. The vibrations continued subtly at first, but became stronger within each warrior as they enjoyed the desert environment and the magical soul energy it provided.

"Keep channelling that wonderful energy, my friends. I can feel you are all doing really well," Blackbeard said. What he observed happening right in front of his eyes would be completely unexplainable to modern science and medicine; the sunburn from each of the soldiers began to dissipate and the injuries on their bodies began to heal. He noticed the scabs on their lips melt away and the cuts, grazes, and bruises fade as they continued in their meditative state. A wry smile came across his face as he knew what their likely reaction would be when they came out of their meditation.

"You are all doing very well. This is what we call the healing meditation. It is possible to heal anything when you get into this meditative state and focus, my friends. By channelling the universal energy through your body, you are effectively repairing yourselves from the inside out. It's powerful stuff. There are a few more things that we can do whilst we are here though before we end the meditations. I want you to all send love to the souls of the people who you have released in battle and in fighting. This is important for you to do in order to restore your heart and soul back to maximum life force and health. Do not think about them with your minds, my friends. Remember, be still and work from the heart. Everything can be healed with love, my friends. Just radiate love from your hearts to all your victims and their families, no matter whether you feel justified in causing their departure from this earth. Keep breathing deeply and focus on your breathing in and out all the time. Radiate from the heart and send love back to Heaven and Earth."

As Blackbeard guided his audience through the loving and healing process, he felt an intense wave of energy radiate from them out into the vastness of the universe. The universal body of love was in full flow through the hearts of these six fine men who had taken the lives of many people during their military careers and were now sending healing love to their victims to release the heavy burden of guilt. He saw each man look visibly lighter and younger as they began to heal their hearts from within with the universal energy of unconditional love.

"Now, my friends, you must transform all the hurt and guilt you are carrying and put down the heavy weights you are all carrying subconsciously. Mother Earth loves enough to carry these burdens for you, so I want you to feel the energy of these emotional drains leave your body and dissipate into Mother Earth. Go ahead now and transform the energy of loss, disappointment, and suffering to love. See and feel this transformed three times. Transform the energy of hurt, death, and trauma to love, light, and joy for all humanity. See and feel this transformed three times."

Blackbeard had a sense of joy in his heart as he saw each man straighten their backs and sit more upright as these huge emotional burdens were lifted from their shoulders. They became young men again from the healing they had just embraced. His own heart radiated love to them, letting them know they were brothers and not enemies.

"Ok, my friends, we are getting towards the end of this part of the journey so I want you to keep your eyes closed until I tell you to open them. Before we end the meditation, I want you to send love and thanks to Heaven and Earth for granting you this healing and for restoring your spirit to full strength. Good, my friends, well done. Ok, take a deep breath and open your eyes." Blackbeard smiled as he waited.

Each member of the Black Widows opened his eyes and took a moment to adjust to the brightness of the fire and emerge from the trance-like state they had just experienced for the last two hours whilst meditating. They looked towards Blackbeard who was partly illuminated by the flames from the fire and partly in shadow against the darkness of the night. Gringo glanced across the semi-circle to the Doc, as his eyes widened in disbelief and his jaw dropped. One by one, the team looked around at each other and at their own hands and bodies in complete amazement. All the bruising, cuts, grazes, and sunburn had disappeared.

The Doc was the first to speak; *"What on earth just happened to us? How did this happen?"*

Gringo quickly followed up, *"I have absolutely no idea what just happened! We're all healed! This is not possible."*

The team were visibly shocked by what had happened to their physical bodies and were touching their own faces and hands to make sure it wasn't a magic trick.

Wedmore was overwhelmed and confused as he spoke to Blackbeard. *"What just happened to us? Is this some kind of magic or witchcraft?"*

Blackbeard was clearly amused at the question as he burst out laughing at the suggestion that something sinister was at work. *"What do you think, my friends? Do you feel this is the work of something other than God and the Heavens? What does your heart say on the matter?"* Blackbeard asked.

"My heart feels at peace right now," Wedmore replied, with a sense of discomfort as the words fell from his lips. For the last day, he was sure the man in front of him was an enemy he would eventually kill. Yet, in the last two hours, he had acted as more of a friend than anyone he had ever met in his entire life.

"I know what you are thinking," Blackbeard said as he read Wedmore's thoughts. *"Why would this man treat us all like slaves and then take us through this process to heal our bodies, hearts, souls, and minds? My brothers, I am sorry to have put*

you through such treatment today but I had to get your attention," Blackbeard continued.

"Our attention?" Wedmore asked. "Well, if you want our attention, you've certainly got it. What do you want with us?"

"I can only show you so much right now as telling you certain things just isn't going to help our situation. You have to experience things like this healing so that you may believe that we are not here to harm you, but to help you," Blackbeard replied.

"What situation are we in? What are you going to help us with? Are you going to help us on our mission?" Wedmore asked.

"My brother, you will have many questions and you will get all your answers in time. For now, understand we are not your enemy. How do you all feel after that experience?" he asked.

"I feel amazing," Hitler said.

"I still can't believe this has happened. I'm in shock," Springbok said.

Kamali had been very quiet up to this point. He looked up to the night sky and saw the most beautiful arrangement of bright shining stars as a smile spread across his face. He placed the fingers of both hands in front of his lips, kissed them, and sent the kiss into the sky. He then said, *"Thank you!"* to the Heavens before turning to look at his friends and Blackbeard with a sense of real calmness and clarity.

"My brother," he said as he looked deeply into the eyes of Blackbeard, *"in my culture, I have heard many legendary tales of this magic healing but no-one has ever been able to show me how. I believed in my heart that it was possible but I have always been overshadowed by the religious opinions of others who say that it is not possible and it is not real. Thank you for sharing this miracle with us."* Kamali's eyes twinkled as he

spoke and all could feel the love radiating from him for his newfound family member.

"Religion is a curious thing," Blackbeard's replied with a big smile on his face. *"You are welcome. I am sorry that you had to endure such hard physical action to find the cure, but I trust you will agree that it was worth it. Your journey will take a very different turn now, my friends. We are all in this together."*

"In what together?" Wedmore asked, keen to get to the bottom of Blackbeard's riddles.

"Patience, patience," Blackbeard said. *"All will become clear this night. First, let us drink in celebration with one another for this blessed miracle that has been bestowed upon us."*

With this, he clapped his hands in the silence of the desert night. Two tray-bearing women emerged from the nearby tent carrying the most elegant and beautiful tall silver teapots the team had ever seen, together with several glasses bearing decorative gold printed designs. They poured a strong mint tea for everyone flavoured with two lumps of sugar. Steam rose from each glass into the night sky as the smell of fresh mint filled the air.

Blackbeard raised his glass first and said, *"A toast, my friends, to Heaven, Earth, Family and above all, The True Healing Power of Universal Love."*

The Black Widows repeated in unison, *"To Heaven, Earth, Family, and above all, The True Healing Power of Universal Love!"* They raised their glasses into the air with smiles adorning their faces before taking a satisfying sip of the fresh mint brew.

Chapter 10

The Heart Knows

LOCATION: Somewhere in Medina
DATE: 1ˢᵗ May
WEATHER: Cool balmy night

As the newfound brotherhood sat in the cooling breeze of the night with only the fire offering illumination and warmth, the calmness continued. Without saying a word, Blackbeard got up and walked towards the tent that the tray bearers had disappeared into. The faint whisper in the distance of Arabic tongue carried across the night sky towards the Black Widows who were once again reunited.

"So Doc, what do you make of this miracle healing?" Wedmore asked.

As the Doc opened his mouth to speak, Kamali interjected, *"It's real! Without a doubt it's real! I have heard of this many times before but believed it to be stuff of pure legend. I know in my heart that it is undoubtedly true and we are in the presence of someone magical to lead us through an experience like that. I believe him when he says that we had to be put through pain and suffering to experience the healing of Universal Love. There is no way that we would have accepted it as real without going through the whole experience ourselves."*

"*I was just about to say the same thing!*" the Doc said. "*In all seriousness, it is a mystery to western medicine why this should have happened, but I am glad it has. I cannot believe we are back to peak physical health in less than two hours. It's truly a miracle!*"

"*So I would suggest that Blackbeard really is our friend and not our enemy. The only question is why we are here and what he now wants us to do,*" Wedmore said. "*We can relax a little more now and trust that he means well.*"

As the group fell silent, the cracking of the fire could be heard as the flames reached up into the night sky. The beauty of the fire and what it meant to be warm in the cold desert night captivated everyone. The flames danced over the charred embers as energy stored within the wood as released and sent to the Heavens, dissipating against the dark background of the night sky. The team sat captivated by the beauty of this phenomenon.

As they were enjoying the moment, Blackbeard reappeared with a veiled tray bearer. They approached the group as Blackbeard said, "*James, I have a surprise for you. Would you please follow this lady of the desert and she will direct you to our leader who would like to talk with you.*"

Blackbeard joined the remaining Black Widows whilst Commander Wedmore stood up and followed her back towards the tent complex. They continued to walk through the large rabbit warren of tents until they came to the main tent. As his companion ushered him inside, Wedmore entered the tent cautiously, unsure of what to expect. The tent was well illuminated and luxuriously laid out with regal thrones within. The desert woman did not follow James into the tent and suggested that he make himself comfortable and wait patiently for their leader to appear.

Wedmore walked into the centre of the tent where he saw the most beautifully embroidered circular tapestry on the ground. The tent was much bigger than the rest. To his left, there was a raised stage with two thrones sporting ornately carved designs of shimmering brilliant gold with plush red cushions. They overlooked the rest of the tent that featured many scatter cushions.

Unsure of what to do, Wedmore sat on the floor opposite the thrones in an attempt to show respect for the mysterious leader he was about to be introduced to. As he sat there waiting, the tray bearer appeared again to offer Wedmore refreshments. She poured him another mint tea and handed it to him without making eye contact or lifting the veil from her face. She appeared to be incredibly shy and not comfortable around him. She turned her back to him and walked out of the tent again leaving Wedmore to his own thoughts, which were now infused with the strong smell of mint in the air. He sat patiently.

After ten minutes, the tray bearer reappeared and walked confidently towards one of the thrones. As she sat down, she looked through her veiled face at a confused James. Without saying a word, she gestured for him to take the seat beside her, which he did so willingly. He looked across at the tray bearer who reached up to remove her veil and looked directly and deeply into Wedmore's eyes with a gentle smile.

Wedmore was gobsmacked. The tray bearer that sat next to him was the same woman he had seen on the first night when they arrived at the camp. He would recognize those eyes and that look absolutely anywhere. His heart started beating rapidly as his palms began to sweat and he grew nervous. This was clearly not the behaviour of a hardened war veteran.

"Who are you?" he asked as he struggled to stop his voice from shaking. He was not sure what was happening, but he was losing control of his emotions.

The tray bearer smiled even more broadly and the spark in her eyes danced beautifully as she did so. *"My name is Sana. In English it means resplendence, brilliance, to gaze or to look,"* she replied in a husky exotic Arabic-English accent.

Wedmore struggled to regain his composure in the moment and quipped, *"I can see why you were given that name with eyes like those!"* He smiled as the words left his mouth and he thanked the Lord that Sana did the same.

"That's a very kind thing to say," she responded.

"It also happens to be true," he continued. *"Yours are the most beautiful eyes I have ever seen. It feels like you can see my soul when you look at me with those deep brown eyes."*

"I can!" she replied with a joyful smile, *"and it's a beautiful soul, James."*

"Thank you. How do you know my name?"

"I know more about you than you know about yourself. My team have brought you here especially so that we can work with you," Sana replied.

"How do you know all about me? Are you the leader here? How do you know what we are working on? I have so many questions!"

"All your answers will come in time, James, but first I must ask you to trust me. Do you trust me, James?"

Wedmore sat silently for a moment. His mind was in overdrive as the adrenaline flooded his bloodstream. How could these people know so much about him when he hadn't even told them his name? What was about to unfold? How could the most beautiful woman he had ever seen be the leader of this desert tribe and what was their mission? Why were they here? What would they work on together?

Suddenly he caught himself and realized he had become absorbed in his own thoughts and had not acknowledged Sana's question. He turned to look at her and found himself looking deeply into her eyes. He felt a stirring in his gut as her gaze captivated him completely. He felt incredibly exposed and vulnerable with no place to hide, yet strangely captivated in his vulnerability. They held one another's gaze as Wedmore sat there dumbfounded at the events that were unfolding in front of him, trying to make sense of it all. His pattern of thought was interrupted.

"James, what does your heart say?" Sana asked.

"I've no idea right now!"

"That's because you are not listening to it, James. You are stuck in your head. Do you know how to tell the difference between your head and your heart?"

"I'm not sure," James said. *"I've never been taught before."*

"The years of military service will have beaten it out of you, James. You wouldn't be able to pull the trigger on another human being if you were listening to your heart. Would you like to find out what it is saying, James?" Sana asked.

"Yes, please help me. I'm a little confused right now."

"Ok. Let me give you some background. Your head is great at making logical decisions in this world as your brain has been trained by the western schooling system to be overactive. Your head speaks in language and it's easy for you to understand because it all makes sense to you. It also has a megaphone and it speaks very, very loudly," Sana said with a smile.

*"Your heart communicates in a very different way. It is usually very quiet and you have to listen very carefully to what it is saying. It only has access to feelings as a method of communicating with you and, unfortunately for you, you have turned

your feelings off, compressed them, and detached from them so much that your heart now finds it very difficult to communicate with you. That's why you are having trouble sleeping," Sana continued.

"So in order to listen to your heart, you have to be very still, like you were earlier, and listen intently. Then it will grant you access to its timeless wisdom. There is something else that is truly special about the heart, James. Would you like to know what it is?" Sana asked.

"I would love to know more, yes please."

"The heart is the seat of the soul and it allows you to connect to the infinite intelligence that is all around you always. When you truly begin to listen to it, it can guide you throughout life and it knows things that are impossible for you to know with the mind alone. Imagine all the knowledge in the universe being available to you at all times whenever you wanted it. You could work out who is friend or foe within a moment. You would know right from wrong. You would know who is telling you the truth and who is trying to deceive you," Sana explained.

"How do you know all of this? I've never heard anyone talk of this before. Is it really possible to know everything there is to know? How can my heart possibly do all of this?" Wedmore asked, clearly confused at what Sana was saying.

"Let me ask you this, Jay. Do you mind if I call you Jay?" Sana asked.

"Not at all, Sana," Wedmore replied.

"How do I know so much about you when we have never met before? How can I possibly know your name and the fact that you have trouble sleeping? How do I know that you are not listening to your heart and listening to your head?" Sana asked.

"I have no idea. Either you have some secret intelligence or it's something else, like some kind of witchcraft!" Wedmore joked.

Sana laughed. As she did so, her head moved backwards revealing the most beautiful feminine smile he had ever seen in his life. The spark in her eyes danced as her nose wrinkled, slightly captivating his heart in that moment. This was possibly the reason why he wasn't listening to his heart because he knew he was rapidly developing feelings for this woman of the desert, despite not knowing her and being a little wary of her.

"Witchcraft!" Sana retorted with a smile. *"You are a funny guy, Jay!"* she continued as she touched him on the arm. Her touch was soft, warm, and deeply feminine. It sent shockwaves throughout his entire body. He clearly was uncomfortable in this position as he shifted his body weight in the seat and crossed one leg over another, pushing against the arms of the chair and leaning away from her in an attempt to regain some composure. He looked at this mysterious woman in awe and racked his brains on what to say next.

"Relax, Jay! It's like this is the first time you have ever seen a woman! What is wrong with you?" she asked.

"I'm not sure what is happening here," he replied.

"There you go again! Your heart is speaking and you're not listening! You are a curious thing, Jay," Sana teased.

Commander Wedmore did not know how to behave. Here he was, a hardened masculine warrior, feeling like a mouse being toyed with by a cat. The Divine Feminine energy radiating from Sana was too much for him. He stood up and walked out of the tent without saying a word. As the cool darkness of the night sky hit his face, he slapped his forehead with the palm of his hand in an attempt to get his mind back on track. He felt like his mind had automatically frozen in her presence and he couldn't think straight. What on earth was happening? He took some deep, slow breaths of the cool air and looked up at the twinkling stars.

As he did so, he felt Sana's arm intertwine with his arm as she pulled herself in towards him. They both stood there looking up into the night sky observing the sheer beauty of the universe in that moment. Wedmore's nervousness took over him in that moment as his throat went dry and he could not even speak.

"It's beautiful, isn't it?" Sana asked.

Wedmore didn't reply. He didn't know how to. He just gazed up into the night sky and mentally retreated to his quiet place of safety. He felt threatened. Exposed. There was no logical reason why someone of his stature and intense masculine energy would be so vulnerable in the presence of this petite and slender woman. There was something about her femininity that transcended his warrior energy and made him feel like a newborn baby in the hands of a warm and loving mother. He hadn't felt like this in decades and could not explain how a feeling he had experienced only once before in an intimate moment could now be brought up in conversation.

"Listen, Jay," Sana emphasized. *"It's there for you to access any time you want. The eternal wisdom of Mother Earth and Father Heaven is talking to you through your heart."*

Wedmore remained silent. He kept looking up into the sky hoping to find some answers to the internal wrangling he was experiencing. His head and heart were in conflict and he didn't know what to do. His gut feeling felt like it was taking over and for the first time in his life, the 'flight' response was greater than 'fight'. What was there to fight in this situation? How could he fight someone who had shown him nothing but loving kindness? He felt like running to hide his vulnerable child-like self away from the woman who could see right through him.

They stood together, arm in arm, for several moments looking towards the heavens. Suddenly a star seemed to shine brighter than all the others and it caught their attention. *"Look, Jay"* Sana said, *"Can you see what I can see?"*

"A bright star in the sky?" Wedmore asked.

"What do you think it represents, Jay?"

"I…. I don't know," Wedmore stammered.

"Do you want me to tell you who the star is?" Sana continued.

"Who it is? What are you talking about, who? It's a star in the sky, Sana, nothing more than that," Wedmore replied, clearly getting a little agitated and his gut feeling starting to indicate he might not like where the conversation was going.

"If that is what you believe, Jay, then that is what it will be, no question about that. However, what if it wasn't? What if it was something else? Or someone else?" Sana insisted.

"Like what, Sana? What are you suggesting it might represent?"

"My belief is that it's your wife shining down on you, letting you know that you're ok, on track and in safe hands," Sana said with a smile.

"My wife?" Wedmore exclaimed, pulling away from Sana and looking visibly vexed. *"How do you know about my wife and why are you bringing her up now? Who are you? What do you want with me?"*

"Please, James," Sana insisted *"children are sleeping close by."*

"I don't give a fuck about that!" Wedmore exclaimed.

They locked intense gazes again. Wedmore was caught up in the red mist of his masculine anger rising within him and projecting towards Sana who met the intensity of his stare with the distilled essence of love, respect, and acceptance of his emotional situation; and the fact that she had inadvertently touched a nerve.

Wedmore instinctively stepped into his masculine energy, straightening his back and standing upright, clenching his fists and gritting his teeth. Sana stood her ground and looked up into the eyes of this fierce, giant of a man with pure compassion and love in her eyes. As she did so, she felt his unresolved pain and associated emotions start to overpower her as tears began to well up in her eyes. She could feel every part of his soul and the torment he had endured since the passing of his wife.

The feelings became too intense for Sana to bear as she turned on her heel and walked back into the tent, leaving Wedmore staring into the void of her absence. Her last teary-eyed look raced through his adrenaline-fuelled mind, as his anger became more intense. His own code of honour made it a Golden Rule to never hurt women and children and here he was about to unleash his anguish on a fragile woman of the desert.

As his aggression subsided because the threat to his vulnerability had retreated, regret quickly swept over him as he realized how frightening it must have been for Sana to be faced with the intensity of his anger. He pulled back the curtain on the tent to find her and apologise. As he entered the tent, she stood in the centre with her back to him, her head bowed and her shoulders shaking, gently sobbing.

"I'm sorry, Sana," Wedmore said as he approached her. *"I don't know what came over me in that moment."*

"It's ok, Jay. I felt your pain and I understand why you were upset with me for bringing it up. She obviously meant the world to you."

"I still don't know how you know about her, but yes, she was my world. I loved her more than anything. She was my safe harbour in the storms of life, do you know what I mean?"

"I have never experienced such love, Jay, but it is clear from how you feel inside that you loved her very much. I am sorry that I touched on such a sensitive subject with you. Please forgive me," Sana said.

"You have nothing to be sorry for, Sana. It is I who must apologise for being angry and aggressive with you," Wedmore said, as he got close enough to her to touch her arm.

She removed her hand from her forehead and looked up with tear-laden eyes into the eyes of the tall soldier stood next to her. It was clear that there was a connection between them. She opened her arms and stepped into the warmth of his embrace, burying her face into his muscular chest and feeling the safety of his strong arms as they gripped tightly around her body. Commander Wedmore stood there holding this slight woman in his arms, the scent of her femininity filling his nostrils and the embrace helping to calm his rapidly beating heart. This is what it felt like to be a warrior: protecting the innocence of those around him with kindness, caring, and understanding, the very essence of which was counter-intuitive for fighting in battle.

He held Sana close and they began to melt into one another, his arms tightening slightly in response to her squeezing him, and his left cheek resting on top of her head. Their breathing calmed and the intensity of the previous emotions drifted away, leaving just the presence of love in their place. Instinct took over and Wedmore kissed Sana on the top of her head to let her know she was safe with him and he was sorry for what he had done. She pulled back slightly and looked up into his eyes. They both saw kindness, love, and generosity in one another. It was a beautiful moment as their hearts connected through their tender gaze and they both felt it. Love and femininity had won the day.

Wedmore opened his arms and set Sana free from his embrace. He then stepped back, picked up some cushions from the floor, and invited Sana to sit with him.

"I want you to explain to me what you meant earlier and how you know all about me, please," Wedmore asked.

She smiled and graciously accepted his invitation as she sat elegantly on the soft cushions facing him.

"Jay, it's actually very simple and nothing mystical. My people here live very simply without distractions and we do not get caught up in the game of wrestling with the mind. That means we know ourselves very well as we spend time with ourselves, understanding our emotions as well as our environment," Sana explained. *"Over time, and by studying the ancient customs of my people, we have accessed the eternal and everlasting wisdom of our hearts. We believe that all knowledge that has ever been, or will ever be, exists in the ether and is all around us, much like radio waves broadcast across the skies. They are there, but we cannot hear them without a device that allows us to receive those signals."*

"My people believe that the creator of the universe blessed us all with something that would allow us to receive these signals, and that is the heart. The challenge is stilling the mind to be able to hear your heart and this can take years of practice in meditation to achieve. It is worth doing though as it allows me to know more about others than they know about themselves by picking up on the signals they broadcast and their energy. It's like mind-reading in a way, Jay." Sana smiled as she explained the simple truths of her way of life and the practice that had allowed her to see straight into the depths of his soul.

She continued, *"When I looked into your eyes, I practiced connecting with you and they say the eyes are the windows to the soul. I see beauty when I look into your eyes Jay, but I also* see pain and I feel for you. I see that you have been tormented by the loss of your love and for some of the decisions you have made in the past, which you now regret. It's not your fault, Jay. You must know that." Sana looked at Wedmore with empathy as she said this and smiled.

"I know the loss of my wife wasn't my fault. It was those bastards from Hezmat who killed her! And you're right, I have made some decisions and done things that I now regret, but there's nothing I can do. What's in the past is in the past," he said.

"Thank you for telling me that, Jay. In my culture, we believe that the past can and does need to be healed in order to obtain peace in the present, otherwise we will continue to torment ourselves over something that has power over us rather than being at peace with it," Sana explained.

"How can the past be healed?" he asked.

"What I am about to tell you will challenge you deeply, Jay, but if you are willing to go on the journey, you will learn a huge amount. Do you trust me to walk by your side during your learning?" Sana asked.

Wedmore paused for a moment and looked at this most beautiful Arabic desert woman once more and wondered what he was about to let himself in for. *"Ok,"* he said, *"I trust you!"*

"Thank you, Jay. I promise I will not let you down. All I am promising to show you is the truth and nothing more. I trust you are man enough to handle it!" Sana said.

As she did so, Wedmore felt a challenge to his masculinity and in true warrior fashion, he vowed to step up in the moment and take everything that was presented to him on the chin.

Sana continued, *"Consider first of all, Jay, that time is the greatest illusion in the world. Like money, time does not have* any bearing on anything else on this great planet of ours other than in the mind of man. When you understand this, you will realize that we are all trapped inside an illusion. If time does not exist, and it does not on a universal level, all things are possible. The past also does not exist. The past is only a present time recollection of a previous event with your mind filling in most of the blanks. It is only your relationship to every event that determines what labels you put on them and like everything, they can be labelled good or bad," Sana explained.

Wedmore looked confused. "What do you mean, Sana?" he asked.

"If we look at nature for an example, it might bring some clarity to you. Consider a lion killing a zebra. If you are the zebra, being killed is pretty bad, but if you are the lion whose cubs have not eaten for a week and will die unless you make the kill, it's a very good day. It's only the labels that we put on things that determine whether they are good or bad," she explained.

"I can see what you mean," he said, "but how do you explain the death of my wife? How can this possibly be a good event?"

"Your relationship to this event will obviously bring a lot of emotions. There are no two ways about it and I am sorry again for your loss. Is it possible that there would have been some good coming from it that you may not have seen yet?" she asked.

"It certainly became my excuse to rid the earth of some terrorist scumbags!" Wedmore said. He was becoming worked up again by the situation.

"There is that, Jay! And how do you feel about that?" she asked.

"Part of me feels good that I avenged her death," he replied.

"*And the other part?*" Sana questioned, sensing there was more that Wedmore wasn't admitting to himself.

Wedmore reflected for a moment bringing his head towards the ground as he did so. "*The other part of me feels empty, hurt, and alone.*"

"*Why do you feel that is, Jay?*" she continued.

"*I'm not sure.*"

For a strong masculine warrior, this was the first time he had ever done any emotional digging around this subject and he was finding it tough. All of a sudden, he was facing his own torment and inner voice along with the deep well of hidden emotions that had not been expressed for many years. The same buried emotions were haunting him every single day of his life and came back in his dreams no matter how much he drank or tried to suppress them.

"*I guess it might have something to do with killing other people. It doesn't feel right, no matter how bad I feel they may have behaved. It feels like a little part of my soul dies every single time I take the life of another person. It's tough, because I am just following orders from my superiors,*" Wedmore explained.

"*Thank you for being honest with me, and more importantly, yourself. I am blessed to be the one you have shared this with. It is the key to making a real breakthrough here. Jay, in my culture, we believe in different levels of consciousness and at the highest levels, there is the belief that we are all one. That level explains why you feel that a little piece of you dies when you take the life of another. I can understand that. Do you think your wife would have wanted you to behave in this way?*" Sana asked.

"*I don't know. She would have wanted justice. She was a big believer in justice,*" he explained.

"I can understand she wants justice, Jay. Do you think that you have achieved justice in her name with the people you have killed?" Sana asked.

Wedmore was dumbstruck. He ran that question through his mind several times for a moment and really let it sink in. He must have killed many hundreds of people in revenge for the killing of his wife when all he really wanted to do was bring the one person who was responsible to justice. He felt that he had also sacrificed a large part of himself in doing so. He bowed his head and looked at the floor again before saying, *"I don't know."*

"Well, if you don't know, why don't we ask her?" Sana asked with a sympathetic smile.

Wedmore looked up at her. *"How would we do that?"*

"Let's go back and look at the shining stars," she replied.

They stood up and walked back outside. Although the tent had no heating, there was a noticeable difference in temperature between the inside of the tent and outside. They looked up at the bright star as Wedmore asked Sana how they would ask the star for guidance.

"Close your eyes, Jay, and feel. Feel for the first time in your life!" she emphasised. *"Connect with the star and feel her wisdom and guidance come through you. Relax and let things unfold naturally. Remember your deep meditative breathing from earlier? Repeat this and feel, Jay."*

Sana closed her own eyes and observed what was happening through her own feelings. In that moment, their energy was fused with the energy of the cosmos as Wedmore connected with the spirit of his late wife. He felt a surge of energy through his body and he opened up the channels of communication through his heart.

"Don't use your mind, Jay," Sana whispered. *"Use the heart. Always the heart. Ask whatever you want through the heart. I will leave you to it."* Sana tiptoed quietly back to the tent leaving him alone in the darkness to communicate with his wife's spirit.

Wedmore stood there in quiet contemplation for a moment making sure that he was in the right breathing pattern and his mind was calm and still. As he did so, he felt the calmness spread throughout his entire body again and he became more centred and grounded. The hard part was letting his heart do the talking whilst his mind stayed out of the picture. He wasn't used to communicating with the intention of the heart, but he reasoned that it was perfectly possible to do so now that he had just experienced the most miraculous healing. His breathing continued deeply as he felt the cool air circulate his body.

Suddenly, he felt an energetic pull on his body and the air around him went quite cold. The image of his wife flashed into his mind as the smiling, beautiful goddess he had once known intimately and whom he missed very dearly every single day. He was stunned as the image was so clear and sharp that it felt like she was right in front of him. Momentarily, he lost his calmness as his mind questioned how this could possibly be. As he did so, the image of his wife drifted from his mind and questions took over. He knew that he had lost his focus, so he took a few deep breaths to become calm and grounded again.

As his breathing returned to calmness and his heart energy took over again, the lucid mental image of his wife returned, smiling as though pleased to see him again after so many years had passed. He felt deep love in his heart again for the woman he had loved and lost in such a tragic way. A smile spread across his face as enjoyed the experience.

"Hi CJ!" his wife said her nickname for Commander James while smiling.

"Hi beautiful!" he replied, with complete joy in his heart. *"It's good to see you again."*

"Good to see you too. I've missed you," his wife said.

In Wedmore's mind's eye, Mr and Mrs Wedmore embraced one another again and the warmth of eternal love consumed his entire body. He felt elated and elevated to a higher level of consciousness in that moment, as though he was in the captivating embrace of an angel. Deep peace and calmness spread through his heart and soul.

"I know you have been hurting since I went, CJ," she said. *"You should know that I am absolutely fine. I am in a very happy place right now and watching over you. You are doing great and I miss you."*

Tears welled up in his eyes as he felt the suppressed pain of his loss wash over him. A lump formed in his throat as a lone tear escaped his eyes and rolled down his right cheek.

"Please don't cry, CJ! It's ok, I promise."

"But I miss you so much!" Wedmore said. *"You have no idea how much love I have for you. I failed in my mission to protect, cherish, and honour you forever."*

"CJ, stop beating yourself up! You didn't fail at all! There is something that you need to know about that situation that will help you understand everything. I cannot give you all the answers, but I can give you some that will help you to find peace in your heart again. You didn't do anything wrong, my love. Before we ever came to earth, we made a soul contract that we had to honour in this realm, which would allow us both to grow. We agreed that we would meet, fall in love, and lose one another so that this soul learning experience could play out for one another. There is nothing wrong with this path that we have chosen and it's all working out perfectly. I am blessed to

have been part of your life and for us to walk through our journey together. I love you."

James tried to prevent his mind from taking over so he could make intellectual sense of the message he was receiving from the Heavens. He took a deep breath and released it very slowly. His wife continued; *"So you see CJ, there is nothing wrong. What happened was just an event, and it has led you to be a war hero and rid the world of some very nasty people. I am blessed to have been sacrificed for this cause because you are the only one that could live this path and the only one who can walk this journey from now on."*

Wedmore straightened his back and took another deep breath, trying to comprehend what was being said whilst dealing with a surge of suppressed grief. It didn't make logical sense that his wife was happy for her life on earth to be taken so that he could live out another path in his own life.

"CJ, you have to know two things; the first is to forgive yourself because you have done nothing wrong and the second is to know that not all is what it seems right now. I cannot say any more than that, my love, as you have to see it for yourself, but I can help you with the first part. Shall we heal that beautiful, kind, compassionate and wonderful heart of yours, darling?" she asked.

"I would love nothing more, sweetheart! I cannot bear to be in this pain and feel this loss any longer."

"Very well, my one true love. Before I help you do this, you must promise me one thing."

"Anything."

"You must promise me that from now on you will always follow your heart and listen to your intuition. It is far more powerful than you can possibly know. And find happiness again…" She took a deep breath before continuing, *"I know*

that you and Sana like each other. Listen to that and see where it takes you. You have my permission to find love again, so don't hold back from sharing that gorgeous heart of yours with another loving soul whenever you can."

"Anything for you, my love. You should know that I will never forget you."

"I know you won't and I know I will always have a special place in your heart. Your journey goes on from here, sweetheart, so you must follow the path that God has laid out for you. Do it with great love and you will see how this all plays out. You are a warrior, my love, and you will always do what is right. Now go make it happen!"

As she finished her sentence, she took a deep breath, and looked at him one last time with intense love in her eyes and the biggest smile on her face. In Wedmore's mind, the image of her got brighter and brighter until she was a blindingly brilliant light that shot into the depths of his heart, physically knocking him to the ground with a thud.

Sana came rushing out of the tent to find him slumped on the ground. She knelt by his side and checked to see if he was ok. He looked up from the ground into her eyes before resting his head on her lap, putting his arms around her kneeling body to pull her close, and sobbing deeply as she stroked his hair.

Chapter 11

A Journey of Truth

LOCATION: Somewhere in Medina
DATE: 1st May
WEATHER: Cool balmy night

As Wedmore sobbed, the pain from the suppressed grief he had kept locked deep in his heart began to dissipate and leave his body. He felt wave after wave of sad and unexpressed emotions flow through him, as years of sorrow and hurt escaped him. Sana remained silent and allowed his vulnerability to show. A hardened and decorated war hero lay on the sandy desert ground with his head in her lap, her skirt becoming moist from the tears of raw emotion flowing from his eyes. His body shook and trembled as he went through this deeply emotional experience. Sana watched over him with a sympathetic smile and love in her heart, only once glancing up to the Heavens to silently mouth the words 'Thank you'. She knew the healing of the emotional scars this great man had carried for so long were taking place before her very eyes. She remained totally present with him in this moment.

After what seemed like 20 minutes of intense sobbing, the tears stopped flowing and Wedmore just lay with his body partly curled around Sana's and his face lying in a tear stained moisture patch on her brilliant white skirt. He felt the soft touch of her hands as they supported his head and stroked his hair to comfort him. He was still shaking slightly from the emotional release, yet a calmness in his heart and mind was now present. He hadn't cried like that since he was eight years old when he lost his mother. Now the intensity of the emotions had gone, he was free from the prison they had kept him in for so many years. He felt renewed and whole again.

He sat up next to Sana and looked at her through tear-laden eyelashes. *"I'm sorry,"* he said.

"Jay, there is nothing to apologise for. I am grateful that you would let me be there for you and your healing. How do you feel now?" Sana asked.

"I feel peaceful. Calm. Still. Like a huge weight has been lifted. That was powerful," Wedmore said.

"I know what you mean, Jay. I am pleased for you. Would you like to tell me about your experience?"

Wedmore dried his eyes and began to explain the mysterious and magical journey he had just embraced to get peace and freedom from the passing of his late wife.

"One thing she said that confused me slightly," he said looking at Sana to see if she could expand more on the learning he had just experienced.

"What was that?" she asked.

"She said that all was not as it seemed. I don't know what she meant by that. You'll be pleased to know that she also told me to follow my heart!" he said with a smile and a twinkle in his eye as he looked at Sana. She looked away with a coy smile on her face.

"What do you think she might have meant by things not being as they seem, Jay?" Sana asked.

"It's puzzling to me," he replied. "I wish there was a way to find out."

Sana paused for a moment and took a deep breath before she looked at Wedmore. "There is another way to access universal truths quickly, Jay. It's not something that I would usually suggest, but with the journey you are on tonight, it might be the best thing to try."

"I don't think there are any more surprises you could possibly throw at me, Sana," Wedmore joked. "I've experienced two miracles tonight, and surely there is much more I could learn from you."

"Ok, Jay," Sana said as she reached out her arm to touch his. "We can prepare a truth ritual tonight for you and your friends if you would like?"

"What's involved in a truth ritual?" Wedmore asked.

"It's an ancient spiritual practice of my people," Sana said. "The truth ritual requires the soul to go on a journey so that you can see beyond the physical reality of your life and understand what is really happening. The local people call it a 'tea ceremony' but it's really called Ayahuasca." Sana explained. "Many people drink Ayahuasca as it takes the mind out of the equation and allows the soul to find its way to universal truth."

"I'm English, and we drink a lot of tea!" he joked again, half-flirting with Sana as he said it. "I've never known a cup of tea allow me to find universal truth!" he continued with a smile.

"You have to try our tea then, Jay! Then you will know the truth!"

"Ok, let's do this!" he said.

James stood, reached out his hands to pick up this beautiful woman, and looked at her with love in his eyes radiating from his heart and soul. He pulled her close to him and kissed her on the forehead before hugging her tightly.

"Thank you," he said, clearly grateful for the experiences he was having in her presence. She gave him a gentle squeeze to let him know that she was also grateful for the experience.

Sana led Wedmore back to the campfire where Blackbeard and the rest of the Black Widows were sharing stories, laughing, and joking under the stars. As Blackbeard heard them approaching, he turned around with a smile and welcomed them back to the group. Sana greeted the rest of the Black Widows as Blackbeard introduced her as their fearless leader and most respected guidance counsellor in their community.

"She knows the ways of the universe, my friends. Sana is a unique woman and we trust deeply in her guidance and leadership. She embodies femininity, love, joy, and respect. She is a fiery warrior woman of the desert, my friends, so don't upset her!" Blackbeard joked.

Sana smiled and looked at the soldiers. She turned to Blackbeard and said; *"We are going to do a tea ceremony for James and his friends. Can you organize this, please?"*

Blackbeard's face lit up as he threw his arms into the air and laughed at the suggestion. *"My friends!"* he exclaimed, *"you are going to love this! We have a real treat in store for you."*

The group smiled at him as he left. Clearly a bond of deep camaraderie had formed between them all since their healing experience. The earlier harsh treatment of them had been long forgotten and had turned to gratitude for being shown the infinite loving power of the universe.

Blackbeard returned a few minutes later with a bottle filled with an orangey brown liquid and a small box of black grapes. He was followed by two of the gunmen who now carried bundles of sage and glasses rather than the rifles they had sported earlier.

Blackbeard was visibly pleased with what was about to unfold. From his pocket, he pulled out six black blindfolds and handed one to each of the Black Widows who were eagerly anticipating what was about to occur.

He sat before them as the two gunmen walked to the campfire to set light to the bundles of sage they carried. They blew out the flames so that a scented smoke arose from the bundles before they walked in circular motions around the gathered group, waving the smoking sage up and down as they did so. As the fragrance of the smoking sage filled the air, Blackbeard began to explain to the Black Widows what was about to happen.

"My friends, the Ayahuasca experience is one that will change your lives forever. It originated from the Amazon rainforest and although it is believed local tribal people discovered it, there are some who claim that extra-terrestrials arrived on earth and told them to brew two plants together for access to otherworldly properties. What we are about to do my friends is to set your soul free so you can fly high and find your truth. This sounds like fun, yes?" Blackbeard asked.

The group nodded to his infectious energy and inviting question. Blackbeard continued, *"We are about to take a hallucinogen and it will play a few tricks on you if you try and control the experience with your mind. You have to surrender and let go to the wisdom of the spirit 'Madré' who is Mother Ayahuasca. She will open the door to allow you to find your truth."*

The Doc looked a little confused. *"I've heard about this Ayahuasca and it's illegal across most of the world!"* he interjected. *"Surely it's dangerous for us to be taking an illegal hallucinogen."*

"When you see how powerful this is, you will understand why it's illegal!" Sana said with a smile. *"Trust me when I say you are in safe hands. You healed yourself within a few hours earlier, so this will be a useful experience for you all."*

"Are you ready, friends?" Blackbeard asked as he began decanting the strange liquid into each of the glasses that he had carefully twisted into the sand to prevent them from being knocked over. He picked up the box of grapes and handed it to Wedmore saying, *"You had all better take a few of these to help you stomach the tea. It's an acquired taste!"*

Wedmore took a handful of grapes before passing the box to his teammates as the sage bearers passed the glasses of tea amongst them. Gringo smelt the liquid in the glass first and turned his nose up at it. *"Wow, that stuff reeks,"* he said.

"It's best to drink it quickly and then eat the grapes to take the taste away," Sana advised. *"It will take about twenty minutes to take affect and it's best to be in darkness with the blindfolds on. I don't know what you will see as you will all go on your own journey, but I can tell you that you will see what you need to for your own journey and your own truth. It is a beautiful experience. Do not try to interpret it or fight it with your mind, as the tea is too strong. Instead, surrender to it and let it take you where you need to go for your healing and your truth. We will play some music around the fire as you go through your journey over the next two or three hours. You may wish to lie down and we have some blankets for your comfort as you journey."*

As Sana spoke, the sage bearers handed each member of the group a thick blanket and a few extra cushions to make everyone comfortable.

"Ok, team," Wedmore said. *"On three, let's do this together. Down in one. One, Two, Three!"*

Everyone gulped down the liquid with various facial expressions detailing what each one felt about the taste and texture of the tea. They each ate the juicy black grapes before getting themselves comfortable and securing their blindfolds in place. They became motionless as they waited for the tea to work its magic. The sage bearers smudged each member of the team personally again before placing another blanket over each of them to keep them warm during their experience.

Silence fell over the company as they all entered the world of Ayahuasca. The sage bearers returned to throw the sage bundles into the campfire, adding more wood as they did so, before providing the group with bottles of fresh water for when they emerged from their experience.

The peace and quiet was broken by one of the sage bearers who had begun playing an acoustic guitar in the background gently whilst his friend sang in Arabic. He sang of the mystical properties of Ayahuasca and the journey of the limitless soul through the experience. He also sang about the universal body of consciousness, of all things being one, and the human experience being an expression of life in its finest form with universal energy and truth being present in the heart and soul of every living thing.

One-by-one, with their eyes closed and deep in blackness from the blindfolds, each began to experience strange flickering multi-coloured lights appearing in their minds, like lines of marching ants walking in opposing directions. As time went on and the tea started to weave its magic through their minds, they began to feel drowsy and their minds were peeled and pulled out of the way so their souls could be set free on a wonderful journey.

As Wedmore lay there, he felt the strangest feeling of his mind being pulled in many directions as the colours he saw before his eyes became much more vivid and bright. He felt his eyes roll back into his head as his mind struggled in vain to hold onto the reality it had created. The colours changed from a procession of marching ants into the most vivid straight lines of all the colours of the rainbow, ebbing and flowing in and out of his mental picture as his body started to curl up on the ground and he rolled over onto his left side. The taste and sensation of the liquid made him feel a little queasy. He used his hands to search in the sand next to his blanket for a stone to grasp to remind him of physical reality as his experience became more and more intense.

As time marched on, his mind felt completely overwhelmed and he couldn't hold on any longer. At one point, he felt like he was losing his mind; a feeling he was familiar with when he had overdosed heavily on drink and was about to lose consciousness. In this moment, he tilted his head back against the pillow with his mouth open and grasped the rock in his right hand tighter and tighter to remind himself that he was just going through a trip rather than a terrifying manifestation of his mind's imagination.

He took a deep breath as he felt the pressure building in his head and his mind being peeled back to remove it from the equation. The drink was clearly stronger than he anticipated and he wasn't ready for the impact it was about to make on him. He really did feel like he was losing his mind as the feeling of unconsciousness passed over him. He could not mentally hold on any longer and gave up trying to wrestle control of the situation. The last words that flashed through his mind were *"God, please help me!"* as he let out a deep breath and mentally passed out in a state of complete surrender. His body became limp and lifeless as it lay on the blanketed desert floor and the tight grip around the rock in his hand loosened.

His internal reality was completely different. With his mind out of the way, his limitless soul was set free to journey, and journey it did. For the first time, Wedmore experienced the complete and utter freedom of being a spirit energy flying through the vast depths of space. His spirit literally travelled from one side of the universe to the other in seconds and he felt he existed within everything and everyone simultaneously. He felt what he believed to be the teachings of all religious masters, which was the feeling of universal 'oneness'. It was the most beautiful experience he had ever felt of complete freedom without constraints or boundaries of physicality at all. He journeyed from planet to planet across the boundless universe and saw things of the most indescribable beauty that filled his soul with joy. A smile spread across his physical body as his heart was lit up by this joyous experience.

As his journey continued, his spirit found itself at the bottom of a dark valley. He looked up and saw a mountain, which he recognized as a symbol for God. His soul floated upwards from the depths of the dark valley to come face-to-face with God who was revealed to Wedmore's soul as a one-eyed mountain that appeared to be in conversation with angelic beings of another realm. He patiently waited his turn to speak with the one-eyed mountain, which eventually turned to him to ask why he was there.

Wedmore's spirit asked God a question he did not fully understand: *"Why are you all the way up here and I am down there?"*

God explained that this was not the case as both he and Wedmore were one and the same. Wedmore seemed confused and didn't understand God's answer, so he asked God to demonstrate what he meant. In that moment, God swopped places with Wedmore, so that his spirit became the mountain and God became Wedmore's spirit. Wedmore could observe God as his own spirit and understood all of God's creations were simply consciousness having an experience in the physical realm. They then swopped places to look at one another from their original perspectives before trading places once more so that Wedmore could get a clear understanding that he and God were one and the same.

As they finally reverted back to their original positions, Wedmore's soul acknowledged God for the experience. God said to him, *"My child, you must understand that you are me and I am you. We are one and the same. There is no difference. You will not find me externally to you because I am within you at all times. I do not ask that you look outwards to find me, but to look within and realise that I am there always and have your best interests at heart, no matter what happens. I will never take you to where my grace will not protect you. You must be careful on your journey through life as there is much darkness that will try to overshadow your light. I always say 'the brighter the light, the darker the shadow'. This is what you must be aware of at all times during your journey on Earth."*

Wedmore asked for some clarification. God explained that it could not be explained in language, but it had to be seen to be believed and he would be happy to show Wedmore if he was open enough to knowing the truth. Wedmore acknowledged that he would be more than happy to be shown what God wished him to see. God was pleased that he had accepted his invitation to look behind the scenes and prepared him for the next stage of his journey by reassuring him, *"My child, I do not offer you an easy path here, but I know that you have the ability to bring about huge change on Mother Earth with your strength of character and fight for justice. If you will hold your faith in a better and more loving environment on Earth, we will co-create it together. I believe in you!"*

God looked to his right. As Wedmore's spirit followed his gaze, he saw the most beautiful angel radiating the most intense amount of love that engulfed Wedmore's spirit and made him feel recharged, re-energised, and completely whole once more.

"This is Archangel Michael and he will be your guide. He is a heavenly warrior of love and light and he will help to pull the veil off what is really happening in the world so you can see for yourself. Brace yourself as its going to be quite a journey for you, but it will prepare you well for what you must do with the time you have left on Earth. I wish you well, my child."

God handed Wedmore over to Archangel Michael to take him on a journey of true enlightenment. As Wedmore observed this enormous Archangel next to him, he felt the vibration of the highest levels of love possible combined with the strongest and most warrior-like spirit he had ever encountered. He noticed Archangel Michael carried a beautifully designed sword that must have been as big as a city skyscraper. It was clear that he was not of the Earth realm. The Heavenly Warrior was face to face with an Earth Warrior and they both smiled as they recognized the resilience, determination, beauty, and need for justice in one another.

Archangel Michael spoke, *"Let me be your guide and show you the real world."*

Despite being confused at the suggestion of what the 'real world' entailed, Wedmore's spirit agreed and they were transported in time and space to an office Wedmore immediately recognized as Rosehill's. They were observing the events unfolding in the office like wizards looking into a crystal ball. It took Wedmore a few moments to realize that the strange visitor Rosehill was engaged in a meeting with was the mysterious gentleman Wedmore had seen before. Wedmore was able to look all around within the office as the story unfolded in front of him. Archangel Michael was silent, allowing Wedmore to get the message for himself.

Wedmore could see the face of this mysterious visitor who was clearly an evil man. He could see the dead, soulless eyes sunken within his grey sneering face. Rosehill addressed him as Lord Childroth. It was clear that this man was not there to do good. However, what unfolded in front of Wedmore left him in complete shock.

He heard the instructions being given to Rosehill, which he acted on without questioning. Wedmore had always thought Rosehill was a tough but honourable man who would always do the right thing, but it was clear that the man in front of him had bought Rosehill. He saw Lord Childroth hand over a briefcase full of £50 notes amounting to several million pounds, along with instructions that suggested The Black Widows would be sent on a mission to take out a so-called terrorist, who was really protecting his country from invasion by foreign forces who threatened to steal their natural resources. He saw how this so-called terrorist leader of Hezmat was fighting to free his country from the financial slavery imposed by the western world who had 'rescued them' by lending an obscene amount of money and food when they suffered the hardship of a famine many years ago.

What struck him as most odd was that Rosehill would take such an action and not do the right thing. Then he realized that Rosehill and his family were also under the threat of death from this vulgar visitor who clearly had a lot of control over other military mercenaries like Wedmore, and would act with fewer morals for more money. The visitor had a briefcase of cash in one hand, a gun in the other, and a picture of Rosehill's family in his pocket. Wedmore reasoned that he would probably make the same choice as Rosehill if he were in the same position, no matter how wrong it may look to an outsider. Nevertheless, to say that he felt let down was an understatement. There was zero reason for him and his men to have been sent on this mission to risk their lives killing this so-called terrorist, other than the profiteering of some western madmen. In fact, it occurred to him that when the west invades a country to seize their resources and central banking system, it's classed as 'democracy' and 'freedom from oppression', but when a country tries to defend itself from an invasion to retain its natural resources for the benefit of its own people, the media calls them terrorists. How ironic, he thought.

It was clear that Wedmore could no longer trust Rosehill to do the right thing. In fact, the mission he had been sent on was a complete sham. He was grateful to have seen this as it answered a number of questions for him. Wedmore turned to Archangel Michael and thanked him. Archangel Michael replied in a booming deep voice, *"There is more to see, Earth Warrior. Come, let me show you."*

They moved through time and space again. Wedmore found himself in a strange city and a setting that he did not recognize. His spirit flew around the immediate vicinity taking in the central area comprising coffee shops, bars, and restaurants. There was an intense hustle and bustle of the public as everyone went about their daily business. The area was clearly very popular with local people and tourists alike. He listened to the language people were talking and it became clear he was in Pakistan. As he continued to observe the central area, he recognized his wife in the crowd walking to lunch with a few of her diplomatic colleagues.

Joy filled his spirit as he watched her effortlessly go about her business. She ordered her usual double espresso with a sparkling water and an avocado salad. She crossed her long, sexy legs as she took a sip of her coffee and looked around at the crowd. She looked as gorgeous as ever and he was proud he had married such a beautiful, kind, intelligent woman.

Then he realized that this was the place that his wife had been killed in a terrorist bomb blast and his emotions quickly shifted from pride to panic, as he did not want to witness the demise of the woman he loved. He looked expectantly at Archangel Michael for reassurance and felt a wave of love and compassion sweep over his spirit.

No one saw it coming. The taxi swung into the square, dropping off a fare-paying passenger. As the passenger stood outside the driver's window paying his fare, the explosion happened. The taxi blew up in a huge cloud of smoke and fire, creating an enormous blast in the centre of the tourist hot spot, sending fragments of people, chairs, glass, tables, cutlery, and pottery in all directions. The intensity of the blast was followed by an eerie silence. There were no screams or shouts, just the deafening sound of nothing.

Moments later, the silence was broken by the sound of car alarms and building intruder alarms being activated from the air displaced by the blast. The whole site looked horrific, with lifeless bodies intermingled with debris and dust, as the crater in the centre of the square was all that remained of the taxi that had caused such devastation. People from the surrounding area came running to see what had happened as the distant sound of emergency services sirens filled the air. Wedmore looked around for survivors and saw none. Anxiety filled his soul as he saw his wife lying there, her soul already moving on to another dimension.

He questioned why Archangel Michael had brought him here to witness the brutal death of his wife. He already knew who was responsible for this atrocity and this was the person he had been sent to eliminate in his current mission. Having witnessed this event unfold, it made him even more determined to avenge his wife's death.

Then Archangel Michael spoke. *"You need to see the truth here. Can you handle it?"*

Wedmore wondered how much worse it could possibly get and swiftly agreed. Archangel Michael held out his two enormous hands in front of him. On the left hand, he saw a vision of the Hezmat leader whom Wedmore was fiercely intent on eliminating. He was incensed as he linked the death of his wife to the actions of this evil man.

However, he witnessed a moving picture of this Muslim man behaving in a truly gentle and loving manner as he embraced his wife and played with his two young children at home. They sat on the floor whilst his children laughed and his wife looked at him with admiration. He could sense peace, love, and generosity. He wondered how such a family man could be capable of such an atrocity.

Then a darker vision filled the open palm of Archangel Michael's right hand. It showed a shadowy boardroom of thirteen grey-faced men dressed in dark suits, white shirts, and red ties. Their plan was obvious: create division, separation, and hatred between people of different races, religions, and cultures to keep people fighting amongst themselves so they could cause even greater distraction and infiltrate every influential position to create wealth for themselves whilst leaving little for anyone else. Wedmore became incensed when he saw how beautifully tailored their plan for world domination was. He saw that these thirteen powerful and evil men were behind every single terrorist act that mainstream media had reported.

By keeping people frightened and fearful, they could manipulate everyone into giving up more and more of their personal rights and freedoms in exchange for more 'security and protection' from their government leaders who were essentially puppets to the organizations the circle of thirteen had created. He saw the erosion of personal liberties through their evil plan to control and manipulate the public and to send men to their death on missions into foreign countries to seize their oil and gold. What surprised Wedmore even more was the fact that these men were also enormous drug lords who infiltrated foreign countries to seize their drug crops and distribute it amongst the west without any repercussions whatsoever. How ironic it seemed to have one rule for them and one rule for everyone else.

It began to dawn on Wedmore that the Hezmat leader was, in fact, not a terrorist, but was actually protecting his own people from those thirteen families who would do them harm and sacrifice whoever they could in pursuit of their bloodthirsty mission of greed and gluttony. It was clear who the real villains were here and they did not reside on foreign shores. They were safely at home in the western world whilst they sent men like the Black Widows on death missions that could result in killing of many innocent people who were just defending their own country from brutal attack and pillage. Then Archangel Michael asked him a question that chilled him right to the core:

"Have you ever stopped to question what you are really fighting for, James?"

Wedmore was stumped, confused, and filled with regret that he had taken the lives of so many so-called enemies who were all doing their best to protect themselves in the face of intense fear and manipulation from the armies of the west. He had to admit that he was wrong.

"It is with great shame that I admit that I have always just followed orders and never thought to question what is really going on," he replied.

"You are not alone, James. Almost all military trained people are broken down during their training so they do not question authority. This allows these thirteen evil men to send good people like you into battle with the false belief that you are fighting the enemy. They know the best way to manipulate

people is to first create a problem that the public cry out for a solution to, so they are then given free rein to implement the 'solution' they wanted to achieve in the first place. They get men like you to do their bidding for them, not caring if the spirit of your life is extinguished in the process. They have manipulated many people like you and it is time for this to stop. You have been chosen to do this, James," Archangel Michael said.

Wedmore was even more shocked. *"But why me?"*

"Do not doubt a mission that God has created for you. He and I will stand by you to achieve it. Much darkness controls the Earth at this moment and it must be overthrown. It has been necessary to serve in the growth and enlightenment of humanity through struggle, but it has gone too far. You will restore the balance of power by removing those who cause harm and replace them with the peace of pure heart and soul that will help elevate brothers and sisters across the world."

"How will I know who they are?" he asked.

"You will know them because we are not sending you on this mission on your own. You are a warrior and a leader, James. You will convince your fellow military colleagues to join the fight for good and overthrow evil."

With that, Archangel Michael clapped his hands and they found themselves in the presence of God again.

God looked at Wedmore. *"You know your mission now, my child. Remember my Mercy will not take you where my Grace will not protect you."*

He spoke in recognition of the feelings of dread and insecurity that had overtaken Wedmore who was already contemplating the size of the mission he was being asked to undertake. Overthrowing the governments of the west and their military powers had already been deemed impossible in his own mind.

At that moment, Sana appeared in his vision, smiling at Wedmore as she did so.

"Sana will accompany you, James," Archangel Michael said. *"She will know who is pure of heart to take over from those who would do evil deeds to their fellow brothers and sisters. Protect and honour her in your mission. You are in this together. Let love be your guide in all that you do. United you stand; divided you fall."*

God interjected. *"My child, you must understand one thing. Men and women are very different. Women are compassionate and nurturing in their approach to life. Men are adversarial and sometimes blinded by their masculinity in their approach to life. However, men literally live to serve women when women truly stand in their feminine energy. All life comes from the feminine and that is why we call it Mother Earth or Mother Nature. Masculine energy protects and does it well. Humanity's progress and growth has largely depended upon man's ability to grow and contribute and it has finally reached a pinnacle of splendour that humans experience today. However, you have seen that much darkness has overshadowed this progress. Men are too easily bought and blinded with money, as they are not as intuitive as women. Women are more in touch with their intuition, or the Divine spark of my spirit, which is within every single one of you. They will not sell their morals for money, and instead strive for love, harmony, and peace. James, it is not until women are in positions of power running the world that humanity shall know true peace. Their motherly instinct protects and nurtures. Masculinity will adapt to serve femininity well. They are far from the weaker sex. This is your mission."*

Wedmore's spirit was troubled by what he was being entrusted to do and he battled with the overwhelming questions and self-doubt that immediately filled his mind. Archangel Michael passed Wedmore and Sana beautiful gold, ruby, and diamond encrusted necklaces in the shape of a winged heart, which they both placed over their hearts. As they did so, they felt a wave of calm, peace, and certainty pass through them and they knew they were connected to a higher realm.

"When you wear these necklaces, you will be guided to do what is right and we will direct you in every step of the way. We will not let you down. Nothing they can throw at you can harm you with our guidance, so have faith. It is time for you to return now, my children. Thank you for carrying out my Heavenly work on Earth. I know it is possible for you to create a Heaven on Earth and stop the division of different religions and cultures separating brothers and sisters. I understand there are some five thousand different religions who worship me and only one of them is wrong for Humanity" God said.

Sana and Wedmore both knew that this single 'religion' was the one that promoted evil and hatred. The many religions that existed on Earth all promoted similar teachings based on loving thy neighbour and not doing anything to our fellow man that you would not wish to be done to yourself. Finally, they understood what had been going on and they thanked God and Archangel Michael for showing them the truth. Whilst it had not been easy to accept, they recognized that the religion of evil had overshadowed the hearts and minds of man, making them susceptible to the negative influences of greed and the pursuit of money. They would restore the balance of power and unite humanity under the banner of love and respect for one another. With that, their spirits returned to their Earthly bodies as the affects of the Ayahuasca started to fade.

Chapter 12

A Mission for Souls

LOCATION: Somewhere in Medina
DATE: 1st May
WEATHER: Cool balmy night

As the Black Widows, Sana, and Blackbeard emerged from their Ayahuasca experience, they began to move their bodies as the feelings of being back in control of their limbs took effect. They moved slowly and then began to sit up as they removed their blindfolds. They smiled at one another as they adjusted to the light of the fire and their minds tried to make logical sense of what they had just experienced.

Wedmore and Sana glanced at one another and the exchange of their look said everything. Sana was as clear in her mind over what she had experienced as Wedmore was. They smiled at one another, her coyness returning as she held his gaze for a moment too long before looking away.

"Was that shit real?" Gringo asked with a smile, taking a large gulp of water as he did so.

"I think so!" the Doc said as he put his head in his hands to shake off the hangover-like after affects of the tea. "It sure was intense though. What did you experience?"

"It was beautiful!" Kamali replied. "I experienced the end of war. No more fighting and no more missions. People were kind *and loving to one another. No one was separated by their label for God and they remembered the teachings of their own religion: honouring kindness and accepting one another. Those that had plenty fed and clothed those who had not enough. It was a magical experience and a place I would love to live in, my brothers."*

Hitler also joined the conversation. *"How weird. That was my experience too!"*

"And mine!" Gringo and the Doc said in unison.

A feeling of confusion swept over them as they felt they could not have all experienced the same dream under the influence of this strange tea.

"It was no mistake, my friends!" Blackbeard said with a smile. *"You saw what you needed to see."*

"I had a very different experience," Wedmore said. He looked at Sana for confirmation of his experience and if she had gone through exactly the same experience as him. She gently nodded back in response without saying a word. Then she stood up and suggested that she and James take a walk to discuss what they had just seen. Blackbeard asked for some food platters so they could feast and discuss the magical world they had all just experienced. Sana and Wedmore walked together in silence with their minds deep in thought. Sana was the first to speak.

"Jay, we have work to do."

Wedmore was clearly confronted by her suggestion. *"How do we even know what we just experienced was real?"*

"I could give you many reasons, Jay, but first look at me and place your hand on your heart."

James did and looked at Sana. As he raised his right hand to place it over his heart, he felt a hard lump between his smock and his skin. His eyes opened wide in disbelief as pulled out the beautiful necklace he had just received on his Ayahuasca journey.

"This...this can't be real!" he stammered.

Sana smiled sweetly before pulling away her headscarf to reveal her own identical necklace. "Now are you a believer, Jay?" she asked.

"But, but, this is impossible! Where did this come from? What did you do?"

"I did nothing, Jay. You were there with me. You saw what I saw. You know all that I know from that experience. God wants us to do his bidding for him here on Earth. Are you with me, Jay?" Sana asked.

Wedmore slumped down on the ground against a sand dune, his mind barely able to comprehend that what was happening to him. Sana sat beside him. He who was clearly having a tough time getting to grips with everything that was not of this world and certainly not part of his former reality. It was a big ask to take him through such an intense spiritual awakening in such a short period of time, but it was God's request that he do so. The journey would serve him well and make more of a man of him. Wedmore held the necklace in his hand and squeezed it tightly to make sure he wasn't still in the dream world. He looked up at Sana.

"How is this possible?" he asked.

"All things are possible with God," she replied. "Think of how each and every single bud on every tree in the world opens at the right time and blossoms effortlessly. Think of every blade of grass that grows. Think of every living thing whose heart beats without any form of intervention from anyone. God orchestrates this beautifully, so I am sure he can make a necklace physically appear in our world as a reminder of your journey," she said with a kind smile.

"Do you remember what we have been asked to do?" he asked.

"Of course I remember, Jay. I was right there with you. What you saw I saw, and together we have to fulfil what God has asked of us. God has granted us life and has chosen us specifically to do this. We must honour that for everyone. It is not about us, Jay, it is about how we live our lives in service of those around us. That is what God wants of us."

"I have so many questions! Where do we begin? I mean, you saw how those evil people were using religion to separate and divide people. That's something you don't mess with! Religion has been around for thousands of years and we are effectively meddling with the worship of the God who has given us this mission. I don't know what it all means," he said, clearly confused by the overwhelming experience and the meaning his mind was trying to give it. His old and new realities were clashing and his mind was vainly trying to make sense of it all.

"We are not meddling with religion, Jay!" reassured Sana. *"We are merely reminding people what they seem to have forgotten. As a Christian, your God teaches you to love your neighbour, right? As a Muslim, we are taught not do anything to anyone that we would not want done to ourselves."*

"You're Muslim?" Wedmore asked. *"You're all supposed to be terrorists! I can't believe I have feelings for you!"*

He blurted the words out before thinking, which horribly upset Sana. She slapped James across the face before walking away from him, leaving him to come to terms with what he had just said. Wedmore stood up quickly and ran after her, grabbing her arm as she tried to pull away.

"Wait, Sana, I'm so, so sorry!" he pleaded.

"Are you crazy, Jay? You just saw that people were being separated and divided by religion and here you go calling me a terrorist because I have a different name for the same God that you believe in and have just met! What are you thinking?" Sana

spat the words at Wedmore, visibly hurt from being labelled a terrorist.

"I wasn't thinking! I'm so sorry! It's the result of past programming. It's what I have been taught to believe and I know in my heart that it's not true. Please forgive me." As the words fell from Wedmore's lips, he fell to the ground on his knees and looked up pleadingly at Sana as he held her tightly by the hands. *"I'm truly sorry. I didn't mean to say it. Next time I will engage my brain before speaking!"*

"Do you know something, Jay? When we were with God and Archangel Michael, they spoke of love being the substance that would unite all of humanity. Do you know what love is, Jay?"

James contemplated the question and his mind immediately jumped to the explosive cocktail of feelings he experienced when he first met her. *"For me, love is finding someone attractive and feeling like I want to protect them. The way I feel about you, for instance."*

"That's cute, Jay!" Sana said, partly blushing as she spoke. *"That's a form of love, but that's more about attraction to a member of the opposite sex. How would you show love to a man you just met?"*

"Erm, I'm not sure. I would probably shake his hand and smile politely," Wedmore replied.

Sana's head rolled backwards as she let out a playful laugh. *"You're so English, Jay! Seriously, think about it for a moment. How would you show love to someone you had just met? This is an important question for someone like you who fights first and asks questions later."*

Wedmore knelt in front of Sana in quiet contemplation, frantically racking his brains for how he would choose to interact with people he didn't know. The truth was, he had very few interactions with people he didn't know in his life. He was either with the Black Widows, his superiors, or perhaps enjoying the company of a woman he had met on a night out. Other than that, his life was insular. Even his shopping was largely done online.

He hadn't quite realized how much of an individual he had become and how alone he felt. The more he turned the question over in his mind, the more he had to admit that he no longer smiled to strangers in a shop anymore. He had seen too much darkness in the world and this affected his spirit and interaction with others by always judging them from first impressions as if they were enemies who might attack first. What a lonely place to be, he thought.

"Sana, I have to say you have me stumped. I have no idea how to answer this question. I knew what love felt like when I met my wife and I know what camaraderie feels like between my team. Other than that, I have little idea. I feel that I have love for my country because that's what I am fighting to protect. I don't know what else to say."

"Do you think your country loves you when they are lying to you about who the enemy is, Jay?" Sana asked.

"I guess not," Wedmore replied with an echo of regret and disappointment that he had offered up his life to a system that ultimately didn't care about him.

"It's ok, Jay, I get it. That's why you have been sent to me on this mission and we can help change the world together. What is love, Jay? Most people have no reference for love in their lives, especially Unconditional Love. Hollywood likes to glamorize love and make it all about a spark between two people leading into an intense inferno of desire and emotions, but that is very difficult to achieve with your fellow brothers and sisters every day. As children, we experienced love from our parents when we were well behaved and it was withdrawn when we were naughty, so most people only know conditional love as some kind of trade. So what's the key to showing love to one another, Jay?"

The blank look on Wedmore's face suggested that Sana continue.

"Acceptance."

A light bulb went off in Wedmore's mind as he got what Sana was hinting at.

"When we accept another, we accept who they are and more importantly, who they are not. We can look at limitations in their behaviour with tolerance, forgiveness, and understanding rather than letting them get under our skin and allowing their behaviour to make us angry! As Gandhi once said, 'no-one can hurt me without my permission'. For another's behaviour to upset us, we must give them control of our emotions, and that is a dangerous place to exist. It's like being a puppet with somebody else pulling on your strings."

"I think I get what you are saying, Sana; but what I saw earlier made me really angry. I mean these people are pure evil. They are purposefully planning death and destruction on this planet. How can we stay calm in the presence of such hate?"

"Calm we must stay, Jay. It's the only way to access the higher levels of consciousness and bring lasting peace and change to the planet. Getting angry with them only allows them to win control over you and you don't want that, do you? By staying calm and grounded, we can keep control of our emotional state and bring about change for the betterment of all humanity. Let us accept these people for who they are, for the significant limitations of their life. It is possible that these people have never experienced the joy of love in their lives and they are angry and upset at themselves and want to destroy the happiness and love others have in their lives. Their life becomes their punishment. We will not give them that power over us, Jay. Emotions are a very powerful experience within ourselves and when someone else is in control of our emotions, they have control over us. It's the same with fear. When we are fearful, it's a weapon they try and use on us all the time to keep us in a state of fear and have complete control over us. When we stand calm, grounded, and complete, they have no control over us, no matter how much they try to manipulate the situation. We have nothing to fear now, Jay. We know what is really going on and we can change it. We have God and the Archangel on our side."

"I admire you, Sana. You see many things that I do not. You are truly kind and loving," Wedmore said.

"It takes practice, Jay. I wasn't always like this. I used to get emotionally hooked by other people and their agendas all the time, and I swung from good to bad emotions every single day! I still do, as you saw from my earlier reaction. It was only when I realized how powerless I was by doing so that I took my power back and began to see the world in a different light. It gives me the power to help lead my people towards the truth. Jay, we have work to do. We need to make a plan to bring God's word to the people. Shall we begin?"

Wedmore took a moment to take in everything Sana had said to him. It had been a very long journey through the night and although he was feeling fine, he felt that a good night's rest would help them get into the best state to make a plan with his team. He had to pinch himself to make sure he wasn't still in a dream. He looked up at the clear starry night sky and felt joy in his heart. He then turned to Sana and looked deeply into her eyes before saying, *"Would you mind if I kissed you instead?"*

Sana was visibly taken aback by his forward suggestion. Before she had chance to reply, he moved towards her without breaking her gaze and pulled her close to him. As they looked at one another, enjoying the moment of anticipation, their pulses started racing. Wedmore leaned in to kiss this beautiful desert woman for the first time. They closed their eyes as their lips touched and a feeling of ecstasy began flowing through their veins. They pulled one another closer in an attempt to join their hearts and souls together in unison. The embrace continued for a brief moment before they pulled apart from one another, their eyes opening to reveal dilated pupils. Sana fluttered her eyelids with a look of breathless anticipation. He then kissed her again on the forehead and pulled her close, letting her know she was safe in his arms. In his heart and mind, he knew he was willing to die for this woman. He would honour her, protect her, and allow her to bring her message of peace, love, and generosity to the world.

"I wasn't expecting you to do that, Jay," she whispered.

"Well, you did say we needed to spread more love into the world!" he replied with a cheeky smile. "I really care about you, Sana, and I want to protect you. I feel like I am falling for you the more time I spend with you."

"Bless you, Jay. I feel the same. I am very grateful to God for bringing you into my life."

"We have had a very long day and night. We can make a plan tomorrow. The team already know the end goal of creating Heaven on Earth and we will all work together to achieve this. For now, let us rest peacefully and embrace the knowledge we have received tonight. Tomorrow is another day, as yet untouched." James smiled as he uttered these words; the phrase used to be one of his mother's favourites. He took Sana by the hand and led her back towards the campfire.

"I agree with getting some rest, Jay, but for the record, we are not sleeping together!"

"You're a fast mover! I was only just talking of developing feelings for you and here you are talking about marriage! It's not a leap year for another two years, so perhaps you can ask me then!" Wedmore joked.

"Very funny, Jay! That's not what I meant. I just want you to know that I have morals and I am not willing to do anything that might compromise them."

"That's fine by me, Sana. You should know that I will wait for you and do everything I can to honour and protect you. I respect you hugely and I am blessed that we have met. I see a very interesting journey unfolding before us. Besides, Love is now my New Religion. Maybe you'd like to join?" He smiled at Sana as he spoke and then kissed her again.

"A religion based on Love!" Sana's face lit up in excitement and wonder as she spoke the words. *"Where all races, religions, colours, and cultures of humanity are accepted for who they are, no matter what their beliefs! I love it, Jay!"*

"Let's not forget a boundless respect and love for nature!" he added.

"What has happened to you, Jay? You are transformed!" she joked.

"I'm a lover, not a fighter!" Wedmore replied with a cheeky smile, clearly enjoying the thought of a united humanity across the world. The possibility of being the one to help bring peace to the world filled his heart and soul with joy and to do so with the woman he loved by his side was a fascinating concept. It thrilled him deeply, as the vision filled his mind and a smile spread across his face.

Sana placed her hand over his heart and closed her eyes. She felt blessed to be with such a wonderful man who would help her to liberate humanity. It was a huge task, no doubt about that, but with such immense higher power on their side, she could relax knowing that it would all turn out how it was meant to.

They arrived back at the campfire to find the rest of the Black Widows and Blackbeard deep in conversation about the endless possibilities of human collaboration and a world without boundaries, fear, or worry. It was a joyous moment to observe these former enemies in deep conversation as friends, ready to help bring deep change to the world.

One question remained: how to do so without more death, violence, and fighting in an attempt to bring peace, love, and harmony to all? This required hours of reflective thought and discussion, but would have to wait until they had all regained their full strength and let their rational minds make sense of the spiritual transformation they had all just experienced.

Blackbeard led the Black Widows back to their tent where they could rest for the remainder of the night. Wedmore waited until his team left before walking Sana back to her own tent. As they stood outside, he hugged her tightly before kissing her once more and thanking her for the experience he had just gone through. As Sana retired to her tent, he walked back towards his teammates who were making themselves comfortable for the night. Before entering, he looked up at the sky and thanked God once more.

Gratitude was in his heart and it was a wonderful emotion to experience. He had finally seen the truth and would stop at nothing to help others find freedom from the evil plan of world domination. This was something that he could throw his heart and soul into, and a mission that he knew would bring more peace, love, and generosity to all. This was his higher calling and he was blessed to be chosen to undertake this mission. He bowed his head and felt the intensity of love in his heart. He felt unbelievably happy. As wave after wave of intense love flowed through his heart and soul, tears of abundant gratitude began streaming from his eyes. He clasped his hands together and repeatedly said thank you. He was finally free of past ties; he knew the truth about the present and would work tirelessly to create a new future for humanity. He punched the air in satisfaction before retiring for the night in the luxurious tent. A new day beckoned action, but now it was time to sleep.

Chapter 13

A Plan for Love

LOCATION: Somewhere in Medina
DATE: 1st May
WEATHER: Hot desert sunshine

The Black Widows awoke to the sound of camels bellowing. It seemed there was a lot of activity around the camp and none of the team were quite sure why. They started to rub sleep from their eyes and felt more refreshed than they had been in many, many years. The events of the night before had clearly had a positive effect on them by restoring their health to maximum vibrancy and freeing them of the emotional blocks of the past. It was refreshing to feel like a newborn baby again within an adult body. They all felt different: peaceful, uplifted, calm, centred, grounded, together with a newfound love for all humanity.

Judging by the noise levels around the camp and the position of the sun in the sky, the team realised it was around midmorning. They went outside to see what was happening. A desert train had arrived at the oasis for refreshments and had brought many items to trade with the local people. As they left the tent and walked towards the oasis, the noise became louder and louder. Amongst the hustle and bustle, they could hear the sound of laughter and singing with everyone very pleased to see one another as they went about their business. It was a magical sight to behold.

The desert train people were trading all sorts of beautiful textiles that had been lovingly hand-woven together with herbs and spices to promote health and healing. Wedmore noticed some of the children playing together and the joy on their faces was a delight to behold. How wonderful, he thought, that these people could treat one another as equals and have fun as they continue to do business. Refreshments were offered to the desert train people to help them recover from their many days of travelling through the harsh desert terrain. It seemed like there was perfect harmony in this beautiful local community. Wedmore smiled at how different it was to local markets in his homeland where people were usually wary of being ripped off by market traders they were unlikely to see again. Why couldn't this sort of thing happen at home? There was just too much emotional distance between people and not enough connection.

His mind flashed back to the events of the night before, the learnings from higher powers, and Sana's words of wisdom. As he caught up in his own thoughts, he looked across to see Sana laughing with some of the market women. He was captivated by her beauty as he observed her lovingly from a distance. There was nothing more enchanting than watching someone you love going about their business oblivious to their admirer. He smiled inside and felt blessed to be alive.

The Black Widows turned and noticed Blackbeard making his way through the crowds with a big smile on his face.

"My friends! Good morning to you!" he said with joy in his heart, clearly pleased to see them. *"I have someone I would like you to meet."*

He turned and led the Black Widows through the crowd towards the centre of the commotion where he stopped at a stall that was nothing more than a blanket on the ground and the most intricate cut-glass vessels carefully arranged to show off their attractive beauty in the sunlight.

"My friends, I want you to meet Dhamar. He is the protector of the desert people and a great man. He will be helpful to you on your quest."

The Black Widows took it in turn to shake Dhamar's hand and introduce themselves with big smiles.

"You are fine men of God!" Dhamar exclaimed. *"It will be an honour to serve with you. Do you have a plan ready to promote the word of The Divine?"*

"Actually, this is something we are still working on. All help gratefully received, brother!" Kamali said with a smile.

There was a real sense of trust and love between the men as they communicated above the hustle and bustle of the marketplace.

"Then there is no time like the present! We can bring many resources to the quest. Come, let us work together now."

Dhamar spoke in a way that instantly commanded respect. He looked towards his son to put him in charge of the market stall as they walked off together to commune in the central tent and work on a plan to bring about God's work to their fellow brothers and sisters. Blackbeard organized refreshments and for some local music to play in the background whilst the men collaborated. Whilst they didn't understand the words of the traditional Arabic songs, they could certainly feel the music promoted love and peace with the most beautiful sounds they had ever heard.

This was a mighty task and one that would require all of Wedmore's brilliance in military planning to pull off. The question that still remained was how to fight fire without fire.

How could they overthrow the evil that was trying to cause death and misery to millions without acting the same way themselves? There was sure to be much opposition to their plan and they didn't have an easy solution. How were they to overthrow governments who were in charge of the military and police forces to end the violence and killing of innocent people?

One of the biggest challenges they knew they would face was how to spread the message of God when the world worshipped over 5,000 different gods. The literal use of the words 'God' and 'Religion' also promoted division and separation as anyone who followed a religion felt that only the word of their God was right and everyone else's was wrong! They seemed to forget that the master teachings of the three main religions of the world, Christianity, Islam, and Judaism were 'love thy neighbour' and 'never do anything to anyone that you wouldn't want done to you'. So why people were killing one another over who had the best label for the same entity was a mystery!

As they strategized for what seemed like hours, they struggled to come up with a plan that would raise the stakes in their favour. The scenario that were causing them the most problems was getting people in the west to believe what was happening against the backdrop of brainwashing mainstream media to ensure their co-operation in the face of potentially taking on the western military monolith with its seemingly unlimited resources and colossal firepower. It became apparent that this task would be near impossible and would almost certainly lead to their demise.

"I like a challenge as much as the next man, but who are we to lead this assault on everything the westerners believe they know based on the lies they have been sold by the media?" Gringo said. *"It seems impossible."*

"Who are we not to, brother?" Kamali asked. *"My people say that one man with courage is a majority."*

"That's sweet," Gringo replied, "but that 'majority' isn't facing the wrath of the controlling governments of the military-industrial complex. Surely they will send people like us to take us out."

"Well the good news is we know all the people like us who would be sent on such a mission!" Wedmore smiled. "The other thing to bear in mind is these people in control are clearly living in fear as they have to surround themselves with such might as a show of strength and make other people fearful to manipulate them. There's no reason why we cannot do the same thing."

"That's fine," Hitler added, "but we are just six men, plus whatever assistance Dhamar can give us. That still leaves us hopelessly outnumbered. Plus, how do we get people to realize what is actually happening?"

At that moment, Sana entered the tent, looked at the men, and suggested that they had more resources than the rest of the military combined. "We have unseen forces on our side, my friends, and they will allow us to bring this mission to completion. There is only one way to get people to realize what is happening and that is for them to go through the same journey you have gone through, to awaken the very essence of humanity in their hearts that they have been desensitized to through countless television programs and films that suggest violence and war are ok. We will make a stand, and as we do so, more people will wake up to realise what is happening and join our crusade. You have the benefit of being awakened and converted from your experiences here. You must understand that others are currently caught up in a reality that makes sense to them and is all they know. As such, they will fight to protect it. Remember a caged bird thinks that flying is an illness. The only thing we can do is to show them the door and trust that *they will walk through it as God intends. We will bring humanity back to all people or we will die trying!"*

Sana's presence clearly made an impact on the group as they listened intently to her words of wisdom. She continued, *"We can awaken small groups and individuals along the way and they will join us in our mission. We cannot do it all at once, but there is hope working a little at a time. When we convince a few key people to join us, they will convince others and the word will spread quickly. This is a test of faith, my friends, but we will succeed. The truth will not be suppressed any longer. This duty rests on our shoulders and God has entrusted us to deliver. Let us not disappoint him."*

The group of men hung onto Sana's words as though they offered the key to salvation. They knew she was speaking truth and had the potential to be the leader in this revolution founded solely on love. They each pledged their service to the cause and knew they would stand shoulder to shoulder no matter what happened or how fierce the opposition was. They had seen the light and would stop at nothing to ensure no more innocent people lost their lives in pointless wars and division over who had 'the best God' when they were all referring to different expressions of the same consciousness. How they would do it would unfold as they marched forward to victory. As the old military saying goes, 'no battle plan survives first contact with the enemy.' They could identify key people to influence, and they trusted the rest would unfold naturally. Their mission was to spread the message of love and acceptance and to allow others to see the issues being created in the world by evil people who would cause the death of others on a whim. They would also bring those people to account for humanity who had been purposefully enslaved by their actions.

Wedmore felt a pang of intense emotion in his gut and fire in his heart. He stood up with adrenaline flowing through his veins, ready to take intense action. *"Alright, you lot, this is how it's going to happen. First of all, we're going to get back to the UK and get hold of that sell out Rosehill and secure his confession. Once he has given us some answers, we can start to work our way up the chain of command and find out who is really the conductor in this nightmare orchestra of madness."*

As he spoke, he clenched both fists so the muscles in his arms were visibly showing. It was clear he meant business and wanted to bring these evil perpetrators to swift justice. Nothing but success entered his mind and he was prepared to risk his life for it. He knew he would be able to obtain all the military equipment he needed to fulfil this mission as he was part of the 'no questions asked' military black ops. He also knew he had a few favours he could call in with other members of secret military personnel and this was definitely the time to do so. There was no doubt about it, excitement mixed with anger and adrenaline were focusing his mind to lead the troops with Sana's help to bring justice and potentially bring an end to war worldwide. If there was one thing he hated most in the world, it was being deceived with lies and falsehoods.

"Dhamar, can you get us to the airbase so we can fly back to the UK?" Wedmore asked.

"Most certainly. We have a jeep that you can use to take you back there. Will you need anything else for your journey?"

"We will need some small arms just to be on the safe side, but everything else we can get back in the UK. Sana, will you come with us to guide us? We really need your support," Wedmore asked.

He looked at Sana as he said this and received silence and a raised eyebrow with a playful expression on her face. *"Ok fine! I need you to guide me on how to make this mission happen. I can't do this without you!"*

A broad smile spread across Sana's face as she agreed to go with the Black Widows and begin the almighty task that lay ahead.

"Great. We leave at 1500 hours today. We will have to relay that we have been successful in our mission as a cover story to ensure the plane is organized for our evacuation. Once we are back in the UK, we can start to put our plan into action. I cannot wait to get my hands on Rosehill!"

"Remember, Jay, Einstein said something powerful when he said that 'you cannot solve a problem with the same level of thinking that created it.' What do you think he meant by that?" Sana asked, purposefully interrupting his habitual train of thought.

Wedmore pondered the question for a moment before answering. *"I would imagine that he means you have to think differently if you want different outcomes. Didn't he also say the definition of insanity is doing the same things over and over again and expecting a different result?"*

"Exactly, Jay! If we are to bring an end to violence and war, we cannot do it with violence. We need another way. I understand that you are angry, and we all feel the same, but there needs to be some space in your heart for compassion, forgiveness, and understanding. This is a hero's journey," Sana said.

"So you're telling me that I have to do this all nice and politely without roughing people up a bit?" Wedmore asked with a hint of sarcasm in his voice.

"No, Jay!" Sana replied, bowing her head slightly and intensifying her gaze towards him. *"That's not what I am saying at all. However, if your plan is to fight fire with fire, someone is going to get burned! Step back into your heart, Jay, and you will find the answers you seek. We have a day or so of travelling for you to work out the best plan. I have faith in you and so does God."*

The rest of the team observed the interaction between Sana and Wedmore and were impressed how she effortlessly used her feminine energy to calm the savage masculine warrior when his emotions ran too high. She had a beautiful way of disrupting his mental thought patterns that were too narrow minded and focused on mission completion with little regard to the consequences or impact of his plan. She was half his size, but commanded twice the respect for her wisdom and calm presence.

"*Ok, I hear you,*" Wedmore replied, feeling a little like the naughty child being reprimanded by a superior. "*Right, team, make sure you are all ready to leave here by 1500. Dhamar, please can you make the arrangements for us to travel safety along with some pistols and a half dozen clips of ammo each. Sana, if there is anything you need to get in place before we travel, please let us know and we will take action on it for you.*"

"*There is only one thing I need and I will sort that for us, Jay. I'll see you later on.*"

Sana left the tent, leaving the men to organize the final details of the transport to the airport. It was going to be an intrepid adventure bringing many mixed emotions, but they were sure that victory could be achieved in their mission, no matter how long it took.

Dhamar organized the jeep along with a sat nav, pistols, ammo, and water to cover any eventuality. He also organized a convoy of an accompanying vehicle with two of his best fighters to ensure they made it safely to their destination. Sana returned to the tent thirty minutes before departure with a small but intricately decorated silver jewellery box with a red ribbon tied into a beautiful bow at the top. She walked up to Wedmore and handed it to him on one knee as though he were royalty.

"*What's this?*" he asked.

"It's something very important to me, Jay. A gift. For our protection. And a small token of my love for you. It will remind you of my people and your desert experience here," Sana replied.

"How could I ever forget my experience here? That's very kind of you, Sana, but you really didn't need to."

"You're so English and polite, Jay! Now be a good boy and open the present!" Sana joked.

The red ribbon unfolded perfectly and allowed him to open the ornate silver lid of the box to reveal a plush velvet interior housing two beautiful aquamarine crystal pendants with leather necklaces that glowed blue as they lay in the box. They caught Wedmore's eye straight away as items of magnificent beauty.

"What are these, Sana?" he asked.

"They are aquamarine crystal pendants for us to wear on our journey. They will give us courage and clear communication with the Divine source of all that is. I thought they would be useful for us to help keep us safe," she replied.

"They are beautiful, Sana. Thank you so much." Wedmore took one of the pendants and tied it gracefully around Sana's neck before kneeling in front of her so she could return the favour. As she completed the knot on his necklace, he looked up into her eyes again and took her hand.

"Sana, no matter what, I want you to know that I will protect you on this journey or I will die trying. No one has managed to get the better of me yet, so you are in very safe hands," he said with a cheeky smile. "I've got your back!"

"I know, Jay. The journey ahead will not be easy but it will be worth it, that much I am sure of. Let us go now and take bold steps into the unknown."

The two spirited warriors exited the tent and headed for the jeep. Their hearts beating in unison, Wedmore felt like the protector of the woman who would spread a message of peace, love, and generosity. He finally had purpose back in his life. His heart and mind were perfectly aligned and it felt like he was walking on cloud nine. Life, he reasoned, had just dealt him a beautiful hand of cards and although it wasn't going to be an easy journey, as Sana had put it, it was certainly going to be the most fulfilling mission he had ever undertaken. Life was beautiful.

Chapter 14

Chrysalis

LOCATION: Somewhere in Medina
DATE: 1ˢᵗ May
WEATHER: Hot desert sunshine

The Doc radioed ahead to the airport and confirmed the emergency evacuation. He explained that they had completed their mission and were being pursued by an enemy vehicle and needed to get away quickly. He also requested assistance to be on standby should they make it back to the airbase and the enemy was still in hot pursuit. At the airbase, the service men and women scrambled to get a plane ready to dispatch the secret military team back home.

The reality of the situation was seven warriors, who were about to bring great change to the world, were plotting and scheming to overthrow the corrupt system that had sent them on this mission in the first place and led them straight to Sana. They were grateful for the spiritual experiences this meeting of minds and hearts had brought them and they were determined to make a stand for good in this world.

The journey through the desert took approximately four hours before they were back onto the main highway. What gave them huge peace of mind was the fact that they knew in their hearts that they could heal themselves whenever they wanted to, so it did not matter what life threw at them from that point forward because they were almost invincible. Not only that, they had seen the truth and nothing could stand in their way. Their hearts were now able to see past the matrix of deceit that had been pulled over their eyes by the corrupt system. Now they had to awaken others and rid the world of this negative influence to allow human consciousness to evolve even further to create Heaven on Earth.

The small convoy gathered speed as they headed in the direction of the airport. With a little bit of luck, the plane would be waiting on the tarmac to fly them back to the UK and they would be at Wedmore's home within the next 12 hours. Wedmore had to address the fact that they had Sana as an additional passenger and needed to get her through security and on board the plane.

"We're going to have to make out that we captured you as the wife of Guisu and that you have valuable information that would be of use to the British government. It's best if we tie your hands up so it looks like you are a prisoner. Please speak broken English, so they don't try and talk to you directly."

"If that's what you think is best, Jay, then I trust you. Just don't tie the rope too tightly."

"Don't you worry, Sana, you're in safe hands. We'll be on the plane in minutes. Once we are airborne, we can cut you loose. There's nowhere for you to run when we are flying!" Wedmore replied with a cheeky smile!

"And what happens when we get to the other side?" Sana asked.

"It's no problem when we get back to the UK. We have Diplomatic Immunity so we will be straight into a military Land Rover and on our way with no questions asked. We don't get questioned when we return from our missions as we report directly to Rosehill. He'll be notified that the mission was a

success, so we had better meet with him tomorrow and make sure that we beat what is really going on out of him!"

There was still a hint of anger and aggression in Wedmore's voice as he spoke about Rosehill. He had trusted Rosehill to always do the right thing and whilst they didn't have the closest relationship, he believed Rosehill when he spoke of the enemy and how Wedmore was performing a great service by taking them out. Sana touched Wedmore on the knee to let him know that everything was going to be fine. The touch brought him back to the reality of the current situation.

Within four hours, they had arrived at the airbase and passed through security. As they climbed out of the vehicle, the passenger of the trailing convoy vehicle stepped out of their jeep and took the keys from Gringo with a smile. The team thanked them for the kind escort back to the airbase and wished them well.

They boarded the plane with Sana as a hostage who acted the part of a prisoner being held against her will surprisingly well. As they made themselves comfortable on the plane, they cut Sana loose and retired to their seats. Military evacuation planes were certainly not first class, but they were better than standing room only. They all had a much-needed hot drink before reclining their seats as the plane sped down the runway. It was too noisy to talk, but there were no shortage of smiles between the Black Widows and Sana at the success of their journey.

As the plane reached its altitude, the drone of the engine was accompanied by snoring noises in the rear of the plane as the six warriors passed out, as was customary on every return flight home after a mission. Only Sana was awake, her gentle, loving gaze fixed on Wedmore, with admiration and joy in her heart for the man who had appeared from nowhere and stolen her heart. She prayed in Arabic to Allah for his safe passage and protection during the most dangerous, heroic mission they were about to take on. She reflected on the journey over the last few days and how he had stolen her heart the moment she first saw him arrive as a captive at the oasis. She knew that she had captivated his too, which made it a true love story.

She wondered what the odds were of two people from completely different countries, cultures, religions, and beliefs falling for one another in a chance meeting. She was glad they were also aligned in their mission to bring about significant world change, even if it meant laying down their lives in exchange for it. They were the perfect team of masculine and feminine energy, both playing to their strengths. She believed that just by standing side by side, they were a true force to be reckoned with.

The monotony of the engine's noise and the fact that the sun was disappearing below the horizon as Sana looked out of the window made her feel drowsy. She relaxed into her seat with peace and calm in her heart and promptly joined her newfound teammates in dreamland.

Several hours passed before the team was woken by the sound of the aircraft's engines slowing down. As they looked out the window, they could see it was foggy and grey. The pilot's landing skills were precision perfect and the plane touched down in the deep fog and darkness of the night with only a minor bump to let them know they had reached terra firma. Wedmore looked around and picked up a hessian sack that was lying on the floor. He turned to Sana and suggested that they put it over her head when they leave the plane so no one would know who she was or what was going on.

"I'm sorry, but needs must, I'm afraid," he said. *"Ok, team, let's get into the Land Rover ASAP and get out of here. We can head to my place and make a plan for the morning,"* Wedmore said as they made ready to disembark the plane.

They could see a vehicle was waiting for them in position with the engine running and lights on. Wedmore threw the door lever and pushed out the small metal staircase so they could all climb down to the tarmac below. As he stepped out, he took Sana's hand and guided her down the steps, talking to her quietly to reassure her.

A young lance corporal got out of the driver's seat of the Land Rover and saluted Wedmore. He responded in kind before walking to the back of the vehicle and opening the door to put Sana on the back seat. Springbok jumped into the driver's seat as the Doc and Hitler sat with Sana, setting the scene that they were keeping her hostage. Kamali and Gringo sat in the rear of the vehicle as Wedmore jumped in the passenger seat ready to leave the base.

The lance corporal observed all of this without question and saluted them as they left the landing site and sped towards the security barrier. Springbok was keen to make sure they were out of there before anyone dared to ask questions. As they approached the barrier, he slowed down as Wedmore wound down the passenger window in anticipation of having to interact with the guards. On approach, the barrier just raised without questions and they turned out onto the service road that would take them to the main road in the direction of Wedmore's home. As soon as they were out of sight, Hitler pulled the sack off Sana's head.

"Good job, team! We made it out and no one is any the wiser. Springbok, get us home as soon as you can so we can work out how we're going to tackle this whole situation."

It took around two hours before they pulled into the driveway of Wedmore's home where he quickly stepped out of the vehicle under cover of darkness to punch in a code to the garage door that allowed them to drive in and disembark without any observation from nosy neighbours. Finally, they were entering

Wedmore's house through the interconnecting garage door that opened into the hallway.

"Anyone who wants a shower can be my guest. You all know where the bathroom is, straight at the top of the stairs. Sana, I'll give you a little guided tour of the place. The rest of you make yourselves at home." Wedmore walked Sana through his home and invited her to make herself comfortable.

"Your home is a little stark, Jay. You need a woman's touch here!" Sana said with a smile as she stepped over some clothes that were lying around on the floor and observed the cobwebs in the corners of the rooms.

"I'm happy for you to help out with all the domestic duties, Sana!" Wedmore joked. They smiled at one another and felt connected and safe in his home.

Hitler was the first to freshen up as he washed the remaining desert sand from his hair. The rest of the Black Widows sat around the kitchen table and started drinking beer as they reflected on the trials of the last few days. They weren't shy raiding Wedmore's stash of beers and hard liquor as they poured a glass for everyone and broke out the smokes. It was good-natured camaraderie.

Wedmore and Sana entered the kitchen as the drinks were being poured. Gringo played host and offered them a drink. "Boss, what will it be? Beer or a whiskey?"

"Make mine a double whiskey! We need a celebration here!" Wedmore replied as he took his glass and offered Sana a drink. The look of disbelief on her face spoke volumes as she saw them downing them in one without a moment of hesitation.

"What are you doing, boys?" she asked with an air of slight superiority. "Do you have any idea what you are doing to yourselves?"

"Jus' a drink, Miss! It's tradition after every mission. Old habits die hard!" Gringo replied with a cheeky smile, yet feeling slightly uncomfortable at being told off by his boss's girl.

"Guys, alcohol causes incredibly low energy and you have just gone through an extreme spiritual awakening. Are you trying to push the reset button and go back to your old ways? We need you to be on top of your game for what we are about to undertake and be in peak physical and mental condition. Alcohol kills your brain cells and makes you stupid! Give it up now!"

It was clear that Sana was becoming agitated. Wedmore sheepishly placed his glass back on the table so as not to incur any of her wrath. There was just something curious about seeing a slight feminine frame taking on six masculine men and cutting them down with her presence. No one dared to argue with her.

"What do you suggest that we drink then? Cups of tea all round?" the Doc asked.

"If your water is filtered and pure, that's fine," Sana snapped.

"There's nothing wrong with tap water!" the Doc said.

"Now I know why you are so stupid! Fluoride!" Sana retorted.

"Fluoride helps create healthy bones and teeth. I should know, I'm a doctor!" the Doc replied, feeling threatened by her challenging his identity as a medical professional.

"You've clearly had the wool pulled over your eyes for too long!" Sana said as she rolled her eyes at this response. *"Do you even know what fluoride does to you? You know the experience you had when you healed in the desert? Well, that was largely you being able to connect your soul to Source with the use of your pineal gland in your head. When you drink fluoride, it calcifies that part of your brain, which makes it impossible to*

connect with the Source. When you can no longer do that, you can no longer heal yourself. Do you want that?"

"But why would it be put into water supplies and toothpaste if it wasn't safe?" the Doc asked, visibly concerned and trying to justify his medical profession.

"Do you remember what we saw when we went through the tea ceremony? You saw the good and the potential that humanity has when we are all in flow and not being repressed, did you not? The truth is, right now, we are being repressed. We're being turned against one another. We're being condemned to obey a ruling elite who would have us kill our brothers and sisters at their whim. All they are interested in is a bloodthirsty game of death and destruction. They want people to be fighting amongst themselves. It keeps them distracted from what is really going on and knowing who is really in charge. It's easy for them to stay in power because if you keep the Jews, Christians, and Muslims all thinking the other is the enemy, then you keep them fighting amongst themselves. They think they are solving the problem by doing so, all while the world's resources are being taken over by others and the world's wealth further concentrated in the hands of the few. This is what we are going to overthrow, is it not? Show the world the truth?"

Sana looked at the stunned men. They knew in their hearts that she spoke the truth. It was schooling time for them as they were reminded of their desert tea experience. They looked down at the table and reflected on what Sana had said. They all wanted to bring about change and were tired of being lied to and repressed by those they trusted to do as good as job as they did and honour the truth. Was there anything worse in this world than having your good nature taken advantage of? Sana suggested that they go and get themselves some bottled mineral water, which would contain less harmful chemicals. Whilst it was not ideal, they could at least get a head start on giving their bodies what it needed rather than poisoning it.

Kamali and the Doc offered to go shopping whilst the others learned more about the journey of spiritual mastery. They were engrossed in Sana's tales of her spiritual evolvement over the last ten years and how she believed that every person you meet in your life is a teacher for you in some ways, especially those you didn't like. She said that whilst part of God was within you, the larger part of the Almighty was there to stimulate spiritual growth for each and every soul on this planet and elsewhere in the universe as it ultimately served God's own growth and evolvement.

"I'd like to ask you a question about that, Sana," Hitler said. *"Why does God allow so much hurt and suffering to take place on Earth? Why does he not hear the prayers of so many people across the world that want an end to suffering and hardship? Should he not just stop it all?"*

*"That is a great question. When I first realized the state of the world as a young lady, I used to pray to God and ask him to stop the hurt, the war, and the suffering. I also asked why someone didn't do something. Then during a meditation several years later, I realized that **I was someone** who could do something, not because I was anything special, but by not standing up for what is good and right in this world, I was turning a blind eye to everything that was evil and consequently adding to it. I also got a message from God saying that humans were praying to him to resolve a problem that they themselves had created. It was not God's place to intervene and therefore we should take it upon ourselves to bring peace, love, and harmony to the world. Humans are too keen to look outside of themselves for some saviour or authority figure to do something about the horrendous situations in this world, but ultimately*

they are giving their power to the same people who caused most of the problems to begin with."

"I see," Hitler said. "There's one thing that I don't understand. How do we resolve the situation of war, hurt, and suffering without creating more hurt, war, and suffering by usurping those who are currently in power, intent on creating evil and wrongdoing in the world? I think we are all struggling with this one! My natural reaction is to go in and take out those in power and rid the Earth of their toxic personalities so we can put good people in their place. Isn't easier to just kill them and be done with it?"

"Nice thinking!" Sana replied with a smile. "There is no doubt about that most people who realize what has been going on are angry about the situation and want revenge, but that just causes more of the same problem. This is important for me to say, so listen carefully."

Her audience leaned in closer.

"It is the absence of love in someone's life that causes them to act in unloving ways towards others."

Sana paused for a moment to let her comments sink in. She watched their facial expressions intently to see the penny drop in their minds. She then continued, *"Simply put, the people who harm others are doing so because they have little, if no love, for themselves. They have simply lost the human aspect of themselves, which makes their behaviour become inhuman. In the absence of love for themselves or not receiving it from others, they have confused obtaining power with obtaining love from others or from another source. We do not know what kind of upbringing they have had; it could have been horrific and they could have been subject to all sorts of abuse from their caregivers. This means they were not encouraged to love themselves which creates a confused and unloved mind that thinks they would never be treated like that again and would be worthy of love if only they had power or success. So, they pursue money, wealth, and power at any cost in order to build a protective wall around themselves to keep more hurt out. At the same time, they treat others badly, especially those who have kindness and love in their lives, by subjecting them to the same kinds of inhumane treatment they had as a child. Hurt people, hurt people. It really is as simple as that."*

"*The longer it goes on, the worse it gets as they believe there is nothing wrong with their behaviour. They rise in power, the protective wall they build around themselves gets bigger and stronger, and they are not subject to any harmful treatment anymore. Inside the prison they have built themselves is a scared little child who has not addressed the terrible issues they faced growing up. If only they had support to face those issues from a higher consciousness perspective, they could see that they were here to serve their higher spiritual growth and no matter what they did or did not do, they were always, always worthy of love. Instead, the scared child acts in selfish and unloving ways trying to protect itself from a world that they perceive is trying to cause them more and more harm. The issue then becomes the fact that the walls of their prison are now so tall and thick that they cannot observe the further destruction their behaviour is causing because they are immune to it. Out of sight, out of mind.*"

"*So, the cycle repeats itself. More and more hurt is spread throughout the world, leading more and more people to seek power, wealth, and money to protect themselves and inflict the same pain they have had in their lives. You see, unfortunately life on Earth doesn't work without a little bit of struggle. There has to be opposites to provide a frame of reference. The caterpillar has to essentially die in order to become the butterfly. Did you know that if you peel back the chrysalis and allow the butterfly to escape, it would not build up the strength* in its wings to be able to fly? As it struggles and fights to break out of its cocoon over several hours, its wings are building up strength to allow it to take flight. Without this, its wings become too weak to be able to fly. How incredible is nature?"

Wedmore interrupted with a question. "*I think I can see where you are going with this, Sana, but I don't know what the butterfly analogy has to do with overthrowing evil on this planet?*"

"*The point is this: the world is how it is for several reasons and if you look at it from a higher perspective, you will see that everything is perfect. We cannot evolve without some element of struggle, and the repression we face now is nothing more than the butterfly faces inside its cocoon. The struggle it takes to break out will be the struggle that allows the whole planet to evolve and lift itself to a higher dimension. We can all do this. It comes from within. It just takes courage!*"

"*I hear what you are saying, Sana, but I still don't know how to sort the problem out!*" Wedmore said with a hint of frustration.

"*Think carefully about this, Jay. The greatest gift we can give these people currently in power is to show them their own humanity and cause a huge spiritual awakening within themselves. Once they see they are truly worthy of love, they will make the changes that are needed themselves without selling their soul in the process.*"

Wedmore buried his face in his hands as he was clearly missing something. It all sounded far too namby-pamby and nice as far as he was concerned. In his mind, these people needed the strongest form of discipline possible and that was something he was usually used to delivering close range from his Desert Eagle .50 pistol. How do you show someone who is wretched and evil to the core that they are worthy of love? He just didn't get it.

"*I have a plan!*" Sana interjected. "*It's very simple, but I think it will also be very effective. Would you like to hear it?*" she said with a knowing smile. Her audience was hanging onto her every word.

"*Well, Jay here is very well connected in the military and whilst we can expect some resistance when news breaks of what we are trying to do, I believe by being forthright and honest with others, we will get people on our side and build momentum to usurp those in power. We then arrest those people who have sought to inflict hurt and suffering on the rest of us and throw them into jail. Once they are all rounded up and replaced in their positions of power with people who will do good, the bad guys in jail will be held there until they have experienced their spiritual awakening.*"

"*You're talking about a military coup of the western world, Sana?*" Wedmore asked in disbelief.

"*Momentarily, yes, Jay. Until everyone who would repress others is taken out of their positions of power and the awakening can begin.*"

"*How on earth do you expect us to co-ordinate something of that scale? We're talking 160,000 military personnel in the UK alone and over one-and-a-half million in the US. And there are seven of us.*" Wedmore was becoming more and more confused by the minute.

"*We're not going to be opposed by that many people, Jay! Besides, it does not matter because we have a force greater than all the military personnel on this planet, remember?*" she touched the winged heart necklace as she spoke as a reminder of their meeting with Archangel Michael and God. "*We want to approach those in a higher position within the military to remind them of their own humanity first before we go further up the chain of command.*"

"*Right, but I cannot see those people giving up their freedom and power easily,*" Wedmore retorted.

Sana turned to Wedmore. Her look alone told him to pay close attention to what was about to be said. *"Jay, I need you. If you are defeated in your mind, you will face defeat in reality. That's the way the world works. You attract to you that which you dwell upon. It's the Law of Attraction in action. Do you understand that?"*

Wedmore nodded.

"You should know that with you or without you, I am going ahead with this mission. I need you, Jay, but if you're not around to help me, I am going it alone. You did swear to protect me when we left my home, so now is your opportunity. We were all born with a purpose and this is mine. If you're with me, great. If not, great. As a team, we stand stronger and you know that I need you. You're either part of the solution or you're part of the problem. So what's it going to be?" Sana asked.

Wedmore bowed his head slightly under the realization that it was now time for action and to stand by the promises he had made. He looked up at Sana and confidently said, *"I'm with you. I'll do it."*

"Jay, you're in your head right now. When the mind is divided, fear usually enters the gap. You need to be aligned completely with our mission. Let's get back into our hearts and realize how powerful we really are."

As Sana spoke, the door opened and in walked the Doc and Kamali carrying their shopping bags filled with fluoride-free mineral water. Sana invited them to join the group and sit peacefully for a few minutes whilst they restored their congruency with their hearts and minds. Sana guided them through the process as she spoke with tenderness and compassion.

"Ok, let's relax for a moment and close our eyes. Take a deep breath in through your nose and hold it for a few seconds then release it. Now, take another deep breath but this time as you breathe, breathe through your heart and focus solely on your breathing. In and out. That's it." Sana tapped into the energy of the group and saw that they had started to relax and the thoughts of fear were leaving their mind. *"Remember what we did previously by connecting to your Heavenly star and protecting yourself with the energy of the Pyramids. Let's do that again and draw the energy down towards you to make sure you are all back into your hearts and not letting your minds take over. Your heart does not know fear when it is aligned with its higher purpose."*

Sana continued to talk them through the meditation to access their higher purpose and bring complete peace of mind. The energy of the room felt lighter, calmer, and tranquil as the warriors became one with the higher intelligence of the universe and harmony in their hearts was restored once again. They mediated for the best part of an hour under Sana's guidance and felt the love surround their bodies as they did so. With their minds relaxed and their hearts aligned, Sana brought them back to reality.

"That felt amazing! Just like being back in the desert again," the Doc said.

"That's why we don't drink fluoride, so we can get that connection!" Sana replied with a compassionate smile. The group all smiled as they realized the practical sense Sana was talking and understood how every little decision they made had a huge impact on their lives. They realised the paradox of being free to make any decision they wanted, but they were not free of the consequences of those decisions. With that, they broke out the water for everyone and Sana blessed it all with the higher vibrations of love and healing.

"Most people don't know that water has a memory and it will take on the properties of whatever you expose it to. So, if you expose it to the blessing of love, you will receive love. If you bless it with hate, it will take on the molecular structure of hate. Our bodies are made up of around 70% water. When you subject that water in your body to the words of your self-talk, your body is always listening and it starts to take on the properties of your self-talk. Think about that for a moment."

The group of men sat in awe at the words of wisdom coming from this woman of the desert who clearly had a mindset they had not witnessed before. She spoke truths they had not previously heard.

"When you consider that your body is listening to everything your mind says, especially your own self-talk, you will see that your body will start to react to the most commonly used words or phrases. This can be positive or negative depending upon how you relate to yourself." Sana again observed her audience before continuing.

"There is an experiment I was shown once by our village Shaman and it fascinated me as a young girl. The Shaman cooked some rice over an open fire for a simple meal that we all ate. They didn't serve all the rice. They kept some back as they explained they wanted to conduct an experiment with it for us to see. After the meal was finished, they took the remaining rice and separated it into three empty glass jars with metal lids. They then placed a label on each jar, which had a different Arabic word written on them; the first was 'Love', the second was 'Hate', and the third was 'Ignore'. The lead Shaman then took each jar in turn, held it up in front of him, and projected the energy of the word on the label to the first two jars. The third jar was just ignored and left to one side."

"Every day for a week, I revisited the same spot in the camp at the same time to witness the lead Shaman performing this strange ritual. For the first two days, I could see no real difference between any of the jars, but as time went on, something very strange started to happen. The jar that contained the 'love rice' did not decay, but the rice started to go mouldy and black in the jar that was labelled hate. This continued over several days. What was more profound was the fact that the rice which was ignored actually decayed much quicker than the jar which had the energy of hate projected into it."

Her audience were surprised and observed her teachings closely.

"How was this all possible, Sana?" Kamali asked.

"I also had the same question, Kamali," Sana continued. *"I asked the Shaman why this would be so. Surely, I reasoned, the rice that was ignored would decay less than the rice that had been subject to hatred. He explained to me that the jar that had received hate had at least received some level of attention and interaction, whereas the rice that was ignored had received none whatsoever. It was a strange thing indeed but I really began to understand that ignoring something living was the worst thing you could do as it dies quickly. It is the same with the flowers that grow in your garden, is it not? Give them attention and they will flourish, ignore them and they will perish."*

She paused for a moment to observe her audience. They were locked deep in thought. She continued, *"If you understand the implications of this experiment, you will understand something much deeper that I was referring to earlier. Humans react in the same way, but it takes some time for the effects to be felt within the human form. If a child is ignored as they grow up, they will perish quickly. The Russian government conducted an experiment on 'children of the State' in the 1960's. Orphan babies were given basic care in terms of food and water, but the nurses were told to minimise physical touch and to avoid eye contact. The gruesome experiment had to be stopped within a few days as the children literally died from lack of human interaction and being denied the energetic connection of eye contact."*

"The same goes for those who inflict hurt on others. As they build their walls higher and stronger, they separate from others. The more they become ignored, the more their soul suffers from neglect. This creates a vicious cycle where the feelings of neglect turn to feelings of hate for others and consequently they subject others to more and more abusive treatment. It will continue until the pattern is interrupted and people realize that what their mind is telling them is not true. That's what we will do, my friends, and this is the gift we will give them in spite of the suffering they have caused others and themselves by their own actions."

The group were speechless at Sana's revelations but understood what she was referring to. They sat contemplating the lives these people must be living and feelings of compassion swept over the group. They didn't realize what pain and suffering these tortured souls had endured and why they had behaved the way they did made sense. With compassion in their hearts, they could see that spiritual transformation was a more effective way of dealing with the situation for everyone involved, and facilitating the personal transformation and evolvement of those souls would allow them to do the right thing for the remainder of their lives.

"So what's the next step, Sana?" Kamali asked, keen to understand more.

"It's quite simple! We get some sleep, as we need to be at Rosehill's office at 5am to start our journey there. Then we will see where our journey takes us."

The group retired to bed with a feeling of peace and excitement that they were taking the very first step to bringing lasting change to the world and allowing love to be their guiding light.

Chapter 15

Beginning the End of Hate

LOCATION: London, England
DATE: 2nd May
WEATHER: Overcast with sunny spells

As the 4am alarm sounded, the troops began stirring within Wedmore's home ready to embark upon the journey of a lifetime. Usually with such little sleep after a mission, it would take them some time to wake up, but everyone bounded out of bed ready to grasp the challenge with both hands. They weren't quite sure what time Rosehill would make it into the office, but he was usually there by 7am at the very latest every day. That gave them approximately three hours to get to his office, break and enter it without being detected by the night security team, and wait for his arrival.

Wedmore smiled when he thought what Rosehill's reaction might be to walking into his office and finding the Black Widows waiting for him. Rosehill was used to being in a position of power and giving orders. To be on the receiving end was going to be quite the experience for him.

The team dressed and grabbed some coffee and croissants that Kamali had picked up the night before, against the protests of Sana who was quick to explain how caffeine was a neurotoxin that cut oxygen flow to the brain by 40% and they were in danger of poisoning themselves.

The team were all carrying concealed handguns with extra clips of ammunition, which were more of a threat and a deterrent and would only be used as a last resort if things turned very ugly. It was unlikely given the circumstances. The one good thing about being the team that Rosehill always instructed to carry out his dirty work was the fact he had no one else to call upon! The element of surprise was on their side and it would create an interesting turning point in their lives.

It dawned on them that by taking these actions, they would be losing their well-paid jobs and more than likely end up having a contract on their heads. They reasoned that there came a point in life when they should really stand up for what they believe in and not continue to be part of the problem by having their silence bought.

They were aware of all the tricks anyone was likely to pull, so were well prepared for such an incident. They would have to spread the word quickly and ensure they had as many supporters of their mission within high-ranking positions of the western military as possible. It was far easier to lead and co-operate with those who would be a danger to them, rather than trying to fight them.

The team jumped into the Land Rover as Springbok reversed out of the driveway and onto the main road. They sped along the road towards the office building where they would await Rosehill. The early morning darkness was beginning to dissipate as the sun rose in the sky. The Land Rover's headlights blazed through the remaining darkness and kept the team focussed on their way towards their target. Springbok turned the heaters on full blast to remove the chill from the air and keep his teammates warm.

"Team, are you ready for this?" Wedmore asked.

"Yeah!" came the unanimous reply, with Sana's soft tones drowned out by the sheer volume of testosterone-fuelled machismo all gunning for payback on their target.

"So, here's the plan. If I remember correctly, there is a disused fire escape at the rear of the office block that will take us up to the fifth floor where Rosehill's office is located. We'll have to break in via the fire door without triggering the alarm and obviously do it quietly so we don't draw attention to ourselves. Then we can lie low and await Rosehill's arrival. Should be a nice surprise before he's had his morning coffee!" Wedmore was visibly excited.

"What's the back-up plan, boss?" Kamali asked.

"Brute force and ignorance!" Wedmore replied.

The team laughed at the proximity to the truth that they knew was usually the last resort in most missions they were sent on. It was also something that they were pretty good at!

"In all seriousness, the second option is to cause total confusion and enter via the front door using the element of surprise. It's more risky and Rosehill might twig that something is not right but there are seven of us and only one of him!"

"I'm willing to take a chance on either," the Doc said. *"I feel we owe him big time for the things he has made us do over the years. He'll know what it's like to be on the receiving end of our 'specialist treatment'."*

"Now, now boys! Calm down," Sana said. *"Remember we are operating at a level of compassion, not revenge. Rosehill clearly had his motives for his own behaviour and as we know, he has been put in some very difficult personal positions that have made it impossible for him to refuse certain instructions. We will achieve far more by having him on our side, rather than against us."*

Having Sana's presence amongst the sea of testosterone certainly had its benefits. The team listened to her truth. There was no room for argument as she gave guidance from her heart, which was connected to, and spoke only of, the universal truth without personal bias. It was the most beautiful quality they had ever experienced in someone and it far outshone her physical size.

The cave man mumble and murmur of agreement that went around the Land Rover suggested that the Black Widows had heard what Sana was saying and were not going to object. It was a new way of being for them and there was always the possibility that their old habits of fire first and ask questions later might just get in the way.

Change, like all things, required commitment, time, and an underlying reason. They certainly had a big enough reason to make the change. Now it was just a case of not being on auto-pilot and being ruled by their old patterns of behaviour. It was comforting that Sana saw their potential to be loving and compassionate people rather than trained killers, and clearly their leader had a vested interest in showing that he was a changed man, however difficult that change might be to make.

The drive to Rosehill's office did not take long without traffic on the roads. As they approached the office block, Wedmore gave Springbok directions to park their vehicle in an alley around the back of the building where they would be out of sight. As they parked up, they surveyed the area to ensure no one was watching. It was far too early for anyone to be working in the adjacent office buildings, so only security might be keeping a keen eye open for any mischief. Their chosen parking spot was also devoid of any CCTV cameras, making it the perfect hideaway.

They climbed out of the vehicle and walked towards the rusty metal fire escape. The design was antiquated, moving with a cantilevered section of staircase that would pivot towards the pavement under the weight of occupants leaving the building, but which was currently suspended in the air out of the reach of vandals and would-be burglars. Hitler and Kamali positioned themselves side-by-side with their backs against the wall as the ever-nimble Gringo climbed on their shoulders to reach the suspended section of the staircase. He was still a good thirty centimetres away from the staircase.

"No doubt about it, you're goanna have to jump at it, Gringo!" Wedmore said as he stood back to watch his progress.

Gringo crouched slightly as Kamali and Hitler braced themselves for the extra pressure of him powering himself upwards off their shoulders. As he leapt upwards with a slight grunt, his hands grasped the last step of the staircase and his body swung sideways in the air carried by the momentum of his jump. The staircase did not move. Gringo heaved himself up and hooked his feet onto one of the banister rails before pulling himself up onto the staircase as the team looked on with mixed admiration and amusement.

The staircase still didn't budge. No matter how much he tried to jump up and down on it without creating too much noise, it would not move. The team were amused at this attempt of breaking and entering, which was definitely not going to plan.

"Is it locked in place, Gringo?" Wedmore asked as he mentally ran through the possibilities of why the staircase wouldn't move.

"Let me check, boss. Ahhh," Gringo said with a knowing realization that he had missed something. The staircase had a one-way activation lever on it that allowed the last section of the metal staircase to pivot towards the pavement under the weight of someone standing on it. As Gringo threw the lever across with a clang, the staircase wobbled slightly before

descending to the ground below. Once the team had walked up the staircase, it would swing back out of the way when it was not under load, leaving no evidence of their ascent.

The team quickly ascended and came face to face with a flush metal reinforced fire door, specifically designed to prevent forced entry from outside. The peeling red paintwork and rusting hinges suggested this door had never been used. Hitler set down a bag of tools he had brought with him and suggested it would be quite easy to gain entry, despite the condition of the door. They knew there was an intruder alarm connected to the other side of the door along with a push bar escape mechanism, which they would have to get around in order to gain entry. Hitler pulled out a can that looked like it contained spray oil yet featured heavy yellow and black hazard warnings on it. He proceeded to spray the hinges with a lime-green gunk, which quickly started to eat away at the metal hinges, dissolving them right in front of the eyes of his audience.

"What is that stuff and where did you get it?" Wedmore asked.

"It was a gift from a friend!" Hitler replied with a cheery smile. Within a minute, both of the hinges had melted away and the door was free. Hitler then took a flexible fibre optic endoscope camera complete with eyepiece and pushed it through the gap towards the top of the doorframe where the hinge was previously. He pressed his right eye into the eyepiece and closed his left as he moved around to observe the environment on the other side of the door.

The push bar would be easily overcome by swinging the door open in the opposite direction, which would be effortless without the binding hinges in place. What was more difficult was not triggering the intruder alarm. He saw two plastic covered contacts connected with wires to the door and the doorframe. The system worked by ensuring that the metal contact between the two points was not broken. If the low voltage electric current that passed between the two points was interrupted, the alarm would sound.

Hitler removed the endoscope and thought carefully about how to take this challenge on. He rummaged in the bag before pulling out a small electromagnetic device and asked Kamali for some assistance. Hitler placed the endoscope back into the hinge hole and guided Kamali as he moved the device into position close to the alarm's contact points. As he got close, Kamali flicked a switch on the device that emitted a small electromagnetic frequency along the flat metallic blade, which was just enough to stick it to the sides of the plastic connectors. As the attraction of the magnets kicked in, Kamali could feel the blade stick to the side of the connectors forming a new circuit. Under Hitler's guidance, he wiggled the blade slightly to position it between the two connector blocks, with the current flowing through the device keeping the circuit complete and not triggering the alarm.

"That's it!" Hitler said as Kamali made contact. *"Just hold it there for a moment."* He bent down again to his bag to remove a crowbar to gently pry the door out of its frame. Gringo and the Doc stepped forward to help take the weight of the door as it moved and eventually pulled it out of its frame to set it to one side. The team entered the building as Kamali held the device in place to prevent the alarm from sounding. After everyone had entered the building, Kamali carefully stood in place whilst Hitler pulled the sensor away and taped the two connecting points together with the magnetic device sandwiched in the middle. He then pulled the door across to close off the opening and cover their tracks.

The team walked through the corridor maze to Rosehill's office as the overhead strip lights pinged on under the direction of the motion sensors. As they got to his door, Hitler prepared himself by removing his lock-picking kit from his kitbag and setting to work. Within a few minutes, the lock clicked and the door was opened. They walked in and closed the door before Hitler re-picked the lock to ensure the door was locked behind them.

Once inside the office, the team had a good look around Rosehill's desk for anything noteworthy. There were various papers and files relating to confidential matters, but nothing that really stood out as obvious. Sana took a seat by the window and enjoyed the view over London as the morning sun rose in the sky and illuminated the commuters heading to work. There was a large glass table near the window, which featured a wooden tray with several glasses and a bottle of water. Sana held up the bottle and blessed it before pouring some water for the team and handing them each a glass. The team took their positions in the room and waited patiently for Rosehill.

Wedmore sat in Rosehill's fine leather captain's chair and with an air of slight contempt, swung the chair around and lifted his feet high in the air before bringing them down hard on Rosehill's desk with a thud. He then relaxed into this position as Kamali pulled a chair directly opposite the door. As he sat down, he drew his handgun and pointed it towards the door, ready to provide some additional encouragement for Rosehill to enter the office.

Gringo positioned himself just behind the door, ready to pull Rosehill into the room as the door swung open. The element of surprise here was key to making the right impact with Rosehill to let him know they meant business. Hitler, Springbok, Sana and the Doc took their places on the large leather sofas that were positioned in front of the window and enjoyed the view as the sun came up.

Once they were in position, silence filled the air and the automatic lights went out in the corridor. No-one dared interrupt the silence. At least the motion sensor activated lights would give them a heads up that Rosehill was approaching.

They were all in position as the clock above the ornate marble fireplace chimed 5am. Rosehill was known as an early riser from his past military days, so it was likely that he would be in his office within the next hour or two at the latest.

As they waited in silence, the room became brighter and brighter as the sun came up and filled the room with its warm golden glow. The team bathed in its beautiful light as they relaxed into its warmth. The angle of the sunlight glaring off the window would provide a useful additional distraction to confuse Rosehill. The team did not have to wait too much longer as they heard the gentle click of the lights being triggered and the faint slamming of a door somewhere along the corridor. The team all straightened up ready for action. They heard footsteps leading up to the door, then the key being inserted into the lock, and watched as the handle began to turn. Gringo edged forward ready to pounce as Kamali trained his gun on the target about to enter the room.

The door swung open as the stooped figure of Rosehill entered. As Rosehill looked up, he felt a firm grip tighten around his right forearm that yanked him off balance. His eyes widened as he saw the gun aimed at him and behind it, a face he vaguely recognized from many years ago when he first met the Black Widows. Gringo's strength had tipped Rosehill off balance and he fell forward onto his knees as Gringo kicked the door closed behind him. Rosehill crouched on the floor before looking up in wide-eyed disbelief. He then raised his hands upwards showing complete surrender. He had not noticed the other parties in the room at this point. He just looked up at Kamali, his eyes showing visible signs of distress.

"Ok, Kamali, put the gun away," Wedmore said.

On hearing the familiar voice, Rosehill turned his head and saw Wedmore looking rather relaxed in his chair with his feet up on his leather-topped desk. His eyes widened further as his mind tried to understand what was happening. He turned his head slightly to the left and saw four more silhouetted shapes, perfectly outlined by the sunshine streaming in through the window, before turning his head around to look at Gringo standing over him. Gringo bent down to pull Rosehill to his feet and thrust him in the direction of one of the seats opposite Wedmore, before taking the seat next to him. Rosehill looked stunned.

With a trembling voice, which seemed quite odd for someone with significant military experience, he spoke to Wedmore.

"What's going on, James? Who sent you?"

It was the first time Wedmore had ever known Rosehill address him by his first name.

"We want to talk to you about the missions you have been sending us on and where your instructions have come from. Bearing in mind we already know the answer to this question, can you please enlighten us?"

Rosehill bowed his head in shame hearing this line of questioning as a lone tear fell from his eyes onto his lap.

"We want to know everything Rosehill, so don't hold back. We're not leaving here until we get our answers."

Rosehill shook his bowed head as more tears of remorse fell from his eyes and formed dark patches on his black suit trousers. A feeling of deep exposure came over him. Nowhere to run. Nowhere to hide. He placed his head in his hands as he thought about where to begin. He then looked up at Wedmore with bloodshot eyes.

"They were all real missions, James. You were ordered to take out the enemy and rid the planet of terrorists." Rosehill's voice trembled as he spoke.

Wedmore wasn't buying it. *"Who gave you the instructions? We have been all over the Middle East taking out so-called Muslim terrorists and I'm doubting that any of them were real,"* Wedmore said.

"I...I can't tell you that. It's serious, James. Very serious. I'll be a dead man if I tell you and my family will be in grave danger," came Rosehill's response.

Kamali pressed the cold metal of his gun into the side of Rosehill's neck to remind him that his fate wasn't looking much brighter if he withheld the necessary information here. Sana walked over to Rosehill before perching herself on the edge of his desk to look deep into his eyes. She waved Kamali away without breaking eye contact with Rosehill. She looked deep into his soul and maintained the gaze for a full minute before Rosehill looked down again. She reached out a hand and touched his chin before directing his head back up towards her gaze.

"Mr Rosehill, you should know that the instructions you have given these men have resulted in the loss of thousands of innocent people's lives who were merely defending their homeland from invasion. Countless fathers have been killed, leaving angry and hostile children wondering why their father never came home and why the west would want to take their fathers away from them. Countless husbands have perished protecting their wives and children from injustice and pillage from the armies you have helped direct into foreign lands under the guise of ridding the world from terrorists. The soldiers you sent to kill others have to carry the burden of taking the life of another for the rest of their days. Their own lives suffer as a result and their own relationships fall apart with their loved ones because of the stress and trauma they are carrying. Many end their lives because the burden of pain they carry is too great. This is not to mention the innocent lives of women and

children who are killed in bombing raids and the lives that are destroyed when someone loses their home and possessions because of a decision that was made thousands of miles away about how some unjust 'justice' should be served upon another. Not to mention the very serious impact it has had causing division and separation between people based on some fictitious links of terrorism with certain religions. Think about that burden carefully, Mr Rosehill, because that is the impact of your words, decisions, and actions. Whatever happened to your humanity? Whatever happened to your moral conscience?"

Sana spoke in such a humble and gentle voice but her words pierced the heart of everyone in the room as they all became present to the incredible impact their actions had on the world. In the heat of battle, it was always easy to be focused on getting the job done, but there was no doubt Sana spoke the truth and the energetic hangover burden they all experienced did affect their mental and physical clarity and gave them countless nights of restless sleep.

Rosehill's eyes welled up as his conscience felt the impact of Sana's truth. His shoulders trembled as he began to sob whilst Sana continued to gently hold his chin to maintain eye contact. Rosehill pulled away from her and took a handkerchief from his pocket. The impact of his actions and decisions was becoming more and more real and the weight of the burden he was subconsciously carrying was enormous. The Black Widows also reflected on what had been said. They were responsible for contributing to the world's problems and this was something they felt obliged to correct, however they could, from now on.

The silence was momentarily broken by the movement of Rosehill under the influence of his emotions as he realized the folly of his actions. It was no defence in this situation to claim that he was just following orders. The impact of his decisions had been brought to bear on him in this present moment and he was no longer able to hide behind any hierarchical military power. It was them and him. He had to face facts; that as a family man, his actions led to the death of tens of thousands of people, many innocent women and children. He would not want to be on the receiving end of his orders or for soldiers to take away the things that mattered most to him: his ex-wife who he still loved, his children, and his home.

It was all too easy to sit behind a desk in his homeland and pass orders off as a 'necessary evil' for the development of the world by sending troops abroad to carry out the dirty work at the request of the higher powers. The young troops were viewed as 'cannon fodder' and he had to admit to himself that he didn't really care how many people returned from a mission as long as the mission was completed and he got his financial reward. The fallen troops would be celebrated in some grandiose arms-length military ritual that pacified the grieving. The real emotional issues were brushed firmly under the carpet, as people were none the wiser to what was really happening or why their young son or daughter had been sent to an early grave.

Rosehill crouched forward in his chair with his head in his hands and his shoulders rocking as more tears flowed. The Black Widows and Sana waited patiently, allowing time for his subconscious to awaken him to the full impact of his actions, which he had kept buried for too long. Without his conscience taking hold within and waking him up, all talk would be in vain. This was a more effective way of dealing with the situation and would lead to the greatest chance that Rosehill would become an ally for their revolutionary mission. The most powerful change always comes from within.

Grief and remorse had begun to take over as he looked around him at the other occupants in the room for some kind of empathy. Wedmore hadn't taken his eyes off him and looked at him with a mixture of compassion and a deep need to know the answers to his burning questions. *"What's going through your mind right now?"* he asked Rosehill.

Rosehill looked at him through frightened eyes before replying. *"It's…it's terrifying to think of the damage I have helped create in the world. I'm ashamed. I bought into all the bullshit of doing my duty for God, Country and The Queen when I really perpetrated the brutal murders of countless innocent people. I am so, so ashamed. I have destroyed lives with my cavalier attitude and hid behind the military without thinking about the consequences. I realize now how foolish that is. I am so, so sorry."*

Wedmore could see that he meant what he was saying. He leaned forward to get closer to Rosehill and spoke in a low voice. *"It's not us you need to apologise to, but you do need to do something. From now on, you're either part of the solution or part of the problem. Which is it going to be?"*

"Part…part of the solution, James," Rosehill said.

"An excellent choice!" Wedmore said with a smile as his hand slapped the desk in an effort to lift the mood. *"We need to know who gave you those orders and who has been instructing you to set up military camps in foreign countries. We are going to remove those people from power and you're going to help us. It's all part of the necessary expansion of consciousness to try and undo the damage of the past. Starting in the UK, we're going to restore peace and brotherhood to one another, bring our troops home from overseas, and help people rebuild their lives that have been torn apart in conflict. I know you're well connected with many other high-ranking military personnel so you can help us to bring them around to our way of thinking and help transform the world."*

Rosehill looked at Wedmore in disbelief. *"That's a lovely vision, James, but you really have no idea who you are dealing with. The problem is too big and powerful now. You'll never overthrow it. We're all destined to be killed if we try. It's hopeless. The people I care about are at real risk if we try to overthrow these people. We're as good as dead."*

Sana interrupted his train of thought with some carefully chosen words of wisdom. *"Mr Rosehill, most people confuse death as a final ending, but it is a rebirth in reality. Therefore, there is nothing to fear. Our exit from Earth is a given, the only question is when. Before you leave, you have a choice to make. Do you want to nurture your soul and help undo your wrongdoings so you can restore the balance of Karma in your life, or do you want to carry the burden of these crimes for many lifetimes to come?"*

Rosehill was confronted and challenged Sana's viewpoint. *"We don't have another life after this! All we have is this one and I want to do all I can to stay alive for as long as possible."*

"That's what they want you to think and that's why you are living in fear. That fear energy contributes to creating more fear in the world and controlling more people through a perpetual state of fear. How ironic that those who do the controlling are the ones living with the deepest of fears. The reality is you are a limitless soul capable of being reincarnated over many dimensions and many lifetimes; the purpose of each life is to grow and learn, always striving to have your soul reach the highest version of itself. You have so much to learn and we cannot go through it all now, but if you make the decision to be part of the solution, you will begin awakening your soul in the process. So what do you want to do?" Sana asked.

Rosehill looked at the floor, then up at Wedmore and finally across to Sana. *"Ok, I will help you in any way I can."*

"*Great!*" Wedmore said. "*So, tell us more about our friends who have been sending us on erroneous missions over the last few years. Who's been giving you our orders?*"

Rosehill looked as though he had seen a ghost as the weight of what he was about to share began to take hold.

"*The man you saw that day was Frederick Marston, one of the controlling elite families in the UK and owner of some of the biggest newspapers in the world. He decides which missions you go on, who the establishment don't like, and who you need to take out. It's nothing more than that. On a whim, if you like. He controls who are the influencers on the world stage and when someone does something they don't like, or they gain too much power, they are squashed through newspaper stories designed to manipulate public opinion. Investigative journalism is dead in mainstream media, so they just repeat whatever stories those in control want to print. The establishment wants everything to stay the same, James. They like having the money and power and see no reason to give it away or let others influence the way things are.*"

"*Ok, so how do we get a hold of Frederick Marston and find out who he is in cahoots with?*" Wedmore asked.

"*James, do you realize what you are asking?*" Rosehill said.

Wedmore leaned forward and glared at Rosehill. "*Listen here, I am tired of being lied to and putting my life on the line for shits like you and this Marston guy who think they can just do whatever they want and be above, not just the law, but the basic fabric of humanity and morality. I have a cause now that I believe in with all my heart and I am willing to die for it. I am not going to let you or anyone else tell me otherwise. So, unless you tell me exactly what I want to know, then you will gain first-hand experience of how efficient we are at doing our jobs. So what's it going to be?*"

Wedmore had never spoken to Rosehill this way before and the power behind his words let him know he meant business.

"Ok, James. It's not going to be easy..."

"I don't give a shit about easy! Easy doesn't feature anywhere in my life or what I do for a living. It's about what is right and protecting lives!"

Rosehill stuttered as he regained some composure. "Well it's not just Marston; there is a whole group pulling the strings behind the scenes and this is an international co-operation, so you need to bear that in mind. Marston appears to work very closely with the British government, but they really control the government and manipulate people through the media to carry out their agenda. The government is a puppet to the systems of control, manipulation, and ultimately money. He works with Trent Darby who owns some of the major broadcasting and television networks."

"It's crazy to think how this whole system works. The TV news programs and newspapers basically lie to the public, telling them what to think, what opinions to have, who to hate, and it all works so seamlessly. Millions of people are having their strings pulled by a small group of people who dictate what is aired on TV and printed in the newspapers. The whole system is rigged to promote division, separation, fear, and conflict and people can't even see it! Even those who claim to be able to see past it all have never understood the true depths of the deceit."

"What's interesting is most people become very defensive when presented with the truth and defend themselves and their opinions as being right when they are merely repeating what has been spoon-fed to them for years through consistent programming. These masters of psychology know that a person's ego will step in and attack anyone who speaks the truth, so the system becomes self-perpetuating and self-sustaining. People don't realise the TV is the monster in their home."

"I'm not finding this as amusing as you are, although it is insightful. It looks like this perfect Matrix of lies has fooled us all. It was nice whilst it lasted, but it's had its day. It's coming down," Wedmore said.

"Sorry! As I was saying, Marston works in cahoots with Darby who does the lying and the covering up for the elite by telling the public non-truths or by drawing their attention to other irrelevant events, whilst not publicizing more critical things. It's the whole reason why sport features so favourably in the media and on TV; it keeps people distracted from what is really going on in the world. It also encourages conflict and division from one another in support of their own teams thinking they are rooting for something good when all the games are largely rigged anyway."

"These two are the frontline men who carry out the big cover-up stories for the families who are really in control; the people who own and operate the largest banks in the world, who manipulate the markets and the economy, and create wars. I don't know their names, as I was never privy to that information, but I can tell you that Marston and Darby will be able to tell you more if you can get hold of them. One thing I should say, James, is they have some very powerful men in their pocket, including the highest ranking military officials, but these men are in the dark about what is really going on and who is really running the country. There are many secret projects that the high ranking military know nothing about and this may very well be your angle to get them on board with your mission."

"Tell me more about these secret projects," Wedmore said. "What do you know about them?"

"A lot is hearsay, James, but it comes from a very reliable source; an old friend of mine from Oxford university who has kept in touch with me over many years. This guy is one of the brightest people I know and was recruited into some of the 'Black-Op' military off-the-record projects that were being conducted in the USA in the 1990's. You wouldn't believe me if I told you some of the things that he's worked on."

"Try me!" Wedmore said.

"Well, after the Second World War, there was a crash involving extra-terrestrial vehicles that were seized by specialist Black Op soldiers in the US working with the UK government who took the spaceships deep underground into an area that most people know as Area 51. Most people think that they were trying to learn from the technologies of extra-terrestrials, but we had the majority of their technology already, we just needed a few missing pieces. This is why technology has taken so many leaps and bounds forward since the Second World War, but honestly, we had many of these technologies decades before."

"What's more interesting are the barriers that have been broken since they captured the vehicles. They were already very close to mastering anti-gravity, but the crashed vehicles gave them the missing pieces of the puzzle. By mastering anti-gravity, they were able to make objects practically weightless, and when you can do that, you are no longer governed by traditional physics that states velocity equates to the mass of the object and the gravitational pull it is subjected to."

"So they were then able to make matter not only practically weightless, but also travel insanely fast, actually faster than the speed of light. This has major applications within the military as it allows a weapon to deliver its payload faster than anything can detect it! The advances that have been made in free energy technology are even more fascinating. Traditional physicists say that over-unity generators could not exist as they could not be

made to produce over 100% energy, but generators have been developed that access the infinite energy that is omnipresent. A cubic centimetre of air could power the entirety of the United States' energy needs for a year through one of these devices. We know that to be true because one tiny little atom has the power to destroy a city," Rosehill explained.

"If that's true, then why don't they use that technology right now? It could help everyone on the planet to access free and clean energy rather than burning fossil fuels!" the Doc asked.

Rosehill laughed to himself at the suggestion. "You've kind of answered your own question there. By doing so, it would render the coal, oil, and petro-chemical industries instantly obsolete. Energy companies the world over would go to the wall and those people who own literally trillions of dollars worth of mineral deposits are not about to see their wealth disappear. So honestly, that's a large part of where you guys come in. Someone threatens the established order by inventing something that could challenge a wealthy person's wealth, and you guys are sent in to take them out. Nice and simple. Of course, if we told you the truth, you wouldn't do it, so you had to be sold some white lies to make you believe they were terrorists."

"I don't believe this! Are you serious?" the Doc asked in staggered disbelief.

"I'm not proud to tell you this, but it's the reality of the world we live in," Rosehill said.

"It was the reality," Kamali added. A deep sadness overcame his heart as he thought about how well the system had played him and his team who had regularly put themselves in harm's way to protect those who fought against the world and humanity. He reflected on an old Buckminster Fuller quote he had read:

"We must do away with the absolutely specious notion that everybody has to earn a living. It is a fact today that one in ten thousand of us can make a technological breakthrough capable of supporting all the rest. The youth of today are absolutely right in recognizing this nonsense of earning a living. We keep inventing jobs because of this false idea that everybody has to be employed at some kind of drudgery because according to Malthusian-Darwinian theory, he must justify his right to exist. So, we have inspectors of inspectors and people making instruments for inspectors to inspect inspectors. The true business of people should be to go back to school and think about whatever it was they were thinking about before somebody came along and told them they had to earn a living."

One invention, like free energy, would be capable of looking after virtually everyone on the planet and would ease their financial burdens or raise their standard of living.

"It was the reality and now things are going to start changing," Kamali continued. *"We're intent on making a stand against the dishonesty and corruption that exists in this world and bring about a better life for everyone."*

Rosehill looked blankly at Kamali. His thoughts lingered on the impossible nature of this task and how standing up to the established order was possibly the shortest route to an early grave.

As if Kamali could read Rosehill's mind, he said *"I would rather die today fighting as a free man than live another minute supporting those who do not care for the good of others and who are fundamentally without a heart. Life is a birthright to all and no-one except God has the right to determine who lives and who dies."*

"Is this not ultimately God's work anyhow?" Rosehill asked.

"God brings people difficult circumstances and challenges to help them grow and I believe these circumstances have partly been brought to bear in order to help raise humanity to a higher level. It is said that when one prays for patience, God provides certain provoking circumstances for them to learn to be patient. However, it is my belief that a certain corrupt group of people have taken advantage of the natural order of things to further themselves and serve their own sick agenda, and this is not God's way. We, the people, have allowed these circumstances to unfold and therefore prayers to God will not rectify the situation. We must take action," Sana said. *"Tell me, Mr Rosehill, where are Mr Marston and Mr Darby? Will you help us find them?"*

Rosehill looked up into Sana's eyes as though he was caught between and rock and a hard place. He hesitated for a moment before acknowledging that he would help.

"Great!" Wedmore said. *"Let's go. Rosehill, do what you need to organize a meeting with them and you'd better tell your loved ones you'll be gone for a few days. We need you with us."*

Rosehill walked to his desk and picked up his desk phone to make a call.

Chapter 16

The Truth

LOCATION: London, England
DATE: 2nd May
WEATHER: Overcast with sunny spells

The Black Widows listened to Rosehill as he made the call to be sure he didn't tip them off. They were uncertain if he could be trusted and the only way to be sure was to watch his actions rather than listen to his words. He had seemed remorseful during their earlier conversation but experience had shown them that people are prone to doing all sorts of things when their backs are against the wall. Rosehill wrapped up the conversation by arranging a meeting at 2pm. This gave them around six hours to kill.

Wedmore strategized how to get out of the building without alarming security. They could hear more and more people entering the building ready to begin their day's work, blissfully unaware of what was happening in Rosehill's office. Wedmore suggested it would be far better if Rosehill and Sana exited the building together via the reception, whilst the Black Widows left via the fire escape and brought the vehicle around to the front to pick them up. It would look a lot less suspicious than all parties exiting via the main reception. Sana could also ensure Rosehill didn't alert anyone or do anything that might jeopardise their next steps.

Sana linked arms with Rosehill and they walked out of the office together, checking to make sure the coast was clear so the Black Widows could walk down the corridor to the fire escape door without being seen. Sana gave the signal for the men to proceed down the corridor whilst she pressed the call button for the lift. She stepped into the empty compartment with Rosehill still attached to her arm. Rosehill had to admit he was feeling slightly intimidated by her, not because he feared her but because he felt she could literally see right through him. Even though his intentions of help were pure, he still felt very exposed.

"Don't be nervous, Mr Rosehill," Sana said reading his energy.

He was even more taken aback as it confirmed his original thoughts. He pulled back slightly from her, unhooked his arm from hers and looked at her in disbelief. *"Are you reading my mind?"* he asked.

"No, not at all. I am reading your energy. There's a difference," Sana said with a smile. *"There's nothing to worry about. I just sensed you were nervous, that's all. Tell me, Mr Rosehill, do you listen to your intuition?"*

"I...I don't really, no. It was drilled out of me in my military training that to do so was not logical and dangerous. In battle situations, we were always told to plan and strategize with our minds. Nothing else matters."

The doors to the lift opened and they walked to the marble tiled entrance hallway to revolving front door.

"It's such a shame that you have been sold on such a lie, Mr Rosehill," Sana said in a soft and quiet voice. *"You might see a different world if you used all of your God-given abilities. The mind is a great servant but a poor leader. Your heart, your intuition, knows all truths."*

Sana linked arms with Rosehill again as they walked outside. They walked in silence for a few hundred metres through the hustle and bustle of early morning commuters to wait for the Black Widows to pick them up. Rosehill was deep in thought and wondering how well he had been played by the system that had ensured he was emotionally blind and lived in servitude to a system that ultimately couldn't care less about him or his family.

The Land Rover screeched to a halt next to them, jolting Rosehill out of his train of thought. The rear passenger door was flung open and Rosehill got in, followed by Sana. Gringo sped off and drove out of town. They knew they had time to kill and they wanted the opportunity to talk more with Rosehill before meeting the men who controlled the nation's media and misled the public.

They drove in silence for several minutes before Wedmore asked Rosehill where they were due to meet later on. Rosehill confirmed that he had arranged to meet Marston and Darby at a disused air base on the outskirts of Kent called RAF Westgate. It was always preferable to hold off-the-record close quarter meetings at disused air bases, as there were invariably never any witnesses. Rosehill mentioned that it might seem suspicious if he didn't show up in his own car, and that perhaps they could set a trap to capture these men so they would be operating under the direction of the Black Widows rather than on their own agenda.

"What makes you so sure they are going to arrive at this meeting alone?" the Doc asked.

"I used the words that always makes these types of people run: it's a matter of national security!" Rosehill replied with a wry smile. *"These words are a code to suggest they really need to hear what is being said."*

"So you're sure they will show?" Wedmore asked.

"If they don't, you can shoot me," Rosehill responded. He was clearly confident that his targets would make an appearance.

Gringo pulled up around the corner from Rosehill's house to pick up his own vehicle and once he was on the road, a gun-toting Hitler joined him in the passenger seat as his personal escort as they followed the Land Rover to pick up supplies and then head towards RAF Westgate.

They arrived shortly before midday, which gave them plenty of time to scope out the terrain of the former RAF base and plan their approach once the other parties had arrived. It was a deserted space with few signs of life. The base had been abandoned since the 1920's and featured a handful of rusting industrial sheds surrounded by overgrown grass, all bounded by perimeter chain-link fence sporting the obligatory bright red 'Keep Out' notices. The UK was full of many air bases that were disused since the end of the world wars. The land was primarily owned by the government that used the armed forces to loosely maintain each base should they ever be needed again in the future. The modern day reality was that the military had moved more towards fighting overseas, bombing from the air rather than using troops on the ground.

Civilian causalities were certainly much higher when carpet bombing techniques were used, but this was considered 'collateral damage' and acceptable as far as military practice was concerned. Being removed from the situation both physically and emotionally made it easier to give orders to decimate a city rather than put soldiers face-to-face with the consequences on the ground. It's what allowed people in the higher military ranks to sleep at night. That, and being told they were serving Queen and Country. If their loved ones were in the area, it would have surely resulted in a different set of orders.

They continued to drive along the main access road leading to the centre of the airbase. There were still five hangers in place, which looked in reasonable condition considering they hadn't been operated for nearly 100 years. There were three short runways spreading out from this centre point that would have facilitated propeller driven planes to take off and land, but they were too short for modern jet aircraft to use. Adjacent to the runways was a disused three-storey Air Traffic Control (ATC) hub. Rosehill parked his Jaguar adjacent to the ATC building and told Gringo to park their vehicle in one of the hangers out of the way. Gringo and the Doc took the vehicle to the nearest hanger whilst the remainder of the Black Widows and Sana walked with Rosehill towards the ATC building being careful not to leave tracks on the moss covered roads, which would be a dead giveaway.

As Gringo and the Doc approached the hanger, they both jumped out of the Land Rover and used brute force to push open the rusting sliding doors. They eased apart just wide enough to allow Gringo to reverse into the hanger. Always battle ready, they had to be sure to have the vehicle ready to make a quick exit if things turned nasty. They took two kitbags from the back of the Land Rover containing rope and a small collection of firearms, which they slung over their shoulders before sliding the doors back into position to hide the vehicle.

The team assembled inside the ATC building. The sunlight streamed in through the cracked dirty windows to illuminate the deteriorating walls and floors of the old building. Cobwebs lingered everywhere, forcing everyone to push them to one side to create a pathway through the central staircase up to the top floor. From here, there was a strong vantage point to observe in all directions.

The team gathered to discuss tactics to extract information and, if necessary, the elimination of Marston and Darby. Whilst they had little evidence that these men were responsible for horrendous crimes against humanity, Rosehill had little reason to lie, especially given his current circumstances.

"How do these meetings usually go, Rosehill?" Wedmore asked, keen to understand more of this mysterious, behind-the-scenes world.

"It's difficult to say at this stage, but they believe I am meeting with them to share more knowledge and information that will safeguard their interests and allow them to profit although they don't know what yet. Their greed and self-interest will lead them here and then it's down to you to do what you want to do," Rosehill replied.

"What exactly did you tell them?" Sana asked.

Rosehill's eyes twinkled at the questioning as he thought about the fabrication that was about to lead these two hated men to their doom. Perhaps after today, he and his loved ones would no longer fear being constantly being watched or persecuted.

"I told them you had succeeded on your last mission and I had news of something that would benefit them enormously. I said you had found a potential 'honey pot', which is code for either precious metals or diamonds. I never mention the real thing in case the phone line is tapped. Whenever we discuss business, we are always careful to ensure we never say anything that could potentially incriminate us. That's why we've arranged to meet here. What are you going to do with them once you capture them?"

Wedmore pondered the question for a moment before replying. "I have a few friends that run an unregulated prison made out of shipping containers on an old oil tanker in the North Sea. I think we'll deposit them there once we have finished questioning them. That should keep them out of the way until we have taken out the main suspects in this whole debacle. I have a feeling we will be collecting quite a few rogues before we can completely undermine their operation and stop the damage they are causing."

"So, the plan of action, gentlemen and lady, is to bag and tag these guys and their entourage so that we can give them the military good cop, bad cop interrogation to extract the information we require. Rosehill, you are the bait to bring them up here, and we will hold positions to surround them. I don't want to mess about with these guys as our time is limited, so let's do what we need to do to get the information we need so we can move on."

"Without killing or hurting anyone," Sana added.

"I can't promise that, I'm afraid, Sana. These guys will need to be roughed up a little to find out what's going on and who is involved. It's probably best that you stay out of the way for this next bit. We know what we are doing."

Sana didn't say anything and just looked deeply into Wedmore's eyes with a look of love and compassion. It spoke to Wedmore's heart. It was clear to him that no matter what these people had done, they still deserved the dignity of humanity and not some typical masculine left-brain, ego-driven response that would make them no better than the perpetrators. She placed her hand over her necklace to remind him what the mission was all about.

"Ok," Wedmore said. "I hear you! We'll do our best! Hitler and Gringo, I want you to bag and tag the main men once they are on the top floor. Me, Kamali, and the Doc will take positions outside to deal with any of their entourage. Rosehill is the bait. Springbok, I want you to take Sana back to the Land Rover and wait for further instructions."

On his command, Hitler knelt down by his bags and distributed the handguns among the team. He then pulled out some plastic ratchet ties and two black hessian sacks with drawstrings, which would be placed over the heads of Marston and Darby.

An hour later, two large chauffeur-driven black Mercedes-Benz limousines cruised up the access road to the military base and pulled up alongside Rosehill's Jaguar. The cars were sporting diplomatic immunity plates and it was not possible to see the occupants as the rear windows were blacked out. The drivers' doors of both opened almost in unison as two very smartly dressed, but clearly ex-SAS drivers got out, scanned the area, and opened the rear doors. Wedmore and the Doc watched them from behind a raised oil tank adjacent to the watchtower. They needed to be sure just how many people were going to be joining the party before they made their move. Rosehill raised his hand to signal a 'hello' from the top floor to the chauffeurs and to let them know it was safe to proceed.

Two men exited the rear of the vehicles. The first man was tall and spindly with an ashen face and thinning hair. He wore a three-piece pinstripe suit with a monocle and a golden chain hanging from the right pocket of his waistcoat to a central button indicating he carried a pocket watch. He had a very aloof air about him as he walked with his head tipped slightly upwards and his eyes beadily scanning the ground. He must have been around 70 and carried a black hardwood cane with hallmark silver ferrule and large pommel handle, which bore an intricate acorn design. His shoes glistened in the sunlight, as he stood tall and erect. He reached back into the car and pulled out a top hat, which he placed upon his head at a slight angle before pulling the white cuffs of his shirt down inside his jacket sleeves to complete his look. Wedmore and the Doc were bemused, as they hadn't seen anyone wear such finery outside a fancy dress party.

The second man was shorter and seemed to carry the extra weight that was missing from the first man. Being slightly rotund in nature, the man was also well dressed in his three-piece suit, which bulged around his waistline. This fellow had flushed cheeks after he had exerted himself from climbing out of the car. As he stood up, he arched his back slightly and pulled at his jacket from the lapels, smoothing it down the front of his body. He too proceeded to don a top hat. His slightly sunken eyes took in the surrounding view with the aid of small gold-rimmed glasses that made him look like a human mole.

"It's like a posh version of Laurel and fucking Hardy," the Doc whispered to Wedmore.

There was no doubt about it, these men had a lot of money and were clearly part of the aristocracy. For all their show of wealth, however, it was apparent to Wedmore and the Doc that these men were hollow and lacked the undefined part of their soul that made them human. The two men walked towards one another and engaged in conversation, just out of earshot. The two warriors were more interested in watching the movements of the chauffeurs who were scoping out the local area to check for signs of danger.

They approached the watchtower, and Wedmore and the Doc suspected their position would soon be compromised. It was obvious from their physique that these guys knew how to handle themselves so they did not want to engage in hand-to-hand combat with them. With hearts beating fast as the adrenaline started to flow, Wedmore and the Doc drew their pistols and brazenly walked out from behind the oil tank with their arms extended and the guns trained expertly on the chauffeurs. This move took the chauffeurs by surprise. They were completely exposed. With zero cover and their own weapons still in their holsters, they raised their hands in the air with a look of disappointment written all over their faces, as they had allowed themselves to be so sloppy.

"Right, boys, you know the drill. On the ground, face down, and keep your hands where we can see them," Wedmore ordered his new captives.

The two men maintained eye contact with Wedmore and the Doc as they stooped down to one knee and then the other, keeping their hands in the air before lying face down and interlocking their hands behind their heads. They were just out of sight of their masters who continued their chat whilst awaiting confirmation from their chauffeurs that it was safe to proceed. Little did they know that their bodyguards had just been captured and were helpless to protect them.

Wedmore kept his pistol and intense stare fixed on the two targets. The Doc took their guns before pulling a couple of thick plastic ratchet ties from the side pocket of his combat trousers to tie their hands tightly together behind their backs. Once he had done this, he rolled the men onto their backs so Wedmore could address them.

"Gentlemen, I know you are both employed to follow orders so our quarrel is not with you; it's with the two men you brought here. There is a great injustice currently taking place in this world and these two men are largely responsible for it. If you allow us to do what we need to do, no harm will come to you. However, if you step out of line, we will shoot you without hesitation. Do you understand?" Wedmore asked.

The two men nodded.

Wedmore continued. *"As ex-servicemen of this country, you may be interested to learn of the biggest lies that you and your fellow comrades have been sold for putting your lives on the line. The lie about protecting Queen and Country and how you are doing the world a favour by standing up for justice, truth, freedom, and democracy against so-called terrorists. We have been protecting the guilty for too long and harming the innocent on the whims of the people running this country. In fact, we have been the terrorists! It's time to have a word with your bosses and you are welcome to hear the truth, if you wish. You have to ask yourself if you are going to continuously put yourself in harm's way for people who do not value your life and view you as nothing more than a pawn on a chessboard. Would you like to know the truth?"*

The two men on the ground looked confused, yet being in no position to argue, nodded again. Wedmore and the Doc helped them to their feet and asked that they remain silent whilst they confronted their masters. Wedmore and the Doc walked out towards their unsuspecting new targets. It wasn't until the two soldiers got closer to them that they realized trouble was brewing. Despite their aloof posterior, both men were visibly shocked to see Wedmore and the Doc walking towards them with their handguns aimed directly at them. They were obviously not used to dealing with situations like this.

"Gentlemen! How nice to see you!" Wedmore said with a hint of sarcasm to his voice. *"It will be a great pleasure to get to know you, but first I have to ask you to get on your knees."*

They looked at Wedmore in wide-eyed disbelief as they saw their bodyguards behind him were helpless to assist in the situation.

"We shall do no such thing!" retorted the tall, skinny man in a tone of voice that suggested he was used to getting his own way. *"Do you have any idea who we are?"*

"I have no idea who you are, but that man up there does," Wedmore replied as he motioned up to the top floor window of the watchtower where Rosehill was observing the situation.

As the two men looked upwards and noticed Rosehill looking down, a look of disappointment and betrayal came across their faces. They looked again at Wedmore and the Doc trying to work out exactly what was going to happen.

Wedmore continued, *"I shan't ask you again, gentlemen. On your knees."*

The short man reluctantly kneeled, but the taller man remained defiant. He took his walking cane in his hand, raised it up as though it were a sword, and waved it at the two soldiers.

"You two obviously have no clue who you are messing with and, by Jove, we will make sure you are hung, drawn, and quartered for this!"

The Doc grabbed the end of the cane and pulled hard bringing the man towards him, causing him to lose balance and stumble forward. The Doc stuck out his right leg causing him to trip up and stumble to the ground, grazing his hands and putting holes in both of his trouser legs at the knees and sent his top hat flying. As he rolled around on the floor nursing his wounds, he screamed, *"Bastards!"* The Doc placed his right boot on top of the man's chest and leaned heavily as he looked down at him with a wry smile.

"Thank you, gentlemen!" Wedmore said in a cheery tone. *"Now that we have your attention, perhaps we can start by getting to know you. Who are you?"* Wedmore asked of the tall, thin man who was gripping his hands together tightly to try and stem the pain from the sudden impact with the ground. He was unresponsive and obviously not used to being treated like this.

"That's Frederick Marston and his colleague is Trent Darby," came the voice of Rosehill as he walked towards them from the entrance to the watchtower. *"These bastards have been giving*

you guys the run around for years and have had me by the balls for longer than I can remember."

The other Black Widows walked behind him, keen to observe the action and establish the next steps. Rosehill took a step towards Marston and kicked him hard in the stomach before walking over to Darby to do the same.

Wedmore signalled to Gringo and Hitler to bring the two ex-servicemen over so they could hear the truth from Marston and Darby. The two men were writhing breathlessly on the floor as they struggled to regain their composure after Rosehill's sharp kick. Rosehill stood over them angrily as he sought revenge for all the years he had silently suffered because of their threats, lies, and deceit. Finally, it was time for some payback. Sana could feel the intense emotions that Rosehill was going through and stepped forward to place a hand gently on his shoulder.

"Do you feel better for doing that?" she asked with a smile.

"I have to say I do!" Rosehill replied. *"It's been long overdue,"* he said with a hint of anger in his voice.

"Remember that if you kill a killer, the number of killers in this world does not diminish," Sana said. Her words of wisdom hit Rosehill and caused him to reflect on his actions.

Sana continued, *"It's understandable that you would meet these two with hatred after what you have told us about them and how they have treated you, but remember this is a journey of growth for you, and believe it or not, these men are responsible for helping you grow. When you start to raise your level of consciousness, I am sure you will see that there is a beautiful gift from the darkness of their actions."*

"I don't follow you," Rosehill said in an angry tone. *"How can these bastards possibly give me a gift with their rotten behaviour?"* As he spat the words with venom, Marston and

Darby looked up from the ground to see how Sana would respond.

"In nature, imagine what a seed goes through. When it is planted, it is pushed into a place of darkness and solidarity where it can be trampled on or eaten at any given moment. Yet, despite all this hardship and struggle, it still manages to thrive and grow into a beautiful flower or a strong tree. You see, sometimes, it is necessary to go through struggle in order to grow. It is the very essence of life, it is nature's way of growth and contribution." Sana's words lingered in the air as both Marston and Darby sat up and looked at her with some apprehension. She turned her attention to them and continued.

"Conversely, when something stops growing and contributing towards others in nature, it is taken out of the equation. It is the same with these two people who are more content with creating misery in the lives of others rather than using their powerful influence to help humanity advance in consciousness. So, tell me, gentlemen, what is it about you that makes you think you can mistreat others and get away with it?"

The two chauffeurs keenly listened. Marston was the first to respond to Sana and retorted in anger with a tone of much superiority.

"You have no idea what you are talking about, woman! You talk as though you live in a fantasy land with absolutely no regard for reality. We tell people what they need to hear to keep an established order in place. It's how civilised society works! We tell them what is going on in the world on a need-to-know basis. They're very happy knowing the sports scores and a watered down view of international politics. They don't need to know everything the people running this country are doing."

Darby then chimed in, *"There are many things that people in this world would not wish to know even if we told them the* truth. Do you think they would want to know that they were little more than worker bees with the sole objective of serving their Queen? They are so engrained in their identities and their fake existence that telling them the truth would cause harm and resentment. We just give them a sugar pill to keep things sweet and to not upset the applecart."

"That all seems very noble of you, gentlemen," Sana replied with a hint of sarcasm. "However, consider that the people you keep enslaved in their own minds with the lies and deceit that you peddle in your newspapers and your television programs are capable of so much more if they weren't so hypnotized by your actions. Consider that if they worked together in harmony with one another that they could house the homeless and end world hunger. They could even build bridges with other nations and people, bringing about a unity of humanity and peace to the world."

"That would never happen!" Marston snapped. "People are inherently selfish by nature and driven by greed. They don't care about anything other than themselves! As long as they have food in their stomachs and are occupied by trivia, they don't care about anything. Caesar was right; give them bread and circuses and they will not revolt."

Wedmore stepped forward with a smile on his face, bending down to firmly grasp Marston's tie with one hand and pulled it upwards so he could look him square in the eyes.

"They say that one's own view on the behaviour of others is generally a reflection of their own level of consciousness. This seems to bear truth for yourselves, gentlemen, as your motives appear to be driven by selfishness and greed to accumulate as much for yourselves and leave little for everyone else. It's quite a tragic poverty consciousness that you have despite your obvious wealth. Why would you not want to end world hunger, *homelessness, or war? Unless there were significant financial or emotional payoffs for you by keeping the status quo, of course."*

Marston and Darby silently looked at one another.

"Do you have an answer for me?" Wedmore asked.

Again, there was silence.

"Ok, gentlemen. You should know that we have become very good at acting on your orders and extracting information from much harder criminals than you on our international missions where we have been chasing alleged Muslim terrorists on your whims. So, if you don't wish to talk, I am telling you now that we will get the information we want whether you like it or not. It's your choice and I am giving you fair warning." Wedmore was insistent that he wasn't going to walk away without knowing everything they wanted to know.

"Go fuck yourself!" Marston spat. *"You're nothing more than cannon fodder and we're not telling you anything. We own you!"*

Wedmore raised his right foot and brought it down on Marston's chest, forcing him back down on the ground, as he drew his Bowie knife from the sheath secured to his right calf. He brought the knife up towards Marston's throat and witnessed how quickly his eyes were filled with terror. The knife glinted in the sunlight as Wedmore crouched into Marston's face, putting more weight onto his chest as he did so, forcing the remaining air from his lungs.

"You appear to have forgotten the situation you are in, Mr. Marston. You and your friend are both on the ground faced with certain immediate death from my team and me so you don't own anything or anyone right now. Your life is hanging by a very fragile thread and my patience is wearing very, very thin. As far as I can see, ridding the world of you two would be

an incredible service, so I'm happy whichever way you want to play this."

Wedmore looked sternly at Marston as he spoke and couldn't help but notice that his eyes were lifeless and lacklustre, soulless even. His grey skin reminded him of a zombie movie he had seen and it looked as though he was nothing more than a skeleton in a suit. A momentary flicker of empathy flashed through Wedmore's heart as he stood up and raised the knife above his head, ready to strike the deadly blow into Marston's heart. He had a fierce look in his eyes as he looked down on Marston who said nothing despite the perilous situation of certain death he was faced with.

"Go ahead and do it! What you can do to us is nothing compared to what would happen to us if we said anything," Marston said.

"Tell us who your masters are and we will take them out to relieve the pain in your life," Wedmore reasoned.

Marston took a deep breath and closed his eyes. Wedmore looked at Darby who looked equally concerned. Springbok stood behind Darby with his own Bowie knife drawn, ready to follow any orders his leader might issue. Both men were moments from certain death unless they started talking. Marston took another deep breath and opened his eyes.

"Exactly what is that you wish to know?" he asked Wedmore.

"We want to know everything. Who is involved in creating the web of deceit and misleading the public? Who are you taking your orders from or working with? Why are we, and everyone else in the military, being sent to take the lives of innocent people under the guise of instilling democracy and freedom when the reality is our home nations are staging the terrorist attacks to justify going to war and pillaging resources? Basically, what the fuck is going on and who is behind it all?" Wedmore said.

Sana was also quick to jump in with the questioning. *"You need to tell us everything and not hold anything back. There are a great many lives at stake here and we have the opportunity to bring about major worldwide change, benefiting billions of people. We are standing at a transformational moment in history and you have the opportunity to undo much of your previous wrongdoing with the choices you make from this moment forward. Either you are part of the solution now or you continue to be part of the problem. One will lead your soul to freedom and the other will keep it enslaved in the personal hell you endure on a daily basis. Which will it be?"*

Marston sat up and looked again at Darby for reassurance for the step he was about to take. He then looked back up at Wedmore, Sana, and Rosehill. Before he spoke, Sana added; *"You should also know that we will know immediately if you are being truthful or not. So please, tell the truth."*

Marston paused as though he had already been caught. Thoughts flashed through his mind over where to begin. Finally, he took another deep breath and composed himself.

"We run almost all of the media broadcasts and publications that the public receive, so we tell them what our masters want them to hear. If they want us to tell people that Russia is the enemy this year, that's what we do. If it's Iran the following year, we produce 'evidence' to tell people that they are harming other countries or threatening our national security and something must be done to stop it. Basically, we highlight the problem in the media to goad the public's reaction, who then cry for the premeditated solution, which was always there. We just needed to engineer the circumstances to rally public support so they wouldn't stop us."

"Our masters then send in troops like you to the chosen country under the guise of fighting for G.O.D. What people don't realize is that G.O.D. stands for Gold, Oil, and Drugs!" Marston said with a wry smile. *"Whilst the public at home are distracted by our coverage of the war on terrorism, our troops are doing the hard work of destabilising the established order within the chosen country. The resources of precious metals, oil, and drugs are taken out of the country and given to our masters. We are then handsomely rewarded for our efforts and our masters' construction companies then win contracts to rebuild the war-torn country. Of course, not before the elite banks have gone in and lent the country a huge amount of money that they can never afford to repay in order to help rebuild it. Once they default on these loans, we can then take even more resources and keep the country in debt servitude forever. You see, it's all just about business, not taking the moral high ground."*

Sana stepped forward and slapped Marston hard across the face. *"How can you say it's all about business? What about the lives of the innocent people who were brutally slaughtered because of the greed of people who already have more than enough. Doesn't that fill you with at least a hint of sadness?"*

"To be perfectly frank with you, we are too removed from the situation to actually feel anything about what's going on. It's just what happens and it's always been that way. People have been killing one another for many generations, so it's all perfectly normal when you look at history."

Sana was clearly angry at Marston's heartless reply. She stood tall and strong and spoke, *"That's exactly the problem. Just because war is legal, people like you think that it's acceptable to carry on this way. People hide behind religious differences and pit one country against another when they forget that we are all part of the same body of consciousness that created all of this.*

We are all one and we need to treat one another as we would like to treat ourselves. History is littered with wars and battles that are unnecessary to settle differences or misunderstandings. It is possible to have two different religions or views of the world without having to go to war and kill one another over it. Now you have explained what is actually happening, I can see why people have a vested interest in keeping the game running this way. However, it has had its time and we will not allow it to continue."

Marston laughed. *"Who do you people think you are? You're only a handful of people up against the might of the ruling elite in this country and across the world. What on earth are you going to do? Do you honestly think that you can stop this? It's been happening for centuries! People are naturally divided by race, culture, and religion. It makes it easier to stir up tensions between people. Just what exactly are you proposing?"*

Sana stepped back and took a deep breath whilst closing her eyes to compose herself. Despite her wisdom, she could feel Marston's comments provoking her. As she opened her eyes again, she fixed a gentle, yet firm stare on Marston.

"All the major religions in this world teach the same principles of loving thy neighbour and treating others as you would have them treat you. These core underlying principles appear to have been forgotten by many people as they have been buried by the media who tell the public who to love and who to hate. People need to be reminded of these core principles to help unite them rather than divide them. For people who don't define themselves as religious, they can still embrace the concept of love and humanity. We are spreading the message of uniting people under the Religion of Love throughout the world, whilst taking away the incestuous element of society that enslaves us in a bloodthirsty and barbaric world."

Marston smiled as he heard Sana's words and vision. "Not all religions subscribe to your fantasy theory of love, my dear. Do you think anyone who believed in God would actually want to go to war?"

"What do you mean?" Wedmore asked. His gut feeling told him Marston was hinting at something sinister.

"You can't possibly believe that a loving God would actually allow all this war and suffering to take place on this planet, do you? Does it strike you as an inalienable truth that the God who created this world would want to allow humans to destroy it? Aren't you missing a piece of the puzzle here?" Marston continued with a malevolent tone and sense of knowing that put Wedmore on edge.

"You're going to have to fill me in on the missing details here," Wedmore replied.

"There are powers and forces at work in this world that you know nothing about and will never know. Those powers are reserved for the chosen few who have received illumination in their quest for knowledge, and thus power over others. Those people are perceived as special and gifted and they control what happens in this world. You cannot, and will never know, the truth of the matter."

Marston's words seemed to be taunting Wedmore as he was clearly in possession of some secret knowledge. Wedmore looked at Marston with a sense of disgust and slight intrigue. Sana observed Wedmore's actions and called him on it.

"Don't let him hook you with his words and actions, Jay. You are better than that."

"You're right, Sana. I'm intrigued by what could possibly be going on when a certain small group of people are granted a higher power over the rest of us yet use it for evil intent? Do you get where he is coming from?"

"We know where he is coming from, Jay, and remember who we have on our side," Sana said. *"He is referring to their false Devil God they worship. He grants them all the money and power in the world in exchange for creating the energy of human suffering to feed their master. Without this energy, he cannot be strong. It's all in the unseen…"* Her speech trailed off as a brief smile spread across her face. *"I just think it's funny that these people would trade their souls in servitude of their master for bits of paper with dead people printed on it! If their actions didn't have such serious effects on humanity, it would almost be amusing."*

As the words fell from Sana's lips, they appeared to ruffle Marston's feathers somewhat. *"You have no clue what you are talking about,"* he spat, although clearly Sana had touched a nerve.

"If that's the case, why would you be so upset with what she just said?" Wedmore asked.

Wedmore turned his attention to Darby who had been notably quiet during the whole exchange. He signalled to Springbok and the Doc to bring him to his feet. They both took an arm each and lifted him up, both men grunting under strain as they moved his heavy frame. Wedmore walked over to him and got up close and personal. He looked deeply into his eyes before asking him, *"What do you have to say on the matter?"*

Darby looked unsettled and unsure. Clearly, he was more frightened to be in this situation than Marston, and Wedmore could see it. This would be to his advantage. Darby remained silent but Wedmore pushed harder.

"I won't ask you again. What do you have to say?" he said, as he lifted his knife up and held it underneath his chin, the sharp tip pressing against his skin causing Darby's eyes to widen from the pain he was now feeling.

Darby started to tremble as beads of sweat formed on top of his brow. Wedmore knew from this reaction that it would be just moments before he started talking. He pressed the knife up a little more as an additional prompt. The trickle of blood spurred Darby's mouth into action.

"Ok! Ok. She's right. There's not much else to say. It's very much what happens."

"So who else is a part of this?" Wedmore asked.

"You would be surprised who is involved," came the reply.

Marston tried to tell him to shut up before receiving another kick to the stomach from Rosehill. He breathlessly rolled around as Wedmore encouraged Darby to continue.

"As I was saying, you would be surprised who is involved. Just about every member of every major government, the major financial houses, medical agencies, every major corporation in the world, and some religions inadvertently worship our god. We get all the money, wealth, and power that we could ever wish for in exchange for helping to create the energy of misery and suffering. The heads of most of these groups are essentially part of secret societies that are strictly off the record and plausibly deniable. No one will ever admit that they are part of them when questioned, and will deny that they even exist. The truth is, they do, and those that are part of them know who the other members are. As such, they will only deal with other members, as they understand the rules of the game. They hide in plain sight and you can usually tell which public figures are part of it when they throw the bull-hand gesture," Darby explained.

"What is the bull-hand gesture? And just what are these 'rules of the game' as you put it?" Wedmore pushed.

"The bull-hand is where you raise your hand above your head with the index and little finger raised whilst the two middle fingers are held down by the thumb. People think it means 'Rock and Roll', but it's really a satanic salute letting others know they are part of the occult. There are also strict entry criteria, as one would obviously expect. You can't have everyone accessing this secret knowledge. It is reserved for those illuminated souls and families who have been worshipping the occult for generations. These families have infiltrated almost every position of power on the planet and their goal is simple: to become exceptionally wealthy and gather as much for themselves as possible whilst ensuring that everyone else has just enough to prevent a revolution. As long as people are fat and distracted with junk television and entertainment gods to worship, they are oblivious to everything that is going on. We're happy and they're sedated enough in their Matrix reality not to care."

"What do you mean, sedated enough not to care?" Wedmore prompted.

"There's a reason why coffee, alcohol, vaccines, and prescription drugs are legal and why homeopathic medicine is not promoted. They keep people in a constant state of enough sedation to ensure they keep towing the line. We don't want people realizing what is going on in the world. As long as they are using their caffeine fix to keep them motivated to do a good job at work and then using alcohol in the evening and weekends to take away the pain of living an unfulfilled and emotionally dead life, they will keep making money for those people in power whilst they get busy with running the world. It's just the way it is and you can't change it!" Darby declared.

"We'll see about that," Wedmore replied. "How many of these families are in these positions of power?"

"No-one knows for certain, but rumour has it there is a council of thirteen families," Darby replied.

"How do we find out who these families are?" Wedmore asked.

"It's quite simple, really. Just follow the major money. Find the people who are profiting from everything being the way it is and you'll know who is in charge. They have significant influence, so it's likely you will be going up against military powers and serious resistance," Darby explained.

"I'm not afraid of that. I am more afraid of living with myself if I don't do something. I can either be a part of the problem by doing nothing, or a part of the solution by doing something about it and I choose to do something about it," Wedmore replied.

He was confident that his military reputation was strong enough to enable other military personnel to see that he was speaking the truth. He could create a following and an army to remove the evil in power and restore balance and harmony to the world. The question was how to bring about a world-shift when he was going up against the strongest military influences in the world. He recalled Sana's earlier comment when she said, *'If you kill a killer, the number of killers in the world remains the same.'* Even though he had participated in enough killing in the name of national servitude, he realized how wrong this was and he was determined to bring this change without further bloodshed. Exactly how remained a mystery, but he had faith in his heart that the journey would unfold perfectly as long as it resonated with his heart and soul.

Chapter 17

The Plan

LOCATION: RAF Westgate, Kent, England
DATE: 2ⁿᵈ May
WEATHER: Overcast with sunny spells

Wedmore looked at his team. There was no doubt that they faced a difficult task, but one that was worth at least striving for. He broke off the conversation with Darby and walked away in quiet reflection. Springbok and Hitler let go of Darby's arms and keenly watched Wedmore with anticipation, wondering what his next move would be. Silence fell. Wedmore stood with his back to the group, and breathed deeply. Sana walked over to him and waited patiently as he collected himself. He turned to look at her.

"You're channelling, aren't you?" she said with a smile.

"I'm doing my best," he replied with a smile. *"I want to be clear on the next steps as I can see a bloody revolution happening if we're not careful. The people of this world deserve to know what is happening to them and the evil people must be removed from power and replaced with those who are pure of heart. Yet, I fear when they are told the truth, there will be anger, upset, and a cry for the heads of these people if we're not careful or even worse, total apathy. That's how I see it anyway. What do you think?"* he asked Sana.

"I think you're right, Jay. You know what the world needs and you have the Good Lord as your guide here. And me of course!" she said with a teasing smile as her eyes lit up to break the heavy mood.

James looked at her with a captivated heart that brought him back into the heartfelt mood of love and appreciation for life, rather than being caught up with the thoughts of injustice running through his mind. He placed his hand on his heart and took another deep breath, slowly releasing his tension to calm his mind and bring him back to centre so he could access Infinite Intelligence.

Wedmore opened his eyes and turned to face his colleagues with a smile. He chose to observe Marston's and Darby's actions from a place of empathy due to their personal limitations. He felt sympathy for them being in such a position of personal anguish that they would choose to sacrifice their souls in exchange for money and power that they mistakenly thought would give them freedom from their internal suffering and emptiness. He could see how emotionally dead they were how they missed the vital essence that would make them a compassionate and loving human towards their fellow brethren. He looked at the chauffeurs and walked towards them. As he approached them, he asked, *"What do you think of your bosses now? Do you still wish to remain in service to them?"*

Both men shook their heads as they realized they had been duped.

Wedmore looked at them with compassion before continuing, *"Don't be hard on yourselves. Part of what is going on here is the power of deception. Have you ever heard of the saying 'repeat a lie long enough and it becomes the truth?' That is exactly what is happening here and there is nothing of value for you in continuing to serve these vagabonds. Will you join us in our quest to restore peace, love, and generosity to the world?"*

Both men gave their word to join the quest and then Wedmore took his knife and cut the men free. He made peace with them for the rough treatment they had received and hoped it would be forgiven in light of the bigger picture. The two chauffeurs approached their respective bosses and resigned by slapping them across their faces and looking at them with disgust.

Wedmore arranged for the chauffeurs to take Marston and Darby to his friend's floating prison to be held there until further notice. He sent Springbok and Gringo to ensure they arrived safely, and then agreed a rendezvous following the drop off.

Once the limousines had departed, the remaining Black Widows, Rosehill, and Sana considered their next move. Wedmore thanked Rosehill for arranging the meeting. Though the situation was clearer, there was still a substantial uphill battle ahead of them to bring change to the world and the unknown quantity of these powerful families was still illusive. Hitler approached the hanger and drove the Land Rover out where he prepared the finest strength military brew on his billy-stove for them. As the group chinked their battered metal mugs together, the conversation started to flow again.

"*Can you believe those fuckers?*" Hitler asked the group. "*Quite unbelievable they would behave that way.*"

"*Unfortunately, it's who they are and they are not alone,*" Rosehill replied. "*We have some understanding of how they think and who they are, but it's not over by a long way. When word gets round that those two have gone missing, those higher up the pyramid will start to get a little nervous and will be more guarded. Our approach will no longer be a surprise and I fear we will have people pursuing us.*"

"*I've been thinking about this,*" Wedmore replied, "*and the only way I can think to deal with this situation is to recruit as* many military personnel as we can to join our cause and use significant brute force to overthrow the council of thirteen families. I do feel a little out of my depth and would welcome suggestions from you all. What would you suggest?"

Sana smiled at James and it was clear from the look in her eyes she was about to provide some more pearls of wisdom. "Do you know the difference between power and force, Jay?"

"I thought they were the same thing," he replied.

"Most people assume they are the same, yet they are quite different. Force carries very low frequency energy so massive amounts of energy are needed to get anything done. Power is effortless and mighty in its approach. You can guess which one is Godly in nature. Force is man-made, whereas nature carries infinite power."

"Ok, so what are you suggesting? We should be 'powerful' in our approach? How do we get more power and how does it compare to the power the wealthy have?

"With pleasure, Jay. A great book was released many years ago by Dr David Hawkins where he reviewed the energetic principles at play in this world. He found that everything in life carried an energetic signature. That's not new news to most people, as they understand what Einstein said about everything being energy. However, it goes deeper than that. He found that energy can be calibrated on a scale related to consciousness and this scale has a tipping point between force, which is low frequency, and power, which is high frequency. When people calibrate at a higher frequency of power, they can achieve far more in the world through consciously affecting others than those calibrating at a frequency of force."

"To give you an example, Ghandi calibrated at a high frequency of power and he was able to stand alone in front of the entire British army and change the course of history by bringing independence to India. He did this without violence or using force of any kind, as he was one person standing for a great cause against injustice. There is no reason why we cannot do the same."

Wedmore reflected for a moment before continuing. *"As much as I don't like my fear to get the better of me, we're a small group of people facing potentially the biggest armies of the world and I'm doubting that the power of our stand will be strong enough."*

"I don't mean to interrupt your flow, boss," Kamali said, *"but knowing what I know now, I would rather die standing alone for something than live and go along with a lie. You said so earlier that living with yourself if you didn't make a stand would be unbearable and we can't let that happen. I believe we are taking bold steps and the more we do this, our courage will grow. They want us to keep us fearful so we don't take action against them when the reality is they are constantly in fear of an uprising from those who realise they have been enslaved by their actions. There is nothing to fear; death is only the start of something more amazing. I say we go for it!"*

The rest of the group nodded in agreement. Rosehill was next to add his thoughts.

"I don't think you quite realize the impact of making those two disappear. It will be substantial and we need to consider that. Questions will be asked of their whereabouts within the next 24 hours and as their chauffeurs and I will have also disappeared, people will start looking. They associate with some of the most powerful people in the world. Be clear, this will have significant repercussions."

Wedmore looked Rosehill square in the eye and said, *"Fuck 'em! Fuck 'em all! We will be victorious. Let's keep our minds and hearts clear and we will come out on top. I am no longer afraid. We will use their weapon of fear against them. Those that use fear are always fearful. We have nothing to fear from their actions. We will be victorious!"* He clenched his right fist and pounded his chest above his heart. He had started to believe in himself, and knew that the mission ahead of his team was the most powerful thing in the world.

The team evacuated the airfield and returned to Wedmore's home to formulate the next part of the battle plan. As the team sat around his dining table with a strong cup of tea in hand, they talked through how to bring this mission to fruition.

Their main concern was how to quickly build a global army to wrestle power from the elite and their pyramid of control. Rosehill made the point that it was better to turn the tables with the current global military resources in place by bringing them on side, rather than trying to recruit and train new freedom fighters to join their cause, which would take a very long time.

Wedmore raised the question of how it would be possible to turn the armies of the western world around to challenge their own governments and their focused discussion covered this topic until Hitler had a brainwave and proposed a possible solution.

"Have you guys ever heard of SOFEX, the Special Operations Forces Exhibition?" Hitler asked. Everyone except Rosehill shook their heads.

"It's basically a huge international weapons and heavy arms trade fair that is held in the Middle East. All the different nations that are effectively at war with one another congregate to sell one another weapons that they will then later use on each other! It's mind-blowingly crazy madness, but that aside, about 300 generals that lead the armies of the world attend every year,

so it could be a good opportunity for us to address them all and get them on side."

"How exactly do you know about this, Hitler?" Kamali asked.

"Where do you think I get all my little gadgets that we carry on our missions from?" he said with a wry smile and a wink. "I have a powerful friend who gets me access to these sorts of things and I can pick up the most amazing pieces of technology. You're supposed to be registered with the authorities, but when you cross the right palms with silver, and I literally mean silver, then access to the event is guaranteed. We should go and recruit a whole bunch of people to our cause. It's the quickest way I know how to access them all in one place."

"How would we address them all?" Wedmore asked.

"There are various speeches given where every general is in attendance. We could storm one of the main events and address everyone there. It's a closed room and despite all the weaponry present, paradoxically because of the type of people there, it actually has little security, so we will be able to take it very easily. If we could bring 10 or so soldiers to our team, the task will be more straightforward, I think," Hitler replied.

"I like your thinking! It's something we can definitely make happen. When is this fair on?" Wedmore asked.

"Coincidentally, it happens in a week, so just enough time for us to make plans and get over there. I can ensure we have clearance to fly over there and enter the event. I'll even come with you and join the ranks under your leadership, Wedmore. I can see where you are going with this and I'd like to play my part," Rosehill said.

"This is a good plan," Sana said. "All I ask is that you respect the rules of no more bloodshed and respect Mother Earth in all that you do. We have no way of knowing how this will all play *out, but know that words and ideas can change the world. It doesn't have to come down to who has the most fire power or military strength."*

Wedmore stood up and inhaled deeply before linking hands with the people either side of him and inviting everyone present to do the same. The congregation rose to their feet other. Wedmore invited them all to breathe deeply in unison with him. As they did so, the energy within the room became calm, clear, and focused.

The collective mind, heart, and soul of the room became elevated and aligned with the highest good. They came together as a team to serve. The mission ahead became clearer and the outcome even more so as they took each deep breath in unison. The vision of peace, harmony, and tranquillity was so real in their minds, it was as though it had already happened. Smiles spread across the faces of everyone present as their hearts filled with joy, peace, love, and acceptance.

Chapter 18

A Crack in the Matrix

LOCATION: SOFEX Exhibition, Al Hizam al Daeri St. 437, Amman Province, Jordan.
DATE: 9th May
WEATHER: Scorching hot sunshine

The plane touched down with a screech of the wheels against the runway in the heat of the midday sun. As the Black Widows looked out the windows, they could see miles of golden sand dunes in every direction, save for the narrow strip of runway and the adjacent prefabricated metal buildings that had been erected especially to serve the world's biggest weapons fair. Rosehill had managed to arrange access into the event through some old contacts who were keen to return one or two of the favours he had granted them over the years.

The group disembarked in civilian clothes, sporting social media press passes on their lapels. They entered the weapons fair with keen anticipation. Their plan was colossal, as they were effectively going to take the most powerful military men and women in the world captive, not just as individuals, but because of the people they led and the countries they served. Their only hope was to appeal to their humanity, compassion, and consciousness, which hardened war veterans were not exactly known for.

The veterans at the conference had lived, breathed, and slept war for thirty or more years, so it was their distinct model of the world. They knew no different and could not see any wrong in their actions. In a perverse way, 'keeping the peace' involved using a bigger stick than the next guy to beat them into submission and get what they wanted. The harsh reality was that convincing those who knew only of death and was definitely going to be an uphill battle. Not only would it directly challenge the way these people observed the world, it would challenge their very identity, which is closely linked to their ego, and therefore something they were likely to defend to the death.

Prior to their arrival at the weapons fair, Wedmore had spoken in great confidence to an old Australian general friend of his, John Wright, who he knew would be an ally. Wright had served his country for many years like his father before him. As a child, all Wright knew was moving from military camp to military camp around the country and sometimes internationally, with his father who glorified the need to 'fight fire with fire' and take 'an eye for an eye'.

Wright entered the military with high hopes of changing the system so that the military were used more for peacekeeping activities rather than serving warlords and pillaging other countries for their resources. Twenty-five years of active military service later and he was starting to bring about some changes that caused some ripples in the current military establishment. Wedmore knew that Wright was the man to help bring massive changes to the system as Wright had often confided in him about the wrongdoings that were happening all over the world.

Wright had agreed to assist Wedmore with his plan and brought over fifty of his top soldiers from Australia to the exhibition under the cover of a top-secret mission. Quite how

Wright had managed to organise this at the expense of the Australian military was not a question Wedmore wanted to ask, but if anyone could do it, he knew Wright could. He just hoped that fifty soldiers and the Black Widows would be enough to gain control of the military exhibition and give them enough time to talk with the generals before things got out of hand.

Despite their casual appearance, the six masculine men found it difficult to relax enough to play the roles of press agents who would be writing articles about the weapons on display as they walked through the exhibition. They knew what most of the weapons were and what they did, and it wasn't pleasant. Before they had gone through their journey towards consciousness, they would have been like kids in a sweet shop, spoilt for choice as to which weapon of death and destruction they would next like to wield on their unsuspecting enemy. Now they knew better, they couldn't help but wince at the inventive ways people had created to take the life of another human being.

Personal close quarter combat was becoming more and more removed, so the latest in military grade weaponry was a lot like playing the latest war-based computer game. Soldiers would soon sit behind computer screens and control drones that would do their bidding for them. Kamali commented on how this would particularly affect a future soldier's psyche, as they would be responsible for taking the life of another without actually feeling anything because they would be physically and emotionally removed from the situation. He thought this would have the same impact as killing a digital character in a computer game. It would only be later on in life when their conscience caught up with them and they realised the full impact of what they had done, that would lead to serious mental health and post-traumatic stress disorder problems. Not that it would matter to the military as the operatives were considered disposable and replaceable by keen youngsters who had grown up killing people on computer games and wanted to be paid for it in adulthood.

What also struck them as very odd was that they knew military and economic sanctions were in place between certain countries such as the USA and South Korea. However, at this particular event, South Korea was being offered substantial financial incentives to acquire their military arsenal from US manufacturers! Moreover, if a particular product was deemed too brutal to be sold to a US enemy, a country could buy the main component, such as a helicopter, from the US using their financial initiatives, and then acquire the other component, like a rocket launcher, from a country that didn't have an embargo against them for that particular weapon. It was a crazy system where a country could sell another the weapons they needed to use against them in an act of war! It occurred to everyone present that war was now about money rather than what was morally right or wrong. They couldn't believe they had laid their lives on the line so many times to support this orchestrated madness!

A thought raced through Wedmore's mind; if war was about nothing more than money, why would the people who were in power, and who could print all the money they wanted, still want war? Could it be because there really were people in the world that wanted to cause terrorist attacks on their own country for no other reason than to enjoy witnessing death and destruction? Or was it really all about those in positions of power wanting more and more power and purposefully enslaving others for their own kicks? Or could it be that they were fighting on behalf of gold, oil, and drugs? What did Darby say about the energies of pain and suffering feeding their master? Either way, he felt the journey they were on would reveal a huge amount of truth as the Matrix reality around them began to crumble.

As the Black Widows continued to walk around the exhibition, they came across more and more horrific weapons, which only served to fan the flames of the mission burning deep within them. Wedmore pulled his cell phone out to call General John Wright. They arranged to meet at one of the military hostage houses built into a recess surrounded by sand dunes, used to demonstrate hostage rescue operations and show off the latest specialist equipment for such tasks. It was also the quietest part of the exhibition and would allow them space to meet and discuss tactics before the critical conference in three hours.

It had been a while since Wright and Wedmore had seen one another. Wright was a tall, muscular black man who was now in his fifties. He had the broadest smile across his face the moment he saw Wedmore. His voice was deep and commanding, yet it carried an air of comforting reassurance, letting everyone knew they were safe in his presence. Wedmore introduced Wright to his comrades in turn and Sana whom Wright was particularly pleased to see after Wedmore had mentioned the role she played in their mission so far.

"So here we are then. The dream team!" Wright said with a smile and jovial laugh.

"We sure are!" Wedmore said. *"It's great to see you again, John. It's been too long! Thank you for agreeing to help us in our mission and for bringing your team. I think we are going to create one hell of a shit storm, but seeing the things I am seeing here, this is long overdue!"*

"It's a pleasure, my friend," Wright replied as he placed a reassuring hand on Wedmore's shoulder. *"You are right that this is long overdue and this madness must end. It is totally in line with the many years I have been campaigning for this, which has fallen on deaf ears. I have every faith in you pulling this one off and bringing peace and harmony to the world. It's*

ballsy but I like it! So, what is it you want us to actually do?" Wright asked.

"At 1500 hours, there is a conference being held in the main exhibition hall that all the generals are required to attend. Our plan is to hold them in the room, tell them what is really going on, and help them come to their senses. Allow them to see the wood for the trees, as it were. Sometimes people are too close to the situation to realise what they are doing wrong. I hope we can show them what is happening and enlist their support in correcting some of the wrongs that have been done to many millions of people around the world. After all, if their own children were facing their consequences, I'm sure they would have something to say about it!

"What we need from you and your men is to be in the room for additional support in the crowd so you can second what I will say and I need your team to keep the doors locked and guarded so no-one can leave and no-one can enter. We won't open the doors until we have agreement from the majority of people in the room to bring about change in the world. It might get heavy in there, so we need to be prepared. Think you can handle it?" Wedmore asked.

"James, if there is one thing I know is that all these generals are used to remaining calm under pressure. They will act as though they aren't scared, but it will have been many years since they were last faced with a front line situation like this, so they will be easy enough to gain consent from. You won't have a lot of time to win them over though, and more than likely some of them will be armed, so you are risking being shot for your actions. Are you prepared for that?" Wright said.

"Fuck it, I am!" Wedmore replied with a smile. "When will we ever get a chance to take advantage of an opportunity like this again?"

"Well, it won't come to this, I'm sure. I have faith in what will be and in God's will. I have to say, James, this plan is genius so let us pray that it will succeed. My men are on standby ready for my orders. It's a simple enough mission. They will cover the perimeter of the conference room and some will be armed inside the room. We will have snipers further away monitoring the situation. Force should not be necessary so let's pray this situation works out well. You're a good man, James. I'm proud of you. Good Luck!"

The two men embraced again and Wright walked off to assemble his team for action. Wedmore turned to his team with a smile and a sense of relief that he had some backup.

"Looks like it's show time, team! Biggest game of our lives so far so let's make it count!" Wedmore said with a smile.

"We're right with you, boss," Gringo replied with a cheeky smile. *"I can't wait to see their faces when they realise what's happening."*

Kamali was keen to go over the finer details of the situation. *"So, while you are talking to the generals present, what exactly will we do?"* he asked.

"I need you guys to be my eyes and ears in the crowd and around the room to suppress any possible explosive situations in the audience. I will speak about everything we know so far and enlist their help in turning the situation around on a global level. Just remember that we are effectively making people in high-ranking positions of power redundant and challenging everything their entire lives have stood for. I can feel that there will be some resistance to the truth, but for the truth to be effective, it must pierce their hearts like an arrow. Chances are, we might end up planting seeds today that will germinate in their minds over the coming weeks and months. They will not have heard what we have to say before so we can expect

resistance. The majority of these people believe that what they are doing is for good rather than evil and this is what I feel will bring the biggest resistance when they realise they are being played by a much more elaborate system," Wedmore said.

Sana walked up to Wedmore and gently squeezed his left arm, offering comfort in his biggest hour. As they looked into each other's eyes, Wedmore felt a sense of calmness and he knew he could conquer the world with her by his side.

She pulled him closer and whispered, *"I believe in you."*

She always knew just what to say at the right moment. Subconsciously, Wedmore's posture changed as he stood taller and his chest began to swell with pride and self-belief. This woman lit his heart up in a way that he had never known before.

Wedmore invited his team to stack their hands on top of his in unison. As they did so, he said; *"For Humanity,"* which the team repeated as they raised their stacked hands upwards in celebration.

The next few hours passed without event as the team performed reconnaissance in and around the conference building. The Black Widows observed a number of high-ranking military officials being plied with champagne and nibbles in an effort to get them to open their large chequebooks and spend millions of dollars on more weapons of mass destruction. The atmosphere was surprisingly cheery, which was an interesting contrast to the main reason why everyone was there in the first place. The team witnessed generals from countries involved in bitter conflict greeting one another warmly and drinking with them. It really did become clear how the Black Widows, and other soldiers just like them, were nothing more than pawns in a rich man's game of real life chess; risking their lives so rich, bored people could play 'soldiers and armies' and move wealth from one country to another.

Humanity and the very essence of the soul didn't matter to them and it certainly wasn't anywhere near the forefront of their mind when they made the decision to go to war with another country. Wedmore thought of the personal emotional pain and distress someone must be in to issue orders for war knowing that it would result in the deaths of thousands of people. The weight of losing just one person from a team was a huge emotional burden to carry, so being responsible for the loss of many lives must be intolerable. How could politicians, or more particularly, those that controlled the politicians, issue such orders? How could they be so emotionally detached from the situation? He knew what it was like trying to sleep when the cost of battle weighed on his conscious mind after he tried to emotionally suppress it.

The fact remained that they were detached from the situation for one reason only: they weren't on the front line carrying out the orders themselves. They never had to witness the horror of holding the blood-soaked body of a trusted and loved colleague as their life slipped away. They didn't know what is was like to patrol the streets of a city that had just undergone airstrikes which were now filled with the bodies of innocent men, women, and children rotting in the heat of the midday sun. They didn't have to deal with the nightmares that followed; they just took their money and moved on, leaving others to pick up the pieces. Humanity truly was living in the dark ages.

Wedmore brought his train of thought back to the present mission as they approached the conference building. He received a wink from Wright who was exiting the building as they entered. He knew this meant everything was in place and they could relax. The room was buzzing with people milling around, all ready for the main event. At the front of the room was a large stage complete with rostrum and seating for an audience of 350 people. Pretty ladies in black silk dresses served champagne to the generals who were laughing and joking with one another whilst they waited for the conference to begin. Press officials were also part of the congregation, eager to report on the main speech being delivered today by top weapons expert Ted Black on 'The Future of the Weapons Industry'. It promised to be an exciting event. They were blissfully unaware of what lay in store for them.

The team split up and mingled with the crowd, doing their best to ensure they were inconspicuous by their actions. They observed all parties present to ensure the room was devoid of any red flags that might otherwise jeopardise the mission. Things seemed to be in order, but only when the doors were locked and Wedmore stormed the stage would the situation potentially begin to change. Wedmore and Sana sat in the front row nearest the stage and his team positioned themselves at the four corners of the room as the Master of Ceremonies announced that the conference would be starting in five minutes. Wedmore turned around to witness two pairs of heavily armed guards closing and locking the double doors at the rear of the building as four more guards took positions towards the middle and front of the room. He was certain these were Wright's men who were armed with machine guns and handguns. No one in the room batted an eyelid. The Master of Ceremonies invited everyone to take their seats. As the chatter within the room died down, Sana reached across and squeezed Wedmore's hand. His heart started beating rapidly as he felt this was one opportunity to make a huge step forward with their mission. If the outcome of a person's life came down to a few turning points in certain moments, this was definitely one of them.

"Ladies and gentlemen, welcome to the SOFEX exhibition," announced the Master of Ceremonies. *"We are very grateful to*

have you here with us in celebration of this amazing time in history! We have an incredible speaker here with us today, so please show your appreciation and welcome Mr Ted Black to the stage!"

The audience erupted in a round of applause as a well dressed, fit-looking man scurried to the stage with a big smile on his face. He thanked the audience for their warm welcome as he briefly arranged some paperwork on the rostrum. There was a large screen on either side of him, announcing his name and the title of his speech.

Black continued to tell the audience how excited he was to be there and how he was looking forward to detailing the latest breakthroughs in weapons science and how he was sure that everyone present would benefit from what he had to say. New technology was making it even simpler to keep an eye on the enemy and to launch a rapid missile strike from greater and greater distances. In line with Rosehill's previous comments made in the privacy of his office, Ted Black stated that they now had patented anti-gravity technology that essentially made rockets much lighter, therefore distorting the traditional model of physics and allowing them to travel at such a speed that they effectively arrived before the enemy even saw them coming!

The audience were seemingly impressed as ripples of whispers filtered around the room. No one seemed to care that these weapons were ultimately for one thing: to end life.

Black was evidently pleased with himself as he turned to his audience with a big smile and announced the fastest and most destructive missile yet: the ZX310b that had a range of over 500 miles and a blast radius of one mile. A video series of the ZX310b flashed up on the screens showing the missile in action as it flew across a desert and crashed into mountains causing significant damage while its operator was sitting peacefully behind a computer monitor with keyboard and joystick in hand guiding the missile to its destination. The audience wowed at the footage as though they were watching the latest Hollywood blockbuster on the big screen.

Wedmore stood and approached the stage. The smile left Black's face and was replaced with confusion as he saw Wedmore coming with a vexed look. He started to edge away from the platform as the audience watched with awe. Kamali also stood up and walked towards the stage as Black stepped backwards towards him. Kamali wrapped his arms around Black's chest from behind, picked him up, and deposited him on the chair he had just left, urging him to be quiet.

Wedmore walked across the stage to the rostrum, whilst Kamali pulled a handgun from his holster and pointed it in the direction of a now terrified Ted Black. Kamali watched with anticipation as Wedmore pulled off his shirt, revealing his muscular physique clad in a tight fitting white vest and his silenced dog collars glinting slightly in the spotlight of the stage. He placed the scrunched up shirt on the podium before pulling his Bowie knife out and stabbing it into Black's presentation papers and the small touch screen monitor controlling the presentation on the big screens. The screens flickered slightly before going out.

"Enough!" Wedmore shouted in a deep voice that silenced the audience immediately. "*All I have heard so far is everyone's support for yet another weapon aimed at causing death and destruction on this planet and you are all offering your support for it! Who would do that? Only those who have a vested interest in taking the lives of others, that's who! Is that you?*" Wedmore scanned his audience with fierce intensity. They knew he meant business.

"*Who are you?*" a voice asked from the rear of the room. "*Some kind of activist?*"

Ripples of laughter filled the room.

Wedmore stood strong and confident. He glared at the comedian before walking back to the podium to grab his knife. The audience immediately fell silent again. Wedmore watched as the colour drained from the comedian's face.

"I'll tell you who I am. I am part of an off-the-record government organisation that has been doing their dirty work for many years. Hired assassins, if you will. I speak from direct experience when I tell you that I have been involved in conflict my entire life, but this is no longer acceptable. I am sure it has been many years since most of you have seen the front lines of conflict and you are all well versed at receiving orders from people in a position of power who tell you where and when to send the troops you are in command of."

"You all know from personal experience that the military model requires initially breaking down subjects so they are incapable of thinking for themselves and will happily follow orders without questioning them, even though they know in their rational mind that taking the life of another is against everything their soul stands for. Soldiers are sent into battle as dispensable pawns and told to face the enemy bravely whilst you high-ranking military officials, and those who give you your orders, sit in your ivory towers immune from the dangers the men on the ground are facing. You sell out on the fact that because you went through it, it's perfectly acceptable for someone else to go through it to rise through the ranks of the military. You conveniently forget the fact that comrades have fallen over the many years of your rise to power, families have been destroyed, and many, many innocent lives lost."

"What was it all for? Democracy? Weapons of mass destruction? Freedom? All bullshit, that's what it was for! You lost sight of the fact that being capable of taking military action means you should also be capable of not taking military action unless your

own country is under attack. Invading another country does not constitute defending your own country; its provocation and we deserve everything we get when we try and meddle with other countries without fully understanding how they operate. We have all been lied to for too many years and lost sight of the truth in the process. It's time we stood up for what's morally right and stop doing the bidding for others who do not care about us or the lives of the fallen. It's time to go back to the principles of honour, morality, dignity, and respect."

A balding Englishman in his fifties stood up, his face red with rage as he unleashed his anger and frustration towards Wedmore. "How dare you speak this way! As a man of the military, you have clearly forgotten your code, your honour, and everything you stand for. You should know better! I am outraged at your outburst!"

"Please tell me that I am wrong! Please tell me where I am wrong in my assumptions of how we are all dealing with the modern age of war? We have drawn fictitious boundaries and borders around our countries and created 'them-and-us' scenarios where we freely slaughter people seemingly unlike us. There is no respect or appreciation for the differences of others or for humanity any more. We are acting on the whims of the wealthy who have us do their bidding for them and who don't give a fuck about our lives or who they kill, maim, or injure in the process."

"If we were really about freedom, justice, and democracy, we would be turning our attention to the people who have conceived this Matrix-like web of lies that we live in and who have deceived us along. Those people who control the media and who tell us all who to hate and who we should justify a war with this week! Those people who go in after a country has been destroyed to pillage their precious resources and take them as their own. Those people who claim to be in support of the war on drugs, yet smuggle the same drugs into their own country through the back door with the support of their friends in positions of power around the world."

"Its utter hypocrisy! Everyone is being bought with money and they are selling their morals and souls for cash. The weak will and scarcity mentality of most people means they are easily swayed with cash, and those who print the money have an abundance of it, whereas the rest of the world does not. It's easy to manipulate people with this system. People's lives become subservient to what is essentially just dead trees with ink on them! How did we come to this? The problem with receiving money in this way is akin to taking heroin. It feels great at first but it destroys your life and soul in the long term. Take a step back and look at yourselves and you will see what I mean. What hard evidence did you ever receive to justify issuing orders to take the lives of soldiers in another country?"

Murmurs went around the room as the generals present realised they never once received first-hand evidence to justify a battle with another country. It was always done on somebody else's say-so. They felt foolish for never questioning their orders.

"I hate to be the one to tell you this, but you all have the blood of countless lives on your hands and your conscience!" Wedmore continued.

At this point, the agitated audience member stood on top his chair and screamed, *"This is an outrage! I order you to stop this outburst immediately!"*

Sana took to her feet and walked over to the stage to join her man in unity and solidarity. The room quietened down in her presence. She stood silent for a moment, leaving the audience intrigued as to what was about to happen. Then, she spoke softly with the air of Divine femininity.

"As a woman who has experienced first-hand the pain and heartache that mindless wars are creating in this world, I can tell you that Jay is right. There is too much mindless killing and not enough moral honouring of your duty. I believe you are all good people and you wish to do the right thing. However, you have been manipulated in the line of duty to go against the very things that your spirit stands for. Millions of men, women, and children across the globe have suffered as a result of war and conflict. Most of this was nothing to do with them, but was a result of two politicians or leaders of different countries having a difference of opinion. I won't be so cynical as to say war is good for business, as that's another conversation. Yet, look at the cost of those differences of opinion. Look at the loss of lives. Look at the displacement of people from their homes. How would you feel if you were on the receiving end of this punishment for crimes you didn't commit?"

The agitated audience member once again spoke up in anger. *"Be quiet! You have no idea what you are talking about! You're not even part of the military!"* he exclaimed.

Sana stood firm on the platform and closed her eyes as she breathed deeply. She raised both hands up into the air and then pushed her hands down towards the ground whilst breathing out hard. The lighting in the room started flickering, causing a little unrest in the audience. Sana continued her deep breathing whilst chanting an ancient Shamanic ritual.

Less than a minute later, the audience members started to wail and ball their eyes out, whilst some began rolling around on the floor in intense pain. These hardened military generals were instantly turned into emotional wrecks as their spirits became interlocked with the tortured souls of those people who had died as a result of their actions and instructions. The temperature in the room plummeted as an icy-cold atmosphere engulfed everyone. The generals continued to writhe in agony.

They were experiencing first-hand what it was like to go through losing the most precious gift God had granted humankind. The impact on them was huge; some had been responsible for giving orders to their troops that had resulted in the loss of tens of thousands of lives and they felt this burden at the deepest emotional level possible.

Then came the deafening screams and cries for help, mixed with sobbing and gasping as the men cried their hearts out at the torture they were now experiencing. They could no longer hide from their actions; they were now living the consequences of them.

Sana allowed this to continue for several minutes, as she believed it was the only way to make these generals realise what they were doing was wrong. Experiencing this suffering would lead to a complete transformation of their thinking and actions from this moment forth. The Black Widows looked on in amazement as Sana continued to work her magic. Wedmore was particularly dumbfounded by the abilities of this woman whom he deeply loved, but did not yet truly know.

Suddenly, Sana clapped her hands together and opened her eyes. The lighting returned to normal and the temperature was instantly restored. Around the room, military generals were wiping streams of tears from their faces as they picked themselves up off the floor. Their bloodshot, puffy eyes accentuated the look of grief and sorrow on their faces. Their postures, which were usually the embodiment of military stiffness and pride, were crumpled and bent as they now carried the huge emotional burdens from their experience. They looked up at this delicate woman with wide-eyed bewilderment, looking for forgiveness and a quick fix to escape the pain they had just endured. Sana read their mood beautifully.

"It is not me you must seek forgiveness from, nor can I offer it to you. You have already made the decisions that have given

you the burdens you now must carry. I have merely given you an insight into the consequences of your actions. The good news is you now have the opportunity to correct the error of your ways. In some ways, it is not your fault, as you acted in good faith. In other ways, you have acted negligently without questioning what is right and good. You have been unconscious in following orders rather than honouring your original duty to protect humanity from tyranny and oppressors. This is the burden you must now bear. If you wish to do right by your previous actions and gain redemption, then we ask that you join us in ridding the world of those who profit from war and who want continued slavery, bloodshed, and conflict in this realm."

"We are going to create heaven on earth, but we must first overthrow those who operate in the shadows and control the governments of the world. We cannot allow the current system to continue to spread fear and hatred amongst the people of the world for their own gains. We are going to spread a message of love, unity, and humanity. So my question is, are you with us?" Sana invited her audience to respond.

Amongst the noise of sobbing and sniffing came a united affirmative response that they would join the mission. They looked to Wedmore and Sana to be their leaders in the way children look to their parents to be led with love and compassion.

Sana continued, "Thank you. Remember, you are free to make any decision you choose, but you are not free of the consequences of those decisions. You can honour your word from this point onward and join us in the mission, or you can retract your agreement once this moment is over. However, the feelings of grief and sorrow will still remain as your burden to carry, so choose wisely. Either decision is fine with us, but remember this; it is not us you will have to justify your actions to. The final *judgement lies in God's hands who is far more powerful than we are. The choice is yours."*

"So, what is the next step?" the formerly agitated audience member asked.

Wedmore stepped in to offer some guidance. *"We are going to launch a worldwide strategy to relieve the current governments of the world of their power. Military coups, if you will. We need to target the governments that are currently at war with other countries and remove them from power. We will imprison the government members initially and allow you fine gentlemen to appoint appropriate representatives to assist you in running the administration of these countries."*

"How will we know who these 'appropriate representatives' are?" another audience member asked.

"Listen to your heart. I know that might sound absurd to you if you've spent your whole life using your head, but trust me on this one. Send them love from your heart when they are with you and monitor what happens. You'll know. It will either be a good feeling or one of indifference. We trust you to do the right thing."

"The next step will be to bring the troops currently operating in foreign lands home and issue an immediate apology to the countries we were in conflict with. We will also write off all debts owed to our respective countries by foreign lands as part of the apology and offer as much support as we can to right the wrongs we have caused. We will listen with compassion to the positions of other countries rather than coming from judgement and ego just because they appear to be different from us. No further acts of war will be tolerated and international treaties preventing war will be ratified as soon as possible."

"Aren't we likely to bankrupt the global economy if we do all this?" an American general at the back of the room asked.

"Most of the loans owed are paper money or numbers on a computer screen. They're not real! Neither is the illusion of bankrupting the global economy. People will always survive even if money as we know it today disappears. It's like the caterpillar being surrounded by a chrysalis; it feels as if the world has ended as it is cloaked in darkness and its old self dies. This is a necessary step to take in order to transform into a beautiful butterfly." Wedmore said as he borrowed Sana's analogy in an attempt to lift the mood.

"The important thing is that we take these necessary steps to stop the current system and stop the senseless killing. As we do this, we will quickly find out who is operating in positions of power and pulling the strings of the current world governments. We will soon flush these people out to face the consequences of their actions. There will be big changes and a lot of upset before the calmness of heaven on earth can exist."

"I also suggest that we eventually abolish all boundaries between countries so there is nothing for us to defend, so people can come and go as they please, and there is nothing for another to conquer. There should be no division of people because we are all global citizens of Mother Earth. We will teach children to be loving and supportive of one another and how to raise their level of consciousness through meditation whilst rebuilding the communities that have been broken down through modern living. Peace and harmony will be the order of the day, not division and separation," Wedmore said.

"This sounds like an excellent plan! I am with you!" said the formerly agitated audience member who stood up to show unity to the cause. *"Who is with me?"* he shouted with his fist raised in the air.

The audience collectively jumped up with excited cheers and roars. They had an opportunity to redeem themselves and they were not going to miss it. Smiles spread across the faces of the

Black Widows and Sana as they realised they had achieved the impossible; they had just recruited the top military leaders to fight for their cause and victory had now just taken a huge leap forward.

"I am pleased to hear it, my friends, and I am sorry that you had to endure such pain in order to see the light. I hope in the fullness of time, you will forgive me for what I put you through. Growth, particularly spiritual growth, does not come without some pain," Sana smiled. *"Keep in mind that the pain you just experienced will be a useful guide from this point forward. Listen to your body as you go about your tasks. If you feel good, you're on the right track. If you get off the right path, the unpleasant feelings will return, so tune in and listen to yourself."*

"I would like to request that you all give me your contact details so that we can co-ordinate our approach in unison. I will establish an international radio frequency to broadcast our movements so this becomes a co-ordinated approach. I also want you to keep it quiet until 48-72 hours prior to us implementing our plan. At that point, you must bring your troops back home immediately and prepare for action. I must warn you that you will no doubt face some resistance from people around you and, at some point, you will be disobeying direct orders that will put your careers in jeopardy. For this, I salute you and thank you for your commitment to the cause. Know that your fellow brothers in arms have your back and if you face any resistance, you must contact us immediately and we will come to your aid," Wedmore said.

The room erupted in supportive cheers as the crowd saluted Wedmore. Their newfound comrades rushed forward to speak privately with Wedmore and Sana about how they would be honoured to support the mission. Contact details were exchanged and the generals emerged from the room with a sense of integrity partly restored in their hearts.

Sana hugged Wedmore. Her heart was bursting with happiness in celebration of a significant win for their cause.

Chapter 19

The Pendulum

LOCATION: Kent, England
DATE: 12th May
WEATHER: Warm and sunny

James Wedmore awoke in his own bed to the sound of early morning birdsong. The sun streamed in and illuminated the room in a half-light. He lay there dazed for a few moments. The events of the last few days ran through his mind as he struggled to gain clarity. It felt as though it had partly been a dream, yet the adrenaline that started pumping through his veins when he remembered what had happened in the conference room at the SOFEX event made him realise that it was all real.

He turned his head to the side and saw the perfect vision of beauty asleep next to him. Sana was dressed in one of his vests and an old pair of jogging bottoms. She looked so peaceful as she slept. His heart swelled with pride and a smile spread across his face as he saw her long dark hair rested on the pillow. Her long eyelashes complimenting her natural beauty made him feel like the luckiest guy on earth. It was a wonderful feeling, loving this majestic woman of the desert and he found it easy to respect her wishes for no physical intimacy before marriage.

Thoughts raced through his mind about how to coordinate the mission ahead of him. Whilst he was pleased that he seemingly had support from most of the military top brass, he knew it would not be a walk in the park to overthrow the oppressors of the modern world. Military presence was great, but it would mean nothing if it was just a show of power that resulted in the loss of life. This whole situation was becoming very daunting and beginning to get the better of his nerves. He then remembered that he didn't have to solve all of the problems of the world in one day and he wasn't alone. He had faith in God that the next step of the journey would be revealed to him in good time. For the time being, he could just enjoy the present moment with Sana.

He looked longingly at the beautiful woman lying beside him. To him, everything about her was perfect. Even more fascinating was the fact that she loved and cared for him too. He wondered what she saw in him in the desert. How did she fall for a man who had lived his life opposite to everything she stood for? It didn't make sense to him at all. His insecurity started to get the better of him again as he wondered if he had got himself into a situation outside his control and influence. Would she leave him if he couldn't pull off this task, or if she discovered what he had really done as a military man his whole life? The waves of emotion and insecurity passed over him again as he lay there wondering if he would eventually lose the woman he had found love with again. It had been a hard journey returning to love after the passing of his wife. Being a lone wolf since her passing had been a lot easier than allowing him to be vulnerable and exposed again.

He gently pushed a lock of Sana's hair away from her face and curved it gently behind her left ear. She stirred slightly and a smile spread across her face as she opened her eyes to see him looking at her lovingly.

"*Good morning, Jay,*" she purred.

He reached forward to kiss her gently on the forehead before saying, *"Good morning, beautiful! Did you sleep well?"*

Sana cuddled up to James and rested her head on his chest before replying, *"I slept really well, thank you. I'm so glad I got to wake up with you, Jay. It makes me happy. How are you?"*

"I'm ok," came his empty reply.

Sana lifted up her head from his chest and looked into his eyes. *"What's wrong, Jay?"*

Sana was concerned that Wedmore wasn't his usual vibrant self. He turned his head to the side and looked back up at the ceiling, avoiding her gaze.

"I'm nervous, Sana. I'm nervous that I will fail at this mission. I'm anxious that you'll soon find out who the real me is and you won't like that person. I'm scared that after falling in love with you, you'll leave and break my heart in the process. I'm feeling a bit insecure right now."

Sana lifted herself up and gently pulled at James's chin to turn his head towards her. She smiled with compassion and understanding at his openness. It's not every day a man has to initiate a global coup and come face-to-face with his own human insecurities and limitations. She placed her hand on his face to offer reassurance as she smiled again and kissed him softly on the lips.

"Jay, you have no idea how amazing you are. Don't take my word for it, look who also believes in your mission!" she said as she showed him the winged heart necklace around his neck as a reminder of the Almighty.

He smiled as he remembered that God had entrusted him enough to go forward on this journey with his team supporting him.

"I see the pureness of your heart, Jay. Your willingness to do what only you were born to do in this world and what no one else can do. I am behind you 100% of the way. You inspire me and you light up my heart like I have never known or experienced before. I love you for who you are, not your physical appearance or rugged good looks that can fade with age, but for the very essence of your heart and soul and all that you stand for. No one else compares, Jay. I love you!"

"What about our mission? What if I fail?" he asked, desperately seeking reassurance and validation from his love.

"Jay, who made it just your mission? Who placed the problems of the world on your shoulders? You have a growing team supporting you and it's down to us all to play our parts. What does it matter if we fail? What does it matter if we don't achieve our vision for world peace? At least we will have tried. At least we will have taken massive action and awoken others to the sins of the world. Do you honestly think any one of those generals will repeat the same orders again without thinking for themselves about the impact they will have on the world? We have impacted their lives positively and given them access to something they would have gone to their graves not knowing. Think of the lives we have saved already. The world will never be the same again. You're in safe hands, Jay. Just do the best you can and God will take care of the rest. I believe in you and I am right by your side until the end."

Sana kissed James again on the forehead giving him reassurance that she was there for him. Wedmore wrapped her up in the warmth of his embrace, holding onto her for dear life. Her words echoed in his mind as he realised there was nothing left for him to do but to go out and give the world his best shot and not worry about the outcome. He felt her heart beating and the gentle rhythm of her breathing. There was something comforting about this experience and he closed his eyes for a moment to savour it completely. After a few minutes, Sana broke the silence.

"You know, Jay, back at home, the elders used to talk to us a lot about how placing too much importance on things can be disruptive to our plan."

"What do you mean?"

"We were taught that the primary law of the universe and Mother Earth is one of balance and so we see a lot of opposites in this world. Good and bad, light and dark, yin and yang. When something gets out of balance in nature, it usually attracts counter-balancing forces, which help to restore the balance. If there are too many predators in one area, for example, and they eat all the animals lower in the food chain, harmony will be restored when the food runs out and the excess number of predators disappears. It sounds quite brutal, but that's how nature is," Sana explained.

"Ok, I see what you are getting at, but how does this relate to importance?" Wedmore asked.

"When we put too much importance on something, such as getting to an appointment on time, it's likely that this excess importance will create a disturbance in the natural laws of harmony so we become a target until the counter-balancing forces of nature appear to restore the balance. If we are standing on the edge of a cliff and we are afraid of falling, this creates excess energy that will be balanced by life, which will result in us either falling off the cliff, or stepping away from the edge so we are safe. Life doesn't care which one happens, only that the excess energy around the important event is actually eliminated. Paradoxically, by actually taking conscious steps to lower the importance we have around something, we create a much greater possibility of the thing happening in our favour," Sana smiled.

"So, you're saying I'm placing too much importance on this mission working out favourably, Sana? How can I not put importance on it? It's a huge mission with a lot at stake!"

"I can see that you are putting a lot of importance on things, Jay, and understandably so. However, by working with the laws of the universe, we have a much better chance of things turning out in our favour. Moving forward without attachment to the outcome of the mission is a crucial element in bringing the universe to your aid in this situation, my love," she explained.

Wedmore let her words sink into his mind. As their embrace continued, a love-induced drowsiness overcame them both as they fell back to sleep, safe in the knowledge they had one another always.

As Wedmore slipped into the depths of a deep sleep with the woman he loved by his side, his mind drifted into a dream world. His mind replayed the events of the last few weeks and how they had managed to take the impressive step of recruiting a large number of the world's military leaders to their cause. He unconsciously replayed the interactions with the crowd over and over again in his mind as it conjured up many different scenarios and outcomes, most of which made him feel restless and uncomfortable. His body started sweating as his mind played tricks on him with worst case scenarios had things turned out differently during the conference. His mind merged images from the conference with previous situations he had found himself in as part of his military heritage: being captured and tortured and coming close to death on a number of occasions. He became restless and began to toss and turn as these images haunted him as he slept.

Just as the images became more and more daunting and overpowering, a bright white light entered his dream. Through the bright light emerged a larger than life figure. As the light began to fade into the background behind this figure, the enemies within Wedmore's dream began to cower away. A sense of calm came over Wedmore as he realised the figure in his dream was Archangel Michael who had come to rescue Wedmore from his plight. He smiled and expressed his gratitude to Michael for showing up when he did in his dream.

"I am glad to see you!" Wedmore said with a smile on his face as he looked up at the monumental figure in front of him.

"Not as glad as I am to see you, James," boomed Michael's reply as a smile spread across his own face. *"We've been watching you and we're very proud of what you have achieved so far. You are very close to victory now, my friend."*

"Thank you, although I am sure I couldn't have done it without your help and without you guiding the right people into my life. Thank you for all your assistance so far," Wedmore replied.

"Let me take a look at you," Michael said. He reached down, placed Wedmore into the palm of his hand, and brought him up to eye level. As he did so, Wedmore felt all the pain, anxiety, and negativity drain from his body as he was surrounded by pure love and light.

"You're looking well, James," Michael said with a smile. *"Is there something troubling you about the next stage of your mission that I can help you with?"*

"To be honest with you, I am nervous about the next step. It seems that we have aligned the right people to be part of the mission and we are ready to shift the balance of power from the corrupt to the compassionate. However, I am concerned that I will fail in my attempts to deliver this. I fear a great war. I fear that I will be attempting to solve the problem by the same methods that created the problem in the first place, through bloodshed, weapons and violence. I know that those in power are not going to give up their positions lightly and they will

have many elements of weaponry and fear mongering at their disposal. I don't know how to solve this problem and I fear that I will let everyone down."

Wedmore poured out his innermost insecurities to Michael who listened patiently to him as he spoke. After he had finished, Michael paused for a moment in quiet consideration before responding.

"Fear is exactly what the dark side want you to feel. It is their best and only weapon. If they keep you in a state of fear, they can manipulate you to do whatever they want. But, you can defeat them at their own game. When you don't fear fear, you are unshakeable and that makes them very fearful!"

"How do I not fear fear?" Wedmore asked.

"There are a few things that you need to be aware of. Remember that there is a real reason why you have been taught that God is the invisible man in the sky watching over everything you do. This has purely been devised by the dark side to keep you from your true power and to keep you looking outside of yourself for things to fill the voids you feel in your life. This is evident when you see people chasing money or material wealth. They have become so accustomed to looking outside themselves for things and possessions that they feel will give them fulfilment, yet they have not thought to look within themselves to find what they really need. The main tools the dark side use to keep you in this state are distraction, deceit, and misinformation. When you realise that, you are on the road to true knowledge."

"What true knowledge should I be aware of?" Wedmore asked as he began to see he had fallen into the same trap as countless millions of others who are searching outside themselves to try and fill the emptiness within.

"The very knowledge that you are God! The essence of God is in the heart of every human being on Earth," Michael said with a smile. *"Would you like me to share a little history of mankind as it has evolved through the ages with you?"*

"I would love to benefit from your knowledge and experience, Michael."

"I've been around for a very long time, so I know how the journey of humankind has unfolded. In the beginning, God had his Angelic realm of which I was a part. All Angels were made of either fire or light. Then God created the first humans, Adam and Eve, from dust. God was very proud of this. He called it his greatest creation so far because of the emotional complexities he had achieved and the ability to have true compassion for all manner of things, which forms the very foundation of humanity. He introduced Adam and Eve to the Angels and asked that all Angels kneel before them as a mark of respect for his finest creation."

"All but one did so. That Angel claimed that humans would be easily corruptible and would not lead a good life. God asked this particular Angel to again kneel before his finest creation to show his respect, but he defied God and would not do so. This Angel was adamant that Adam and Eve would go against God's word to live a decent and good life and create Heaven on Mother Earth. He did not believe it was possible for humans to be good people and follow the word of God."

"God became furious. He could not hear anything bad said against his creation. In his fury, he banished this Angel to Earth to live alongside humans to witness this first-hand how good his people were. The twist was, the now Fallen Angel resolved to show God how easily his creation could be led into temptation and how their offspring would fight with one another and cause separation and division rather than unity. Ever since, humans have been manipulated by the Fallen Angel

who is hell bent on proving to God that he was right. You might have heard of the early stories of Eve being tempted by a talking serpent to eat the apple from the Tree of Knowledge. Well, that was the first attempt at proving he was right, and it worked. From that point on, he has sought to bring corruption, division, and separation to humanity in order to justify his righteousness. It's a sad thing really, as before that, he was one of the best Angels and God's favourite."

"So, you're telling me that this Fallen Angel is the one leading all the cruelty and corruption in the world? Why didn't God put a stop to it?" Wedmore asked.

"God has sent many prophets to Earth in an attempt to correct the errors of humanity and to get them back on the right track. Buddha, Jesus, Krishna, even Ghandi were all prophets sent to Earth to do God's bidding to give humans access to the very essence of their humanity and steer them in the right direction. Some were successful and others took a fall because they conflicted with what the Fallen One had brainwashed humans to believe. He's a clever trickster and the great deceiver. What fascinates me is he masterfully plays both sides of the coin, leaving humans caught in a web of deceit and deception. He plays both the devil and God on the Earth realm and has played this role so well that many people unwittingly worship him," Michael explained.

"How is this possible?" Wedmore asked.

"'Well consider the three main religions on Earth, which approximately 50% of the world's population subscribe to. That's around three-and-a-half billion people who are Christian, Jew, or Muslim. The foundational teachings of the three main religions are exactly the same:; love thy neighbour and do not do anything to anyone else that you wouldn't want done unto you - what we in Heaven refer to as The Golden Rule," Michael explained.

"Sana says exactly the same thing," Wedmore said.

"Do you really believe all those people who claim to be religious and follow the word of God would fight in wars with other people who also claim to be religious and follow the word of God?" Michael asked.

Wedmore paused for a second and had to admit he was completely stumped. In the end, he acknowledged that it would only be possible if they were defending themselves against the other 50% of the world's population that weren't following the word of God and were attacking them.

"That's a good answer!" Michael replied with a smile. *"Even so, do you think they would still kill or injure others if they were operating from a place of love thy neighbour? Look at Jesus as the example. When he was sentenced to death, did he fight with or kill his captors, or did he graciously go along with their painful plans and ask for God's forgiveness for their sins? We know it was the latter and even when he was barbarically crucified, he still chose to stand for peace, love, and light for humanity, rather than cruelty and revenge!"* Michael said.

"He did not stand for spreading the word of his teachings through bloodshed or taking from others less fortunate or who did not believe in the word of God. Man has stood for that. The problem is that morally weak humans have high jacked religion and made it serve their ulterior purposes, rather than honouring the original word of God. Jesus was not a Christian and he certainly never told people to read a Holy book or go to church. He told people to go out and do good. God gave everyone a conscience, which is their internal moral compass to help guide them to establish whether or not they are doing well. Humans know when they are doing good because they usually feel good in their heart and soul. It's a deep and honourable feeling. Doing harm to your fellow man might massage the ego in the short term and there is an initial gain, but the long-term

effects are catastrophic. I believe you have felt this yourself, James?" Michael asked.

He was referring to the endless nights of waking up sweating from the many dreams of previous missions where he thought he was doing good, but was actually killing innocent people. Wedmore acknowledged that he knew what Michael was talking about.

Michael continued, *"So, here is the problem. The Fallen One has become very good at playing both sides of the coin and has encouraged many humans to slowly manipulate the word of God over countless generations, making slight changes, time and again, creating watered down truths and leaving people powerless. The ultimate crime is convincing everyone to look outside themselves for God, rather than realising he is within. Every human possesses a timeless spirit or soul connected to the Divine that cannot be harmed or destroyed! Unless, of course, they decide to sell their souls!"* Michael added.

"Do people really do that, Michael?" Wedmore asked.

"Of course! It's all very real. Here is the part that would be very funny were it not so serious. Some individual souls have a particularly arduous life journey, and they are put through certain challenges as part of their growth. God will never put anyone through anything that he doesn't already know they can handle. In fact, we have a saying, 'The Grace of God will never take you where the Mercy of God will not protect you.' However, certain souls lose their faith and believe that because of their human experience, they are unable to continue on their journey, so they resort to prayer. Rather than praying to the God within for the resilience and strength to continue, they 'sell out' and ask to be saved from their plight."

"The Fallen One naturally obliges and even appears to be a friend to help these souls in their time of torment. He is able to

give them whatever they want in exchange for their soul. If they want fame and money to ease their pain, it's easy for The Great Deceiver to provide that for them. Politicians and musicians are a classic case of this; they get illuminated for their contribution to the Fallen One so they gain more followers and influence, while the Fallen One is pulling the strings of their actions behind the scenes, dictating what they do for his own agenda. When the time comes, The Fallen One gets them to do his dirty work and they are powerless to resist. That's how the circle of corruption keeps on growing! For all his faults, he's actually very clever at manipulating people by first appearing as their friend and then taking from them when they are at their weakest."

"*I am shocked!*" Wedmore replied. "*I had heard the stories but never really knew it was true! How long has this been going on for?*" he asked.

"Ever since God created man. Perhaps The Fallen One was right when he said man would ultimately be corruptible, but that is a side to mankind that co-exists with their loving humanity, which you see whenever someone is in trouble or a natural disaster strikes a community. Unfortunately, one of the impacts of modern life is that people become detached from their inner emotions through the pursuit of wealth or a career, which, of course, the media tells them to do. When this detachment happens, they are no longer able to listen to the inner voice of their conscience or their heart so they mentally override it. That's why so many people are suffering from depression and anxiety. They know within themselves they are doing something that is not in alignment with their higher selves or they are aware of things going on in the world that they are morally against but do not do anything about. This causes a conflict with their internal emotions as their logical left-brain gives them all the reasons why they should carry on with what they are doing. It's a sad state of affairs.

"Thankfully, some people are released from this hypnotic state when they see others suffering and their compassion takes over, giving them access to love and understanding. They ultimately extend the hand of friendship to help them through troubled times. People forget they have a God-like essence within their own hearts. Unfortunately, they have been taught by the Great Deceiver that God is in the heavens above them, judging them because they are a sinner, so they pray to the sky instead of listening to their hearts for guidance where they would be all powerful," Michael explained.

"I see what you are saying, Michael, but I am not sure I am connecting the dots between humanity and my own path to bringing enlightenment to the people whilst stopping the corruption that exists worldwide. What am I missing here?"

"Ok, my friend," Michael said with a smile. *"I will explain the great mystery of life to you that eludes so many people during their lifetimes. Life at its very essence is a binary deal; it's a simple yes/no or one/zero equation, much like binary code on a computer. What humans do not realise is they are ultimate creators of the worlds they live in based on the level of consciousness they vibrate at on a daily basis. Going deeper than that, everyone's actions are based on one of two emotions: love or fear. It really is that simple. Where it starts to get more complicated is that once a decision has been made by someone rooted in either emotion, each step they take from that point onwards brings about more of the initial emotion."*

"So someone making a decision based on fear can only create and amplify more of that initial fear. It's what leads to people self-sabotaging because they don't realise what they are doing and the feelings continue to grow until they become overwhelming. You see, you can run and hide from other people, but you will always have to live with yourself. It's the inner voice that drives most people crazy. Either they aren't

listening to it or they can hear it when everything in their life is quiet, until it completely overwhelms them and it drives them insane."

"Where it helps you, my friend," Michael continued, "is that even though you are concerned about what the future will hold with your mission, you have a choice to make on how you emotionally approach the situation. Do you want to approach it from a place of fear or from a place of Love?"

"I want to operate from a place of love, Michael, but I don't know how to do this when the mission is so scary and overwhelming in my mind. What if I don't deliver the result we all want? What if I get killed? It's like nothing I have ever done before. I'm public enemy number one in the eyes of those who would maintain power and do away with my mission for good. Now you mention The Fallen One as well, and that really concerns me. How do I maintain love in my heart when I am faced with this challenge?" Wedmore said as honestly as he could.

"That is a great question and one that I am glad you have asked. Remember, the journey down the path to love starts with the initial intention. If you have love in your heart when you make the first decision, it's like planting a seed of love, so the more you tend to it and nurture it, the more it will flourish. Start with a definite relaxed intention that you will operate from love. From there, let the journey unfold without attachment or judgement by your mind or your emotions as you progress."

"Remember everything is perfect no matter what happens. The journey will be worth it. You have us behind you, so there really is nothing to worry about. Go lead those gracious people who want a better life and show them what is possible. Break the hypnotic spell mankind is under. Do it with the intention of love for that is the highest frequency you can resonate at. Many people think that the enemy is hate, but it's actually fear.

It's a state that those who would rule the world would have you operate in daily given half a chance. That negative energy feeds those entities like sugar feeds the growth of cancer."

"What entities do you mean, Michael?" Wedmore asked.

"Are you familiar with the concept that everything is energy, James?" Michael asked.

"I remember that was something Albert Einstein said and I think I understand it," Wedmore replied.

"That's quite correct and Einstein knew a thing or two, didn't he?" Michael smiled. "Try not to get too concerned with what I am about to tell you, but in order for The Great Deceiver to carry out more of his work on Earth, he created a group of energetic beings called pendulums. These energetic beings help create situations by setting up conflicts with other people or creating situations that generally result in negative energy or emotions being released. So, when you are driving down the road and someone cuts in front of you, this is usually a pendulum at work."

"They are called pendulums because they usually work through provocation; something happens to a person when they least expect it, which they consider is completely unjust, so they push back and that starts the pendulum swinging. Each push back from one person to the other creates more momentum, escalating the conflict higher and higher, while the pendulums harvest the negative energy from the conflict."

"I'm not sure I follow you exactly, Michael," Wedmore said. "Are you suggesting these situations and conflicts are set up by entities manipulating people and are not directly due to people acting of their own accord? Where does all this energy go?"

"These are wonderful questions, James, and I am glad you are thinking deeply about it. As I say, it can be a difficult concept to understand. Ultimately, the energy is like growth hormone for these pendulums, so the more they harvest, the more they *grow and continue to set up more and more conflicts between people. Not all interactions between people are as a result of pendulums in action, but most people are on auto-pilot throughout their day, so they are not aware they are being manipulated or provoked by a situation that is not of their making. Imagine a waiter accidentally spills soup on a businessman; his knee-jerk reaction is to give the waiter a public dressing down and vent his own frustration at the waiter. Both parties walk away from the interaction in a foul mood, which can impact wider relationships between co-workers, or even their families when they get home. I'm sure you have seen something relatively minor happen to someone in the morning and they are still annoyed about it by the time they go to bed. Imagine the energy they are feeding the pendulum throughout the day. Worse still, think about the impact they have on others they interact with. It's a constant spiral of negativity,"* Michael explained.

"*Yes, I have met people like that. Something minor happens to them and they spend all day brooding over it. I wonder what they would be like if they had to encounter something serious like the perils of being behind enemy lines or walking through a war zone,*" Wedmore reflected with a half-smile.

"*Exactly, James! And can you imagine the energy that something like war generates for pendulums and the master of the dark side...*" Michael's voice trailed off as he looked expectantly at Wedmore.

Wedmore was stunned. Thoughts raced through his mind. Had he really spent his entire life being manipulated to work for the dark side? Had he really been duped by the Great Deceiver into thinking he was fighting for his country and God when all he was doing was creating conflict in the lives of others, some of which would take years if not generations to overcome and heal? Had he really personally fed these energy-draining machines and spent every day of his life so far making it bigger and stronger to ultimately tip the world's balance in favour of the dark side? The thoughts were too much for him to bear and he became angry as he contemplated what it could all mean.

"The thoughts you are thinking now, James," interjected Michael; *"Are they loving and harmonious thoughts supporting the spread of good throughout the world, or are they feeding the pendulums?"*

Wedmore took a deep breath as he reflected on everything that Michael had said.

"James, there's something else to ponder here before the lesson is over. The rhetorical question I would ask you is where your thoughts come from? If you think about this for a moment, your ego might try to take control of the situation and say they come from within you, but do they?"

"You see, most people don't realise that the mind is a sending and receiving station for thoughts, something that writers in the past have described quite accurately. However, the mind can only receive thoughts based on the frequency of consciousness a person is tuned into. Just as a radio can only play a station it is tuned into, the mind can only think thoughts based on the frequencies it is aligned to."

"Another job of the pendulums is to keep people's mind attuned to a lower frequency of thought. Just as an airplane can be tossed around at the mercy of the weather if it flies beneath the clouds, it can be in permanent sunlight and above the perils of the lower altitudes if it flies above the clouds. The mind works in a similar way and if you tune your mind to higher frequency levels, you can also be in permanent sunlight.; That's why they call it enlightenment," Michael joked.

Wedmore laughed. *"Yes, I see what you're saying, Michael. So these pendulums are quite sneaky really. You're saying that if I am going about my day without being conscious of what I am thinking, I could be manipulated into a situation by a pendulum where I will either be thinking lower vibration negative thoughts, or be caught up in an unjust situation with someone else that could escalate and leave us both emitting negative energy that is then harvested by the pendulum?"* Wedmore asked.

"The worst case scenario is both could happen or you could affect more and more people with your low mood, leaving them feeling anxious or angry. They can then transfer this to others and cause a ripple effect around your community, country or the world at large," Michael explained.

"Wow! Yes I can see that the impacts of getting caught up in one negative interaction can be huge. How do we prevent these pendulums taking our energy?" James asked.

"That's a great question and exactly how you should be thinking. The first step really is to be aware that they are in operation at all times, waiting for a chink in your armour, or for you to have a lapse of concentration before striking. It's a bit like being in a conflict situation where the enemy could attack you at any moment," Michael explained. *"Once you know that they could be ready to strike at any moment, your next task is to be aware of your thoughts and keep them at the highest vibration of love that you can. If you do get embroiled with a pendulum's provocation, and it is likely to happen from time-to-time, the best thing to do is to practice a form of mental aikido. You don't want to react to it by pushing back, so step to one side and allow it to swing past you. Don't react, don't take the bait, and don't get caught up in thoughts of how unjust the situation may be. Just step to one side and allow it to pass you by."*

"If you don't react, like any pendulum that needs energy to keep pushing against it to gain momentum, it will extinguish itself quickly and you can move on with your life. In most instances, an apology, even though it may not be your fault, is all you need to move on and walk away from the situation. You

don't need to do any more than that really. A quite serious situation, such as a mugging, means you have to respond accordingly and the best situation may be to hand your money or valuables over and let them walk away rather than fight. You can then send that person love and be grateful that the situation didn't turn out a lot worse. Keeping love in your heart is one of the best ways to help raise your vibration of consciousness high and not react to the pendulums that just drain your energy and make the cause you are fighting against even stronger. I hope that makes sense," Michael said.

"That makes perfect sense to me, Michael, and it's something that I really do need to practice on a daily basis," Wedmore replied.

He closed his eyes and counted ten heartbeats as the chatter in his mind started to quieten down and stepped into the emotions of love. He felt it radiate from his heart and surround the world, giving love to every person and connecting directly with their hearts. As the love flowed from his heart, he felt it return tenfold and a smile spread across his face as his own energy levels increased. The fear melted away and peace came to his soul. He opened his eyes and looked once again at the ever-patient Michael who smiled.

"That's excellent, James! There's just one more thing to say before you go. There is a difference between walking the path with doubt or fear in your mind, and walking the path with certainty. If you walk the path with the certainty that you will be a success in your mission, then you are stacking the odds in your favour that things will work out for the best. If you walk the path uncertainly, with doubt and fear in your mind, then you will attract what you do not want. It comes down to your initial intention of love or fear when you are making that first decision. Do you understand?"

"I completely understand," Wedmore replied. *"Thank you for your wisdom and patience, Michael. I feel more confident and enlightened about the mission ahead of us now."*

"You are more than welcome, my friend. Now go and do what you were born to do and don't worry. Remember, having the intention of certainty with the heart and mind unified by love is the path to creating the future that you desire," Michael replied.

He looked into Wedmore's eyes to make sure he understood. The moment of silent exchange through the windows of the soul ensured Michael he could now send the warrior back to the task ahead.

They bade each other farewell. Michael raised the tip of his right finger towards Wedmore's chest and gently placed it in front of his heart. Wedmore felt a surge of the most heavenly energy flow through his heart before engulfing the rest of his body with pure unconditional blissful love. A smile spread across his face as he raised his arms and tilted his head to bask in the feeling. He felt superhuman in every cell of his body. As the initial overpowering emotion began to subside, Wedmore felt certainty in his heart. He looked again at Michael who noticed Wedmore's eyes had changed from hazel to a grey-green colour.

A feeling of freedom and ease ran through Wedmore's body as every cell had biochemically anchored itself to the success of the mission. There was no room for doubt or uncertainty; the very essence and fibre of his being knew that he would successfully lead the greatest mission in the world. He thanked Michael again. Moments later, he vanished leaving Wedmore floating in mid air.

He wanted to enjoy the moment even more so he lay back and envisioned what the world would look like once the mission was completed and the veil of worldwide corruption had been lifted. He smiled as he hoped everyone alive would get to experience this incredible deep feeling of love and connection with the Divine and know they were being taken care of, no matter the circumstances. This was certainly something he wanted to bring to the world as part of his gift and he vowed he would spend the rest of his life helping others to walk the path towards enlightenment and love whilst dispensing with fear, hatred, and intolerance.

Chapter 20

Capture

LOCATION: Kent, England
DATE: 12th May
WEATHER: Warm and sunny

Wedmore awoke to a soft hand rubbing his shoulder gently. He looked up to see Sana looking adoringly at him with a loving smile on her face. On the bedside table were two steaming mugs of tea, some orange juice, and some freshly buttered toast. Wedmore stretched as he shook off his slumber. He took hold of Sana's arm, pulling her closer to him so he could kiss her on the cheek and give her a big cuddle. They lay there holding one another, feeling lovingly connected in perfect unity.

"Did you sleep well, my love?" Sana asked.

"It was incredible!" James replied. *"I drifted into another world and I had a wonderful conversation with Michael about the mission. Sana, it felt amazing to be in his presence again and he spoke many words of truth to me. He left me feeling so powerful and connected to the most wonderful outcome of this journey ahead of us, it was unreal! We're so blessed, sweetheart!"*

Sana rolled over in the bed to face Wedmore with a smile on her face and her heart full of joy as she listened to him speak.

"That's amazing, darling! Well done you. I'm so proud of you. What did he s...Jay! Your eyes are a different colour! What on earth happened?" Sana asked.

"They are?" Wedmore said. "I have no idea!"

Wedmore leapt out of bed and looked at himself in the full-length mirror hanging from the bedroom wall. He pulled the skin beneath his eyes down gently to get a clearer view of his eyes and was shocked to see they had actually changed colour.

"I...I have no idea how this happened, but it must be something to do with the feeling of euphoria I felt when Michael put his finger on my heart. Honestly Sana, I have to tell you that the experience he gave me felt absolutely incredible and it's left me with so much certainty over the future of our mission. I just know it's going to unfold beautifully as we walk this path." Wedmore said.

"Jay, I can feel there is a real difference in your aura! I can feel you're in the most incredible space and I am so confident you will achieve everything you set your mind to. It feels amazing being around you! I sense peace, calmness, love, and connection with you. It's incredible! We are very blessed to have you leading us."

Sana's eyes were full of joy and love as her pupils dilated in the presence of her man who was now radiating at a higher level of consciousness, solidly grounded in love.

"Sana, I can't begin to tell you how great I feel! Calmness and certainty are definitely strong emotions, but I also feel at one with everything around me. I can feel the connection with you, with everything in this room, with the house, and the universe at large. I feel as though I have arrived home to a state of blissful loving unity with everyone and everything. Fear and doubt have fallen away to bring love, acceptance, and peace to the surface and I feel invincible as I stand here before you. I don't mean that in an arrogant way; I just mean that I am not fearful of what the opposition may or may not do. I'm in a very beautiful place, Sana," Wedmore explained.

"I can see that, Jay!" she replied as she looked at him in awe. "You are emitting the most beautiful emotions and it's a joy to be in your presence. Come here and let me hold you!"

Sana walked over to her man and they held each other tightly.

Sana looked up into Wedmore's eyes. "Jay, I have only felt this once before when I was a little girl in the presence of a very enlightened being. I don't remember his name, but I do remember how he made me feel. He was from a long line of yogis in India and he passed through our village on a pilgrimage, if I remember correctly. It was as if he didn't walk, but glided along and he was the most peaceful and humble person I have ever met. He was hugely enlightened and radiated love and connection from his heart wherever he went. He would sometimes sit and meditate by the fire at night and it brought the most peaceful space to the whole village as everyone felt the subtle affects of what he was doing. Even the animals would fall silent the moment he started meditating. It was no coincidence. Peace, love, and harmony fell like a rainstorm from the heavens. It was beautiful being around that energy and you've just reminded me of that same feeling. You're a very special being and I'm blessed to be by your side."

Wedmore smiled hearing Sana explain how she felt and kissed her gently on the forehead. He felt his heart swell with pride that she felt him worthy of comparison to such an enlightened being. Although his journey of growth had not been an easy one so far, it was certainly worthwhile to be firmly grounded and totally present in the moment with the woman he loved whilst his whole being was free from the past torturous thoughts and emotions that had haunted him for so long.

He gathered Sana up in his arms, smiling like a mischievous child as he looked down at his wide-eyed woman who was beaming with joy. He swung her round as Sana playfully screamed for him to stop. He gently dropped her onto the soft mattress and laughed like a child. Joy was such a pleasant emotion to experience through being playful with someone he cared about deeply. It had been many years since he had last experienced these emotions and it felt strangely wonderful.

The thought flashed through his mind that being an adult somehow meant disconnecting from the emotions of childlike joy and happiness as though these emotions should be suppressed because they were deemed immature. Living an adult life seemed to be an emotional rut of shallow feelings, and avoiding feeling too deeply to avoid the pain of being hurt by life. This meant shutting ourselves down from experiencing the highs to avoid the lows. Why was it a requirement to be serious and emotionally stunted as an adult?

Wedmore kissed Sana again before announcing he would like to go for a walk around town alone. He wanted to spend a few hours in this state of emotional bliss to observe the outside world through new eyes. Wedmore pulled on his well-worn blue denim jeans, slipped a white v-neck t-shirt over his head, and thrust his feet into his trusty Caterpillar boots.

As Wedmore walked, he became more aware of the world around him. He looked up for the first time in as long as he could remember to see the endless light blue sky and brilliant sunshine that warmed him to the core. He heard the birds singing in the trees and observed nature in a way he had never experienced it before.

It occurred to him that the essence of being human was experiencing a range of emotions. He knew his experience of the world was directly related to the thoughts he was thinking and the feelings he was feeling. Previously, he had experienced the world as a dark and oppressive place, which reflected his emotional and mental thought patterns at the time. As he strolled down the street full of loving energy, without a care in the world observing the abundantly beautiful and effortless nature around him, he felt very different. His hometown was physically the same, but his emotional experience of it was now one of calmness, peace, and surrender. There was harmony in every step he took and it felt great.

As he approached an old couple walking arm-in-arm towards him, he decided to do something he hadn't done for years. He looked at them both whilst smiling and said, *'Good Morning.'* They both responded in kind as he walked past them. He placed his hand on his heart as he was momentarily overcome with emotion at the sheer beauty of humanity. Here he was, just walking down the street and two kind strangers had gone out of their way to wish him a good day.

This was so far removed from the environment he had operated in for too long that his left brain began to wrestle for control of the situation, flooding his head with thoughts of why people weren't to be trusted and why he was justified in losing his faith in humankind. He relaxed as he let the thoughts come and go, releasing them without attachment. As he did so, he realised the essence of who he really was did not consist of his thoughts or feelings. At the core, he was eternal, endless and ephemeral; everything else was borne out of the human experience in flesh and blood and all of the thoughts, feelings, and emotions that came with it.

Wedmore continued his walk feeling blessed to be getting these incredible breakthroughs. He smiled at everyone he saw and felt joy and harmony as he did so. Every smile he flashed at a passer-by was responded to in kind, lifting his spirit higher, and he wondered why he had waited so long to enjoy this feeling of giving others these little gifts wherever he went. It was a far more empowered way of living and he wanted to tell everyone how great it felt to encourage everyone to enjoy the same state of bliss he now experienced.

He toyed with the idea of becoming a public speaker once his final mission was complete so he could encourage others to access this state. He hoped the journey for others would not be as painful as his own, although he recognised there were many blessings in disguise from everything he had personally experienced in his life. Perhaps others could receive the same gifts, if he gave people the right context with which to reframe the sometimes painful experiences of life. By allowing people to view events from a higher state of consciousness, he could show how these events actually served people on their own journey of growth and contribution to others and ultimately uplift humanity. Perhaps it was just a dream, but the idea of adding value to the journey of others certainly appealed, particularly if it allowed them to access even a glimpse of the ecstasy he was currently experiencing.

As Wedmore approached a tall tree in the local park, he was stunned at how beautiful the vibrancy of colours shining through its canopy looked. He stopped walking for a moment to admire the gnarled tree trunk he guessed must have been well over 100 years old. He contemplated what changes that tree must have witnessed in its time on Earth. He looked at its magnificence as it towered above him, breathing fresh oxygen out for him to enjoy, all for free!

He wondered if the person who originally planted the tree all those years ago knew what a magnificent specimen it would grow to be, providing shelter and food for many insects and animals. His mind stretched further thinking about the nutrients the leaves would return to the soil when they fell from the tree in autumn, providing a rich and fertile ground for other plants to grow. He marvelled at the magnificence of how everything in nature seemed to live beyond itself to support the community that surrounded it. How wonderful that nature was so perfectly designed to do this in harmony with its natural environment and yet here was man, arguably God's finest creation, arguing about who had the 'better God' and destroying the very nature their God had created! Was this the work of The Fallen Angel poisoning the mind of man to work against one another and even nature itself, or was it a sickness of the human condition that Mother Nature would correct to restore the balance sometime in the future? It was time to create a different way of life based on harmony. As Wedmore breathed in a lung-full of fresh oxygen, he renewed his determination to deliver this to the world once again.

Wedmore thought about the possibilities of what could happen on Earth if people were kind and loving towards one another. He reflected on how fortunate he was to have someone like Sana in his life and how she had changed him. As his thoughts lingered on Sana and her divine feminine beauty, he felt uneasy.

Now accustomed to listening to this inner knowing, Wedmore became very concerned and started to jog home. In his playful behaviour before leaving the house, he had decided against taking his phone as he wanted to be present and in the moment to really experience life, rather than being distracted by a flashing screen. With no way to call Sana, he picked up the pace.

As he turned the corner to the road where he lived, he scanned ahead to look for signs of trouble. He was breathing heavily from his run and beads of sweat had formed on his forehead. He hoped he was wrong, but as he got closer to home, the unsettled feeling became more intense.

He hopped over the dry stonewall and pushed his way through the small bushes, keeping his eyes alert for possible signs of danger. Backed into the driveway was a black Mercedes 4x4 with the engine running. Wedmore crouched and looked for signs of activity within the house. He could not see any faces in the windows on look out, nor could he see any signs of unrest. His gut feeling had been validated and he was pleased he had listened.

He stooped his way towards the front of the house. The front door was slightly ajar and he could hear Sana's muffled screams and the clatter of furniture as she resisted whatever was happening. Wedmore's heart pounded as he realised she was in trouble and there was very little he could do. The likelihood was they would be armed and dangerous and his weapons were either upstairs or in the garage, neither of which would serve him in this moment.

He knew that in hostage situations like this, challenging the perpetrators now could result in things turning sour very quickly. The adrenaline running through their systems would be at its highest right now, so the captors would not be capable of rational thought in the heat of the moment. Besides, if he challenged them now, he would be shot, or taken hostage too, neither of which would help Sana.

He cursed himself while listening to his woman being mistreated in his own home. He was angry he had left her home alone and the rest of the team were some distance away. Besides, his phone was lying on the bedside table and he needed to act fast.

"I'm not going to let this happen again!" he muttered. *"There's no way I am going to lose another girl to these bastards."*

He heard footsteps and more muffled screams, so he took a few steps back and hid behind a tall potted shrub to conceal his position. He watched in horror as Sana was dragged kicking and screaming by two men in balaclavas out of his home and towards the 4x4. Sana was gagged and had a black hessian sack over her head and her hands had been zip-tied behind her back. Despite the physical size difference between her and her two captors, she put up a feisty fight as she was dragged to the vehicle. A third man exited the house, looking around as he did so before following the trio back to the SUV.

As soon as the terrorists were out of sight, Wedmore leapt into action, running into the house and sprinting upstairs to grab his phone to call for backup before running back downstairs. As he approached the bottom of the stairs, he noticed a letter on the back of the front door held in place by a six-inch Bowie knife. He pulled hard on the letter as he left, letting the paper tear around the blade.

He ran towards the driveway, taking care to stay out of sight but making a careful note of the vehicle's number plate as it screeched onto the tarmac road. Wedmore sprinted into the garage and snatched his Desert Eagle .50 pistol and two magazines, holstering the gun into the back of his trousers and slipping the magazines into his pocket. He grabbed the key to his Honda Fireblade motorbike, firing it into action and slipping his helmet quickly over his head.

Wedmore revved the engine and flew out of the garage, pulling a wheelie before leaning left to navigate the gatepost as he forced the bike to make the turn onto the country road. Although he was a minute or two behind the captors, he knew he would be able to catch up very quickly on his high-powered machine. He opened the throttle up as the bike lurched forwards and the engine screamed. Up through the gears he went as the bike sped along the road. The rapid movement of air passing over his body quickly chilled his skin.

He could see the rear of the Mercedes disappear around a corner approximately a mile ahead. Although the lanes were quite winding, he knew them like the back of his hand and would quickly catch up, although he wondered how to do this effectively without spooking the occupants and causing Sana even more problems.

He clenched his teeth as he twisted the throttle even harder to gain quickly on the SUV. The lanes twisted and turned as he rode in hot pursuit of the 4x4. The terrain over the next mile was treacherous with multiple blind bends up ahead. He had to keep the pace up but he hoped that fortune was on his side and there would be no oncoming traffic.

He rounded the next corner at 60 miles an hour and suddenly saw a low-slung Toyota MR2 heading rapidly towards him. Everything happened so fast; he glanced at the two young boy racers inside going just as fast as he was through the country lanes. Their faces turned to horror as they saw the bike heading for a head-on collision.

In his peripheral vision, Wedmore noticed the road was slightly hunched, so with reactions that would make a fighter pilot proud, Wedmore kicked down a gear, opened up the throttle and hit the bump in the road while simultaneously lifting the bike up with his body weight to try and jump the car.

Almost in slow motion, the bike left the road as the MR2 approached the point of impact. The front tyre of Wedmore's bike skimmed the top of the windscreen as the rear wheel made full contact with the bonnet. The momentum of Wedmore's bike, combined with the rear wheel finding grip on the bonnet, launched the Fireblade over the windscreen and sent it flying several feet through the air. The two boy racers watched in sheer amazement, before slamming on the brakes.

Wedmore held on as the Fireblade soared through the air, before coming back into contact with the ground with a bump and sending his heart rate even higher. He just about kept control of the bike before ensuring it was pointing in a straight line and applying the power once more. He smiled to himself before disappearing around the next corner and continuing his pursuit.

The Mercedes came back into sight so Wedmore eased off the throttle and fell into a reconnaissance pursuit position a respectable distance away so as not to arouse suspicion. He wondered where they might be taking her and who they were. He also wondered on how to rescue her once he established where they were taking her. He knew that he was emotionally hooked and had placed a lot of importance on the situation, so he had to be careful that he wasn't setting himself up for complications in the rescue mission. He needed his mind to be clear.

He followed the car for several miles on the main roads leading towards the nearby village of Ruckinge where the 4x4 indicated left to turn off towards a farm track. Wedmore also indicated and pulled the bike off the road into a small lay-by before the entrance to the farm. As the bike came to a standstill, he spotted the Mercedes through a hedgerow as it continued down the bumpy track. He kicked the bike stand out and turned the ignition off as the 4x4 disappeared from view.

He pulled out his phone to call Kamali. After three rings, Kamali picked up as Wedmore crouched down out of sight.

"What's happening, boss?" came Kamali's friendly and reassuring voice.

"It…it's Sana. She's in trouble!" Wedmore stammered as he saw the vehicle park up in a distant farmyard and the occupants disembark. Sana was dragged out of the back seat and manhandled towards the nearby farmhouse.

"What do you mean? Trouble in what way?"

"She's been kidnapped! She was taken from the house earlier today when I was out. I've no idea who they are or what they want with her." His voice trembled as he spoke.

Crouching in the hedgerow out of sight, he remembered the note on the back of the door. He grabbed the letter from his pocket and frantically tore it open to read its contents as Kamali asked him questions.

"Where are you now, Wedmore? I'll rally the troops and we'll come immediately," Kamali replied as enthusiastically as he could, realising the emotional turmoil his friend was under.

Wedmore's mind was on the note, which simply read 'An eye for an eye'.

"Wedmore, are you there?" he asked.

"Sorry, Kamali, yes I'm here. Can you bring the guys over quickly? They're holding her outside of Ruckinge on the B2067. There's a small lay-by outside the farm and my bike is parked there. I don't think you can miss it. I don't know how much time we've got, so I'm going to try and get a bit closer to do some re-con."

"Right. We'll be with you in thirty minutes tops," Kamali said.

He was keen to get the team together and help save Sana. Wedmore stood and looked around for cover that would allow him to get closer to the farmhouse. There was nothing to be seen. There was a distinct lack of cover between his present position and the farmhouse, so he elected to commando crawl through the long grass of the pasture fields surrounding the farm buildings.

He took a moment to roughly chart his course through the long grass and get himself to a vantage point that would allow him to observe what was going on in the house without being spotted. Breathless with anticipation, Wedmore walked through the farm entrance before beginning his crawl through the field. The long wet grass quickly soaked his already sweat-drenched clothes. He crawled towards the rear of the closest barn. With a lack of cover and moving in broad daylight, he felt quite exposed so he had to move fast.

As he reached the barn, he pressed himself upright and took a moment to check to ensure he hadn't been seen. He took hold of his Desert Eagle .50 gun from the back of his jeans, and cocked it ready for action. Breathing heavily as more adrenaline started to flow in anticipation of a confrontation, he took a few deep breaths and tried to steady his mind. He had to be careful not to turn this into a revenge mission.

Wedmore took his phone from his pocket and turned it off so there was no danger he could be compromised. He knew the team would be on their way and would want to contact him, but he wasn't sure how long Sana had.

He took another deep breath before slowing walking towards the end of the stone barn to get closer to the house. The muddy ground made walking difficult. As he reached the end of the barn, he carefully peered around the corner to see if he could gain any more information on the whereabouts of Sana.

The old farmhouse looked as though it hadn't been lived in for many years. It was double fronted with an entrance porch in front of the main door. The rotten, broken windows overlooked a square courtyard flanked by two barns; the smaller of which he was now pressed up against in an effort to get closer to the house. He noticed a side door that opened into what he believed would have been the original scullery. The concrete courtyard was covered in moss with the lone Mercedes was parked close to the front of the farmhouse. Wedmore couldn't hear anything within the house and he couldn't see anyone on lookout near the windows. He was still confident that the people who took Sana were military professionals and he had to be on his guard.

The gravel pathway to the side of the house was covered in old leaves and moss. It showed some signs of recent disturbance that suggested the side doorway was in use. Around thirty feet away was an old corrugated steel outbuilding, which would give him a better view of the side of the house and was less exposed than his current position. He paused for a second to listen intently and kept his eyes fixed on the two side windows of the house for any movement that might indicate he would be caught by his next move. He glanced across at his target to check for any trip hazards and then back at the house before making a dash towards the outbuilding. His feet squelched on the soft ground, but he made it unscathed to the tattered outbuilding.

Once inside the rickety old structure, he gained a much better vantage point of the farmhouse as the rusty corrugated panels that formed the structure had drifted from their original positions and provided plenty of peepholes. He could see nothing, but continued to observe for a few minutes to ensure he hadn't been caught in the act.

Wedmore heard a faint buzzing noise in the distance that sounded like a small swarm of bees. The noise came from the road and was distinctly audible over the sound of passing traffic. He turned and saw a small drone flying towards the house before passing over its roof. He lost sight of it, but he hoped it was his back up. He kept his eyes and ears peeled toward the sky for any sight of the drone. It wasn't long before he saw it fly back into sight over the courtyard and directly above the house again before heading out of sight back towards the road.

Wedmore looked back at the farmhouse to see if anyone had noticed the drone and then heard the drone return. This time, it chartered a much lower flight path and Wedmore saw it was carrying a small package. The drone reached the derelict outbuilding he was hiding in and dropped a small cardboard package.

Wedmore now felt sure that it was another piece of technology that Hitler had obtained and hoped that he also had a few extra tricks up his sleeve. The package was about five feet away from him. He looked back at the farm to check again before he emerged from cover and grabbed it. He then spun around quickly and dashed back to the cover of his hut.

The package contained a stainless steel earpiece and pair of futuristic folding glasses. He slid the earpiece into his left ear and pushed the glasses onto his nose as he hooked them behind his ears. Then he heard the familiar voice of Gringo through the earpiece.

"How's it going, boss?" Gringo asked.

"I'm relieved to hear your voice, Gringo!" Wedmore whispered.

"Don't worry, boss, the cavalry are here! Want some help?" Gringo asked.

"Tell you the truth, I don't think we have much time and I think being mob-handed will do more harm than good. With your support, I'm going this one alone," Wedmore replied.

"No worries, boss. We've got some cool kit here to help you and if you slip your glasses on and flick the switch on the left arm, you'll get a view of the drone's camera," Gringo said.

A small screen sprang to life on the left side of the glasses, giving Wedmore a crystal clear view of the drone's camera, which was hovering near the road.

"Wow, this is great!" Wedmore said.

"You ain't seen nothing yet, boss! How do you think we found you?" Gringo replied. "We've got thermo-imaging X-ray cams on board that show you where people are within the house so you can get in there safely ASAP! We've even got stealth mode, so we can cut virtually all the noise from the propellers. What do you say? Get going!" said Gringo. "We've got your back!"

"Ok, let's do this. Can you fly that thing over to this side of the house to see if there's anyone near the side door?" Wedmore asked.

"Sure thing. We've got you on loudspeaker here and Hitler is piloting the drone so he can go off your directions. Switching to stealth mode now," Gringo replied.

"Great. Once I'm closer to the house, I'm not going to be able to say anything, as I don't want to give away my position. So, if you could do a couple of laps around the house to locate everyone, I should be able to view it on these glasses and make my approach. Ok, I'm going in."

Wedmore walked towards the door of the outbuilding as the drone flew silently towards the house. He watched the camera images flashing in front of him before the image changed to a greyish outline of the house with faint yellow and orange pixels as the thermo-imaging camera kicked in. The drone passed the side of the house so Wedmore could see there was no immediate threat near the door. He could now walk confidently towards his target, yet he kept a firm grip on his gun.

As he got closer to the side of the house, he watched the images from the camera as the drone flew slowly around the property. He could essentially see inside each room. There was a group of people in one of the upstairs rooms and a single person in one of the ground floor rooms. The lone person was at least fifteen feet away from the side door and all parties upstairs appeared to be stationary.

Never one to rely solely on technology, Wedmore crept up to the side door and looked for any obvious signs of the door being alarmed or anyone the camera hadn't picked up. He approached the door preparing to enter the country hideout.

Chapter 21

Rescue and Reveal

LOCATION: Kent, England
DATE: 12th May
WEATHER: Warm and sunny

Wedmore placed his left hand on the rusty doorknob and slowly twisted it clockwise. He held his gun ready to engage anyone lurking in the darkness on the other side. The door latch clicked back as the door opened slightly. Suffering from years of neglect and being badly swollen, the bottom of the door began to scrape against the scullery floor as the rusting hinges creaked. He leaned into the door doing his best to keep noise to a minimum, but caused more creaking. Wedmore began to fear he would quickly reveal his position. He took firm hold of the door handle and lifted as hard as he could to stop contact with the floor before again pushing against the door. He kept the upward pressure on the door for a few moments longer to create an opening that he could just slip through.

Standing momentarily in the scullery listening intently and observing his surroundings, he could smell dampness in the air. He saw green algae growing from some of the stonewalls where water leaks had left the place damp and run down. The floor was caked in dust with a network of footprints leading to and from the external scullery door and the internal door into the adjacent room.

Wedmore looked at the images flashing on his glasses as the drone continued its circular movements around the house. The lone ranger hadn't moved from his previous position, which meant Wedmore's entry had gone undetected.

He walked into the next room where the same dust trails showed the foot traffic throughout the room. The room showed remnants of a former kitchen that had been smashed to pieces and set alight by vandals in years gone by. There was a door to the side of the room hanging off one hinge that led into a hallway with a broken, grimy window overlooking the courtyard. Wedmore felt a cold draught of air blowing throughout the house.

He watched the images in his glasses as he moved closer towards the hallway, his gun held ready to fire at a moment's notice. He could not allow the visions to be a distraction or a substitute for his years of military experience in a precarious situation like this. He looked across the hallway through a crack in the opposite doorway and saw the lone ranger tending to an open fire. The room featured a couple of deck chairs and a battered old leather sofa placed around the fireplace. He didn't want to engage the lone ranger when there was a danger Sana could be harmed or killed if the kidnappers realised there was an intruder in the house.

Instead, he turned his attention to how to scale the old pine staircase to the right of him, which looked as though it would start creaking and give way if he looked at it for too long. The steps leading upstairs were in poor condition and some parts of the staircase were missing. He counted fifteen steps in total and figured that if he walked closest to the edge of the staircase, it would lessen his chances of creating a disturbance. It did concern him that it could take several moments to walk up the stairs, which could leave him exposed should the lone ranger or the others see him.

He felt he could climb the balustrade to the side and pull himself up onto the landing, but that would assume the balustrade would hold his weight without creaking or giving way. He felt this was his best option so he stepped forward to get a secure footing on the staircase before reaching up to the landing floor to steady himself. With a few swift moves, he hopped onto the balustrade and hauled himself up. He landed quietly and crouched into position to prepare for action.

The thermal images revealed four people sitting in a small circle in a bedroom. The floor between his current position and the door to the bedroom had several missing or damaged floorboards. He would have to be sure-footed as one false move could cause him to trip up, or worse, send him crashing through the floor.

He could hear three male voices. Wedmore wondered if he could get a little closer to the room without being discovered. Across the landing was a doorway into another vacant bedroom and he couldn't see any evidence of anyone within the room from the thermal images. He tiptoed across the broken floor with his gun trained in the direction of the bedrooms. As he shifted his weight from one foot to another, the floorboards creaked, but barely enough to be heard.

He was alert, but the discussions continued uninterrupted. As Wedmore got closer to the vacant bedroom doorway, he prepared for any unpleasant surprises. He peered into the darkness of the room. He couldn't see the floor clearly enough to ensure a solid footing, so he slid his feet along the ground to test for any holes. All he wanted to do was to hide behind the reveal wall to listen in on the conversations next door so he could find the perfect opportunity to strike.

He felt the edges of broken floorboards and found a large hole just behind the door. He reached across the void and felt solid flooring on the other side. Although not ideal, with a slightly stretched stance, the hiding place would conceal him should anyone walk in or out of the room. Wedmore positioned himself against the cold, dank plaster wall, and listened in.

He could only make out a few words. It appeared as though the captors were interrogating Sana. Thankfully, he could hear her voice occasionally and she sounded quite calm, so he felt reassured that she wasn't being mistreated.

The drone circled around the house once more and hovered in a position almost directly opposite Wedmore's location. The images showed the dark outlines of the bedroom walls with four orangey-red figures still sitting in a circle. Unfortunately, he had no idea which of them were the kidnappers and which was Sana. He was mindful not to go in guns blazing because he didn't want to hit her with a stray round or risk her being killed by one of the captors. Also, Sana's voice was on repeat in his head warning him to do things peacefully and to not kill people. This was without a doubt the hardest mission he had faced for a long time as the woman he loved was being held against her will and he had no real plan to help her yet.

As he ran certain scenarios through his mind, his heart began to race as more adrenaline was dumped into his bloodstream. His palms began to sweat, making it difficult to keep a firm grip on his weapon. He took a moment to wipe the handle of his gun with his t-shirt and ran his palms down his jeans. He wondered if striking the villains in the bedroom was the best place to attack as he had no idea if Sana was in a booby-trap situation. He was also mindful of the lone ranger downstairs who would come running, armed and dangerous, on hearing gunshots.

He reasoned that a peaceful approach was out of the question and the only way would be to try to injure the bad guys with flesh wounds and try to stop them firing back at him. If he burst through the door, he would have to size up everyone in the room and deliver three rounds at a rapid pace within a split second.

Deep emotions crept into his thinking. What if he shot Sana by accident? What if one of the captors shot her during the commotion? What if she was rigged in an explosive vest? The maddening scenarios caused him to lose his cool. Maybe he should wait until some or all of them left the room, or maybe he could chance it and peacefully take the room through the element of surprise. The difficulty would be covering the room as at least one, if not two, people would be obscured from view behind the door as it opened into the room. Doubt started to get the better of him.

Wedmore took a deep breath and closed his eyes. He rationalised that he didn't need to rush things as Sana wasn't being harmed and everything seemed reasonably calm. If he allowed matters to unfold, there was always a chance that one or more people might leave the room to go downstairs, or the lone ranger might come upstairs to join them, which might present a better opportunity to strike. He had some time to play with. He didn't need to make a rushed decision amped up by a ton of adrenaline and masculinity to save her.

As he was absorbed by his thoughts, he heard the click of the bedroom door opening. Wedmore was jolted out of his train of thought. With an elevated heart rate, he inhaled slowly and deliberately through his nostrils to fill his lungs fully before holding his breath in an attempt to bring a state of calm to his body. He couldn't see anything from his hiding place, but he could hear that someone had left the room and was standing literally inches away from him. Wedmore pressed himself into the damp plaster wall. Although he wanted to peek around the edge of the doorframe to watch, he resisted the temptation and instead listened intently to the rustling of a jacket and the heavy breathing of his enemy.

Wedmore removed the glasses from his face and slid them into his back pocket. Now he would rely on good old-fashioned instinct, balls, and combat experience. He readied himself. As he listened for more movement, it became clear to him that the person on the other side of the wall was making a phone call. Although he could only hear one side of the conversation, the call appeared to be about Sana.

"Yeah, gov. It's Wilson," the deep East-End London accent said. *"Yeah we've got the girl. We snatched her from the house but nobody else was there. We were expecting a real battle, but it was easy. He wasn't around. What do you want us to do with her?"* Wilson asked… *"You want us to ask her about who, gov.? Yeah, the signal's a bit shit here. Say that again. Who were you talking about?"… Darby and Marston, is that right?"*

Wedmore recognised the names Darby and Marston, but couldn't place them. His thoughts were interrupted by the continued monologue of Wilson.

"Alright, gov. We'll ask about them fellas Marston and Darby. Once we've got the info from her, what do you want us to do with her?"… "Kill her, gov?"… "Alright, no problem. Anything else?"

These words sent chills down Wedmore's spine as he realised what this was all about. Marston and Darby were the media barons he previously met with Rosehill at the airfield. Rosehill did warn that their disappearance would cause some repercussions, but he wondered how they had traced it all back to him and Sana.

"Alright, gov. Yeah, we got that. Leave it with us. See ya."

Wilson looked down at the screen for a moment as he went to hang up. As he did so, the shining metallic silver barrel of

Wedmore's gun invaded the space between his face and his mobile. Wedmore brought the gun up towards Wilson's forehead and could see he was clearly caught off-guard. With eyes full of disbelief, Wilson looked at Wedmore standing opposite him as though he were a ghost. This was the last place Wilson had expected to encounter confrontation.

Wedmore brought his index finger to his lips signalling for Wilson to be quiet then motioned for Wilson to place both hands on top of his head. Wedmore pressed his gun into the back of Wilson's head before leaning forward slightly to whisper.

"Right, Wilson, we're going back into that room and your friends are going to surrender or this will be the last thing you remember. Clear?" Wedmore asked.

Wilson nodded before slowly walking towards the bedroom door. Wedmore kept his gun firmly fixed into the back of Wilson's head as they moved in unison. Wedmore noticed that his new friend had a handgun holstered on his left hip so he removed it and held it in his left hand. Having two guns might give him a split-second advantage as they entered the room. Wilson gripped the door handle and hesitated for a second before feeling the second gun press into his lower back. He opened the door and stepped into the room with Wedmore keeping himself hidden behind Wilson's ample frame.

Wedmore scanned the room over Wilson's shoulder and could see two men sitting opposite one another. They looked up at Wilson as he entered the room, slightly confused why he had his hands on his head. In the periphery of his vision, he could see Sana to the right of him. With three enemies to manage in the room, Wedmore delivered a sharp kick to the back of Wilson's knee and sent him crashing to the ground, revealing himself with guns trained on both seated kidnappers. The element of surprise always worked well in these situations as

Wedmore uttered the words, *"Nobody move!"* to his new audience.

The sound of Wilson crashing to the floor made the lone ranger shout to his colleagues to ask if everything was ok. Wedmore kicked Wilson again and told him to answer him.

"Yeah, gov!" Wilson shouted. *"It's these fucking floors! Just tripped up, that's all."*

Sana, who was relieved to see her man, took her cue and relieved the gunman closest to her of his machine gun. Wedmore motioned to the other gunman and told him to surrender his machine gun as he holstered Wilson's handgun in the belt at the back of his jeans. He then spoke quietly to his captives as Sana kept her machine gun pointed at Wilson.

"Ok, you three. I want you all on the floor together face down. No sudden moves and no tricks or we'll shoot you. You first."

Both kidnappers obediently got down on the floor next to Wilson so they were all lying parallel to one another. Once they were all face down, Wedmore quickly flashed a smile to Sana, glancing at the machine gun she was holding and then looking at her smiling face before saying, *"That's kinda hot!"* with a cheeky grin.

Despite her ordeal, Sana giggled at his ability to bring humour to a horrendous situation. Wedmore shushed her from making too much noise by pressing his lips firmly against hers; a kiss that tasted sweeter after the ordeal they had both been through. Wedmore then began inspecting the kidnappers for any other weapons. He removed an assortment of handguns and knives before fortuitously finding a number of black ratchet ties in the side pocket of Wilson's combats. He used them to tie their hands behind their backs, before telling them to sit up with their backs against one another. As they shuffled themselves into position, he took more ratchet straps to tie all of their hands together before he stood up.

Wedmore looked around for something to gag the men with so they wouldn't call out to their friend downstairs. The only thing he could see was a pair of torn, mouldy old curtains, which he thought might make the captives convulse involuntarily, so he took one of the knives he had recovered moments ago and approached Wilson. Sana became concerned and tapped him on the shoulder to ask him to stop.

"Relax," he assured her. *"It's not what you think."*

He took the knife and started to cut the sleeves from the captives' shirts, then wound them into makeshift gags. Once in place, he stood up and whispered to Sana.

"I'm going to head downstairs to apprehend the lone ranger. Then we can call in the cavalry as the boys are waiting on my command. Stay here and mind these three. Here, let's take the safety off this thing! Keep it pointed at them and if they move, shoot them." Wedmore showed Sana how to turn the safety off the machine gun, and noticed she was looking at him with some scepticism.

"You remember I am a warrior woman of the desert, don't you, Jay?" she asked him.

"Erm, yes! Just checking!" he replied. *"This is the real deal, Sana! You can either shoot them or tell them one of your jokes."*

Sana laughed again and playfully hit him on his arm.

"Ok, I'll be back in a few minutes."

He reached forward and kissed her quickly before leaving the room. It felt great to know that she was safe and he had rescued her. Once back out on the landing, he placed the machine gun on the floor with Wilson's handgun. He started to plot his approach before deciding to brazenly walk downstairs and act like one of the lone ranger's teammates. The lone ranger would definitely not be expecting confrontation, so he was confident that the element of surprise would again work in his favour.

He strode confidently across the landing and quickly walked down the stairs. On hearing footsteps, the lone ranger called out, *"You're just in time. I've just got those rat packs cooked up."*

Fucking ration packs, Wedmore thought. He didn't miss those. Without reply, Wedmore gripped his Desert Eagle and let it lead his way into the room where the lone ranger had his back to him, oblivious to the danger and innocently cooking the ration packs in aluminium pots over the open fire. Wedmore glanced across the room to see the lone ranger's weapon resting across the arms of his deck chair, which was at least two strides away from him. Wedmore purposely cleared his throat, causing the lone ranger to turn around. As he saw the gun trained on him and realised it was a hostile situation, the colour drained from the lone ranger's face.

"Hands up!" Wedmore instructed.

The lone ranger dropped the wooden spoon as Wedmore took a step to one side of the doorway and instructed his new captive to go upstairs. Hanging his head in disappointment, the lone ranger walked passed Wedmore with his hands up and began to walk upstairs. Wedmore momentarily thought about calling the cavalry in, but decided to play it safe and get all possible elements of danger under control first.

Wedmore called out to reassure Sana they were approaching. They entered the room where Wedmore tied the lone ranger's hands behind his back, but didn't bother gagging him. He then walked over to the window and looked at the camera on the drone outside. He signalled 'OK' to the camera and asked his teammates to join him. In the moments they had together before the Black Widows descended on the house, he took Sana into his arms and gave her a reassuring hug.

"I'm so sorry this happened to you, Sana," Wedmore said in a voice that was tinged with regret.

"Worry not, Jay. It's all part of the master plan!" Sana replied, as cheerful and wise as ever.

They were interrupted by the sound of a Land Rover hurtling down the farm track and screeching to a halt in the courtyard, as five familiar faces leapt out, armed and ready for battle. They stormed into the house, double-checking all of the rooms before arriving in the upstairs bedroom to join Sana and Wedmore.

"Looks like we are a little late to the party, boss," Gringo said.

"I've gotta say that it looks like the boss has still got it!" Kamali said with a smile as he patted Wedmore on the back. *"Good job, my friend."*

"Couldn't have done it without you boys, and thank you so much for the extra 'eye in the sky', Hitler. I really appreciate it. That technology is fucking awesome! Never had an X-ray view of a target's hideaway before."

"You're welcome," Hitler replied. *"It was great to finally use it for something other than spying on my hot neighbour!"* he joked, only to receive a disapproving raised eyebrow from Sana.

"Ok, let's get back to business" Springbok said. *"Let's find out what these fuckers have been up to and why they snatched your girl, boss."*

"I heard that one on the phone say it's got something to do with Marston and Darby," Wedmore said as he motioned in Wilson's direction. *"Remember those guys we sent to the floating prison from the airfield? Rosehill warned us that there

would be repercussions. I think that's why they're here and why they came after Sana."

"*Is that so?*" Springbok asked. He knelt on the floor next to Wilson who began to look somewhat uncomfortable in his presence. "*Does anyone have any objections to me starting the interrogation?*" Springbok asked.

"*Be our guest,*" the Doc said.

Springbok took his Bowie knife, and slowly and deliberately, began cutting the shoelaces of Wilson's boots. One by one, the loops of his laces were severed by the sharpness of the blade as Wilson looked on in horror. As the last loop was cut, Springbok slid the boots and socks off Wilson's feet and began to smile as he reached into his shirt pocket to remove a box of matches.

The rest of the team looked on with some amusement as they knew what was about to happen. Sana was somewhat bemused and stepped closer to Wedmore, interlocking her left arm with his right. Springbok carefully placed four matches in between the toes of both Wilson's feet before saying, "*Here's how this is going to work. I'm going to ask you some questions and you're going to tell me the truth, because if you don't, I'm going to light one of these matches and its going to get very warm on the tender underside of your feet. Do you understand?*"

Wilson nodded rapidly.

"*Good!*" Springbok continued as he untied the gag from Wilson's mouth. "*Now that we understand each other, I want you to tell me who sent you to our boss's house to kidnap his girl?*" Springbok tossed his right thumb over his shoulder to point at Wedmore and Sana as he kept his steely gaze fixed firmly on Wilson.

Wilson took a breath to gain some composure before saying, "Yeah, well, it's the guvnor, innit? I mean like, he's the one that told us what to do, yeah."

"And who is your governor?" Springbok asked.

"Well, I don't know his name, mate. He's just the one I get my orders from and who I report to. Never seen him, though to tell you the truth, mate, so I wouldn't know him from Adam," Wilson said.

"That's a lie, Springbok. I heard him talking on the phone to his boss earlier and he definitely knows who he is," Wedmore said. "I say we light one of the matches," he continued, gently nudging Sana to provoke a reaction. Sana remained quiet and watched with anticipation.

As Wilson protested, Springbok lit one of the matches and firmly held onto his leg as the match burned away. Moments later, the smell of singed skin filled the air as Wilson yelped in pain.

"Alright, alright!" Wilson shouted. "Christ, that fucking hurt! I do know who it is. He's a strange man, and if I tell you this, I know he'll kill me. He's a guy called Childroth. Hemplock Childroth. I think he's also a lord and he's one mean son of a bitch!" Wilson winced and writhed under Springbok's restraint as the pain shot up his body.

"And where do we find this Childroth?" Wedmore asked.

"He's a little difficult to tie down because he's always on the move. But he is expecting us to take you to him shortly," he said glancing in Sana's direction. "The gov was asking us about some people called Darby and Marston. Do you know anything about 'em?" Wilson asked.

"Hmmm, and why do they want to know about them?" Wedmore asked.

"The gov said they went missing recently and seems to think you are responsible for some reason," Wilson replied.

"Where are you meeting Childroth?" Springbok asked. "I think we should all go and pay him a visit."

"We ain't due to see him for a couple-a days, but maybe we could go see him sooner like, if we tell him we can't get any information out of the girl. We can tell the gov that we're bringing her to him to see if he can get her to talk," Wilson suggested, trying to win the trust of his captors by thinking on his feet whilst also trying to work out the motives of the mysterious group stood around him. Wilson had little idea of who they were or what he was caught up in.

Springbok looked towards Wedmore for some direction. Wedmore thought for a moment before turning to his girl and cheekily asking, *"Fancy playing hostage again?"*

Sana looked into Wedmore's eyes with a smile before teasing him by saying, *"Is this some kind of kinky fantasy you've got going on, Jay?"* They laughed together before she continued, *"If you think it will help then let's do it!"*

"Alright, here we go, this is what we'll do," Wedmore said. "Let's play captives and go and find Mr Childroth. Then we can wrap this thing up once and for all and get back on track with our mission. Wilson, get on the phone and arrange a meeting with your governor."

Wedmore turned to Hitler and asked him to secure their position before leaving the room with Sana. Hitler fished around in his rucksack and pulled out four thick rubber hoops, which he began to fix around the necks of the captives.

"What's this?" Wilson asked.

"They're exploding head collars," Hitler replied. *"Basically, if you attempt to turn on us in any way, then we detonate these*

devices and it's goodnight Vienna. They're to ensure your co-operation."

Hitler took a moment to secure the collars in place before switching them on. A small led light shone green for a second on each collar before going out. Hitler then adjusted the collars of their shirts to cover as much of the devices as he could.

"We're also removing all ammunition from your weapons so you can stage the hostage situation with our boss and his girl in front of Childroth. Any funny business and our boss will flick a switch and they'll all explode. You have been warned!" Hitler then took his knife and cut the zip-tie holding Wilson's hands together. *"Wilson, make your call,"* Hitler said as he handed Wilson his phone.

Wilson took the phone from Hitler and dialled Childroth's number. Springbok ensured the phone was on loudspeaker so they could all hear the call.

"Alright, gov. It's Wilson again. Yeah, we've got a bit of a situation here. We've tried to crack this bird here, but she ain't saying a word. We've tried everything, except cutting off her fingers and toes. The thing is, gov, a couple of the lads went back to the house and they've managed to grab the guy as well. They're both here and we've done all we can, but neither of them is saying anything."

Wilson paused for a moment to see if there was a reaction from Childroth. The voice at the other end of the line cleared his throat before speaking.

"Very well, bring them to me. We simply must find out what has happened to Marston and Darby. I am convinced they know something about their disappearance. I have a little something here that I know will make them talk," Childroth replied.

"Alright, gov. Where we bringing 'em to? You got an address for us?" Wilson asked.

"Yes. Bring them to the Pharmakul building on Robinus Street. Approach the back door of the warehouse building and I'll be waiting for you," Childroth instructed.

"Alright, gov. We'll bring them over now. See you in half an hour," Wilson said.

"Good. There'll be nobody around so we can work without interruption. See you shortly. Goodbye," Childroth said as he ended the call.

Springbok snatched back the phone. The Black Widows emptied a couple of handguns of ammunition before handing them to the captives as Kamali cut them free from their bonds. The remainder of the guns, knives, and ammunition were placed in Hitler's holdall whilst the machine guns were slung over the shoulders of the Black Widows. The Doc opened the door and led the procession downstairs with Hitler, Kamali, and Springbok close behind, keeping them at gunpoint.

The group joined Sana and Wedmore in the courtyard after the couple completed a thorough inspection of the Mercedes 4x4. They had been looking for weapons or anything that could put them in a compromising position.

"Looks like it's all clean, guys," Wedmore said. "Let's saddle up and you guys can follow us. I've still got the earpiece in, so you can communicate with us as we get closer to our destination."

"You'll need this as a little insurance policy whilst you're travelling with our friends," Hitler said, handing Wedmore the detonator for the head collars.

"Let's hope I won't be needing this, gentlemen," Wedmore said, addressing the four captives who were now holding their ammo-less handguns. "Ok, let's get going."

Chapter 22

The Devil's Breath

LOCATION: Kent, England
DATE: 12th May
WEATHER: Warm and sunny

The journey to Robinus Street took an hour. Wedmore and Sana were in the rear passenger seat of the Mercedes 4x4 with their captives, with the Black Widows following closely in the Land Rover. The vehicles turned off the main road into an industrial estate. The sizeable Pharmakul building was directly in front of them, the bright neon sign standing out against the duskiness of the early evening. The Mercedes passed through the entrance to the side and pulled up near the shutter door at the back whilst the Land Rover parked in the shadows nearby.

A quick honk of the horn sent the shutter door clattering into action before the Mercedes disappeared out of sight from the Black Widows. They listened intently to the sounds from Wedmore's earpiece.

The Mercedes parked and everyone disembarked as they were approached by a tall, spindly looking figure wearing a white lab coat. The lanky man wore brown corduroy trousers and matching brogues and had shoulder length curly hair and metal-rimmed glasses. Wilson addressed him as Childroth. His brogues clicked against the grey warehouse floor as he walked towards Sana and Wedmore. Childroth sneered as he prepared to disclose his plan on how to get the couple to talk. He pulled a small orange container from his pocket and held it up to the couple as the fake captors stood around watching.

"This is a new product we've been developing called 'Devil's Breath' and it's a very powerful compound. Once you inhale from this container, you will be forced to tell me the truth and do exactly as I say. If you thought you could withhold the truth from me, then you've got another thing coming," Childroth said with contempt in his voice.

He was clearly proud of himself and his achievements, yet completely oblivious of what was about to unfold.

Wedmore reached around to the back of his jeans and pulled out his Desert Eagle .50 gun, aiming it straight at Childroth's face, changing his sneer to shock. He looked towards Wilson and his colleagues for support, but they were helpless. Wedmore stepped forward and whipped the container out of Childroth's hand and pushed him to the ground. He flipped the lid off the container with his left thumb before thrusting it under Childroth's nose. Childroth tried to resist inhaling, yet as Wedmore knelt on his chest to force the air out of his lungs, he had no choice. Sana stepped closer to observe proceedings, enjoying seeing her man in action and also curious to observe the affects of Devil's Breath.

Childroth coughed a couple of times before a slightly glazed look came over him. Wedmore was keen to find out more about this mysterious character and his interest in Darby and Marston. Wedmore stood up and pulled Childroth to his feet.

"So tell me Mr Childroth, what's your interest in Mr Marston and Mr Darby? And what led you to think we had anything to do with their disappearance?"

Childroth spoke in voice that sounded similar to someone being possessed. *"They are very powerful people who control* what happens in the national and international media. They have been instrumental in creating an environment of anxiety and fear in the collective mind of the western public. They ensure everyone is compliant and distracted while we constantly provoke them with a barrage events in the world that are unlikely to affect their lives but give them something to talk about."

He continued, *"They have been useful servants of mine for many years and kept the status quo functioning as it should throughout the western world. By keeping the public distracted, we continue our work in the shadows serving our master."*

Wedmore was amazed at the honesty this drug had quickly created as he asked, *"Who is your master and what work are you doing in the shadows?"*

Childroth tilted his head back as he looked towards Wedmore with soulless eyes. His possessed voice continued, *"We serve the enlightened one, Lucifer. He blesses us with knowledge of the light and keeps us in our lucrative positions of power. He is everywhere and sees everything at all times. The all-seeing eye, if you will."*

"And the work you do in the shadows? What is this?" Wedmore interjected.

"We carry out the work of Lucifer by inflicting pain and suffering on the weak, innocent, and unsuspecting. We do this to release 'Loosh energy' of pain, misery, and suffering that feeds him. The more we create for him, the stronger he grows and the more we are rewarded with power and material wealth. People think it's all about money, but the reality is we're after people's energy."

Sana stepped forward and was keen to interrogate Childroth. *"How exactly do you create this Loosh energy?"* she asked.

"The best way is by hiding in plain sight and masquerading as something else entirely," Childroth replied. *"One of the ways we do this is by seemingly offering to do good for others with an evil or harmful intent in the background. To get the most Loosh energy over a person's lifetime, we always target the children, so their pain and suffering will generate an enormous amount of energy. Evil does its best work when it's masquerading as good."*

"If a man saw another man sexually abusing a child, the observer would no doubt step in and physically reprimand or harm the offender. But, if the paedophile is part of a church and masquerades as a good-guy, then his wrongdoings can go undetected for many years and generate lots of energy for our master from many children. The best emotion we can keep people trapped in is the feeling of shame as it keeps them compliant and always second-guessing the world they live in. They emit an enormous amount of anxiety, frustration, and fear."

Sana reached out to stop Wedmore from punching Childroth's face. *"No, Jay, don't get drawn into their world. Stay with me!"*

Childroth continued unfazed, looking almost a little pleased with himself; *"We also get much energy from the work we do here at Pharmakul. People who take our quick-fix medicines and injections without questioning them put themselves in harm's way voluntarily. It's the greatest scam ever! Who would have thought you could get people believing they could inject health into themselves? We convince them so much that they actually line up to inflict damage upon themselves!"* Laughing to himself, Childroth continued, *"Darby and Marston sure did a fine job of brain-washing the public with that one!"*

Wedmore was becoming increasingly agitated as Childroth spoke, yet Sana remained her usual calm self as though she was finally hearing the truth about what she had long suspected was a problem. She held her partner's arm tightly as she leaned forward to put the final pieces of the puzzle into place. *"Tell me, Mr Childroth, how many more people know about the disappearance of Mr Darby and Mr Marston?"*

"None, only me. Our Council of Thirteen who serve Lucifer is aware that I organise the strings to be pulled in the media, but they don't know who does it."

"How do we know who else serves Lucifer?" Sana asked.

"It's simple really. Most, not all, but most of the people who serve him are in high-powered positions across the world and they look great on camera as they seemingly do their bit of good for humanity. You can always tell which ones are part of it as they usually give very visible hand signals. One is the 'OK' symbol, which shows the index finger and thumb making a circle with the middle, fourth and pinkie fingers forming the body of a 6. This shows three 6's on the hand, which is a clear sign of worship to their master. The other is the 'rock and roll' hand gesture where the index and little fingers are extended and the thumb holds down the middle and fourth fingers. It's amazing how these gestures of worship have been made fashionable by the Luciferian rock bands. Many millions of people are willingly throwing these hand signals around thinking they are being cool but are unwittingly showing their allegiance to Lucifer. It's quite amazing what we have been able to achieve over the years. Millions of people hypnotised, unquestioning, and believing anything put in front of them," Childroth said.

"Aren't you worried about the karmic comeback from operating in this way?" Sana asked.

"Ha! Karma!" Childroth mocked. "Here's the funny thing about karma. It only applies when you don't tell someone what you're doing to them. The moment you show or tell them what is happening, all karmic comeback ceases to exist. That's why films, television shows, music videos, video games, printed newspapers, and magazines are so powerful. We program the sheeple with what is happening to them in a variety of ways, and not only do they turn up in droves to watch the latest film, they actually endorse what is happening."

"We see it all the time when there is a call for war and people give their public approval as they've been brainwashed into believing it is ok. Or they rave about the latest film showing how the weather could be weaponised, which people pass off as a work of fiction, not realising we have been manipulating it for years. People are too glued to their smartphones to look up to the sky and see what is really going on."

"How are you able to manipulate the weather?" Wedmore asked.

"It's simple really. An additive is mixed into airline jet engine fuel that causes white chemtrails behind the airplane. This creates an ionising affect in the atmosphere, which attracts water molecules and causes cloud cover. We are then able to manipulate this cloud cover to control the amount of sunshine and even the wind speed through the use of wireless transmitters stationed around the world. These transmitters emit a certain frequency that alters the weather patterns in different parts of the world to our liking," Childroth responded.

"Why would you want to manipulate the weather?" Wedmore asked.

"There are many reasons. It started as a program for bringing water to areas suffering from drought. Once we had the technology for doing good, it wasn't long before we could bring it into our world and create more Loosh energy. Think about how many topics of British conversation are about the weather! The dark clouds, the rain, the storms, they all make life a little miserable. We know how much happier people are in the sunshine, so if we take that away from them as much as possible, it reduces their personal power and keeps them depressed. We could even create enough cloud cover to form another ice age, completely depriving the earth of sunlight and killing off life as we know it. The only reason we don't go that far is because it would starve our Lord of the Loosh energy he needs to survive. The best part about it all is that when someone realises what is going and they try to tell others about it, they sound like lunatics and are dismissed. It takes a strong person to continue to spread the truth of what is happening in the world when there is so much ignorance. It's true that people have actually become happy in their slavery. No public outcry. In fact, no-one is taking action against the situation. Total public inertia!" Childroth sneered.

"Well, that's what you think, Mr Childroth, but I can tell you there is a storm brewing," Sana said.

"Good luck with that!" Childroth snorted. "We have infiltrated every position of power in the world, so you're going to have to remove us from the most powerful governments, authorities, militaries, and financial systems worldwide. I don't see that working out too well for you!" Childroth mocked.

"We'll see!" Wedmore said through gritted teeth. "We've got a special place for the likes of you and with any luck, you'll get a front row seat to watch the action unfold."

Sana and Wedmore turned around to realise their captives had disappeared during their interrogation of Childroth. Wedmore quickly frogmarched the intoxicated Childroth towards the Mercedes and flung him into the back seat before running with Sana towards the open roller shutter door. As they ran out into the concrete service yard area, they were greeted by the Black Widows who had recaptured the men as they had tried to sneak out of the building unnoticed.

"Don't worry, boss, we've got them!" Springbok said.

"Good work, team. Glad I can always rely on you guys!" Wedmore said. "Looks like we've got an extra few visitors for our friends at the floating prison. Let's get this riff-raff over to them tonight and we can get things back to normal. I think we should also give them the Merc as a thank you gift for taking care of these degenerates and keeping them out of our way."

"Aye-aye, Captain," Gringo said with a mock salute as he entered the Mercedes to take the men to prison. As the Mercedes exited the building, Wedmore went to the back of the Land Rover and removed a jerry can full of fuel. He then walked back into the warehouse towards a large number of pallets of medicine and poured the fuel over the pallets before setting light to them, much to Sana's protests.

"Sorry, sweetheart," he said with a stern look in his eye. "Nobody fucks around with my girl and gets away with it. This should put their operation out of action for several months. Evil fuckers!"

"Oh Jay! You're such a man when you're angry!" teased Sana as they headed towards the vehicles to get their mission back on track.

• • • •

Wedmore and the Black Widows scrambled their associates to initiate Project Peace and Love (PAL). They had to act now to provide a united and co-ordinated worldwide approach to prevent their mission from being thwarted by allied countries potentially using their armies to stop the unification from taking place.

It was a stressful time as they worked around the clock to organise the most trusted personnel from across the world who were joining their mission and who were sworn to secrecy to prevent any more authority figures from finding out their plans. Clearly, a breach of trust would be devastating and potentially lead to the Black Widows being assassinated in their attempts to overthrow those who would continue to use evil and corruption to suppress the lives of humanity.

Wedmore had to take the time to focus on his daily routine to ensure he was in peak mental and emotional shape. He was acutely aware of the enormity of what they were going to do and knew it could quickly overwhelm him, which would start to drive thoughts of negativity into his mind if he wasn't careful. He started most mornings reading the 'Tao Te Ching', a book Sana had brought for him to help give a greater insight into life. As he read each paragraph, it prompted him to really reflect on what the words were saying. It distilled ancient wisdom into simple paragraphs, yet provoked intense and reflective thoughts and feelings on how the teachings could be applied to everyday life.

Wedmore wrote in his journal every morning to manage his mind whilst reflecting on the wonderful journey of life he was currently enjoying. He felt blessed and grateful to be in the fortunate position to take this mission forward, but hearing the fears of others invariably triggered some negative thoughts of possible consequences in his own mind. A major breakthrough Wedmore experienced was to realise that people could only ever project their model of the world in conversation with him, which was always based on the experiences they had endured throughout their life journey so far. It was futile for him to expect everyone he spoke to in confidence was going to jump at the chance of joining their mission, particularly as many were military men who faced severe consequences for insubordination and financial penalties for standing against the current system.

No matter how many negative thoughts and feelings were expressed by those he spoke with, he realised that he could either buy into the fear and insecurities of others and give up on his mission, or have empathy for them and trust they would be in a position to join the mission if it was part of their life journey. The Tao Te Ching allowed him to realise that not everything he was going through had to have a huge amount of meaning and emotion attached to it, so he choose to be in control of his own emotions and act accordingly.

The combination of the journaling and reading in the morning was working wonders to manage his mental and emotional state prior to getting heavily involved with his day. He also took the time to sit in quiet meditation every morning for about half an hour so he could calm himself and begin to broadcast a powerful intention for how his day would go. He personally viewed this as the most powerful thing he could do, as he believed it really was a space to create an internal conversation with God. It opened the channels for Divine communication with the Creator and allowed him to see whether he was on track with the mission and his life in general.

One powerful thing that emerged was the knowledge that he could start to read and interpret energies of people without even speaking with them. He had begun to listen to his heart in every way, which proved particularly helpful for knowing if people genuinely wanted to be part of his mission, or whether their heart wasn't in it, or if they were going to betray him. To do this, he would first still his mind and hold a vision of the person in his mind's eye. He would then take a few deep breaths to calm himself completely and then tune into his heart to pick up the messages the image was sending him. As he listened for the signals he received, which were interpreted through his feelings, he sent love from his heart to the person he was thinking of and monitor what feelings came back to him. If the feeling was good, he would know he could trust them and if the feeling was bad, he wouldn't even think about contacting them no matter what potential assistance they could offer. By following this procedure with many people he had known for several years, and tuning into his heart to send them love, the results he received back surprised him.

The team were planning to take action in a few short weeks with Wedmore co-ordinating the lead of teams from both America and the UK. Their plan was to march on Parliament Square in London, the White House in Washington, and Wall Street in New York. So far, he and his team had managed to recruit an army of 150,000 soldiers who had various ranks within the military and who desperately wanted to see change in the world. They were tired of being ordered to slaughter innocent people for corrupt evil people with loaded personal agendas.

He felt he could recruit around 1.5million soldiers. It wasn't the biggest army in the world, but by approaching multiple cities at one time, Wedmore hoped to cause enough disruption that they would gain many other supporters for their work.

Their plan was essentially a military coup; overthrow those in positions of power and take control of the central points of authority within each country, namely the financial institutions and legislation making facilities. They would then determine who was the most qualified to run the respective countries with the best interests of the people in their heart. They would jail all politicians and bankers and would not tolerate any abuse of power.

The hub of their operations was a hive of activity with the Black Widows hitting the satellite phones and talking to their colleagues and trusted referrals worldwide. Their secure encrypted messaging service allowed them to contact anyone and to finalise arrangements for the march. Conversations were difficult to open with those generals who had not been at the

SOFEX exhibition because of their indoctrination into the military system and their years of service to something they firmly believed in. However, even some of these veterans had begun to have their doubts about the orders they were receiving. Their conscience had already led them to doubt whether they were doing the right thing. They began to look beyond the reports given in the media and by their superiors to be part of an agenda they had not signed up for, nor had they pledged their life to defend. Many had lost valued colleagues and friends in wars around the world, all of which appeared to be based on lies and deceit. There was a growing sense of dissatisfaction with their roles on the world stage.

What was more distressing was not the loss of life during the conflicts, but the amount of soldiers taking their own lives after they returned home. The rates of post-traumatic stress disorder (PTSD) in soldiers returning from combat were skyrocketing. The overwhelming and unrelenting feeling of guilt for being associated with the death of innocent people and the sight of dead bodies, some dismembered and blown apart, were playing on their minds constantly. The visions of death and destruction from battle haunted them and they felt the only way to escape it was to end their own lives.

This was something the Black Widows knew all too well and were it not for their healing experiences in the desert, they would no doubt have found themselves in the same position. Life was incredibly precious and no-one had the right to take the life of another. The fact that so many generals witnessed the loss of soldiers in their command through suicide gave further support to the mission and they vowed to break rank and send their troops in to support the uprising.

The biggest hurdle was not a show of might or strength; it was the non-violent approach of a peaceful revolution. Trying to suggest those who wanted to show their support for the movement should do so peacefully and unarmed was dismissed by those who believed they needed to 'always be prepared'. Fear ran through those who felt they would be met with fierce military opposition in their march to freedom. Because of this, they chose to keep the exact date and time of the movement absolutely secret until a few days prior to the march. They had managed to secure the commitment of 'ready when you are' from a number of parties and their numbers were growing by the day.

One of the key people Wedmore had personally spoken with was his longstanding friend in the US Military, Admiral Richard Byrd. Byrd and Wedmore met during a covert military operation in former Soviet Russia. They were there on a fact-finding mission to understand the strength of the Soviet military for their respective governments. What they witnessed was far different from what they had been led to believe they would find. They had been told of the iron fist that ruled Russia and how its people were suppressed by the dictatorship, living in poverty and misery whilst their government creamed off the wealth and resources for itself. The images that filled the media at that time were not long after the Chernobyl nuclear power disaster, giving people a false impression of what Russia was really like. Desolate wastelands and destroyed buildings were all they expected to find with its citizens dressed like village paupers out of a Robin Hood movie. What they found was almost the exact opposite. The citizens largely happy and supportive of one another and well turned out. Sure, the country had made its fair share of mistakes, as any country of its size would do, but nothing of the order and magnitude they had been led to believe. Their military operation was proud and organised, yet they were not interested in threatening other countries and just wanted to defend their homeland; the true nobility of military forces.

Admiral Byrd had been a good friend to Wedmore in the intervening years and was well respected by high-level brass in the US military for his outstanding bravery and dynamic leadership. Byrd was fifteen years older and had been a good mentor as Wedmore's career unfolded and he was drafted into more and more secret missions. Whenever Wedmore and his team found themselves in situations where they needed particular emergency help, or military support, their first call was to Admiral Byrd. He commanded several hundred thousand troops across the world and always had a team available for an emergency evacuation close by.

Byrd was particularly intrigued by Wedmore's plans and Wedmore was keen to secure his support. They spoke at length for several hours as Wedmore appealed to Byrd's interest. Byrd pledged to bring at least fifty thousand men to join the team at the White House. His support meant they could overcome any number of challenges. Armed with Byrd's support, Wedmore felt confident his long-time friend and ally would pull out all the stops to make things happen.

Chapter 23

A Revolution for Peace

LOCATION: Washington D.C., USA
DATE: 4th July
WEATHER: Overcast as though a storm was brewing…

The day the team had finally been waiting for was suddenly upon them. Doomsday had arrived. Wedmore and his team had pulled off the most incredible effort to rally over two million soldiers to join them to overthrow corruption internationally. As the sun began to rise over the horizon, Wedmore and his team were already awake and focussed on the monumental day ahead. They had arrived in Washington two days prior to ensure all systems were go.

Confirmation had been received from all parties that they were ready and, over the course of the three days prior to the march on Washington, generals from the British and American armies had been issuing their orders to recall troops from foreign missions back to base under the pretence of the next top-secret military mission. No one but the privileged few generals and those in high command knew what was about to unfold. For Wedmore and his team who were leading this revolt, their hearts were in their mouths.

"This is it, team! Today's the day," Wedmore said in an attempt to sound enthusiastic, but realising his voice was quivering as he spoke.

"It sure is boss! And we're with you all the way!" Gringo replied in his usual upbeat tone. Somehow, the magnitude of the situation was definitely not going to throw his cheeky attitude.

"I have to be honest and say I am feeling nervous!" Wedmore said with a wry smile. *"I'm anxious to see how things play out."*

"It will all go well, Jay. Have faith. Look at what you have achieved over the last few months. You have rallied huge support from people all over the world and now you just need to take the stand and speak for what you truly believe in. You're not doing this for you, you're leading this movement to bring greater fairness, equality, and justice to the world and to stamp out evil in the process. Don't make it about you, make it about a bigger cause and you'll be fine. We're by your side as always, Jay!" said Sana with a big smile.

She was pleased that the big day was finally here and her man was about to lovingly realise his purpose. She felt strongly in her heart that her destiny lay in supporting him through this day of adventure.

"Thank you, Sana" Wedmore replied, still struggling to fake the confidence he felt he needed in the situation.

Kamali reached out across Wedmore's shoulders. He looked him straight in the eyes with a look of stern conviction. *"Look, brother. We've all come a hell of a long way to get here. We have stood by your side through it all and we're not about to back down today, of all days. We trust in you and we will follow you to our death if needs be."*

As he spoke, the team formed a circle around Wedmore and looked at him with smiles and appreciation for everything he stood for. They nodded in silent confirmation of Kamali's words that spoke the truth for them all. No matter what the outcome of the day, they were with him every step of the way.

A tear of overwhelming gratitude formed in Wedmore's right eye and rolled down his cheek. *"Thank you,"* he said.

"Our pleasure, man! Now let's go and kick some butt!" Gringo chirped.

The group laughed together as they began to gather their things and load their fully customised truck ready for the mission. The truck was fitted with amplifiers, loudspeakers, a microphone and an elevating stage that would allow Wedmore to address everyone present. This would give Wedmore an elevated view of everything going on around him and allow him to address the troops to direct their efforts. The intention was to show strength in numbers, not forceful might, and to be peaceful in doing so. The message from this point would be loud and clear; come peacefully to be detained or resist and be detained anyway! Hundreds of thousands of troops as well as many innocent bystanders would be present, so the Black Widows knew clear communication would be of paramount importance to keep the situation under control. The whole march was structured to be peaceful in every respect, but should they encounter resistance, Wedmore would need to be able to direct the soldiers on the ground to carry out his orders. Without this, chaos would likely take over and despite there being well-trained military personnel present, loss of order would quickly result in the loss of life, which Wedmore was very keen to avoid. There was no point in being part of their system by fighting. This was a revolution of peace and their mission was to spread love.

The team boarded the truck with Gringo taking the wheel. Wedmore had contact with his main generals on the ground who were also leading their own platoons of men. It would be a sight to behold as tanks, armoured personnel carriers, and thousands of uniformed men and women marched in the streets towards the White House as early morning commuters looked on aghast.

Hitler had managed to hack the local ABC television network in Washington and was shortly due to release an urgent message to all local residents advising them to stay indoors. He had created a short video of numerous historic presidential speeches, which he had spent many hours editing to keep local residents off the streets during the march. As the team boarded the truck and set off, Hitler planned to patch into the ABC television network and launch the video. They knew that other local television networks would also start to play the video shortly afterwards as they wouldn't miss out on a breaking news story. One thing that could always be relied upon was the exceptionally repetitive nature of the media that would replay it many times over the next hour as the Black Widows and their thousands of supporting troops made their way towards the White House.

Simultaneously, Colonel James Major, a long-standing friend of Wedmore's who supported his mission fully, was leading a march with British troops on the Houses of Parliament in London. Their message was about to break on the BBC news network, which had been skilfully hacked by one of his technology wizards who was used to creating propaganda campaigns against various countries they were instructed to invade for "western intelligence". The two-pronged approach would ensure their mission was a success in the west and would provide a clear warning signal to other governments the world over that enough was enough. No more war.

It was time for a new era where humanity and human consciousness expanded to the next level and for people to start practicing the main teachings of the majority of world religions: to love thy neighbour and to not do anything to another that you wouldn't want done to you. Every other challenge could be resolved from this place of enlightenment by people talking to one another with respect and love rather than with an agenda loaded with expectation and ego. This would be a major step forward.

As the vehicle pulled onto the highway, Hitler cracked open his military grade laptop and connected to the nearest satellite to begin his broadcast. With a few expert strokes of his fingers across the keyboard, he completed the hack into the ABC television network and was ready to upload the video. He turned and slid open the glass screen between the driver's cabin and the rear compartment of the truck to tell Wedmore he was ready. Wedmore took a deep breath, closed his eyes for a moment to soak in the reality of what was about to unfold, and then told Hitler to do it. Hitler tapped the keyboard a few more times and completed the patch into the network, which instantly uploaded the video. He had a separate window open on his laptop as a preview screen for the news network so he could see when the takeover message began to broadcast.

Moments later, the news presenter in mid flow about some wholly irrelevant trivia was dropped like a hot coal as the screen went fuzzy for a moment before the video burst onto the scene with an announcement by JFK advising all personnel in the Washington area to stay indoors. Hitler punched the air with a smile and yelled, *"YES!"* as he saw the result of his handiwork being aired across the nation. The message was bright, bold, and striking, which made it absolutely apparent it was not a hoax. Hitler wondered what it would be like to watch the producers' faces when they realised their network had been hacked and there was no way to take the story off air. He imagined the panic breaking out at the station and knew within minutes, every other news station would broadcast the story across the USA.

Hitler leaned forward and switched on the radio. He pressed the search buttons a few times and did not have to wait long before a newsreader interrupted their usual broadcast with an urgent announcement that ABC's network had been hacked and the perpetrators were using a message from previous presidents advising people to stay indoors in the Washington D.C. area. Hitler, Gringo and the Doc were high-fiving with cheers of joy, realising that the first stage of their plan was complete, whilst Kamali, Springbok, Wedmore and Sana remained somewhat more reserved as they realised it was now game time.

As the truck continued its journey, more and more media stations broke the news about events unfolding in Washington and surprisingly, a similar situation unfolding in London. As a consequence, the roads were unusually quiet with few people milling about in the streets. Those that were there appeared panicked and were running to get home as quickly as possible. More and more army trucks were now driving towards the White House in convoy.

Underneath their composure, the Black Widows breathed a huge sigh of relief that at least they now had some physical back up for their mission. To arrive at the White House and find out they were on their own, or worse, to be greeted by a bunch of people they trusted but who were now standing in opposition to them, would be a devastating scenario.

As they got closer, the roads were filled with military trucks heading towards the White House. Their approach led them in on Interstate 395 which passed The Pentagon, so as soon as they had traversed the 14th Street Bridge, the convoy divided into two, moving towards the White House and Capitol Hill where all politicians would be placed under military arrest.

From there, the Black Widows and their military general friends would assemble a temporary government of the most trusted men and women to lead the country through the forthcoming turmoil and instigate true reform. It was time for ethics, morals, and humanity to take over.

Very soon, the roads were flooded with military vehicles as the huge convoy moved towards the centre of Washington. Kamali reached forward and tuned in their military radio to the secret frequency being used to communicate the plan of attack. This frequency, 11.1Hz, had only been given to those in command of troops who would relay messages to Wedmore as events unfolded. Everyone was instructed to keep the airwaves as clear as possible to avoid possible confusion and to allow Wedmore enough time to process what was going on in different parts of the city. Voices started to break the radio silence as the troops and their commanders descended on the area. Wedmore picked up the hand-held radio to begin directing his men on the ground. Roads were being blocked off to prevent civilians getting close to the scene and foot soldiers were taking their positions to begin their advance on the centre of administration.

Any civilians present were quickly turned away and advised to return home immediately. The local businesses, shops, and offices were empty and the streets were eerily quiet, save for the rumbling of the huge numbers of military vehicles all heading in the same direction. The breaking news had clearly done its job in keeping people away. The convoy was minutes from their rendezvous as some trucks began to pull over to the sides of the road to unload their cargo of soldiers. Wedmore and his team took this opportunity to drive forward and lead the operation from the front.

The streets were now awash with green military berets, polished boots, and assault rifles, complemented by an array of trucks and tanks. Kamali and Wedmore cleared the curtained sides and roof of the truck as people fell into position within their platoons. It really was a sight to behold! At the very front of the soldiers were two rows of tanks taking up both sides of the highway.

Behind the tanks, approximately five hundred thousand men and women all proudly fell in line ready to serve their worthy cause. Gringo positioned the truck between the first rank of soldiers as more and more soldiers surrounded the vehicle. Gringo hit the brakes and waited for a few moments as the two most trusted military personnel, Richard Byrd and John Wright, joined Wedmore in the back of the truck whilst Springbok and Kamali jumped in the front of the cramped cab with their teammates. As soon as the men were on board, Wedmore manoeuvred the platform into place above the driver's cab and took his position at the rostrum with the microphone in hand. The platform was surrounded by railings, which the men and Sana held onto tightly. Wright and Byrd were in contact with their men on the ground and Wedmore stood proud on the platform ready to lead the mission.

With a flick of a switch, the loudspeakers hummed into life and he was able to address the platoons of soldiers that surrounded him. He turned away from the microphone to clear his throat as Sana took a step forward and rested a reassuring hand on his forearm. He glanced briefly at the two trusted men to his right before turning to his left and smiling at Sana. Standing tall and erect with his chest out, Wedmore prepared to give the speech of his life.

"My friends," he began, *"I want to acknowledge each and every one of you for coming here today."*

As he spoke, his amplified voice echoed off the walls of the buildings on both sides of the road as it was carried through the airwaves to each supporting general in the nearby streets.

"What you have chosen to do here today is to take a stand against all that is wrong in the world. You have chosen to stand for peace, justice, love, and freedom and to take the necessary steps towards ending war. Have no doubt about it, we are taking the first of many steps towards creating Heaven on Earth. Whilst it will get darkest before the dawn, we must stand strong together and be the change we want to see in the world. You stand beside your fellow brothers and sisters united, with no thought of separation through racism or prejudice from differences in religion, creed, culture, or upbringing. We stand together as children of God and we want to honour the right to life for everyone the world over. We will have victory today and we will bring about the change that is long overdue."

"The darkness has had its day. Now it's time to bring love and light into this world. I salute every single one of you for your bravery and ask that you stay true to this mission of peace and love long after today has passed. Practice it daily in your encounters with everyone you meet. Spread the message of peace, love, and generosity with everyone you meet. Greet them with a cheerful smile and take an interest in their lives whilst being mindful not to judge them through comparison."

"Love your families and friends in the same way you would want them to love you and most importantly, love yourselves. Love yourselves so much that you would not allow yourself to be, do, or have anything that hurts you or your soul. Love yourself without limits because by doing so, you subconsciously allow other people to love themselves too. Your individual acts of love will create a ripple effect that will extend beyond the boundaries of your physical bodies and will begin to uplift all of humanity. We all play a part in this, my friends. I know that most of you are war veterans and you have seen and done some things that were not in your best interests because you were following the orders of someone else. Take the time you need to heal from these experiences; take the time to own the shadow

within you and learn from the wisdom it grants you to now always do the right thing. Take the time to love yourself completely as you are, knowing that the experiences you have in your life are all whole, complete, and perfect. They will be the transformational events you need to become the very best version of you."

"*I love you all unconditionally, no matter how this turns out today, and I want you know that God Loves you all too. We have been entrusted to deliver this mission and we shall not fail. Have faith, friends, the new dawn beckons.*"

Wedmore paused for a breath. He had no idea where those words came from as he hadn't prepared a speech. He spoke from the heart and allowed the words to flow. It was as though the words were being channelled through him from a higher power and were perfect for the occasion. He received reassuring nods and smiles from his friends on the platform and even Gringo stuck a 'thumbs up' out the window to let Wedmore know his message had been well received. Silence fell before Wedmore finally roared, *"Right, let's show these guys we mean business!"*

The drill sergeant at the front of the platoon screamed *"Quick March!"* The tanks roared into action as the foot soldiers fell into double time behind them. Gringo revved the engine of the truck in enthusiastic celebration before engaging first gear and keeping pace with the soldiers. As they moved forward, the thundering roar of helicopter blades sounded above them as TV crews descended to report the scenes as they unfolded.

They had to cover at least three miles on foot to break the cover of the buildings and get towards the 14th Street Bridge where the platoon would fall into a uniform march towards the target. There was a strong sense of confidence in the air. Sana hooked her arm around Wedmore's as he leaned against the rostrum for balance. She squeezed him tightly to let him know that she was there as his emotional rock. Wedmore turned and kissed her head and they looked at one another lovingly. *"I love you, Jay!"* Sana mouthed above the noise of the engines, helicopters and troops' marching boots that surrounded them. A smile spread across his face as his woman's love distracted him momentarily.

Byrd and Wright were both on their radios issuing instructions to their sergeants on the ground who ensured their men followed an orderly line through the narrow streets towards the 14th Street bridge. It was a formidable and overpowering sight to see them all advancing together. Inside the cabin, Hitler's computer screen showed international news reports of troops descending on the Houses of Parliament in Westminster, London and it was truly a sight to behold. The team cheered to witness the unison of people under this common cause of fighting for their own liberty and the freedom of their fellow man from oppression.

Wedmore scanned the horizons and the skies for possible signs of trouble. He wasn't wearing any body armour and had faith his protection would come from honouring his mission and the alignment of what was meant to be. He didn't want to be the hero, but he also didn't want to die either. He was well aware there could be snipers and he would represent a highly visible target. He had maximum exposure and zero protection. As the thought went through his mind, the feelings of fear started to escalate and he felt goose bumps as he began to grip the rostrum harder.

Feeling his left arm tense up as she clung to it, Sana looked at her man with reassurance and love, kissing him on his bulging triceps to let him know that it would all be just fine. If today was the day they were going to pass, it would all have been worth it to experience the love they had shared over the last few months. She had never felt more alive or on purpose than giving the best of herself in support of her man and the mission they had been entrusted with. Being the Goddess to her Warrior made her life very fulfilling; the balance of their respective masculine and feminine energies was pure harmony as she experienced true love. She knew her man was ready to give his life to protect her.

As the convoy rounded the corner and continued towards the 14th Street Bridge, the platoon slowed from their double time advance into a more orderly march. Part of the platoon of soldiers broke away from the main group to completely surround the Pentagon. As they did so, a pair of F-16 fighter jets flew overhead at low altitude. The noise of their engines bounced off the surrounding buildings and created a thundering rumble that shook everyone to the core. The soldiers did not flinch; they were used to such scare tactics. This was usual protocol for any impending approach or attack on the White House, Capitol Hill, or the Pentagon, and it was a clear sign that the breaking news had alerted those in power there was mutiny in the streets.

As the road straightened out, it became apparent their path towards the White House was not going to be a clear one. The procession was greeted by a number of opposing tanks and soldiers standing firm on the opposite side of the bridge. Wedmore and his trusted advisors kept their calm as the convoy approached the impenetrable boundary and took in the scene that awaited them. They saw many thousands of soldiers standing strong with heavy artillery guns stationed at either side, and at least twice as many tanks as they had on their side. They had expected some resistance, but Wedmore's gut feeling told him this was different. The sheer numbers of soldiers and artillery waiting for them suggested they had received inside information. The F-16s flew over again at a much slower pace and far lower to the ground, so that the road itself shook under their thundering vibrations. The ears of the soldiers screamed as the deafening noise passed overhead.

Wedmore's platoon advanced to the edge of the Potomac River where the tanks stopped and the soldiers were ordered to 'Halt' by the commanding drill sergeant. The idling engines of the tanks on both sides of the bridge filled the otherwise silent air as Wedmore and his two trusted men surveyed the standoff in front of them. Wright and Byrd stepped toward Wedmore whilst Sana took a step back to hold the railing next to her for balance. Wedmore looked around him for clues of how to proceed. As he did so, he noticed two US Navy ships making their way along the Potomac River, the turrets of their guns pointed firmly at Wedmore and his allies. Wright was the first to break the silence.

"What do you make of this?" Wright asked Wedmore.

"I'm not sure what to say," Wedmore replied. *"They've definitely had advanced warning of our arrival. There is no way they could have assembled this many men from the moment the news broke this morning. Most of the local troops are with us anyway, so this doesn't make sense. Who would have told them we were coming?"*

"I've no idea, but now that we're here, what should we do?" Byrd asked.

Wedmore paused for a moment to assess the situation. His pulse rate was rising as he felt he was walking into an ambush. He didn't want things to turn nasty and war to break out on the streets of Washington. This was a standoff, but who knew what would unfold next. He looked to both of his friends who were patiently looking to him for some direction. He then turned to look at Sana who responded with a loving smile and touched her heart in silence.

Another wave of goose bumps ran up his spine as he straightened his back and inched towards the microphone on the rostrum. He listened to his inner voice uttering the words calmness and love.

He reached forward to adjust the microphone with his hands to buy himself a moment or two of extra time as he took a deep breath to deliver a speech to all those present.

"My fellow citizens, we come in peace. We do not mean you any harm. We have merely come to arrest the evil perpetrators who would cause us to harm our fellow man through their web of lies, deceit, and trickery."

His amplified words echoed from the loudspeakers and bounced over the highway towards the soldiers on the Western bank of the Potomac. Silence fell, only to be interrupted by a strong gust of cold wind that blew through the air. There was no reply from the other side. Moments passed that felt like an eternity as the standoff continued. Wedmore felt the thudding of his heartbeat grow stronger as he tried to figure out his next move. Overhead, the roar of more helicopter blades filled the air as TV networks tried to capture the scenes unfolding. Each of them were vying for the best possible position in the sky to report what was taking place in the capital to horrified viewers. Hitler was still tuned into the news networks in London watching similar scenes unfolding there, with rival army soldiers standing strong against the advancing troops. A standoff was in place on both sides of the pond.

"My friends!" Wedmore continued with a forced smile. *"I need you to pull back the veil of deception that has been drawn over your eyes. This is something that only you can do for yourselves. As fellow high-ranking special ops soldiers, I can assure you that we are not being told the truth. We are being sent to war to control other countries for reasons that are fundamentally wrong. We have put our lives at risk for people who could not care less about us, our families, or our livelihoods. We have lost valued friends and comrades being pawns in a rich man's game. Wives have lost husbands, children have lost fathers, and for what? So we can steal oil and resources*

from a foreign land? Give control of their banking system to the elite that run the world? Why are we doing this? For fake paper money that's ultimately worth fuck-all? We say it's to support our families or some sense of duty to our country, but ultimately, we know deep down we are being used and abused as somebody else's bitch! We're worth more than this, aren't we?"

"I implore you to think about the decisions we have all made in the past in the name of following orders. There is no doubt we have all participated in the atrocities of warfare, which would make the worst horror movie look like a fairytale. There is no doubt that innocent men, women, and children have lost their lives in the crossfire of our conflicts. For every good deed we have done, there have undoubtedly been numerous action that have undone our good work."

"The media pumps propaganda into the public to support the drive for endless war, but they are detached from the realities of it. We are the ones who have to deal with the horrifying nightmares night after night, haunting us and leaving us in pools of sweat! We all know valued colleagues who have taken their own lives after returning from combat because they couldn't cope with the haunting memories running through their minds continuously. Is this what it means to be in service to our country? Are we really looking after our families if we return from conflict mentally and spiritually broken with the risk of taking our own lives and leaving our loved ones to clean up the aftermath and live with the heartbreak? I say you're all worth more."

"Don't get me wrong. I believe that representing our country is worthwhile if we are protecting ourselves from attack or invasion. However, our own governments facilitate an on-going war in the Middle East and have orchestrated the so-called acts of terrorism we have supposedly witnessed. We have all been

stationed out there at some point in our careers, and to what end? So we can secure oil and opium for our country's consumption? Then we blame those nations for acting with hostility towards us? Can you blame them? How would we feel if one of them invaded our home or killed our loved ones? Would we not be entitled to feel enraged? To want revenge? To want to take from them what they took from us? Put yourself in their shoes! Have compassion for these people. Deep down, I know you know what I am talking about."

"We are told these people are different to us because they seemingly worship a different God. They dress differently or speak a different language and our media portrays them as wrong for doing so. That they should be somehow feared for having a different skin colour, religion, or way of being. We are brainwashed into believing they are the enemy. That their lives are worth less than ours. That they are expendable. It's a war based on division and separation."

"We all know that if we want to defeat a strong enemy, our motto is 'Divide and Conquer' and this is being used against us so we are fighting amongst ourselves. We say we fight to liberate other nations from oppression, when the true oppressors are working behind closed doors in our homeland, enacting laws and policies that enslave us into a police state or make us live in endless debt while we sedate ourselves with junk food and alcohol and watch thousands of meaningless TV channels. I believe there is a higher calling for each and every one of us here, and our lives all matter. Otherwise, we wouldn't be here. I say, if the politicians and elites want war, then let's send them to deal with it instead! Let's give them weapons and send them on to the battlefield themselves. I guarantee they wouldn't last five fucking minutes!"

Wedmore's dramatic pause after delivering this last line was designed to have a lasting impact. The soldiers following his command cheered a mighty cheer, which he knew would have a dramatic affect on the morale of the opposing side. He knew his military comrades on both side of the river were subjected to horrendous mental torture as a result of following orders and none of those pen-pushing politicians would last a day in the field. This was where he believed he could create unity amongst the soldiers on both sides to fight for the same cause. He took another deep breath before continuing.

"My friends, I don't believe the people who hold office are necessarily bad, but they are human, and as such, they are subject to the low vibrational influences of money and corruption. I believe the majority probably came to office in their youth with a vision that they were going to change the system in some positive way. But, over time, after many years of being in the same environment with others who have been tainted by easy money and lavish lifestyles, they too have become shadows of their former selves and turned a blind eye to corruption because it's easier to do so than to be constantly exhausted trying to change something no-one has a vested interest in changing."

"A short time ago, myself and my colleagues here were at the SOFEX exhibition. There are US manufacturers selling arms to countries we are at war with. I mean, how does any of this make sense? We go to war with a country, yet we sell them the arms they need to fight us? Do you have any idea how expensive these rockets are? One rocket costs more than you make in a year as a soldier and we fire them at people who don't make what we make in a year over their entire lifetimes! When the rockets explode, the surrounding damage is enormous, so the cost is not just financial; it's moral and ethical when there's innocent blood on our hands. And, we're asked to risk our lives for this shit? Are you fucking kidding me? You couldn't even make this shit up!"

"People's lives are worth more than explosive rockets, surely? Is your very life and soul not worth more than the cost of carrying this guilt with you forever? I ask you to look beyond the veil of deception to see the world for what it really is and the madness we have been sold as the price for living in a civilised country. This is not what you pledged to do when you signed up for the military. This is not protecting your country; it is bastardising the lives of others. My brothers and sisters all, you are worth far more and it's time to make those men and women in suits who sit behind expensive desks paid for by your tax dollars to answer to us, whose lives they have endangered by their selfishness and greed for too long."

A huge roar of acknowledgement went up from the crowd of soldiers as Wedmore stood back from the microphone breathless and relieved his words had been well received. He sensed a shift in energy and that his speech had made a firm impact on the other side. There was no doubt that his words would have got underneath the skin of even the most hard-core and devoted marine because they were coming from someone with experience in the field, not from a hippy who was pushing a 'peace, man' agenda. His two comrades both uttered compliments to acknowledge the impact he was making with the crowd. He now felt like he was winning and soon they would be on their way to completing the mission they had started.

As the streets fell silent and the noise of the crowd dissipated, Wedmore was just thinking of his next move when suddenly a response came from the other side. A cackling laugh came over the airwaves as a man in his seventies held a microphone to his mouth and began to respond to Wedmore's speech.

The man stood on an elevated platform to one side of his own troops but was audible enough for all to hear. Sana passed Wedmore a pair of binoculars so he could get a better view of who was speaking. The man, who looked as though his very life force had been drained away, had wrinkled grey skin. He was dressed in a very smart three-piece suit with a white shirt and spotted silk necktie, as though he was due to make a court appearance. A sly smile adorned his face framed by thin pursed lips that were almost purple in colour which was the only colour to his face save for the yellowy-whiteness of his sunken bloodshot eyes. His silver-grey thinning hair had been swept back and stuck down to the top of his head with Brylcreem, and his yellow-white crooked teeth were marginally visible from his mouth as he spoke. Wedmore's gut wrenched as he looked at this man, suggesting all was perhaps not well with what was about to unfold. He sensed evil was very much doing its dirty work through this empty and hollow individual. Wedmore mentally nicknamed him 'The Straw Man', depicting his emptiness.

"What a pathetic speech!" the Straw Man mocked. *"Do you really think those words are going to carry any weight with anyone? You have no idea what you are talking about! You're just a washed-up, alcoholic, former black ops soldier who is well past his prime, and after being unceremoniously dismissed, you have conjured up some bullshit story to bring everyone here today to try and seek revenge."*

He continued, *"You don't want to listen to a man who walked away from his duties and his team, leaving them all exposed; with some captured and executed by the enemy live on television. He practically supports terrorists with his actions and should be considered an enemy of the state. There is no way that you can trust someone like him. His record of desertion speaks for itself."*

Wedmore knew the Straw Man's words were false and did not describe any aspect of who he was, but it still didn't stop him from getting angry. He gripped the rostrum hard. The knuckles on both hands turned white and he started to grind his teeth with clenched jaws. Sana stepped forward to try comfort him from being publically humiliated by mistruths.

The Straw Man continued, *"Your actions today are treason and I will personally give one million dollars to whoever brings me your head! You have no place being here and inciting hatred against those who would honourably serve the public from their place of office. You, sir, are a conspiracy theorist of the highest order and you should be taken into custody or put in a mental institution immediately."*

The troops on both sides of the bridge were now very motivated to bring the head of James Wedmore to the Straw Man. Wedmore felt very exposed.

Just as he was gathering his thoughts on how to play the next step in this monumental game of chess, he heard a scuffle behind him. He turned to witness his long-standing friend and ally, Admiral Richard Byrd, push John Wright off the platform into the crowd below before drawing his gun and pointing it directly at Wedmore. With wide-eyed disbelief, Wedmore looked at Byrd for some clues as to what was happening. This wasn't part of the script and he was very confused. Byrd waved the gun sideways between Sana and Wedmore and ordered her to step down from the platform or he would shoot her. Wedmore encouraged her to do as Byrd had ordered, whilst Byrd kept the gun trained firmly on Wedmore.

Almost speechless with disbelief, he asked Byrd, *"What the fuck is going on?"*

Byrd had a glazed look in his eyes as he responded, *"He's right, James. You have committed treason today. I have no idea what possessed me to go along with your mad idea. We're all totally fucked if we try anything else and I have a family to take care of. I choose the money."*

"But, you know the real reason why we are here today, Richard! How long have we known each other for and why would you betray me now? The money doesn't mean anything when you consider the innocent blood you have on your hands by carrying out the requests of madmen like this. You're a slave to their system. Money won't buy you anything when your conscience isn't clear! We have the opportunity to make a change today, Richard. Stand with us! You owe it to your wife and children and future generations. Let no more innocent people perish by carrying out the orders of these pricks! Let's be the change we want to see in the world."

"These 'madmen' happen to pay my bills and they employ me to keep the country free from terrorists like you! I am just doing my job, James. Enough is enough. It's an elaborate fairytale and it was never going to work. You're not smart enough and you forgot to watch your back. Now come with me. We can do this peacefully so you live, or we can do this the hard way and I can pull this trigger. Which would you prefer?"

Wedmore bowed his head with disappointment at this betrayal in this moment more than any other. Of all the contingency plans he ran prior to the mission, never once did he think he would be betrayed by one of his closest allies and turned over to the authorities to face their wrath. It was a massive blow to his confidence. He had an insight into how Jesus must have felt being betrayed by Judas and it hurt him to the core. He looked up at Byrd pointing his gun at him.

This was not what Wedmore wanted and he was in no doubt that despite all the soldiers surrounding him on his side, Byrd could pull the trigger and end his life at any time. Byrd motioned for Wedmore to put his hands on his head, and turn around to face the direction of the Straw Man. As he did so, Byrd walked up behind him and removed Wedmore's gun and knife. Wedmore could not believe this was happening but did his best to remain calm under duress. Byrd held the gun to Wedmore's temple and leaned towards the microphone.

With cowardice in his voice, he spoke, *"I have him, sir! He is under my control and I shall bring him in for public arrest."*

It was then that Wedmore realised how they knew of his plan and were waiting for him. Byrd must have given the game away and informed the authorities. Rather than take him out prior to today, they chose to make a public embarrassment of him in front of millions of TV viewers around the world, showing them what would happen if anyone else tried to bring about a civil uprising against the established order. It was all there right in front of him. The betrayal was just as public as the execution of Jesus. Twenty-plus years of friendship had just dissipated in an instant and there was little Wedmore or any of the Black Widows could do to reverse the situation.

All around the lorry, soldiers were stirring and getting restless as they witnessed what was unfolding above them. Wedmore was concerned that one of them might attempt to shoot Byrd so he uttered a few words to save his old friend.

"You might want to let me talk to my platoon here as they have sworn with their lives to protect me. Right now, you're surrounded by several hundred thousand men and women who could take your life in a heartbeat. Let me tell them not to take any action and then you can take me in and get your reward. I'll go peacefully."

Wedmore looked into Byrd's eyes with compassion, realising that Byrd's moral threshold was considerably lower than most. He had been bought with fake paper currency and the promise that the system, which was now protecting him and telling him he was a good and decent man for following orders, would later turn on him and dispose of him when it suited. Byrd couldn't see the depths of the corruption for what it was, as unfortunately he had been indoctrinated too deeply into their system. He saw the fixed look of fear in Byrd's eyes as he held the gun to Wedmore's face.

Byrd took a step back to allow Wedmore to talk to the crowd. *"Ok, but make it quick."*

Wedmore shuffled towards the microphone and announced to his followers, *"My friends, please do not shoot. I repeat, DO NOT SHOOT! We are not going to become as bad as the system we are dealing with here and I don't want this man's blood on your hands. I will go peacefully. Once again, Do Not Shoot."*

The Black Widows were confined to the lorry's unit and opened the doors to see what was going on when they heard Wedmore's words. Byrd ordered Hitler and Gringo to step away from the vehicle or he would shoot Wedmore. Byrd felt threatened in his position and was hugely exposed. Both men put their hands up in and took a few steps back from the vehicle. Byrd took to the microphone again and ordered all the troops in front of the lorry to move out of the way so they could drive through.

The drill sergeant on the ground ordered his men to carry out the request and, like the parting of the Red Sea, thousands of soldiers started moving to the sides so the lorry could pass through. Byrd then ordered Gringo throw his gun to the ground before getting behind the wheel of the vehicle and driving it towards the other side of the bridge. Gringo did as he was ordered and jumped back into the lorry.

However, Byrd had missed the fact that the Doc, Springbok, and Kamali were still in the front seat. The Doc had drawn his weapon and aimed it towards the roof of the truck. He looked out of the passenger window towards Hitler for some direction on where he should be pointing. Hitler motioned gently with his hands in the air to help the Doc cover his blind shot whilst making eye contact with Wedmore to silently let him know what was about to unfold. The synergy between them meant a fleeting glance was all they needed to relay what was about to happen.

The Doc fired his weapon as Gringo revved the engine and engaged first gear. The blind shot tore through the thin metal roof of the truck, through the plywood floor of the platform, and embedded itself into Byrd's right foot. Byrd didn't know what hit him as the searing white-hot pain ran up his leg from the impact. As soon as Wedmore saw the impact of the shot, he gripped the handrail and kicked Byrd hard with both feet, sending him crashing to the ground below where he was quickly apprehended by Hitler. Wedmore ordered Byrd to be taken away for emergency medical assistance before resuming his position on the rostrum.

"*My friends,*" he continued with a smile. "*As you were! We shall not be defeated today!*"

The soldiers cheered once more and rapidly fell back into formation, ready to advance under the command of Wedmore once again. They were undeterred by the financial reward on offer having witnessed how easily corruptible people could be. Sana re-joined her man on the platform and embraced him for his bravery. The magnificent couple stood side-by-side once again, ready to complete their mission.

Through his binoculars, Wedmore could see that the Straw Man was not deterred in his advances despite how things had turned out with his spy. The Straw Man coughed a few times to clear his throat before shouting into the loudspeaker.

"*I want this man dead or alive now! He will be taken down and treated as the global terrorist he is and made a public example of. We will not tolerate such insolent behaviour. He is a threat to National Security. I order you to do whatever it takes to bring this man to justice!*"

Wedmore reflected briefly on the 'National Security' comment. Did he really mean the security of the United States or was he referring to the fact that Washington was actually a separate legal entity and not part of the USA? He remembered Kamali telling him a few years ago that Washington D.C., London, and the Vatican were actually classed as separate legal countries from the nations they were physically domiciled within. This had played on Wedmore's mind for years, wondering why this was necessary.

Wedmore stood firm in his conviction that what they were doing now was required more than ever, particularly after his most recent experience. Once again, he addressed his team.

"My friends, we have all just witnessed an example of how their system works and how they would treat us given half a chance. It's the same system that pits us against one another. Just for once, would you not prefer peace in the world? Would you not rather be with your families knowing you were not endangering your life playing out some uncaring rich man's game of war? Wouldn't you rather be honouring your oath and protecting vulnerable people? Today, my friends, it is your moral calling to do the right thing and bring an end to this nonsense. There is a better way and its roots are founded in love and compassion rather than hate and suppression. Are you with me?"

The deafening cheer from the crowd demonstrated their support as the soldiers were rallied into a frenzy, knowing they were finally standing for something that brought peace to their hearts. The Straw Man became vexed at the support Wedmore was receiving and the fact that Wedmore was so rooted in love for humanity that he would keep on fighting for the greater good no matter what was thrown at him. The Straw Man's face turned purple with rage as he gave the order to fire at will and bring the resistance crashing down.

As the words fell from his lips, there was a mighty roar of the most deafening thunder overhead as the sky turned pitch black with dark clouds. Intense rain started to fall as the thunderclaps became more and more intense. A blinding flash of lightening upstream on the Potomac River caused everyone to look over as a huge tornado appeared out of nowhere and began to cause chaos to the flow of the river. The river's water was drawn up into a vortex. The two US Navy ships with their turrets trained on Wedmore's men were immediately sucked up into the vortex and tossed high into the air. The ships flew round and round in the air as the tornado moved towards the 14th Street Bridge.

The Straw Man went crazy, shouting orders for everyone to fire and not to be distracted by the weather. Tanks began firing heavy shells and soldiers began offloading shots in the direction of the resistance as the heavy storm bore down on them. The noise the wind made was disorientating and prevented people hearing any commands. The tornado was so strong it drew the bullets and shells into the vortex, where they spiralled round and round in the air without ever reaching their intended targets. Wedmore's troops stood fast and refused to fire on the innocent.

As quickly as the storm had appeared, it disappeared once the tornado hit the bridge, planting both ships down onto the freeway with their turrets facing towards the Straw Man and the soldiers supporting the authorities. It began raining bullets and tank shells onto the surface of the road and the helmets of the nearby soldiers. Both sides were stunned as the firing stopped.

Wedmore smiled deeply, as he knew who had created the perfect storm. He ordered his men to continue their advance. As they moved forward, he witnessed the soldiers on the other side of the bridge lay down their weapons and retreat, believing black magic was against them. The Straw Man, in his flustered state, continually shouted at his men to keep firing, but once a few men had begun fleeing the scene, the fear spread like wildfire and the opposing soldiers dissipated in all directions.

Wedmore, with the support of his thousands of troops, began to advance over the 14th Street bridge to arrest those operating in public service within the Pentagon, the White House, and Capitol Hill. He ordered that all personnel be rounded up and taken away for questioning in a non-violent way. Hitler had received word from London that their allies had also managed to overthrow the oppressors with similar support from Mother Nature.

The victory was theirs for the taking as hundreds of government employees were marched out of their offices and placed under military arrest in a special holding place. Wedmore could not believe it.

He turned to his girl with the biggest smile and said, *"We did it! I can't believe it! We actually did it!"*

"Yes Jay, you did it! And it happened exactly as you wanted it to. I'm so proud of you. You were so brave in the face of adversity and I admire you so much for it. You showed us what it means to stand strong rooted in love, even when fear tried to overshadow you and stack all the odds against you. You're a true hero."

Sana was gushing with pride for the man who had the courage to follow his dream and have faith in God supporting him all the way. She threw her arms around his neck and hugged him tightly with the most radiant glow of love beaming from her. They had been entrusted with the mission of a lifetime, and with a little help from Archangel Michael at the right moment, the situation unfolded beautifully without loss of life and only one injury.

"Come now, Sana, we must say thank you to the Lord for allowing this to happen."

They closed their eyes and placed their right palms on their hearts, feeling the spark of the Divine beating within them. They spoke words of kindness and gratitude to God for guiding them through the mission, for the support granted by the thousands of men and women who believed it would be possible, and for Archangel Michael's help at the right moment.

As they opened their eyes to look towards the heavens, a beautiful butterfly appeared. It circled their heads before landing gently on Sana's nose, making her giggle. It flapped its wings twice, showing the beauty of its colours before flying off. Wedmore noticed it had pure white wings with a beautiful red heart-like shape across the middle of them. Smiling broadly at one another, they realised their prayers had been heard.

Afterword

In the aftermath of the weeks and months following the victory at Potomac where hundreds of politicians, diplomats, and government workers were incarcerated and awaiting trial, Wedmore worked around the clock with his team to ensure a temporary government facilitated a relatively smooth transition from the previous regime to one that would be guided by the principles of love. He put General John Wright in charge of diplomatic relations with overseas countries and together, they helped to bring about peace and harmony to otherwise battered relationships with countries the USA and the UK had been at war with for many years. The dramatic western military coup demonstrated to foreign lands how serious Wedmore was at restoring morality in western politics.

Their first action was to immediately order all troops to return from overseas missions, unless they were there to sincerely support rebuilding countries following any intervention from the west. They also issued unilateral apologies to every country the west had ever been in conflict with and forgave them any debt they had subsequently been saddled with.

At first, this latter policy was met with strong resistance from the Federal Reserve as well as the Bank of England who did not wish to write off these 'assets' on their balance sheets. Wedmore had little patience for the greed of bankers and immediately had all parties running the Federal Reserve and the Bank of England arrested and incarcerated whilst nationalising both privately-owned institutions, turning them into public bodies held in trust for the good of the people. The debt was forgiven and all countries that had suffered the impact of previous actions were given interest free multi-million dollar grants to help rebuild.

Whilst this caused some impact in the global financial markets, Wedmore ordered a six-month suspension of trading on all stocks and shares, and western currencies whilst they ironed out the issues. Despite an outcry from Wall Street, he ignored their greed and gluttony and carried on dealing with the bigger picture. After all, they had been responsible for most of the world's financial problems with their careless risk taking and dodgy financial instruments, such as their sub-prime loans rolled into packaged mortgage-backed derivatives that later caused the global financial crisis. Even so, the banks had previously been bailed out by the good citizens of the west, so it was high time they were held responsible.

With the troops returning from overseas, Wedmore cut military spending significantly and instead of encouraging troops to train for combat, he issued a nationwide program to help the homeless and those less fortunate in their homeland. Soldiers were sent out into the streets in civil uniform and tasked with finding people who were homeless or living in poverty. One by one, people were taken off the streets, fed well, given warmth, clothing, and housing before being given the opportunities they needed to begin rebuilding their lives. Those people in poverty were given financial support at home to make ends meet, increased social security pay-outs, and child support to help those who wanted to return to work, knowing their children were being well cared for.

Understandably, the people of the west were somewhat nervous that their governments had been overthrown by a military operation and Wedmore appeared at many press conferences to reassure them it was all for the right reasons and there was no need to be concerned. The majority of daily life remained as it was previously, but he encouraged everyone to try to be a little more loving as they went about their daily lives. He encouraged people to be kind, sensitive, and warm to one another. He suggested that everyone we know is dealing with a personal circumstance that we don't perhaps know about, so the least we could do is be kind and cheerful to spread compassion, joy, and love, so that one day it may return to us many times over. He also argued that it made life just that much more pleasant for everyone when we all understand each another.

Despite all the changes, none of them compared to the sheer brilliance of the next stage in Wedmore's master plan. He had contemplated what to do with the politicians and bankers who had sought to cause misery in the lives of others with their greedy, selfish ways. Although he had toyed with the idea of sending each one to trial for their misgivings, the burden of proof would potentially take years to pull together and even then, it would not change them in any fundamental way. He meditated on it one morning to find an answer, but he was still none the wiser.

Sana could see he was perplexed and asked him what was on his mind. He explained how he had been meditating on the idea of what to do with all the people who had been jailed awaiting trial but had not found any answers.

"Jay, do you think you are maybe trying a little too hard to come up with the answers? You know what to do: breathe and let go. The answer will come to you soon enough."

"You're right," he replied. *"I do need to figure something out soon, otherwise we will have to let them all go. It's not really practicing what we preach to keep them locked up without charge. I was hoping the meditation might give me the ans.........THAT'S IT!"*

He jumped up and hugged his beautiful girl. *"You're so wonderful! Thank you! I knew there was a reason we were together!"* he joked.

"What, Jay? What is it?" she smiled back at him.

"Meditation! That's the answer!" he said. *"That's how we bring about the change in these people. We help bring them to a state of enlightenment without them even realising it. When they get there, they alone will realise their wrongdoings and will want to make amends themselves. It's far more powerful than anything else we can do. Far more powerful than punishment, or long-term imprisonment. They will make changes of their own accord and facilitate humanity's shift to a much higher level of consciousness."*

"I don't disagree, Jay, but how do you plan to do this?" Sana asked.

"I remember reading something on the internet years ago about a professor of psychology who practiced meditation in a prison he worked at. The prison was full of the worst offenders in the world: serial rapists, murderers, and all kinds of evil people. What he did was to focus his daily meditations on one unsuspecting subject at a time, and over the course of several weeks, he noticed unprecedented shifts in that person's personality and behaviour. This was to the point that these people found God, repented for their sins and became calm, peaceful, and loving when they were once the most feared people in the institution. I think we can do the same with these people," Wedmore replied.

"That sounds good, Jay, but that could take several years with you and I just focussing on a few people. How are we going to do this with several thousand men and women in a short time?" Sana asked.

"I think the best thing we can do is to bring together some of the best monks and lamas in the world and ask that they meditate outside the prison walls whilst focussing their energies on the inmates. I think if we do this, the transformation will happen quite quickly. Then we can release them once they understand what they have helped to create in the world. With

their knowledge and expertise, I am sure they can help us to implement all of our other plans for peace on earth."

Wedmore was clearly excited as he unveiled his vision to Sana who was fully supportive of his proposals and encouraged him to action them immediately.

By the end of the week, literally thousands of monks, lamas and high-level practitioners of meditation had been flown into the USA and UK from all over the world. They were brought to Washington and London where the offenders were being held in the maximum-security jails. All offenders were brought into the recreation yard and told to sit quietly in uniform rows on the ground for several hours at a time every day.

The meditation practitioners formed uniform circles around the prisons and got to work with their deep, connected meditations. It was fascinating for Wedmore, Sana, and the rest of the Black Widows to witness what happened as the group consciousness formed and everyone was aligned in the meditation. It was as though a serene calmness descended upon all present, with peace and tranquillity vibrating all around the prison. The guards, management, and inmates alike all reported feeling much calmer and happier as they went about their day. Within four weeks of this continued practice, they reported feeling happy and joyous in their work.

It took a further two weeks of continued meditations to trigger the beginnings of remorse. Thousands upon thousands of confessions of the worst order came from the inmates as they revealed the lives they had been living and the wrongs they had purposely done to others in pursuit of power and money and in service of their dark master.

What was even more revealing was the fact that the overwhelming majority of these people pinpointed defining turning points in their own lives that caused them to behave in a certain way, most noticeably, the distinct absence of love in their lives growing up. Almost everyone who had sought to mistreat his fellow man, either subconsciously through actions founded in hate or fear, or purposefully by enslaving people in debt, did so on the basis that their lives had been lacking any major form of love in their childhood. As such, their view of the world in their formative years was tainted and they didn't see why others deserved a loving connection of family and friends, so they purposefully tried to take it away from them any way they could.

Their mindset became so distorted that they believed money and power would eventually bring them the happiness they desperately craved. Paradoxically, no matter how much wealth they created and how much they sought to take love and joy away from the lives of others, they never found happiness or fulfilment in their own lives. They suppressed their emotions deep within their human psyche, which constantly haunted them in every way possible, leading them to live lives of misery and unhappiness.

Being exposed to the peaceful meditation surrounded them in a blanket of acceptance and Unconditional Love that some were experiencing for the very first time. This caused an overwhelming tidal wave of suppressed emotions to come flooding out though confessions of their previous behaviours and how wrong they had been to try and take away from others what they sought for themselves. Endless tears of sorrow flowed from the inmates over the coming weeks as they came to terms with the lives they had created and the impact they had on others.

Men and women, who were once portrayed as being made of steel, were devastated now their own conscience had caught up with them. Most sought to publicly apologise for what they had done, and wanted the opportunity to right some of the wrongs they had created. People not only gained a deep insight into their own psychology, they were able to use this understanding of their own behaviour and motives as a gift. They realised what they thought they never received themselves could be something they could give to others. Those who felt they had never received love had a real insight into what it felt like to live without the love they needed; therefore, they could have compassion for others who were also in need of love. They actively sought to be the expression of this gift of love and give it to those who most needed it. Men and women, who had previously been guilty of the most inhumane wrongdoings, were now keen to make amends and work with those less fortunate to bring about love, peace, and harmony. It was truly transformational.

This had to be the biggest victory the Black Widows had ever had the pleasure of witnessing because the impact of it sent ripples around the world. The meditation programme was rolled out across all of the correctional facilities within the UK and USA. Outstanding results were reported with a 100% 'cure rate' of all inmates who found relief from their past and who were now drawn towards a new future full of hope, love, and possibilities. Other countries that observed the results of the meditation programmes were keen to follow suit and eventually correctional facilities began to close due to the decline in the number of new and repeat offenders. Meditation was introduced to all scholastic environments as a non-religious topic allowing children to find peace and harmony in their own lives. Bullying and stress within academic institutions disappeared as the tone set at the grass roots level led to a monumental shift in the behaviour of young adults leading to the elevation of consciousness for all humanity.

With the availability of interest free currency, the pressure of rising personal debt became less and less of an issue for families, and more people were able to find emotional freedom from the ties of being indebted to financial institutions. The personal lives of many millions of people improved dramatically as a result, facilitating a fall in the divorce rate as money was no longer the major issue and stress for couples it once was. People seemed a lot happier, as they were encouraged to live as shining examples of the universal body of consciousness that they are, rather than made to fit into corporate organisations to work for money just to pay bills. People were supported getting their own businesses off the ground and encouraged to pursue meaningful work in their lives. More and more people veered away from the materialist life in order to find fulfilment in their own hopes and dreams. This was particularly apparent for the number of people who were affected by the earlier suspension of stock market trading and the impact it had on financial and banking institutions.

Health was put firmly back on the agenda for the nations of the west and all genetically-modified food was banned. Natural farming methods were encouraged and organic farming was incentivised to become the norm. The reduction in the number of pesticides being used was significant, whilst chemical-laden pharmaceutical drugs were put through more stringent tests to ensure they were a valid choice against the viable natural alternatives of herbal homeopathic medicine.

Wedmore's administration lifted the ban on medical marijuana, which had tremendous healing properties for people suffering from a variety of seemingly incurable medical conditions. Healthcare practice was reversed from a place of trying to secure patients for life for pharmaceutical companies, to helping patients get back on their feet as quickly as possible. All patients had to attend mandatory classes dealing with their personal mind-set and belief systems as this was the single most important parameter in the patient's ability to heal themselves.

In response to repeated public calls to be more kind to the environment, policies were put in place to urgently end the world's dependency on fossil fuels. Renewable forms of energy were given their proper place as forerunners in the energy world after it was determined that just five days of sunshine would provide the west with its annual energy needs. These policies helped to phase out the reliance on oil for transportation and lessened the need for nuclear reactors for electricity generation when more suitable alternatives such as solar and wind power could be used effectively without damaging the environment. There was also zero possibility of oil spills or nuclear reactor fall-outs as these forms of energy dependency were phased out. Over-unity and quantum energy generators were also funded to create an abundance of clean energy, driving down costs for all concerned.

What was more interesting was the way people felt as a result of these changes. People were no longer despondent about the future of the world, nor did they find themselves in jobs where they were selling their souls for cash. With a rise in personal happiness, no-one was being tormented by pendulums that manipulate their unhappy state to cause conflicts, leading to misery, upset, and depression. In turn, this dramatically reduced the level of Loosh energy being released to feed The Fallen One, Lucifer. With their master starved of energy and their systems of control within former western administrations gone, the Council of Thirteen no longer had power. The old structures of control perished and the soulless entities who had sought to suppress the human spirit fell by the wayside.

People became happier and were more pleasant to be around as they now saw a brighter future than was previously being painted under the old regime. Freedom in the true sense of the word had been afforded to them, which made them feel very good. People also became more accepting of one another as stress and irritability began to dissipate from the human experience. People no longer vented their stresses and troubles on others as they took responsibility for their emotional wellbeing through self-care, meditation, and living in accordance with their Divine purpose. This further led to something no-one ever saw coming: the eventual abolition of borders between countries.

In an act similar to the fall of the Berlin Wall, borders between countries began to be removed to facilitate free travel from country to country. Whilst there was undoubtedly significant periods of adjustment, the ability for people to freely travel without the need for passports or control of any sort was widely accepted as a radically brilliant idea. As there was now little need for people to identify themselves with any particular country, there was zero need to defend those previous identities. People could be free to be the true essence of who they really were and could travel freely to meet new people and have greater experiences of the world and what it meant to be human. As people experienced different cultures, they no longer feared those who appeared to be different from themselves and identified more closely with their similarities instead. Everyone smiled in the same language!

Ultimately, the love, kindness and compassion shared by everyone from formerly different backgrounds, religious beliefs, and cultures showed humanity that love really could be the new religion.

——— THE END ———

Resources

Baer, Greg. *Real Love*. Gotham Books 2004.

Baer, Greg. *Real Love for Wise Men and Women*. Blue Ridge Press 2007.

Bale, Christian. *The Big Short*. DVD. Directed by Adam McKay. Universal Pictures, 2016.

Cherniske, Stephen. *Caffeine Blues: Wake Up To The Hidden Dangers of America's #1 Drug*. Grand Central Publishing 1998.

Christoff, Jason. Vaccines and Autism - Is There Any Connection? (article 2017) https://www.jchristoff.com/vaccines-and-autism-is-there-any-connection/

Clason, George S. *The Richest Man in Babylon*. Signet 2002

Connett, Paul and James Beck and H Spedding Micklem. *The Case Against Fluoride: How Hazardous Waste Ended Up in Our Drinking Water and the Bad Science and Powerful Politics that keep it there.* Chelsea Green Publishing Co. 2010.

Davies, Paul and Kirk Rutter. *Meet Your Strawman!* Infomaticfilms.com via YouTube 2010. https://www.youtube.com/watch?v=ME7K6P7hlko

Dispenza, Joe. *You Are The Placebo*. Hay House Publishing 2014.

Dispenza, Joe. *Breaking The Habit Of Being Yourself*. Hay House Publishing 2012.

Dyer, Wayne W. *The Power of Intention*. Hay House Publishing 2004.

Elrod, Hal. *The Miracle Morning: The 6 Habits That Will Transform Your Life Before 8am*. John Murray Learning 2016.

Emoto, Masaru. *The Hidden Messages in Water.* Simon & Schuster 2005.

Engelhardt, Tom and Glenn Greenwald. *Shadow Government: Surveillance, Secret Wars, and a Global Security State in a Single Superpower World.* Haymarket Books. 2014

Fels, Gabby. *Healing in a Maximum Security Prison.* http://www.kinesiologyshop.com/eqintro2.htm

Freeland, Elena M. *Chemtrails, HAARP, and the Full Spectrum Dominance of Planet Earth.* Feral House 2014.

Hawkins, David R. *Power vs Force.* Hay House Publishing 1995.

Harris, Russ. *The Happiness Trap.* Robinson 2007.

Harrar, Sari. *The Sugar Solution: Balance Your Blood Sugar Naturally to Beat Disease, Lose Weight, Gain Energy and Feel Great.* Rodale Books 2004.

Hill, Napolean. *The Law of Success In Sixteen Lessons Complete.* BN Publishing 2007.

J. *The Unholy Trinity of Globalist Control: The Vatican, The City of London & Washington D.C.* (article 2017) https://wakeuptothetruthsite.wordpress.com/2017/04/25/the-unholy-trinity-of-globalist-control-the-vatican-the-city-of-london-washington-d-c/

Kinslow, Frank J. *The Secret of Instant Healing.* Hay House Publishing 2008.

Kinslow, Frank J. *The Secret of Quantum Living.* Hay House Publishing 2012.

Lewis, Michael. *The Big Short: Inside the Doomsday Machine.* Penguin 2011

Lipton, Bruce. *The Biology of Belief.* Hay House Publishing 2005.

MacDonald-Bayne, Murdo. *Beyond The Himalayas*. L.N. Fowler & Co 2012

MacDonald-Bayne, Murdo. *The Yoga of The Christ*. L.N. Fowler & Co 2012

Marie, Stephanie. *Heartmath: The heart is more powerful that the brain.* (article 2013). https://wearechange.org/heartmath-part-1/

Mitchell, Stephen. *Tao Te Ching by Lao Tzu: An Illustrated Journey*. Frances Lincoln 1999.

Paget, Antonia. *Desperate former soldiers suffering from PTSD are stretching 999 services to breaking point.* (article 2017) https://www.mirror.co.uk/lifestyle/health/desperate-former-soldiers-suffering-ptsd-11468895

Perkins, John. *Confessions of an Economic Hit Man*. Penguin 2004.

Pert, Candace B. *Molecules of Emotion*. Simon & Schuster 1997

Peter. *Emoto's Rice Experiment* (article 2014) http://www.lifeintherightdirection.com/emotos-rice-experiment/

Reeves, Keanu. *The Matrix*. DVD. Directed by The Wachowski Brothers. Warner Home Video, 1999.

Smith, Shane. *The Business of War: SOFEX*. VICE via YouTube 2012. https://www.youtube.com/watch?v=QL_3Qg-SADY

Wakefield, Andrew. *VAXXED: From Cover-Up to Catastrophe*. DVD/Vaxxedthemovie.com. Directed by Andrew Wakefield. Cinema Libre Studio, 2016.

VACCINE Peer Review: *The History Of The Global Vaccination Program In 1000 Peer Reviewed Reports And Studies 1915-2015*. http://vaccine-injury.info/pdf/vaccinepeerreview.pdf A Jeff Prager Publication 2013.

Walton, Kenneth, David Orme-Johnson and Rachel S Goodman. *Transcendental Meditation in Criminal Rehabilitation and Crime Prevention*. Routledge 2003.

Wikipedia. Subprime Mortgage Crisis (article)
https://en.wikipedia.org/wiki/Subprime_mortgage_crisis

Young, C. *The Truth About Hair and Why Indians Would Keep Their Hair Long.* (article 2011).
https://www.sott.net/article/234783-The-Truth-About-Hair-and-Why-Indians-Would-Keep-Their-Hair-Long

Zeland, Vadim. *Reality Transurfing Volume 1: The Space of Variations.* O Books 2008.

Zukav, Gary. *The Seat Of The Soul.* Rider Books 1990.

Printed in Poland
by Amazon Fulfillment
Poland Sp. z o.o., Wrocław